ABUSE OF DISCRETION

Books by Pamela Samuels Young

Vernetta Henderson Series

Every Reasonable Doubt (1st in series)

In Firm Pursuit (2nd in series)

Murder on the Down Low (3rd in series)

Attorney-Client Privilege (4th in series)

Lawful Deception (5th in series)

Dre Thomas Series

Buying Time (1st in series)

Anybody's Daughter (2nd in series)

Abuse of Discretion (3rd in series)

Short Stories

The Setup

Easy Money

Unlawful Greed

Non-Fiction

Kinky Coily: A Natural Hair Resource Guide

PAMELA SAMUELS YOUNG

ABUSE OF DISCRETION

For my grand-nieces Anyah Samuels and Temple Samuels,
and my grand-nephews, Blake Samuels and Roman Samuels,
may you always be safe in this technologically complicated world.

"Children have never been very good at listening to their elders,
but they have never failed to imitate them."

— James Baldwin, novelist and social critic

CHAPTER 1

Graylin

"What's the matter, Mrs. Singletary? Why do I have to go to the principal's office?"

I'm walking side-by-side down the hallway with my second-period teacher. Students are huddled together staring and pointing at us like we're zoo animals. When a teacher at Marcus Preparatory Academy escorts you to the principal's office, it's a big deal. Nothing like this has ever happened to me before. I'm a good student. I *never* get in trouble.

Mrs. Singletary won't answer my questions or even look at me. I hope she knows she's only making me more nervous.

"Mrs. Singletary, please tell me what's wrong?"

"Just follow me. You'll find out in a minute."

I'm about to ask her another question when it hits me. *Something happened to my mama!*

My mama has been on and off drugs for as long as I can remember. I haven't seen her in months and I don't even know where she lives. No one does. I act like it doesn't bother me, but it does. I've prayed to God a million times to get her off drugs. Even though my granny says God answers prayers, He hasn't answered mine, so I stopped asking.

I jump in front of my teacher, forcing her to stop. "Was there a death in my family, Mrs. Singletary? Did something happen to my mama?"

"No, there wasn't a death."

She swerves around me and keeps going. I have to take giant steps to keep up with her.

Once we're inside the main office, Mrs. Singletary points at a wooden chair outside Principal Keller's office. "Have a seat and don't move."

She goes into the principal's office and closes the door. My head begins to throb like somebody's banging on it from the inside. I close my eyes and try to calm down. I didn't do anything wrong. It's probably just—*Oh snap! The picture!*

I slide down in the chair and pull my iPhone from my right pocket. My hands are trembling so bad I have to concentrate to keep from dropping it. I open the photos app and delete the last picture on my camera roll. If anyone saw that picture, I'd be screwed.

Loud voices seep through the closed door. I lean forward, straining to hear. It almost sounds like Mrs. Singletary and Principal Keller are arguing.

It's only an allegation. We don't even know if it's true.

I don't care. We have to follow protocol.

Can't you at least check his phone first?

I'm not putting myself in the middle of this mess. I've already made the call.

The call? I can't believe Principal Keller called my dad without even giving me a chance to defend myself. How'd she even find out about the picture?

The door swings open and I almost jump out of my skin. The principal crooks her finger at me. "Come in here, son."

Trudging into her office, I sit down on a red cloth chair that's way more comfortable than the hard one outside. My heart is beating so fast it feels like it might jump out of my chest.

The only time I've ever been in Principal Keller's office was the day my dad enrolled me in school. Mrs. Singletary is standing in front of the principal's desk with her arms folded. I hope she's going to stay here with me, but a second later, she walks out and closes the door.

Principal Keller sits on the edge of her desk, looking down at me. "Graylin, do you have any inappropriate pictures on your cell phone?"

"Huh?" I try to keep a straight face. "No, ma'am."

"It's been brought to my attention that you have an inappropriate picture—a naked picture—of Kennedy Carlyle on your phone. Is that true?"

"No…uh…No, ma'am." *Thank God I deleted it!*

"This is a very serious matter, young man. So, I need you to tell me the truth."

"No, ma'am." I shake my head so hard my cheeks vibrate. "I don't have anything like that on my phone."

"I pray to God you're telling me the truth."

I don't want to ask this next question, but I have to know. "Um, so you called my dad?"

"Yes, I did. He's on his way down here now."

I hug myself and start rocking back and forth. Even though I deleted the picture, my dad is still going to kill me for having to leave work in the middle of the day.

"I also made another call."

At first I'm confused. Then I realize Mrs. Keller must've called my granny too. At least she'll keep my dad from going ballistic.

"So you called my granny?"

"No." The principal's cheeks puff up like she's about to blow something away. "I called the police."

CHAPTER 2

Dre

"We haven't heard much from you this afternoon, Dre. How've you been making out?"

I instantly straighten up from my slouched position on the therapist's too-soft couch. This clueless chick has no idea how much I hate being here. Her suffocating, windowless office with its mint green walls, inspirational sayings and shiny cement floor make me feel like a caged animal. Almost like it felt when I'd been caged up for real.

"I'm making it." I squeeze my niece's hand. My sister Donna is sitting on the opposite side of Brianna, looking as worried about me as she is about her daughter.

Having to participate in this kumbaya session with this over-articulate sister who keeps pressing me to bare my soul—something I ain't gonna do—is almost painful.

If I'd met her in a club, she definitely would've piqued my interest. Cute face, nice tits, and thick around the hips, just the way I like my women. But as I stare across the room, that's not what I see. She might as well be one of those annoying, yellow happy faces because that's how she comes off.

The therapist folds her arms and rests them on her enormous boobs. "Oh, c'mon, Dre. You can surely dig a little deeper than that."

If this chick tells me to *dig deep* one more time, I swear I'm gonna kick her ugly-ass purple coffee table across the room. She seems to believe that constantly picking at my scabs will cause my pain to seep out and float away like the excrement that it is. Everyone in this room knows that's bull. Nothing—not even time—can heal this hurt.

My lips curve into a tight smile. "As long as Bree's good, then I'm good."

This is only our third family counseling session, but it feels like the thirtieth. Whenever the urge to bolt hits me—like now—I tell myself that after everything Brianna's been through, spending an hour a week listening to this psychobabble is the least I can do.

"But we want to know if *you're* good," the therapist presses. "Brianna wasn't the only victim. This was a traumatic experience for you too."

I inhale as the silver plaque on the wall above her head catches my eye. *Life is lived forward but understood backwards.* Yeah, tell me about it.

"As I've said before, I'm dealing with it."

"Actually, he's not dealing with it at all," my sister volunteers. "The Shepherd's in prison, but Dre wants him dead. To be honest, I'm more worried about my brother than my daughter."

My baby sis is such a drama queen. Except this time, she's right on the money.

As much as I've tried, I cannot wrap my mind around the fact that children like my thirteen-year-old niece—babies really—are being sold on the street like dime bags of weed. Before Brianna's kidnapping over a year ago, I knew nothing about the world of child sex trafficking. Now I could teach a college course on the subject. My niece was literally snatched off the street as part of a Facebook scam run by a thug called The Shepherd.

It pisses me off that the dude only got a measly twelve years. He's even in a low-security federal prison. From everything I've heard, that's basically summer camp.

The therapist is waiting for me to say something. Unlike most people, she's quite comfortable with silence. To get her off my back, I pretend to open up.

"Most of the time I'm fine." I fake a long sigh and lower my head, but my voice starts to quiver all on its own. "Then I think about what Brianna went through and I get pissed off."

Brianna pats my hand. "I'm okay, Uncle Dre. And you're gonna be okay too."

A warm sensation sweeps across my face and my heart. This little girl has such a hold on me. I lean down and kiss the top of her head.

The therapist gives Brianna an encouraging smile. "I'm proud of your progress, Brianna. How's everything between you and your mother?"

"Um, pretty good." Brianna gives her mother a quick sideways glance. "But she still won't let me have another cell phone or an Instagram account. She won't even let me sleep over at my friend Kendra's house."

"I'm with your mother on the cell phone tip," I say, turning to my sister. "But you could back up off her a little bit. Why don't we give Instagram a try and see how it goes? All the kids do is post a bunch of pictures on it. I trust her not to do anything crazy. Right, Bree?"

"Right," Brianna says eagerly.

"Yeah, okay, I guess," Donna says, full of reluctance. "But I'm getting one of those programs so I can monitor everybody you're talking to and everything you post."

Brianna gives her mother a kiss on the cheek. "Thanks, Mommy!"

"But I'm still not ready for a sleepover," Donna insists. "Whenever Brianna's out of my sight, I still get nervous about somebody kidnapping her again. I can barely handle her being back in school."

"Let's try this," the therapist suggests. "How about having Brianna spend the night at her grandmother's house first? Then we'll go from there."

Donna grimaces.

"You do trust your mother to take care of her, right?"

"Yeah, I guess so."

Brianna's face lights up. "And when you and Angela get married," she says, nudging me with her elbow, "I can have a sleepover at your house too. Don't you think it's about time you bought Angela an engagement ring?"

Outwardly, I chuckle, but on the inside, dread slithers through my veins like a warm shot of heroin. My girl Angela is the best thing about my life these days. But the timing of us finally getting together couldn't be worse.

Neither Angela nor my family knows about the call I received from my cousin this morning. From behind prison walls, The Shepherd put the word out on the street that he's gunning for me.

This poses a problem on multiple fronts. I promised Angela that my life of crime was behind me. And, at the time, I meant it. But The Shepherd's threat changes things. Angela's a lawyer who walks the straight-and-narrow. If she knew what was going on, she'd want me to report it to the police. That ain't my style. I'm gonna handle *my* situation *my* way.

My top priority for the moment is keeping myself and everyone around me safe. Unfortunately, Angela and I recently decided to move in together. She texted me this morning about checking out a rental house in Leimert Park. I have to find a way to slow her roll, at least until this situation is resolved. If we shack up now, she could end up as collateral damage.

Brianna's voice punctures my thoughts. "And when you propose to her, you better get down on one knee."

"You're a little smarty pants. You know that?"

"Yep. And I'm also smart enough to know that you're going to be okay. Just like me."

Brianna presses her right cheek against my chest and hugs me tight.

My niece's words are soothingly prophetic. I will indeed be okay. As soon as I find a way to kill The Shepherd.

CHAPTER 3

Graylin

The police!

My mouth is as dry as sand. "I don't have a naked picture of anybody on my phone, Mrs. Keller. I swear, I don't. Why'd you call the police on me?"

"I had no choice."

My right knee won't stop bouncing up and down. "Who said I had a naked picture?"

"I can't disclose that information."

There's a knock on the door. When two police officers step into the room, I almost pee on myself. They introduce themselves to the principal but ignore me.

One of the cops is short and Asian with biceps that look like two boulders. He turns around and mean mugs me. "Is this the student?"

Principal Keller nods and hands him a piece of paper. He reads it, then turns back to me.

"I'm Officer Chin and this is Officer Fenton," the Asian cop says, referring to a tall white man with slicked-back hair who's staring down at me too. "We need to talk to you."

Officer Chin opens the side door leading into the principal's private conference room and tells me to go inside. I'm so nervous it feels like I'm walking on toothpicks.

The white cop sits in the chair next to me and turns sideways. He's sitting so close to me that his knee keeps brushing against my thigh. I want to ask him to move back, but I don't. Officer Chin sits on the other side of the long table, glaring at me like I shot somebody.

"So, Graylin, do you know why you're here?" Officer Chin asks.

"Nope," I mumble. Then I hear my grandmother's voice. She's old school and is always telling me to be respectful to adults. "I mean, no, sir."

I don't like looking at the Asian cop. If they try a good-cop, bad-cop act on me, he's probably going to play the bad cop.

"First, I need to tell you that you're in some major trouble," the mean one says.

I've already decided that's what I'm going to call Officer Chin—Mean Cop—because that's what he is.

I don't say anything since he hasn't asked me a question.

"How old are you?"

"Fourteen."

"Your principal got a report that you have a naked picture of one of your classmates on your phone."

"But I don't." *Not anymore.*

"Do you know Kennedy Carlyle?"

"Yes."

"Is she your girlfriend?"

I screw up my face. "No." Kennedy is way too stuck-up to be any-body's girlfriend.

"Well, how do you know her?"

"She's in my English and algebra classes."

I don't want to talk to them because I know they aren't on my side. I watch a lot of TV crime shows with my granny. The cops always act like they want to help you, but they'd rather shoot a black kid than help him. That's why we need Black Lives Matter. They just need to read me my rights and—*Oh snap!* I suddenly remember what my dad told me to do if the police ever stopped me.

I sit up straight and try to look brave. "My dad told me not to talk to the police without his permission."

Mean Cop rolls his eyes. "Is that right? Does your daddy know you have a naked picture of one of your classmates on your phone?"

But I don't. I want to smile, but I know that will get me in even more trouble.

Mean Cop grips the edge of the table and leans forward. "If I were you, I'd want to defend myself. So, if you want us to hear your side of the story, you better start talking."

I don't know what to do. I want to defend myself, but my dad gave me strict instructions. *If a cop stops you, don't say a damn word.*

Officer Fenton bumps my thigh with his knee again which makes me flinch. "Look, Graylin, we need you to be honest with us. If you do, we can cut you some slack."

Even though I wish he wouldn't sit so close to me, at least he talks nice to me. Still, I keep quiet.

"According to the report we received," Mean Cop continues, "you've been going all over the school showing people a naked picture of your classmate."

Before I can stop myself, I blurt out, "No, I didn't! Somebody's lying on me!"

Of course, I'd *planned* to show the picture to my best friend Crayvon, but you can't go to jail for something you were only thinking about doing.

"If you have the picture on your phone," Officer Fenton says, "just be truthful about it and we'll see what we can do to keep you out of trouble."

They must think I'm stupid. I do what my dad told me to do and keep my mouth shut.

Mean Cop pounds the table with his fist, making me jump two inches out of my chair. "Where's your phone?"

I still don't answer. Everybody has the right to remain silent, even kids.

"I said where's your phone?" Mean Cop repeats.

I hide my hands underneath the table, so he can't see them shaking.

Officer Fenton pats me on the shoulder. "C'mon, Graylin, you seem like a good kid. I bet you make good grades, don't you?"

I nod and start to tell them I got honors certificates in math and science last year, but I figure they still won't let me go. "My dad"—I start to stutter—"my dad told me not to talk to the police without his permission."

"Why don't you help us out here?" Officer Fenton says. "We really need to see your phone. We'll take a quick look and if there's no picture, we'll send you back to class."

A squeaky voice comes out of my mouth. "It's…it's in my backpack."

As soon as the words are out, I want to kick myself. Now I've just lied to the police. Again.

"And where's your backpack?"

"In my locker."

"Why don't we go with you to your locker, so you can get it?" Officer Fenton says.

"My dad told me not to talk to the police without his permission," I say for the third time.

Officer Fenton frowns. "This is a very serious matter, son."

Mean Cop thumps his fingers on the table. "Why don't you just—"

The voice of Young Thug singing *RiRi* fills the room.

Ah-ah-ah work

Do the work baby do the work

Tonight baby do the work baby do the work.

When I hear my ringtone, my stomach lurches up into my throat. I'm about to throw up the oatmeal I had for breakfast.

Mean Cop scrunches up his face like a WWF wrestler. "Did your daddy also teach you to lie to the police? Give me the damn phone!"

I shakily pull it from my pocket and set it on the table.

Officer Fenton picks it up, taps the screen, then looks over at me. "What's the password?"

I stare down at the table.

"I said what's the password?" Now he's turning mean too.

"LeBron forty-three."

"For your sake, young man, I hope you're telling us the truth."

I keep my eyes on the table. A bead of sweat falls from my forehead into my eye, but I don't wipe it away.

"Why're you sweating?" Mean Cop says. "You afraid we're going to find that naked picture?"

After a couple of minutes, Officer Fenton looks at Mean Cop and shakes his head. "Nothing in his photos or texts. I only see a few recent emails. Nothing there either." He sets it back on the table.

Mean Cop grunts. "Let me look." He stretches one of his short arms across the table and grabs my phone.

He taps the screen a few times, then starts smiling. "Well, well, well, what do we have here? Looks like you forgot to check his deleted pictures, partner."

Mean Cop holds up my phone and shows me the picture I thought was gone forever. A warm trickle of pee runs down my left leg.

"You're quite the little liar, aren't you?" Mean Cop yells at me. "Where're the rest of the pictures?"

"There aren't any more," I stutter. "That was the only one I had."

"Did you take it?"

"No."

"You lied about your phone being in your locker, you lied about having this picture, and you're still lying now!"

"My…my dad"—I can't get my words out—"my dad told me not to talk to the police without his permission."

"When your daddy told you that, he didn't realize you'd be in this kind of trouble. If you didn't take this picture, how'd it get on your phone?"

"Somebody sent it to me."

"Who?"

"I don't know."

My throat hurts and it feels like somebody's pressing down on my chest. If the table wasn't in the way, I'd hug my knees to my chest.

Mean Cop pulls out his handcuffs and dangles them from his finger. "Stop lying and tell us the truth," he barks. "If you don't, you're going to jail."

CHAPTER 4

The Shepherd

If you have to do time, Seagoville Federal Correctional Institution outside Dallas—or *The Low* as we call it—isn't a bad place to spend a few years.

I'm in the yard, sitting at a picnic table, gazing down at my chess board, contemplating my next move. The sun is shining and the birds are chirping. The only thing spoiling this day is the heat. The Texas humidity is thick enough to butter a roll.

Marty Geller, a pudgy, ex-hedge fund manager, sits across from me. Everybody calls him Wallstreet. Few guys go by their real names at The Low. A full name is too much information to give up to just anybody. I only know Wallstreet's full name because he's my cellie.

The opportunity to rub shoulders with the criminal elite is what I like most about The Low. We have our fair share of low-level drug dealers and con men, but there's also a guy on my floor who's a Harvard grad convicted of embezzlement and a couple of doctors who wrote too many illegal prescriptions. When this is all behind us, Wallstreet and I have already made plans to do a deal or two.

Once I make my move, Wallstreet shoots me a grin. "You sure that's the move you wanna make, *Rodney*?"

I chuckle. Real names are a no-no around here. Everybody calls me Cali because that's where I'm from. Saying my real name is part of Wallstreet's tactic to unnerve me, but I'm not easily rattled.

I move my queen to the opposite side of the board and wait.

On the street, I had a solid rep as a strategist. I ran my operation like a business—and not just any business—but like a Fortune 500 corporation with checks and balances. I'm not like most guys who pursue criminal activities. I rarely lose my cool, I respect the concept of patience and I understand that all money isn't good money. I'm also a college graduate.

Wallstreet places a finger on his rook, waits a few seconds while he triple-checks himself, then zips it horizontally across the board.

I taunt him with a smile. "Are you sure that's the move *you* wanna make?"

"You can't bluff me," he says. The uncertainty in his eyes undercuts his response.

I pretend to study the board, then make a move that I put in place three turns ago. "Check..." I like stringing out the words "...mate."

"What?" Wallstreet leans in for a closer look, then chuckles with brotherly admiration. "Okay, you got me. You got me good. *This* time."

He starts setting up the board again, but I stand up. "I need to take a stretch."

I begin a leisurely walk across the compound. This place looks more like a private college campus than a prison. Manicured grass, leafy trees, paved walkways. Brick buildings that could pass for college dorms. Cells with actual doors, not bars. But it's the freedom to roam the place—within limits—that I appreciate the most.

My given name is Rodney Merriweather, but I'm known as The Shepherd on the street. The feds convicted me of sex trafficking—the politically correct term for pimping nowadays. The guys I associate with at The Low know that trafficking is the reason I'm here. But that's all they know and I prefer to keep it that way. Criminals have a strange code of ethics. A man can stab his own mother in the heart and get a pass. But some dudes think pimping little girls is akin to being a chomo—the prison nickname for child molesters. Even though my conviction for trafficking requires me to register as a sex offender once I get out of here, I'm not a chomo. I'm a businessman who was smart enough to capitalize on a product that happened to be in high demand.

Because I had no prior criminal record and no history of violence, my point total—the way the feds determine whether a convict will end up in a low, medium or maximum-security prison—qualified me for The Low.

I spot my target. Correctional Officer Sims is walking out of unit 5. As I get closer, he gives me an almost imperceptible nod as he walks past.

That's the signal I've been waiting for. I pick up my pace and head inside the building. I walk to the end of the hallway and open the door of the Education Department, where I work as a copy clerk. All inmates at The Low are required to work at least four hours a day. The minimum wage in federal prison is $5.25 a month. If you have a high school diploma, a job like mine, where I spend my days making copies for the Bureau of Prisons, pays a whopping $100 a month. If you can swing a gig with Unicor, the company that makes clothes for the entire prison system, you can make upwards of two or three hundred dollars a month.

Old School is waiting for me. He's a sixty-plus serial burglar from Decatur, Georgia, with nobody who cares enough to put any money on his books. So he hustles anyway he can.

Without words, he moves to the doorway and acts like he's talking to me. What he's really doing is serving as my lookout. If he sees the police—that's what we call the correctional officers behind their backs—he'll give me a signal.

I dash over to the third file cabinet on the north wall and retrieve the iPhone Sims left for me in a folder.

It was harder than I expected to find a correctional officer to buy off. But after bonding with Wallstreet, he introduced me to C.O. Sims. Like any working man, Sims has bills to pay and mouths to feed. I have needs too, like decent food, Michael Kors underwear and regular access to a cell phone. It was well worth the two grand. I had one of my guys wire the money to a special bank account Sims set up in his brother's name.

I dial Willie's number.

"How's the new project working out?" I never offer a greeting. Willie knows my time is limited.

"I found a new guy who can get to work on it right away. Everything's in motion."

Willie's been running my trafficking operation since my arrest. Prior to my hiatus, he handled security at my now-defunct strip club, City

Stars. I promoted him to my second-in-command out of necessity, not because he has the requisite skills for the job.

"You doing much advertising?"

"Yeah. I practically announced it from a bullhorn."

That makes me smile. I can see Dre Thomas now. Cowering someplace wondering when my guys are coming for him, never anticipating my bait-and-switch move. Before we get to him, we're actually snatching his niece Brianna for a second time.

The man brought all of this on himself. He should've been grateful to get the kid back and moved on. Instead, he had the balls to testify against me in court. And for that, he's going to pay.

"Sounds like you have everything under control. How long before the project is operational?"

"A few days at the most."

"And the new guy is somebody you trust, correct?"

"For sure."

"How's the other business working out?"

"Like butter, baby." I can almost see the smile on Willie's thick lips.

He's referring to my Birmingham operation. After the feds shut me down, I shipped the few girls I had left down south.

Once we snatch Brianna, she'll be headed there too.

CHAPTER 5

Dre

Two of the people I trust most in the world are kicking it at my crib right now.

Mossy is sitting on my couch, while I'm slouching in an easy chair across from him. My cousin Apache is standing with his back pressed against the door. Every few minutes or so, he lifts the edge of the curtain covering the picture window and peers outside.

"I'm telling you, man, it's all over the street," Apache says. "It ain't no bluff. The Shepherd put the word out. He wants you dead."

A long, braided ponytail runs past his shoulder blades. He earned his nickname because of his Native American features: bronzy skin, shiny, coal-black hair, and a bold, fearless demeanor that defies his small stature.

"I'm hearing all of this," Mossy says, his face drenched in disapproval, "but I ain't hearing no solutions."

My buddy is a large, chunky dude who sports a smooth, bald head like me. Mossy is a careful guy. He prefers to analyze all the pros and cons of a situation before making a move. "So what's the plan?" he asks.

Apache grins eagerly. "The plan is to kill his ass. That's the only way to shut him down for good."

Mossy smacks his lips. "Man, how you gonna take out a dude in federal prison?" He glances my way for confirmation that my cousin's statement is crazy.

When my eyes meet his and Mossy realizes I'm on board, he retreats.

"C'mon, man, I'm all the way down with having your back. But I ain't trying to go down for no murder." He hooks a thumb toward Apache. "And certainly not with this cowboy."

"Ain't nobody going down for nothing," Apache says. "I know how to handle my business. If you wanna punk out, the door is right over there."

"Dude, you're full of—"

"Hold up!" I shout. "This ain't helping. We're just talking. Considering our options."

This whole scene feels like *deja vu*. We convened here after Brianna went missing. We were successful then and we'll be successful this time too.

I understand Mossy's reluctance about working with Apache. So if he bails on us, I won't hold it against him. My cousin can be a bit of a renegade. He's likely to ignore any agreed-upon plan and go off on his own tangent. But Apache does have his strong points. He knows the streets of L.A. and has both direct and indirect ties to the criminals who run them. More importantly, he's the most loyal, fearless dude I know. When somebody he cares about needs help, Apache transforms into a flame-retardant super hero, willing to run naked into a blazing building.

"We should've taken him out when we had the chance," Apache complains. "I could've caught his ass walking into that courthouse and busted a cap right in the middle of his forehead."

"That would've been a real smart move," Mossy says.

I rub the back of my neck and slowly twist my head from side to side. In stressful situations, tension always settles deep in my neck.

"Whatever we do," I say, "we have to be smart about it."

Apache nods his agreement, then takes another surreptitious peek out of the window.

"Why you keep looking outta that window?" Mossy grumbles.

"For The Shepherd's dudes. We don't know when they gonna strike."

That reality sends another spasm through my already-tight neck muscles.

"You know he's still running little girls from prison, right?" Apache says.

My head jerks up. "You serious?"

"As a heart attack. Shep's got a whole new trafficking operation down south in Birmingham. He also owns a bar over on Central called

Craps. The dude who used to own it was going bankrupt. Shep bought him out and lets him work there. The dude's name is on the paperwork, but it's really all Shep. Ain't that a mother?"

"Where's Gus?" Mossy asks.

Gus is more like Mossy, a rational, out-of-the-box thinker. But if somebody pushes his button, Gus can be even more volatile than Apache.

"Graylin got into some trouble at school," I say. "Hopefully, Gus'll be here any minute."

Mossy nods. "As much as he's paying to send Graylin to that private school. I hope he ain't down there screwing up."

"Naw," I say. "That boy's college material for sure. I wish some of his smarts would rub off on Little Dre."

"So back to the problem at hand." Apache's focus is solely on The Shepherd. "The first thing we need to do is go on the offensive."

Mossy's about to say something when my phone rings. I grab it from the table and start moving toward my bedroom. "It's Angela. Give me a minute."

Before I can say hello, Angela's excitement gushes through the phone. "Did you get my text? When can you come look at the house? It's a three-bedroom on Edgehill. It's *so* cute."

I suck in a deep breath.

"Dre? Are you there?"

"Yeah, babe."

"The real estate agent has two other people interested in it. So we have to act fast."

My fingers tighten around the phone. "Can't do it today."

"Okay, what about tomorrow morning?"

I count off five long beats. "We'll see."

"*We'll see?* What does that mean?"

I love black women. They can transition from syrupy sweetness to outright indignation at the flip of a switch.

"I have a lot going on at the moment."

"Look, Dre, you're the one who brought up moving in together in the first place. If you've changed your mind, you need to tell me now. I don't want to waste any more time looking for a place if—"

"Hey, young lady, hold your horses," I say with a chuckle. "I haven't changed my mind. I just have a few things I need to handle first."

"What few things?"

"Nothing I have time to explain right now. Can we talk later?"

I let the silence linger. Angela's a classic Type A. Impatient, proactive, always in control. She hates being in the dark about anything.

"Dre, if it's about money and you don't have your half of the deposit, I can—"

"It's not about money, babe." My tone hardens. "Give me some time to handle my business. Okay?"

Strong women dig strong men. Whenever I toughen up, she goes soft. But only temporarily.

"Okay," she says hesitantly.

I rush her off the phone and head back into the living room.

"Like I was saying," Apache starts up again, "first thing we need to do is show him you ain't running scared. Let's step to his bar and let his peeps know that Shep's the one who needs to be watching *his* back cuz Dre got people in the joint who can make things happen."

"But he don't," Mossy points out.

Apache puffs out his chest. "I got connections to all kinda dudes who can get the job done."

Mossy moves to the edge of the couch. "Hold up. Whatever we do, we need to be smart about it. The more people involved, the more potential for problems."

"You're underestimating me, my brutha," Apache declares with a crooked smile. "Need I remind you that I'm the only one in this room who ain't never seen the interior of the county jail, much less a prison? There's a reason for that."

I smile to myself. Mossy has no comeback.

"I like the idea of showing up at Shep's bar," I say. "Let's do it tomorrow night."

CHAPTER 6

Gus

I've been sitting in a hard-ass chair outside the principal's office for almost 15 minutes now, getting more and more irritated. I don't know why, but something doesn't feel right.

What the hell did Graylin do?

I tried calling him, but got no answer. He must have his phone on mute since they aren't allowed to use it in class.

The door to the principal's office opens and Mrs. Keller shows me inside.

"What's going on? Where's Graylin?"

"Why don't you have a seat, Mr. Alexander?"

I sit down, but I'm still on edge. "I need to know what's going on with my son. Where is he?"

"I'm sorry to have to tell you this, but we received an anonymous report that Graylin had an inappropriate picture on his cell phone."

"What kind of inappropriate picture?"

"A photograph of a female classmate." Mrs. Keller swallows. "Naked."

I'm momentarily taken aback. My son's no angel, but this isn't something I would've expected from him. But then again, in this day and age with everything kids are exposed to and all this technology mess, who knows what they're up to. I start to breathe a little easier. A naked picture of a girl isn't the end of the world.

"Okay. I'll handle it. Who took the picture?"

"We don't know."

"Well, what did Graylin say about it?"

"He denied having it."

"Did you see the picture?"

"No."

"Then how do you know he has one?"

"As I said, we received an anonymous report."

"Did you check his phone?"

"No."

I'm not one of those parents who thinks my kid is an angel, but this sounds like something blown way out of proportion.

"So what you're telling me is that you don't even know if the allegation is true." And that's all it is as far as I'm concerned. An allegation and nothing more.

"You have to understand that when we receive a report like this, there's a certain protocol we have to follow."

I exhale. This is a bunch of crap. I can't believe I had to drive all the way down here for this bull.

"I'll talk to him. Where is he?"

"He's being interviewed by the police."

"Police?" I shoot to my feet so fast the chair topples backward, banging into the wall. "Like hell he is! The police can't talk to my son without my permission. Take me to him. Now!"

I hear yelling coming from the door to my right. Before the principal can stop me, I burst through it.

"What the fuck!" My son is in handcuffs, a white cop gripping him by the forearm.

"Dad! Dad! Please help me!" Graylin cries. "Dad, please don't let them arrest me!"

I charge up to the cop holding Graylin. "What are you doing to my son?"

"Sir, you need to calm down," yells an Asian cop. He extends his right palm toward me while his other hand grazes the butt of his gun. "Please back up, sir!"

I defiantly stay put. "I asked you what you're doing to my son. You can't interrogate him without my permission."

"I told you to step back!" the Asian cop yells, twice as loud as before.

When I still don't move, he snatches his Beretta from its holster and points it at me. "I said back up! Now!"

"Oh my God!" the principal cries. "Please, Mr. Alexander. Please step back!"

"Dad, Dad, please go back!" Graylin's sobbing hysterically now. "They're going to shoot you. I'm okay! Please, Dad, go back! Please!"

The *only* reason I take two small steps backward is because the cop's hand is so unsteady I fear he might actually shoot me. But I'm way madder than he is nervous.

The cop lowers his gun but doesn't return it to the holster.

Heat stings my face. "What are you doing to my son?"

"Sir, you need to lower your voice," says the cop restraining Graylin.

"You can't talk to him without my permission."

"We don't need your permission," the white cop says.

"Please, Dad!" Graylin cries. "It's okay! I'll be okay. Please, Dad! I don't want them to shoot you! Please do what they say!"

The Asian cop looks past me at the principal. "We found the picture."

Principal Keller gasps and cups her mouth.

I'm so pissed off my vision is blurry. But it's my son's terror-stricken face, not the Beretta still in that cop's hand that forces me to regain control of my senses. I take a few more steps back, lower my voice, but amplify my outrage.

"Why is my son in handcuffs?"

The Asian cop eyes me with contempt. "Because he's under arrest."

"For what?"

"Possession of child pornography."

CHAPTER 7

Willie

I'm bringing my new sidekick Bones up to speed on our assignment from The Shepherd.

"We have to do this thing by the book," I tell him as we relax in a booth at Craps, nursing two fingers of Jack. "The Man don't want no mistakes."

"You've said that three times," Bones gripes. "I don't make mistakes. I ain't no rookie."

Indeed he is not. A career criminal who enjoys his work, Johnny "Bones" Battle is neither particularly bright nor inquisitive, which makes him the perfect candidate for this job. Don't ask, don't tell, just do. Bones lives by the hour, never looking ahead, not even as far as the end of the day. Where Bones grew up—dirt poor, deep in the backwoods of Alabama—days weren't promised to anybody.

He leans back and looks me up and down. "Why you always dressin' up? It's the middle of the day, and you look like a TV preacher."

I flash him a smile with my flawless implants. I appreciate it when somebody notices the care I take in presenting myself to the world. My slender frame is always adorned in the best: Italian suits, silk ties, and cap-toe Oxford shoes. I also take proper care of my temple. I refrain from pork and fried foods, get monthly facials and have standing appointments with my barber and manicurist every Wednesday afternoon. I'm pushing fifty, but people tell me I could pass for forty-five. Bones, by comparison, drapes his bulky body in jogging suits and wrinkled T-shirts.

"When you look good, you feel good," I say.

Bones grins, revealing a spacious gap between his two front teeth. A horseshoe-shaped bald spot rests on the crown of his head, which is as round and brown as a coconut. His pointy, caricature-like ears frame small, oval eyes that are too close together.

"To do this thing right, we gotta do our research first."

Bones scrunches up his face. "Research? What kinda research?"

"This ain't gonna be a typical snatch and grab. We need to follow the girl for a few days. Figure out her routine. Then strike when we know it's safe."

"I thought The Man wanted it done right away."

"He does, but Sh—" I catch myself. I don't trust Bones enough to let him know this is The Shepherd's operation. "The Man ain't calling the shots, I am. Taking a few more days to do this thing right won't hurt nothing."

Bones nods. "Whatever you say, bruh. Just make sure The Man has my money ready as soon as the job is done."

I don't bother to mention that Shep already transferred the money to my account. I also neglected to mention to Shep that Bones is doing the job for three grand, not five.

"Dre Thomas lives in those apartments at the corner of Slauson and LaBrea. His niece is in Compton on Magnolia Street." I hand him a piece of paper with both addresses.

"What I need his address for? I thought I was just snatchin' the girl."

"After we get the kid, we're going after him next. We might as well figure out his routine now, so when The Man gives the word, we'll be ready."

"Whoa," Bones says. "I'ma need some more money for a second job."

"How about another grand since I'll be helping out on that one?"

Bones is quiet for a minute. I'm guessing he'll ask for another five hundred dollars, which I'm prepared to pay since I'm getting five grand for that job too.

"I think I should get half the cost of the first job," he says. "Fifteen hundred."

I grunt like I'm upset. "Okay."

Bones smirks, happy because he thinks he's put the squeeze on me.

"Oh, yeah, I need to borrow your Escalade. My car is in the shop for a couple of days."

This time my frown is real. "How'd you get down here?"

"Uber."

Working with a criminal who has to rely on a ride-sharing company to get around isn't a good thing. This job better go well.

"Don't worry, man," Bones says. "I'll take good care of your ride. At least I didn't ask to borrow your Lincoln."

I don't mind parting with my Escalade, but *nobody* drives my Lincoln. That would be akin to letting some dude wear my silk boxers.

"I'll take you to my place to pick up the Escalade. Start following the girl in the morning. I'll trail the uncle. In a couple of days, we'll switch off and I'll follow the girl and you watch Dre. Once we figure out their routines, we can discuss our next move."

"I never had a job where I had to do all this undercover stuff," Bones complains.

I take a sip of my drink. "Well, you do now."

"I don't understand why The Man don't take both of 'em out and be done with it. Having me kidnap that girl and drive her all the way down to Birmingham seems like a lot of work."

"That's because you're not a businessman. If he ships her down south, he can make some money off of her first."

Bones licks his lips. "It's a lot of girls out there. Don't make sense to put all this time into this one."

"You don't need to know all the hows and whys. The Man wants to mess with their heads. Terrorize 'em."

"Whatever," Bones says, draining his glass. "Just have my money ready the minute I dump that kid down south."

CHAPTER 8

Graylin

Possession of child pornography?

"What?" I cry out. "I don't have any child pornography!"

Principal Keller looks just as shocked as me and my dad. She's hugging herself and rubbing her hands up and down her arms.

This is all your fault! Why'd you call the police on me?

My dad backs up all the way into Principal Keller's office and Mean Cop finally puts his gun away.

"Please, Dad, don't let them take me to jail!" My face is wet with tears and snot. "I swear I didn't do anything wrong. I swear, I didn't!"

My dad's fists are clenched tight, which is how I know he's really, really mad.

"I can bring him down to the police station," he says. "You don't have to arrest him."

Officer Fenton pulls me past my dad into the main office. Once we're outside in the hallway, it seems like half the school has lined up for a parade. As the cops march me toward the front entrance of the school, everyone stares and points at me.

"What happened?"

"What did Graylin do?"

"Graylin's too smart to get arrested."

I glance back over my shoulder and I'm relieved to see my dad following us.

They tug me down the steps to a police car parked in front of the school. Officer Fenton opens the back door, palms the top of my head like a basketball and pushes me into the seat.

My dad moves toward me, but Mean Cop grips the butt of his gun. "You need to stay back, sir, and let us do our jobs."

I'm crying so hard I feel like I might throw up.

"Where are you taking him?" My dad's voice sounds muffled through the thick car window.

"Eastlake Juvenile Hall," Officer Fenton says. "They'll call you."

"Can I go with him? He's just a kid. He's only fourteen."

"It doesn't work like that."

The two cops climb into the front and slam the doors. As I stare up at my dad, the unbelievable sight in front of me sends a chill through my whole body. Tears are streaming down my dad's face. I've never seen my dad cry. When my Uncle Diddy got shot, I thought my dad was going to cry, but he didn't. Not even at the funeral. So I didn't think my dad *could* cry.

As the car pulls away from the curb, he starts jogging alongside it.

"I'm coming to get you!" my dad yells. "Don't talk to them! Don't say nothing to nobody!"

Simone

I can't wait to show Kennedy the new cell phone cover I bought her in New York. I'm certain she'll be the only eighth grader at snooty Marcus Prep with real diamonds on her phone.

As soon as the plane touches down at LAX, I unbuckle my seatbelt. I love flying first-class. It's not just the extra attention from the flight attendants, the superior food or the cushy seats. I simply despise sitting in the back of the plane with the common folk.

The minute I take my phone out of airplane mode, it starts pinging with texts and emails—all from work, of course. I'm the only black V.P. in my division at AT&T and I love my job.

The flight attendants open the doors and I'm the first one to step into the jetway. I'm reading a text from my assistant when my phone rings.

"Hello, Mrs. Carlyle. This is Gloria Keller. From Marcus Preparatory Academy."

I stop cold, forcing the man behind me to swerve left as he curses under his breath.

"Oh my God! What's the matter? Is Kennedy okay? What happened?"

"Kennedy's fine."

I instantly relax, a little embarrassed about my panicked reaction. She's probably calling about the spring fundraiser. "You don't have to ask," I tell her. "We're good for five grand."

Percy and I have donated close to twenty thousand dollars to the theater program at Marcus Prep. Little good it did us. Despite our generosity, the principal did absolutely nothing when I complained about Kennedy not getting the lead role in *Beauty and the Beast.*

"Mrs. Carlyle, I'm not calling about the fundraiser. We've had an incident."

The click-clacking of my pink Jimmy Choos on the airport tile abruptly stops. "What do you mean by *an incident*?"

I hear Keller suck in a gulp of air. "We received an anonymous report that one of our students had an inappropriate picture of Kennedy on his cell phone."

For the next few seconds it's as if someone has pressed a mute button, silencing the airport's background noise.

"What kind of inappropriate picture?"

Keller waits several beats. "Well, um, a naked picture."

"What? Is it true?"

"According to the police, it is. They've arrested the boy."

"What's his name?"

"I'm not at liberty to provide that information. He's a minor and—"

"I don't care. If some boy is sending naked pictures of my baby all over that school, I have a right to know his name. Is he some peeping Tom? Did the school fail to secure the girls' locker room?"

"Please, Mrs. Carlyle, calm down. The report only mentioned one picture, not multiple pictures. And we don't have any information that he sent it to anyone."

"I don't care if it's one or ten. I bet it's all over the internet by now."

"The police will be conducting an investigation. I'm sure—"

"What kind of place are you running down there?" I drop my professionalism and use words that more accurately convey my disgust. "I put my child in that school because I didn't want her exposed to a bunch of ghetto-ass hood rats. And you let this happen? I'm suing that little bastard, his parents, *and* the school."

"I can assure you, Mrs. Carlyle, no school personnel had any involvement in any of this."

"Where's my child? Put my baby on the phone!"

"She's with one of our guidance counselors. We thought you or her father should be here when we told her what happened."

"Well, at least you did one thing right. I just landed at LAX. It'll take me about thirty minutes to get over there. In the meantime, you tell that boy's parents they don't need to be worried about the police. They need to worry about *me*."

"Hold on, Mrs. Carlyle, there's no need for any threats. The school is doing everything it can to—"

"I don't care what the school is doing. The only thing that matters is what *I'm* going to do. This is *my* child you're talking about. And that boy is definitely going to pay."

CHAPTER 10

Graylin

The backseat of the police cruiser smells like the bums that sleep outside the Quickstop Liquor Store on Manchester. And that makes me want to throw up. I can't stop crying and my teeth are chattering even though I'm not cold.

"We're here." Mean Cop glances back at me as the police car rolls to a stop. Two giant steel gates slowly open and I can't help thinking we're driving into a dungeon.

Mean Cop opens the back door, grabs my arm and pulls me from the car. It's hard to keep my balance with my hands cuffed behind my back. I dip my head and try to wipe the snot off my nose with my shoulder, but Mean Cop acts like I'm trying to escape and squeezes my arm real hard.

They walk me inside where three men are standing behind bulletproof windows like at the bank. Mean Cop walks up to the counter, spouts off my name and starts filling out some paperwork.

A gruff-looking Mexican man steps out from behind the counter. I hold my breath. I swear I can't handle another evil cop.

"I'll take it from here," he says in a harsh tone. "Take off the cuffs."

"He's all yours." Mean Cop unlocks the handcuffs, then follows Officer Fenton out of the door.

"I'm Mr. Cardoza," the man says, as I massage my sore wrists. "I'm a detention services officer." He talks nicer to me than he did to the cops. "I'm going to explain the rules to you, okay?"

I nod as he starts patting me down.

"I'll need you to answer *yes* or *no* so I know you understand me, okay?"

I nod again. "I mean, yes, sir."

"This your first time here?"

"Yes, sir." I'm not crying anymore because I cried so hard I don't have any tears left.

"I thought so."

"So is this the jail?"

He smiles. "No, this isn't a jail. This is Eastlake Juvenile Hall. Take a look at that sign." Mr. Cardoza points at a poster on the wall. "Can you read?"

"Yes. I get mostly A's."

"That's good." He gives me a wink. "Take a few minutes to look over the rules, then we'll read them together."

I'm a fast reader, so it doesn't take me long to read all 15 of them, which are in English and Spanish. No profanity, no gang slogans, no fighting or horse playing, no weapons or drugs, and no loud talking. A couple of them seem kind of lame, like no sex talk, mother talk, escape talk or race talk.

Mr. Cardoza comes back and we spend another 10 minutes going over the rules one by one. There's no way I can remember all of them, but since I never do that kind of stuff, I don't even try.

Mr. Cardoza uses a key on his belt to unlock a door and leads me down a long hallway.

"Where are we going?"

"To the Boys Receiving Unit."

I want to ask what that is, but I don't. I hope it's not like it is on *Lockup* where you have to take off all your clothes and bend over so a guard can look inside your butt.

"Um, do I get a phone call. I want to call my dad."

"Sure, as soon as we get you processed."

That makes me so happy I almost start crying again. I'm surprised that juvenile hall looks a lot like my old elementary school. Everything is beige and old with lots of windows. They even have grass and plants. We stop near an open doorway where a black woman is sitting behind a desk. She reminds me of my aunt Macie because of her dark skin and short hair. All of the staff, including Mr. Cardoza, are dressed in beige khakis and dark-blue golf shirts. Since they don't have guns, maybe this really isn't a jail.

"This is Graylin Alexander," Mr. Cardoza says. "A first-timer. He's an A student."

The woman smiles at me. "I'm Ms. Turner. Here's your towel roll. You need to shower and change into the clothes wrapped inside that towel." She points at a man standing a few feet away. "Mr. Winston handles the boys."

I wish Ms. Turner could stay with me, but I'm too afraid to ask her to.

I look through a big window and see two gangbanger-looking boys sitting on a bench. One of them has tattoos all over his shaved head.

"The showers are over there," Mr. Winston says.

He points to a gray cemented area with four shower stalls that don't have any doors. I put my towel roll on a bench underneath a small window. When Mr. Winston doesn't move, I realize he's going to stand there and watch me.

"Let's go. We don't have all day."

I unwrap the towel roll and find a white T-shirt, briefs, socks, gray sweatpants and a gray sweatshirt. Turning my back to Mr. Winston, I pull my shirt over my head, then strip off my underwear, which reeks of urine.

They didn't give me a face towel, so I guess I have to use my hands. I take several pumps from a soap dispenser outside the shower stall and step inside. The warm water feels good and I want to stay here forever.

"That's long enough," Mr. Winston says, after only a few minutes.

I step out of the shower and run over to the bench to grab my towel. Our bathroom at home has a heater, which I miss right now because it's freezing cold. I quickly dry myself off with the towel, which isn't thick and soft like the ones we have at home. I always put on deodorant and Vaseline after getting out of the shower, but I guess they don't have any here.

After I'm dressed in my sweatshirt and sweatpants, Ms. Turner asks me a bunch of questions.

No, I don't take any medications. *No,* I don't have any allergies. *No,* I don't have asthma or seizures or lice. *No,* I'm not autistic and *no* I don't have any mental conditions or health issues like ADD. After what seems like fifty more questions, she leads me down another hallway to an office with two desks that seem too big for such a little room. A man with an Afro stands up and shakes my hand.

"I'm Mr. Jackson. What's your full name?"

"Graylin Michael Alexander."

"Okay, Graylin, have a seat. I'm your Detention and Control Officer. You'll also be assigned a probation officer."

Probation officer? I haven't even had a trial yet. How can I be on probation already?

I know my dad told me not to talk to anybody, but I have to ask. "Why do I have a probation officer? I haven't even been convicted of anything."

Mr. Jackson laughs. "Every kid gets assigned a probation officer. I'll explain how it works in a second."

"The other man"—I try to remember his name but I can't— "the one who told me all the rules said I could call my dad."

"You sure can. I have a few things to go over with you first."

Mr. Jackson types something into his computer, then turns back to me. He tells me that the police arrested me for possession of child pornography, California Penal Code 311.1, then he starts reading me my rights.

"You have the right to remain silent," he begins. "Anything you say can and will be used against you in a court of law…"

I'm mad because Mean Cop should've read me my rights before they took me in that conference room. Then I wouldn't have said anything or given them my phone. The words sound just like they do on TV, which makes me want to start crying again because I'm not a criminal.

"Do you understand the rights I've just read to you?"

"Yes, sir." I'm not too sure I understood everything, only the part about being silent.

"Would you like to speak with me?"

I can hear my dad yelling at me through the window of the police car, telling me not to talk to anybody. But Mr. Jackson is being so nice to me, I don't want to make him mad.

"Um, no, sir." I try to sound respectful so he won't get upset. "I want to be silent."

"This is a chance for you to tell me your side of the story. Are you sure you don't want to speak with me about what happened at school?"

I *do* want to explain everything to him so he can let me go home. But I have to do what my dad told me to do.

"My dad told me not to talk to anybody."

"Okay, that's fine."

I'm glad Mr. Jackson doesn't seem mad. Now he starts asking me almost as many questions as Ms. Turner.

I tell him the name of my school, my age, my grade, my birthdate, my address. *No,* I'm not a foster kid. *No,* I don't have a social worker. *No,* I've never been arrested or suspended from school or picked up for truancy.

Then he starts asking me about my family. I tell him that I'm an only child, that I live with my dad and my granny, and that my mama is on drugs and we don't know where she is.

"Do your father or grandmother drink alcohol in the home?"

That question makes me kinda nervous. "Only my dad. But he never gets drunk."

"What about drugs?"

"My dad and my granny don't do drugs. Just my mama."

"What about weed? Does your dad smoke weed?"

My dad has never smoked weed in front of me, but I've smelled it on him a couple of times. I don't want to lie again, but if I tell the truth, my dad could get in trouble. Maybe if I hadn't lied about that picture, they wouldn't have arrested me. Then I remember that weed is legal in California now. It's the same as drinking alcohol, so they can't arrest my dad for that.

"Um, I think my dad smokes weed, but not in front of me."

I expect Mr. Jackson to look surprised, but he just moves on to the next question.

My head is hurting by the time I finish giving him my whole life story. Then he goes over the same rules the other officer made me read, even though I told him we already did that.

"Can I call my dad now?" I ask when we're done.

"Sure." Mr. Jackson picks up the telephone receiver from his desk. "What's his number?"

My mind goes as blank as a computer screen. I always call my dad from my Favorites. I try to concentrate, but his number won't come to me. I can't even remember my home number so I can talk to my granny.

"I don't know my dad's number." Tears start falling again and my chest is hurting now. "It's…it's in my phone."

Without my phone, I don't know *anybody's* number.

CHAPTER 11

Angela

Most people hate sitting in traffic, but I welcome the downtime. The bumper-to-bumper congestion on Slauson Avenue right now gives me a chance to think.

After bugging me for weeks about living together, Dre's suddenly too busy to check out the place I found. Is he suffering from cold feet or is he about to ghost on me?

My phone rings and I brighten with relief when I see that it's Dre. Maybe he's changed his mind about seeing the place.

When I pick up, his words come at me like he's firing them from a machine gun.

"Dre, slow down. I can't understand a word you're saying."

"Graylin got arrested!"

"Arrested? For what?"

As Dre explains the situation, I feel an eerie sense of foreboding. I've read about kids charged with possession of child pornography for sending naked selfies. Kids as young as twelve and thirteen.

"They took him to juvenile hall. We have to go down there and get him out."

"Which one?" There are at least three juvenile facilities in the L.A. area.

"Eastlake. Gus is with me. We're headed there now."

I make a left on LaBrea and head for the Santa Monica Freeway. "I'm on my way."

As soon as I'm on the freeway, I get to work on something Gus hasn't yet asked me to do—finding legal representation for Graylin.

Since I practice criminal defense in addition to employment law, Gus will probably want me to handle Graylin's case. But my practice is almost exclusively in state and federal court. Juvenile court has totally different rules and I don't speak the language.

I call a couple of friends and ask them to recommend a top-notch juvenile defense attorney. "I want the attorney you'd hire to represent your kid," I tell them.

Within twenty minutes, both of them call back with three names. Only one name appears on both lists: Jenny Ungerman.

I transition to the Harbor Freeway north, hop off at 9th Street and pull into a metered parking space so I can Google Jenny's name. Her website boasts of multiple victories and even provides helpful videos for parents about the juvenile justice system. I look up the other attorneys as well. I'm also impressed with them, but Jenny is the clear standout. I get back on the road and call Dre.

"Graylin's going to need an attorney. I have someone who comes highly recommended. Her name is—"

"Why can't you represent him?"

"I don't practice in juvenile court."

"You were a federal prosecutor. A juvenile case should be easy."

"It doesn't work like that, Dre. I don't know the rules or the players. I'd almost be committing malpractice by handling Graylin's case. Just trust me on this. Put me on speakerphone so I can talk to Gus."

After getting his okay, I give Jenny a call. When I start gushing over her reputation, she abruptly waves off the praise. "Tell me what's going on."

She listens to the few facts I can provide, then sighs long and hard.

"Don't worry. Graylin's father can pay your fee." I'm not sure that's true since I haven't asked about her rates.

"That sigh wasn't reluctance to take the case. It was frustration. So far this year, I've had eight cases where the D.A.'s office went after kids for sexting."

"That many?"

"Yep. And they're not just charging them with possession and distribution of child pornography, they're actually locking them up. My last client, who was fifteen, got a year for convincing his girlfriend to pose nude and then sending her picture to his best friend, who put it on Instagram. It ultimately ended up on some underground pedophile site."

"You couldn't plead it down to a lesser charge?"

"I tried, but the asshole D.A. wouldn't budge. Prosecutors have a lot of discretion as to who gets charged. Some of them read the statutes literally and will go after anyone in possession of a naked picture of a kid, even if it's a thirteen-year-old child."

I pray to God Graylin hasn't taken a naked picture of some girl. "So will you take the case?"

"Yes, of course. It'll take me about forty minutes to get down to Eastlake."

"Thanks. It sounds like Graylin might be in some serious trouble."

"If he has a naked picture of an under-aged girl on his phone, there's no *might* about it," Jenny says. "These days, a smartphone in the hands of a kid can have more devastating consequences than giving them a loaded gun. And the average parent doesn't have a clue."

CHAPTER **12**

Simone

I have to wait far too long for a cab and when I finally climb inside one, it stinks of cigarette smoke. To add to my stress, I can't reach my worthless husband. Rather than call Percy a third time, I send him a text.

URGENT. CALL ME RE KENNEDY. IF YOU EVEN CARE THAT IS.

As my finger hovers over the *send* button, I have a sudden and rare change of heart. Antagonizing Percy usually brings me tremendous joy. But even *I* have to admit that now isn't the time for heightened discord. I delete the last sentence.

Seconds later, my phone pings with a return text.

ALREADY KNOW. PICKED K UP FROM SCHOOL.

What? I wanted to be there when they told Kennedy. That principal called Percy because she didn't want to face me. I plan to give both of them a piece of my mind.

Twenty minutes later, I charge through the front door like I've arrived to put out a fire. Kennedy's in the den, sitting on the couch next to Percy.

"My baby!" I call out, pulling her into my arms. Her eyes are puffy and her bangs are matted to her forehead. "I'm so sorry this had to happen to you."

"Oh, Mommy, I'm so embarrassed. LaShay says everybody at school is talking about the picture. I'm never going back to that school again!"

I glare over her head at Percy. "I can't believe you didn't wait for me to get there."

"Now's not the time, Simone." He peers down at Kennedy. "Honey, we need to talk about what happened. Was this kid your boyfriend or something?"

"Boyfriend?" I scream. "Percy, you know darn well Kennedy's not allowed to date until she's sixteen."

Percy pats Kennedy on the shoulder. "Everything's going to be fine, sweetie. But I don't understand how that boy got a naked picture of you? Do you even know him?"

I pull Kennedy closer. "How in the world would she know how he got it? He's probably some pervert."

"Please turn off the drama machine for a second, Simone. Okay? I'm just trying to get to the bottom of this."

"His name's Graylin Alexander, Daddy. He's in two of my classes. I don't know how he got my picture, Daddy. I promise."

"Where was the picture taken?" Percy asks. "Has anybody even seen it?"

"I don't know," Kennedy sniffs. "LaShay said they arrested him because he had it on his phone. Daddy, I'm so embarrassed!"

"Sweetie, you know you can tell us anything, right," Percy continues to push. "You haven't let some boy take pictures of you, have you?"

"Percy! Are you out of your mind?"

"Look, Simone, we have to ask. One of my law partners found out his daughter was sexting a boy at her school. She was only a year older than Kennedy."

"What that little fast girl did has nothing to do with my child."

"No, Daddy. I didn't sext anybody, I promise."

"We know you didn't," I tell her. "I'll have Zala make you some chamomile tea. Zala, get in here!"

"I don't want any tea!" Kennedy sobs. "I just want to go to bed and never get up again!"

Our Ethiopian *au pair* scurries into the room, her hands clasped in front of her.

"Do you know anything about this?"

"About what, Mrs. Carlyle?"

"Some kid had a naked picture of—"

"That's enough!" Percy yells. "Zala, this doesn't involve you. Please help Kennedy to her bedroom."

Zala takes Kennedy by the hand and walks her out of the room.

I'm not happy with Percy right now. "Why in the world would you interrogate your own child like she's some hostile witness?"

Percy rubs his forehead. "I'm just trying to understand how this could've happened. Maybe it's a fake picture. Her head on somebody else's body. That's pretty easy to do on a computer."

"Whether it's fake or not, we're suing that school and that boy's parents."

"We're going to handle this," Percy says. "But let's not make a federal case out of it."

My head rears back like a stunned cobra. "What did you say?"

"Let's wait until we have all the facts. I'm not sure suing anybody is the best thing for Kennedy."

"Oh, this is interesting. Mr. Big Time Lawyer sues people every day of the week, but wants to run and hide when his daughter's reputation is on the line."

"My daughter's reputation is *exactly* what I'm thinking about. A lawsuit means publicity and publicity will only cause more embarrassment for Kennedy. We need to address this quickly and quietly. Can we please focus on what's best for our daughter rather than your penchant for payback?"

"I guess you also expect me to sit back and do nothing while you continue screwing your little associate."

Percy stands up. "I've told you a thousand times, I'm not seeing anybody. Jesus Christ! Your constant badgering me over this nonsense is exactly why I left."

My husband moved out three months ago claiming we'd *grown apart*. He's supposedly been working on a high-profile securities fraud case with a junior associate at his law firm—a thirty-something Latina. The fourth time he came home after midnight, I stopped accepting his excuses about the complicated brief or the burdensome discovery responses. What angers me most is Percy's refusal to admit that he's having an affair.

"We should put her in a new school," Percy says.

"I don't want her at *any* school right now. We can homeschool her."

His brow arches. "Really? So you're going to be around to do that?"

"You're not going to make me feel guilty for having a career. Zala can make sure she gets her work done every day. I'll review all of her assignments. If I'm out of town, we can Skype."

"That's just like you. Job first, family second."

"How dare you—"

Like always, Percy is out of the door before I've had a chance to say my piece. I hate the way he so easily dismisses me.

I grab my cell phone from the table near the door and start scrolling through my contacts. We're major campaign donors and have a ton of important political connections. And I'm about to call in some favors.

That little hoodlum Graylin Alexander deserves to be in jail for what he did to my child. And I'm going to do everything in my power to make sure that's where he ends up.

CHAPTER 13

Angela

Thirty minutes and two wrong turns later, I finally make it to Eastlake Juvenile Hall. The only parking spot I can find is almost a block away.

From a quick Google search, I learn that Eastlake—also referred to as Central Juvenile Hall—sits on more than twenty acres in the Boyle Heights section of Los Angeles. It's the oldest youth detention center in the country, established back in 1912. Most of its residents are black and Hispanic. Only about twenty percent are female.

A security guard waves me through a metal detector, while a different one checks my purse. I'm barely inside the tiny lobby before Gus and Dre rush up to me.

I give Gus a hug as I squeeze Dre's hand. Gus has a burly build and is just under six feet. He and Dre did time together at Corcoran State Prison. Since then, they've both committed to a crime-free life and now team up rehabbing houses.

"Jenny should be here any minute. She'll explain how everything works and get us in to see Graylin."

Just then, a tall, slim white woman with shoulder-length auburn hair steps through the metal detectors. As she heads our way, she walks with a lawyer's confidence and has the polished prettiness of a TV news anchor.

"Are you Angela Evans?" the woman asks.

I nod. "And you must be Jenny Ungerman. Thanks so much for getting here so quickly."

Jenny's wide brown eyes and pert smile convey a friendly, easygoing vibe. After short introductions, we all sit down and Gus starts bombarding her with questions.

"How soon can we post bail and get him outta here? And why were those cops talking to him without my permission? I don't understand how—"

Jenny raises her hands. "Mr. Alexander, I know you're concerned about your son. But we need to discuss a few things before we proceed."

Gus sighs, then nods.

"First, my retainer to handle Graylin's case through adjudication is twenty thousand dollars. If there are any special hearings, it could be more."

Dre and Gus pin me with a stupefied look that says, *This chick is all about the money.* But Jenny is doing what she has to do. When you're a defense attorney, your fee has to be the first order of business. If the client can't afford you, there's no need for any further discussion. Attorneys don't work for free, especially not the good ones.

"What's adjudi—what's that mean?" Gus asks.

"That's what a trial is called in the juvenile system."

Jenny's fee is a little on the high side, but not outrageous. "Would you be willing to accept a small retainer, and the rest via monthly payments," I ask.

"As a professional courtesy to you, I'll do that. But I'll need a cashier's check for five thousand dollars before making my first court appearance."

I pull Gus and Dre off to the side. "Twenty friggin' grand?" Gus says. "Are you kidding me?"

"Can't he get a public defender?" Dre asks. "It ain't like he's facing a felony or something."

"I know some great public defenders, but you don't get to choose the one you want," I tell them. "From everything I've been told, Jenny's worth every penny."

"I'll kick in," Dre says to Gus. "And I know your sister Macie will too."

Once Gus tells Jenny he'd like to proceed, she pulls a retainer agreement from her satchel and says he should call her if he has any questions about it.

"Now, to your questions," Jenny begins. "First, there's no bail for juveniles."

Gus' forehead creases. "I can't bail him out? How long will he have to stay here?"

"The lack of a bail system is a good thing. Unless a kid is accused of a violent crime, has trouble at home or a prior record, he'll usually be released to a parent or guardian."

Gus leans back in his chair and exhales. "So I can get him out of here tonight. Thank God."

"I didn't say that," Jenny says. "We won't know for sure until I speak with one of the detention officers."

"Graylin's a good kid," I say, hoping to reduce some of Gus' anxiety. "I'm sure they'll let him come home."

Jenny fixes me with a scorching glare that I don't quite understand. This is Graylin we're talking about. He's a model child. Of course they're going to let him go home.

"What I wanna know," Gus says, "is why those cops were interrogating my son without my permission. They should've—"

"The police don't need parental consent to question a minor in California."

This time, Dre speaks up. "For real?"

"That's always a shock to parents," Jenny says. "And the school also doesn't need probable cause to search him, just reasonable suspicion, which is a much lower standard. Did a teacher take his phone?"

"We don't know," I say.

Jenny directs her attention to Gus. "Mr. Alexander, I need to explain something else that's sometimes a little difficult for parents to understand. Even though Graylin's a minor, if you hire me to represent him, he's my client, not you."

Gus cocks his head. "And what exactly does that mean?"

Jenny forces a smile. "It means that even though you'll be paying my bill, my only obligation is to Graylin. I can keep you updated about the case, but only to the extent Graylin allows me to do so. And to be completely clear, I'll be following Graylin's directions, not yours."

Both Gus and Dre look over at me as if I'm pranking them.

"That's nuts," Dre says. "Graylin's just a kid."

I jump in to head off a confrontation. "Let's listen to everything she has to say. What else, Jenny?"

"You shouldn't have any substantive conversations with Graylin about his case. There's a privilege between husband and wife, but not between a parent and child. If Graylin admits something incriminating, you could be compelled to testify against him."

The creases in Gus' forehead deepen into crevices. "Lady, don't talk to me like I'm stupid. Even if Graylin did tell me something, I'd never testify against my own son."

Jenny shows no reaction to Gus' hostile tone. She's obviously done this dance before. "I couldn't allow you to lie under oath, Mr. Alexander. So, it's best that you don't have any knowledge of the underlying facts."

"Are you saying I can't even ask him if he did what they're accusing him of?"

"Yes, that's what I'm saying."

Gus glares at me again. "And this is who you want to represent my son?"

I place a hand on Gus' forearm. "Let's just get Graylin out of here tonight and take it from there."

Jenny stands up. "Let me go see if I can make that happen."

Dre waits until she's out of earshot. "Are you sure this chick knows what she's doing?"

"Yes, I'm sure."

We stand in a huddle for another thirty minutes before Jenny returns. The stern look on her face telegraphs that she doesn't have good news.

"I'm sorry, but they're keeping him here until his arraignment and detention hearing. A judge will have to decide whether he can go home."

Gus' face tightens with tension. "And when is that going to happen?"

Jenny pauses. "Detention hearings have to be held within forty-eight hours of arrest, not counting weekends. Since this is Friday, he probably won't see the judge until Tuesday."

"Are you kidding me?" Gus shouts. "He has to stay here for four friggin' days!"

In seconds, the security guard darts across the lobby and is standing only inches from Gus. "Is there a problem here? You'll need to keep your voice down, sir."

"I'm sorry, officer," Jenny says with a stiff smile. "Everything's fine. I had to give this father some disappointing news about his son and he's understandably upset. We'll keep it down."

Gus rubs his forehead.

"Why are they keeping him?" I ask. "What happened?"

"When a kid is charged with certain crimes, remaining in custody until the detention hearing is mandatory. They've added a second charge." She briefly looks away. "Making a criminal threat."

Gus slumps into the nearest chair and doesn't say a word.

Dre blinks several times. "What criminal threat?"

"An anonymous note started all of this. It said Graylin threatened to beat the girl up and embarrass her by putting her picture on Instagram."

"I know my kid," Gus says. "And that's not him. How can they lock him up based on some anonymous note?"

"Like I said," Dre repeats through clenched teeth, "what criminal threat?"

"I know it sounds crazy," Jenny continues, her tone apologetic, "but in this day and age of sensitivity about bullying, when a kid threatens to beat up somebody and embarrass them on social media, it's considered a criminal threat under the California Penal Code."

Nobody says a word. Jenny wisely gives us a few seconds to let this sink in.

"But I do have some good news for you, Mr. Alexander." Jenny smiles for the first time.

Gus slowly raises his head.

"They're going to let you see him. In fact, Graylin's waiting for you right now."

CHAPTER 14

Bones

I try not to slow down too much as I ease past the little girl's house for the third time. The front curtains are closed, so I can't tell if anyone is even home.

I decided to get a jump on things rather than wait until tomorrow morning. So after picking up Willie's Escalade, I got a bite to eat and headed over to Compton.

This gig is posing a problem I didn't think about and, I assume, neither did Willie. Kids don't play in the yard like they did when I was coming up. That's why most of 'em are fat slobs. No exercise. That girl is probably inside with her eyes glued to a computer screen.

I park the Escalade near the east corner of Magnolia Street behind Mario's Fish Market and climb out. I'm wearing my black jogging suit, so I don't look out of place as I stroll down the street. I'm just a guy getting some exercise. I gotta remind Willie to dress down when it's his turn to follow the girl. All his fancy duds will draw attention.

I walk casually past Brianna's house but on the opposite side of the street. It's still early afternoon and the house looks quiet. I don't see a car in the driveway, but it could be in the garage.

An old Mexican woman opens her screen door and steps onto the porch of the house next door. She's checking me out and I'm checking her out too. Nobody knows their neighbors these days, so for all the woman knows, I live in the neighborhood. Our eyes meet. I smile and wave. She doesn't wave back.

I'd planned to make a U-turn at the corner and walk back on Brianna's side of the street to see if I could get a look into the backyard. I change my mind because of that nosy neighbor and make a right and head down the next street, circling the block to get back to Willie's Escalade.

I open the window, light a cigarette and call Willie.

"I don't know how we gonna snatch this kid," I say. "Kids don't play in the yard these days."

"What are you doing over there now?" Willie huffs. "I told you to wait until tomorrow."

"I just wanted to check things out. I'm still comin' back in the morning."

"Get there early enough to follow her walking to school."

"Man, we gotta come up with another way. Kids don't walk to school no more. Her mama probably drops her off and picks her up too."

"You don't know that for sure. Anyway, let me think on it."

As I hang up, I feel something cold and hard jammed against my temple. My cigarette tumbles into my lap.

"Don't move, motherfucka! Put your hands on the steering wheel!"

Damn! I can't believe I'm about to get robbed by some crackhead. I'm too afraid to turn my head to look.

"Look, man, I ain't got no money on me. So you wastin' your time." I feel the lit cigarette burning a hole through my sweatpants. I rub my legs together to snuff it out.

"I saw you walking up and down the street, like you casing the place. Look like you was doing a whole lot of staring at one house in particular."

The blood drains from my fingers. Was I *that* obvious?

"Dude, I don't know what you talkin' about?"

"What you doing in this neighborhood anyway?" the man demands.

"I was takin' a walk. That's all."

"Keep playing stupid if you want to. You drove over here just to park and walk up and down the street? Don't they have streets where you live?"

This crackhead is asking way too many questions.

"Man, people are probably watchin' us. I bet they've already called the police. I would hightail it out of here if I was you."

"But you *ain't* me. Take one hand off the wheel and give me your wallet. And don't try anything stupid because I'd love to blow your head off."

When I hand this fool my wallet, he looks at my driver's license then tosses the wallet back into my lap.

WTF?

"Okay, Johnny Battle, I got a message for your boss."

"My boss? I ain't got no—"

The man cracks the gun against the side of my head so hard that my eyes roll around like two marbles fired into a wall.

"Ow!"

I take my left hand off the steering wheel to massage my temple when I hear the gun cock.

"I told you to keep your hands on the wheel. I'm delivering a message from Dre Thomas," the man says.

My spine straightens like a metal pipe.

"I assume you working for The Shepherd. Well, I work for Dre. You need to stay the hell away from him as well as his niece Brianna. Both of 'em have twenty-four-hour protection. And now that I know your name and address, Mr. Johnny Battle, if anything happens to either one of them, I'm coming for you."

"Man, I told you, I don't know what you talkin' about. I don't have a boss and I don't know nobody name Shepherd."

"You keep insulting my intelligence with your bullshit and I'll bust a cap in your ass right now."

I'm trying hard not to move, but my whole body is shuddering like I got Parkinson's. The gun is pressed so deep into my temple I can feel it scraping bone. If this fool's finger slips, my brains are gonna spray-paint the inside of Willie's truck.

"My name is Apache," the man continues. "Ask around about me. Anybody who knows me or know of me will tell you I don't make idle threats. I actually *like* shooting people."

"Man, you got it all wrong. I was—"

"I know The Shepherd's kicking back in the federal pen still pimping little girls," he says, talking over me, "but tell him he's the one who needs to be watching his back."

He lifts the gun from my head. By the time I turn around, he's disappeared. I never even got a look at him.

It takes me a full minute to catch my breath. I try to light another cigarette, but I can't steady my hands.

I must be slipping. I've never let nobody walk up on me like that.

This Apache dude is even crazier than me. And that's a problem.

CHAPTER 15

Miguel

I listen to the voicemail message from my boss and high-five the air. I'm about to be called up to the big leagues.

I've only been a juvenile prosecutor for eight months, but it's not uncommon for the shinning stars—like me—to get promoted to adult court on the fast track. Unlike most of my colleagues, I come in early, stay late, deal with the political crap and never complain when I have to take over a case another deputy D.A. screwed up.

Walking in long, proud strides, I head for the elevators with a serious pep in my step. I have the thin, taut body of a long-distance runner because I am one, logging more than forty miles a week. I wear boxy black glasses I don't actually need in a deliberate effort to appear older than my thirty-one years.

"Have a seat, Martinez," my boss says when I knock on his open door.

Deputy-in-Charge Sol Stein is a chubby-faced man with graying hair and a portly build.

My boss never wastes time on small talk. He doesn't care about the personal lives of the prosecutors who work for him, so he never engages in chitchat about their families or their plans for the weekend. I appreciate that.

"We have another sexting case," Stein says, scratching his balding crown. "And we need to go hard on this one. It's a wobbler, but file it as a felony, not a misdemeanor."

My jaw goes slack as my dream of a promotion dissipates like a puff of smoke. *Not another sexting case.*

Of the handful of sexting cases I've handled, I only went to the mat once. The victim was so devastated about her naked picture being blasted all over her school and the internet, she swallowed a handful of her mother's Vicodin and nearly died. I made sure the boy paid the price. He was locked up for two years.

But that case was the exception. I've prosecuted my share of teenage thugs who were as hardcore as any convict at San Quentin, but kids who take nude selfies aren't criminals and I hate throwing the book at them.

"And why do we have to *go hard*?" I ask, still stunned at the unexpected left turn this meeting has taken.

"This boy made the mistake of getting caught with a naked picture of a girl whose father and mother are close to the mayor."

This is not how the system is supposed to work. Rich kids get special treatment, while black and brown kids get shafted.

"Is the kid in custody?"

"Yeah. He was arrested at school earlier today."

Today? My eyes ricochet off my legal pad. If this kid was just picked up, the police report hasn't even made it to our office yet. This girl's parents must be *really* connected.

"So is the victim pretty messed up?"

Stein shrugs. "Nobody mentioned that."

"Who're the parents?"

Stein pulls a piece of paper from one of the messy piles on his desk. "The father's Percy Carlyle, a partner at Morgan Lewis. The mother, Simone Carlyle, is a V.P. at AT&T. Their daughter and the boy—Graylin Alexander—were classmates at Marcus Preparatory Academy."

Marcus Prep is a well-regarded private school. "White victim?" I ask, assuming she is.

"Nope. Black. The boy too."

"How old are they?"

"Both fourteen."

"Did the boy convince the girl to strip for him?"

"Don't know. The police confiscated his phone with the girl's picture on it. So it's an open-and-shut case for possession. You'll need to see how the evidence plays out on distribution. No telling who he sent it to."

"Is it a boyfriend-girlfriend thing? Is that why the parents are going nuclear?"

I had a case last year where some Beverly Hills professionals weren't thrilled with their daughter's South Central boyfriend. So, when they found a picture of his penis on her phone, they went for the jugular. But that was before the boy's parents turned over a ton of X-rated selfies their sweet little daughter sent not just to him, but several other boys.

"Don't have any other facts," Stein says. "The rest is your job. A lot of the naked selfies these kids are sharing end up in the hands of predators, who find the pictures online, then target the kids. If we make a public example of this boy, maybe he'll get the help he needs. And when other parents hear about the case, maybe they'll wake up and start monitoring what their kids are doing online."

What a load of crap. This is about politics and payola. The girl's angry parents called the mayor, the mayor called the D.A., and the D.A. called Stein.

"I need you to handle the girl's parents with kid gloves. Would be nice if you could pay them a visit tomorrow. Show them a little TLC. Let them know the D.A.'s office is taking the case seriously and so is the mayor."

That kills my hiking plans for Saturday.

As I stand up, a rancid feeling swirls like a tornado in the pit of my stomach. I hate these cases, but they just keep coming. The juvenile court purports to rehabilitate, not punish its young wards. But no kid who spends a year at the California Youth Authority ends up better for it. I'm almost at the door when I decide to say what's on my mind.

"It's crazy for us to bring these kids up on pornography charges. If I'd had a camera phone when I was fourteen, I would've been taking pictures of my girlfriend's boobs too."

Stein chuckles. "I didn't write the laws. Until the state legislature does something about it, it's our job to prosecute these brats."

My shoulders slump from the weight of this travesty. Stein apparently notices.

"I thought you'd be more excited about this case. Maybe you're looking at it all wrong."

"Am I?" I wait for him to blow more smoke up my ass.

"You're first in line for the next transfer to adult court. Getting the Carlyles the justice they deserve for their daughter could cause that transfer to happen sooner rather than later."

He winks, rocks back in his chair and continues. "The mayor will be following this case since the Carlyles are friends. Putting this kid away could be a feather in your cap."

My boss is blatantly bribing me. My blank expression gives him no hint of whether I'm willing to play ball. This must make Stein nervous because he does a one-eighty.

"Now, I want to be clear," he says, steepling his fat fingers, "you're still first up for the next transfer, regardless of how this case turns out."

Yeah, right. You're just covering your ass.

I want out of juvenile court, but not if it means locking up some kid who doesn't deserve it.

CHAPTER 16

Angela

When Jenny and Gus start following a staff member into the facility, I fall in step behind them, but the security guard stops me.

"Only parents and attorneys. You his mother?"

"No. His attorney."

A hint of a frown glazes Jenny's lips.

"Can I see your bar card and driver's license?" the guard asks.

He glances at them, then hands me something to sign.

Dre steps in line behind us. "I'm his uncle," he says. Though not by blood, Dre does fill that role.

The guard grimaces. "Don't matter. Parents and attorneys. That's it."

The guy takes us from the waiting area down a wide hallway. Gus is looking the place up and down, from the beige walls to the gray linoleum floor tiles. I sense he's feeling the same relief I am. Except for the locked doors, the place has the feel of a school, not a jail or a prison. We walk past a wall with motivational words stenciled in English and Spanish. *Respecto. Respect. Orgullo. Pride. Sobresalga. Excel.*

We're taken to a small oblong room inside the Boys Receiving Unit. It looks more like a storage closet than an office. A minute later, the door opens and Graylin flies into his father's arms.

"Dad, please get me out of here! They're lying on me. I'm innocent!"

"I know, Little Man, I know." Gus pulls him close. "Don't worry. We're gonna get you outta here. I promise."

Graylin's a beefy kid with a round, innocent face. I'm always teasing him about his cute dimples, which are not on display right now.

"Can I go home with you? Please, Dad. I don't wanna stay here!"

Jenny and I stand with our backs to the door while Gus and Graylin remain locked in an embrace.

"We only have a few minutes," Jenny says. "I'd like to go over a few things with Graylin." She offers her hand to him. "My name is Jenny Ungerman. I'm your attorney. Your dad hired me to represent you."

Graylin squints as if he just realized we were in the room. "How come Ms. Angela can't be my attorney?"

"Jenny's an expert in juvenile cases," I explain. "But I'll be helping out as well."

Jenny's tightly pursed lips tell me she's not thrilled about what I just said. My words are as much of a shock to me as they are to her. I hadn't planned on participating in Graylin's defense until the words spilled out of my mouth.

"You're not going to be able to go home tonight," Jenny explains. "The judge won't decide whether you can go home until Tuesday."

Graylin whips his head in his father's direction. "I have to stay here all the way to Tuesday?" His voice crumples. "How come I can't go home with you? Can't you bail me out?"

Gus pulls him close again. "I know this is hard, but I need you to man up. Just do what Ms. Jenny says and everything's going to be okay."

"It's very important that you don't talk to anyone about your case," Jenny says firmly. "That includes other kids you meet in here. Absolutely no one, except me."

And me, I want to add.

"Not even my dad?"

"Not even your dad. If you tell somebody something about your case, even your dad, they could be forced to testify about what you told them in court. Even if you tell it to them in secret. So it's very important that you don't say *anything* to *anybody* about what happened. Do you understand?"

Graylin nods weakly. "I understand. The police put snitches in your jail cell to try to make you incriminate yourself."

"That's right," Jenny says.

"And I want you to understand that you're my client, not your dad. Even though your dad may be paying me, you make the decisions about your case, not anyone else. Do you have any questions?"

Graylin pauses like he expects his dad to object.

"Um, aren't you going to ask me what happened so I can show you I'm innocent?"

"I'll be back tomorrow afternoon to meet with you. You can explain everything to me then."

"Can my dad come to our meeting?"

"Your father can visit you tomorrow," Jenny says, "but for our first meeting, I only want to meet with you. Your dad can attend our future meetings as long as it's okay with you."

Gus scratches his jaw and inhales.

"Five more minutes," says a voice from outside the door.

Graylin grabs his father and presses his head against his chest.

"We'll let you two have these last few minutes alone," Jenny says.

I follow her into the hallway.

"Your comment about helping out with Graylin's defense threw me for a loop," Jenny says the instant the door is closed. "I didn't realize this would be a two-member defense team."

"I didn't either until I said it. But I think I'd like to be involved in Graylin's defense."

"Well, I guess we'll just have to see."

We'll just have to see? My friends forgot to mention that this chick is a prima donna.

"Yes," I reply. "We will."

CHAPTER 17

Dre

On the ride home from juvenile hall, Gus doesn't say one word. I want to console him, but I don't know how. So I keep my mouth shut.

When I pull up in front of his apartment building on Hillcrest in Inglewood, Gus doesn't open the car door. He just sits there staring through the window.

"They almost shot me," he says quietly.

"What? Who almost shot you?"

He describes what went down in the principal's office. "And the crazy part is, I was so pissed off I almost dared that cop to do it. Then I heard Graylin crying and begging me to step back." His voice cracks. "I've made a lot of mistakes in my life, but my son is the one thing I've done right. I was determined to make sure he never saw the inside of a jail, much less a prison. And now he's mixed up in some craziness that already seems way out of my control."

I reach over and squeeze his shoulder. "Graylin's gonna be fine."

My words sound so worthless I wish I could take them back. I know what Gus is feeling because I felt the same helplessness when Brianna got kidnapped. Words do nothing for you at a time like this.

After he climbs out, I head back to my place to pick up some clothes, then drive to Angela's apartment in Ladera Heights. She opens the door to let me in dressed in shorts and a tank top. I follow her into the kitchen where she's fixing a bowl of bran cereal.

"Want some?"

Angela knows I hate bran cereal but refuses to buy the high-calorie, sugary stuff I like.

"I'll pass." I pull out a chair and take a seat at the kitchen table.

We're both dog-tired. There's tension in the air and it has nothing to do with our mutual concern for Graylin. This is like bracing for an earthquake you know is about to strike any second.

She turns her back to me and pours milk into her bowl. My eyes gravitate to her muscular thighs. An excitement stirs in me that brings to mind an activity that could significantly lower my stress level. But the attitude on Angela's face signals that sex won't be on the menu tonight. I know she can't hold out much longer.

One thousand one, one thousand two…

"I need to know what's going on, Dre." She turns around to face me, her butt pressed against the cabinet. I wish her ass was pressed up against me. "Why'd you change your mind about moving in together?"

"I haven't changed my mind."

"Then why won't you go look at the house I found?"

I mull over whether it makes sense to come clean. It takes me two seconds to decide that it doesn't. Angela's about to be tied up defending Graylin and doesn't need the additional stress of worrying about me too.

I massage the back of my neck. "Like I said, I need a little time to handle a few things."

She takes a spoonful of cereal, finishes chewing, then asks, "What few things?"

We've had this conversation already and I don't want to have it again.

"I can't say right now."

Angela slams down the bowl on the counter, splashing milk every-where. "I don't understand you and maybe I never will! Do you know how it makes me feel when you refuse to confide in me?"

"I just need you to trust me."

"Here we go again. How am I ever going to be comfortable with—" She stops herself mid-sentence.

"My criminal past?" I say, finishing the sentence for her. "It's going to take time. I'm going to prove to you that all of that is behind me. I don't deal drugs anymore, Angela. I need you to trust me."

"Does this have anything to do with The Shepherd?"

I pause for a beat. "No."

"Does it have anything to do with *any* kind of criminal activity?"

I hate it when she jams me up like I'm on the witness stand. Before I can answer, she cuts me off.

"Fine. Never mind. Your silence just answered my question."

She wipes down the countertop, dumps the rest of her cereal into the garbage disposal, and marches out of the kitchen.

I want to follow her, but I don't. Our relationship has been on a rocky path from the start. We've ridden out one storm after another and now this thing with The Shepherd is threatening to sink us once and for all. I'm beginning to wonder if there's ever going to be a time when we can just concentrate on each other and sail off into the sunset.

I hate lying to my woman, but the way I see it, I don't have a choice. I just pray she can hang with me until The Shepherd is dead.

CHAPTER 18

Graylin

I don't know how I'm going to survive in here for four whole days. And I still don't understand how they can put somebody in jail when you haven't done anything wrong. As soon as I find out who sent me that picture, I'm going to make sure my attorneys put *them* in jail.

Mr. Morris, the guard who took me to see my dad, is taking me to my unit. I'm trying to keep up with him at the same time that I'm trying to check out everything around me. It really does look like a school except that there are some high fences and you have to have a key to go through almost every door.

"How come the guards don't have guns?" I ask Mr. Morris.

"Because we're not guards, we're staff. This ain't a jail."

We walk near a grassy area toward a brick building with *GH* on the front. Mr. Morris uses his key to open the glass doors.

"This is the day room," he says, showing me inside.

It's a wide-open area about the size of my aunt Macie's den. Along the back wall is a smaller room with a large glass window. Behind that, I see a tiled wall with showerheads sticking out.

Two black kids and three Hispanics, all dressed in gray sweat suits like me, are sitting at a long table like the one in my school cafeteria. Until a second ago they were watching the TV hanging near the ceiling. Now they're watching me.

"This is Graylin Alexander," Mr. Morris says to a black man who walks out of a glass enclosure. It seems like almost everybody who works here is either black or Mexican.

I peer behind him and see lots of buttons, computer screens and TV monitors. It reminds me of the dashboard at the sound studio in Hollywood where my cousin Trey recorded a rap album.

"I'm Mr. Dennison," the man says, shaking my hand.

"He has a detention hearing on Tuesday." Mr. Morris rolls his eyes. "Another sexting case."

"I didn't sext *nobody*," I say. "I'm innocent."

Mr. Dennison nods as if he's heard this before. "Let's go over the rules."

I press my hands to my face. "I went over the rules already. Twice."

"And now we're going to do it one last time to make extra sure you don't forget."

I barely listen as he tells me the same rules all over again.

"You're in room number seven."

I peer down a long hallway and see pairs of tennis shoes outside some of the rooms. "We can't wear shoes in our cells?"

"They ain't cells, they're rooms. And no, you can't wear shoes inside your room. Set them outside the door so the staff knows you're in there."

Mr. Dennison hands me a cloth bag containing deodorant and lotion.

"Dinner's at five. After dinner, once you get your homework done, you can watch TV until it's time to shower at seven-forty-five. Lights out at nine."

I wish he would hurry up because I'm tired.

"Wakeup time is six-fifteen," he continues. "You need to have your bed made and room cleaned by seven. School starts at eight-thirty. We all leave the building as a group. Everybody walks in lines of two. Did you understand everything I just said?"

"There's school tomorrow on Saturday?"

Mr. Dennison smiles. "Sorry about that. No school tomorrow. And wake-up time is at seven on weekends. There's church on Sunday in the chapel if you want to go. So did you understand everything I said?"

"Yes, sir."

Mr. Dennison raises an eyebrow. "A kid with some manners. I like that."

"How many inmates are in here?"

"None. This ain't a prison. We have twelve rooms, but only eight other boys are here now." I follow him down the hallway. He opens a door with the number seven on it.

"This'll be your room for the next few days."

The room looks kind of like the prison cells on TV, except there aren't any bars or a toilet. My bedroom at home is about six times as big. There's a rectangular window on the door about the size of a sheet of paper. My eyes widen at the slab sticking out from the wall.

"I have to sleep on that hard cement without a mattress?"

Mr. Dennison laughs. "No, I'll get you a mattress."

"Do I get pajamas?"

"No pajamas. Sleep in your underwear."

"Do I have a cellmate?"

"No, you don't have a *roommate*. When the lights go out, the doors are locked from the outside."

My eyes get wide. My granny says never lock the doors from the outside. You can die in a fire like that. "But what if there's a fire? How do I get out?"

"We've never had a fire. Don't worry, we'll get you out if that happens."

"Can I keep the lights on?" I'm too embarrassed to tell him that I have a night light in my room at home.

He points up at the ceiling. "There's a dim light up there."

I look around. "Where's the light switch?"

"There isn't one. We control the lights from the booth up front. That one stays on all night so we can look into your room and check on you."

Mr. Dennison leaves and returns with a thin blanket and a worn, striped mattress about as thick as a double cheeseburger. I look up at him. "This is the mattress?"

"Yep. You'll be fine. You're just in time for dinner."

As soon as he says that, I realize that I haven't had anything to eat since breakfast and I'm suddenly starving. We go back into the day room where eight boys are now sitting around the table.

"We got a new kid on the block," one of them says as they all seem to approach me at once.

"What's your name?" somebody asks.

"Graylin."

A skinny, light-skinned black kid steps forward. "I'm Tyke. What you in for?"

I hesitate. "My attorney told me not to talk about my case."

"I don't care what your attorney told you. I asked you a question."

The other boys snicker. Tyke is obviously the bully of the group.

I stand a little taller and try to look tough. "I can't talk about my case."

"You think I'm a snitch or something? Cuz if that's what you trying to say about me, I'ma have to do something 'bout that."

My head starts to hurt. I don't need this bully bothering me on top of everything else I've been through today.

Before I can respond, Mr. Dennison walks up and Tyke changes his tune.

"Hey, Mr. Dennison, whazzup?"

Mr. Dennison ignores him as he removes plates from a metal container and hands one to each of us. We all sit down at the table to eat. I unwrap my plate to find chicken steak, tater tots, and broccoli. It tastes about the same as the food at school. My plate is empty in seconds.

I sense someone behind me and turn around to find Tyke hovering over me.

"Don't think I'm done with you," he whispers. "You can't call me a snitch and get away with it."

"I didn't call you a snitch."

"So now you callin' me a liar?"

I know it will only get worse if I let him know how scared I am. So I try to act hard. "Get outta my face."

The other boys start whooping with laughter, which makes Tyke's light skin darken like he's been sitting in the sun too long.

"You better not let me catch you alone," Tyke seethes. "Cuz if I do, I'ma fuck you up."

CHAPTER 19

Willie

It's early Saturday morning and I've been sitting in my car on Springpark Avenue in Ladera Heights for the last hour. I'm pretending to read the newspaper, but I'm on the lookout for Dre Thomas.

Last night, I parked outside his apartment building not knowing whether he was even there or not. Just when I was about to call it a day, he pulled up in a cheap-ass Jetta. I watched him go inside and come out only ten minutes later carrying a small duffel bag. My first thought was that he was dealing drugs again.

I followed him west on Slauson, then south on La Cienega to Centinela. He disappeared inside an apartment building on Springpark. I hung around for a couple of hours, then split, figuring he was in for the night.

It was around seven when I got back here this morning. Dre's Jetta was still parked in the same spot. It's now well after eight and I'm getting antsy. All this waiting ain't my thing.

I'm ready to call it quits for the second time when I see Dre and a woman walk out of the building.

Okay, this makes sense. He spent the night with his lady.

Dre walks the woman over to a silver-blue Saab. When he gives her a peck on the lips, the chick rolls her eyes, says something, then gets into the car and drives off. Dre just stands there with his arms folded, looking pissed.

Trouble in paradise?

My plan was to follow Dre for most of the day, but without giving it much thought, I decide to trail this chick instead. Depending on how tight they are, The Shepherd might want the 411 on her too.

The woman heads east on Centinela to LaBrea, where she makes a right. Only minutes later, she turns into an office building not far from the Inglewood Courthouse. I keep a safe distance behind as she pulls into the parking garage.

I make another snap decision and decide to follow her into the building. I'm dressed in one of my finest suits, a gray gabardine, so I should blend in just fine. I look around for security cameras and I'm happy not to spot any.

It's almost nine o'clock on a Saturday morning, but people are already going in and out of the building. Stepping onto the elevator with the woman and two other men, I watch her punch the fourth-floor button while one of the men presses the third floor. Dre's woman is glued to the screen of her phone and hasn't noticed me or anyone else in the elevator. She's still looking at her phone when I step off behind her.

I hang back until she disappears inside double doors that read *Law Offices*. I study the four names on the plaque to the right of the door. One female and three males. Since there's no law firm name, I assume the attorneys have separate practices but share office space.

Is this chick a lawyer or a secretary?

Inside, a long counter takes up most of the small reception area. A young girl with tiny braids is sitting behind the desk. She has yet to look up from her computer screen. To the left, is a tall door that I assume leads to other offices.

"Good morning." The receptionist smiles up at me. "How can I help you?"

"I'm looking for an attorney who can help me with a real estate matter? Do any of the attorneys here handle real estate law?"

The woman shakes her head. "Sorry. All of our lawyers do criminal defense work. But I think there's a guy on the first floor who handles real estate cases."

"Okay, I'll head down there." I notice four business cardholders on the counter and take a card from each stack. "Never know when I might need a criminal attorney."

"Let's hope not," the woman says with a laugh.

"Who's the best criminal attorney here?"

The receptionist leans forward and lowers her voice. "Angela Evans hands down."

"Is she the one who walked in here a few seconds ago wearing jeans and a yellow blouse?"

"Yep. She used to be a federal prosecutor. She's smart and nice too. Always has extra work for me to do on Saturdays. Thank goodness."

I study the business cards as I head back outside. "So, Mr. Drug Dealer is banging an ex-prosecutor," I mumble to myself. "That's some information Shep would want to know."

My phone rings as the elevator doors open. I step inside before answering.

"Man, I should've called you last night, but I was too shook up," Bones says in a hoarse voice. "I had to go home and have a few drinks and I'm just now wakin' up."

If Bones has messed up and done something stupid, I swear I'm going to shoot him. "What happened?"

"This dude Dre Thomas ain't no joke! They're on to us, man. Snatchin' that kid ain't gonna be easy. While we watchin' them, they watchin' us!"

He starts telling me about his run-in with Apache.

I know the name well. Anybody in L.A. with even the most tenuous criminal ties knows all about Apache. Bones is lucky to be alive. Apache has a rep for shooting first and asking questions never.

"How did they even know we was watchin' them?" Bones asks. "And who is The Shepherd? Is that who you always callin' The Man?"

I can't let Bones know who we're working for. He's likely to slip up and mention Shep's name to the wrong person.

"Naw. I don't know who he's talking about."

It was a mistake to let Dre Thomas know we were coming for him. A surprise attack would've been more effective. But Shep had to feed his ego by announcing it to the world.

"So what we gonna do?" Bones asks.

"Let me think."

I'm dreading my next conversation with Shep. He won't be happy to hear about this. Maybe I won't even tell him. If I do, he'll blame me for selecting the wrong sidekick for this gig. But I'm already kicking myself for that.

"You still there?"

Bones is acting way too panicky.

"Yeah. Hang tight and don't make another move. I need to talk to The Man."

Since Dre and the kid have protection, we need another plan. If Shep really wants to send a message, it might make more sense to kidnap Dre's woman. She'll be a much easier target.

I'll just have to convince Shep of that.

CHAPTER 20

Miguel

I park my Volvo along the curb in front of the Carlyles' home on Valley Ridge in the View Park section of Los Angeles. The striking brick home is the length of two houses in my neighborhood. The homes here sell for over a million dollars and, for as long as I can remember, the neighborhood's been overwhelmingly black. That's why I'm surprised to see a white woman jogging behind a stroller and a thirty-something white couple walking a terrier.

As I'm about to get out of my car, a black BMW pulls into the driveway. A man climbs out and waits as I head up the brick-lined walkway.

"I'm Percy Carlyle. Kennedy's father. You must be from the District Attorney's Office. Thanks for coming by so early, and on a weekend, no less."

Mr. Carlyle is clean-shaven with angular features. He looks like a big-firm lawyer even in khakis and a Polo shirt.

I wait for him to pull out a key and open the door, but he knocks instead.

An attractive black woman answers and introduces herself as Simone Carlyle, Kennedy's mother. Her hair is pulled back in a tight bun and she's wearing dark jeans and a starched white shirt that's as stiff as the smile on her face. She acknowledges Percy Carlyle with something short of a nod.

The first thing I notice when I walk inside is the elevator. The living room is the size of a two-car garage and is full of antique furniture with high backs and textured fabrics in deep red and burgundy. Heavy velvet curtains cover almost a complete wall, giving the room the feel of a funeral parlor. A teapot, tiny cookies, and expensive China sit in the middle of the coffee table. I wonder if it's intentional that the pink and yellow sprinkles on the cookies are the same color as the stripes along the rim of the teacups.

"I'd like you to know that the District Attorney's Office is taking this case very seriously," I begin. Mrs. Carlyle insists on pouring me some chamomile tea even though I declined. "We regret what happened to your daughter. I'll be prosecuting the case against the boy who was arrested. One of the things—"

"His name is Graylin Alexander, right?" Simone asks.

I hesitate. "He's a juvenile, so we try to keep his identity confidential. How did you find out his name?"

"It's all over the school. That boy put my baby's picture on the internet. Everybody needs to know his name."

I lean forward. "You have evidence that the picture is on the internet?"

"No, she doesn't," Percy says, shooting Simone an annoyed side glance. "Go ahead. Finish what you were saying."

I tell them about the anonymous note and that the defendant is charged with making a criminal threat as well as possession of child pornography.

"How many cases have you tried and how many guilty verdicts did you get?" Simone interrupts.

Percy rolls his eyes. The couple has yet to say one word to each other. I assume they're divorced and that it wasn't an amicable breakup.

"They're called adjudications, not trials in the juvenile system and the judge determines whether a kid is delinquent. Technically, there's no finding of guilt."

"I have no doubt the little thug is a juvenile delinquent. You still haven't told me how many cases you won."

"I have a very solid record of success, Mrs. Carlyle. But you need to understand that the goal of the juvenile system is rehabilitation, not punishment."

"That boy needs to be punished."

This woman is way beyond pushy.

"As I explained on the phone," I say, trying to regain control of the conversation, "I'd like to interview Kennedy. Is she here?"

Percy stands up. "I'll go get her."

Simone's eyes trail Percy out of the room. It's almost as if she's uncomfortable with him roaming the house unsupervised. After a few seconds, she gets up. "I don't know what's taking him so long."

I understand now why the man doesn't have a key. He doesn't want one.

Percy and Simone escort their daughter into the room, each holding an arm. She's a skinny girl with bangs and a long ponytail that extends past her shoulder blades. She looks dazed, as if she's just been roused from a deep sleep.

I want to speak to Kennedy alone, but I suspect that won't go over well with Mrs. Carlyle, so I let it go for now. I introduce myself and ask a few harmless questions about her classes and teachers to put her at ease.

"Do you have any idea how someone could've gotten a naked picture of you?" I ask after five minutes or so.

Kennedy lowers her head and answers in a shaky voice, "No."

"Do you know Graylin Alexander?"

She nods. "He's in two of my classes. But we're not friends or anything like that."

"Has he ever approached you or tried to talk to you?"

"No."

For the next twenty minutes or so, I ask a series of questions that yield nothing super helpful.

"Thanks for speaking with me. I'll need to talk to you again later on, but right now I'd like to speak with your parents."

Simone escorts Kennedy to her room.

"As you can see," Simone says when she returns, "this has been a very traumatic experience for my daughter. I don't know if she'll ever be the same."

I nod, hoping to appear empathetic. "I have a copy of the picture they found on the boy's phone. I'd like to see if you recognize the background. We need to determine where it might've been taken. I didn't want to show it to Kennedy yet, considering how fragile she appears to be."

"I don't want to see it." Percy gets to his feet and stalks out of the room.

"He's such a weak man," Simone hisses as she takes a sip of tea. "Let me see it."

I open a folder and hand Simone an 8x10 color photograph. "This is an enlargement, so it's a little blurry."

"Oh my God!" Simone presses her right hand to her chest. Percy flies back into the room. "That's Kennedy's room! That boy took that picture through my baby's bedroom window!"

CHAPTER 21

Graylin

I wake up to a loud voice and banging on my door.
"Time to get up! Time to get up!"

It takes me a few seconds to realize where I am. When I do, sadness swoops down on me like someone slapped a hood over my head.

Mr. Dennison is stomping down the hallway unlocking doors. "Time to get cleaned up and make up your bed. Be in the day room for breakfast in thirty minutes."

My granny has to come into my room at least two times before I finally climb out of bed. When I sit up, pain shoots across my back, probably from sleeping on that skinny mattress. The room feels as cold as the inside of a refrigerator.

I step outside my room and head into the day room. Two other boys are already in line for the bathroom.

"What you lookin' at?" Tyke says, appearing from nowhere and breathing down the back of my neck.

I ignore him.

"I ain't forgot about you dissin' me."

It's my turn, so I wash my face and brush my teeth as fast as I can and go back to my room to make up my bed. When it's time to eat, we walk up to the cart and Mr. Dennison hands us trays with sausage, hash browns, orange juice and a fruit cup. I feel Tyke watching me, but I refuse to make eye contact. I want to sit as far away from him as I can, but the day room isn't that big. A white kid with tattoos crawling up his pale neck calls out to me.

"Sit over here, homie."

The boy's greeting feels almost as good as a warm hug from my granny. He tells me his name is Andrew.

"What you in for?" he asks, even before I get seated on the bench.

"For nothing," I mutter, happy to have someone nice to talk to. I'm about to say I can't talk about my case, but I don't want a repeat of the situation with Tyke.

"They said I sexted a naked picture of a girl at my school, but I didn't."

"Aw man!" His blue-green eyes almost start glowing. "You goin' down! My friend got a whole year at C-Y-A for that."

"What's C-Y-A?"

"California Youth Authority. Juvie prison."

I open my orange juice. "I'm not going nowhere. My dad hired me an attorney. Two attorneys. They're getting me out of here."

Andrew presses his fist to his mouth like it's a bullhorn and laughs. "I don't care how many attorneys you got. You crazy if you think you gettin' off."

I now regret sitting down next to Andrew and wish he would shut up.

"So you know your dad?" he asks.

I squint as if something's in my eye. "Of course I know my dad. He's coming to see me today."

"You rich or something?"

"No."

"I never met my dad," Andrew says with a shrug. "Don't nobody visit me."

Now I feel kind of sorry for him. "What about your mother or your granny? They don't come to see you?"

"Naw. I got a foster mother, but she can't get off work."

"Why are you in here?" I ask.

"Got into a fight with my foster brother and ran away. Broke his jaw." He puffs out his scrawny chest. "They charged me with assault and being a runaway."

He's smiling like he should get a prize or something. I want to tell him that's nothing to be proud of, but I don't.

"Stick with me," Andrew says, getting up from the table. "I'll show you what's up. And don't worry about Tyke. He always messes with the new kids. Just ignore him."

Since it's Saturday, we get to go into the yard. As soon as we step outside, I hear my name being called. "Graylin, you've got a visitor."

When I see my dad coming up the walkway, I run over and hug him so tight we almost fall over.

"How you making out, Little Man?"

"I'm okay." I was going to tell my dad about Tyke messing with me, but I figure he's worried enough about me. I take him into my unit and Mr. Dennison lets me show him my room.

My dad looks all around, but doesn't say anything. We go back outside and sit on a bench by ourselves.

"When can I come home?" My voice gets shaky even though I'm trying hard not to cry.

"After your hearing on Tuesday. I'm sure that judge will see you don't belong in here." My dad goes quiet for a long time, then stares at me real hard. "I need you to tell me what happened."

I wring my hands. "But Ms. Jenny and Ms. Angela said I wasn't supposed to talk about my case to nobody. Not even you."

"I don't care what they said!" My dad's nostrils get bigger. "I'm your father. Did you take a picture of that girl?"

I want to do what my attorneys said, but I can't disobey my dad. Anyway, I want him to know that I'm not guilty. "No."

"Then what was it doing on your phone?"

"Somebody sent it to me?"

"Who?"

"I don't know."

"What do you mean you don't know?"

"They sent it on Snapchat."

"What the hell is Snapchat?"

I try to explain how Snapchat works, but I can tell my dad isn't getting it.

"Well, if the picture disappears, why was it still on your phone?"

"Because I took a screenshot of it."

My dad brushes his hand down his face. "This is nuts. I don't see how they could punish you for having a picture when somebody else sent it to you. Everything's going to be okay." He pulls me so close he almost smothers me.

"My friend Andrew says his friend got sent to juvie prison for a year for sexting."

"Friend? These hoodlums in here ain't your friends! Didn't Ms. Jenny tell you not to talk to nobody about your case?"

"I didn't tell him anything."

"You better not. And don't be listening to these thugs. You ain't going to nobody's prison, you hear me?" My dad's voice is so angry that it scares me. "That ain't gonna happen because I ain't gonna let it happen."

CHAPTER 22

Angela

I agree to meet Jenny at Woodcat, a trendy coffee shop on Sunset Boulevard in Echo Park. It's only twenty minutes away from Eastlake Juvenile Hall, where we'll be interviewing Graylin in a couple of hours.

When I walk in, I see Jenny seated at a table in the back. It's a small place with orange and gray walls and pictures of birds everywhere. Everybody in the place is bent over a laptop.

"I was able to get a copy of the police report," she says, handing it to me before I can even sit down. "According to the report, Graylin did have a naked picture on his phone. I'll have to get the hows and whys from him."

It's a good sign that Jenny's willing to share the police report with me, but a bad one that she's still using the pronoun *I* rather than *we*. I was hoping she'd give my offer to help some consideration overnight and come to the realization that two heads are better than one.

I go to the counter to order coffee and an oatmeal cookie, then return to the table and start reading the police report.

"I don't know whether a prosecutor's been assigned yet," Jenny continues, "but Judge Jaynie Miller will most likely handle the detention hearing. That's both good and bad. She's in her early fifties, sharp as a whip and down-to-earth. She's notorious for letting you know exactly what's on her mind, even if you didn't ask. She also doesn't think kids should be prosecuted for sexting. And luckily for us, she's the mother of two boys close to Graylin's age."

"That's obviously the good part. What's her downside?"

"She used to be in-house at a corporation. After years of pulling down a fat six-figure salary, she retired and set her sights on being a juvenile judge as a way of giving back."

"I still haven't heard anything bad yet."

"She wants to know every minute detail of your case, even stuff that has no bearing on the charges. Nobody can un-hear something, but Miller thinks she can. She's also a proud NRA member."

I understand how the judge's overreaching could be problematic, but on balance she sounds like a decent draw. I'm about to ask a question when Jenny beats me to it.

"As I mentioned last night, it came as quite a surprise to me that you wanted to be part of Graylin's defense team."

She certainly likes to cut to the chase.

I turn the police report facedown. "Frankly, *I* didn't realize I wanted to participate until the words came out of my mouth last night. If you're worried about splitting the fee, that's a non-issue. I'm doing this *pro bono*."

"I'm sure you know this, but it's not always a good idea to represent someone close to you. Emotion can interfere with legal judgment."

"I agree. It's not *always* a good idea. But it shouldn't be a problem in this case since I won't be the lead attorney." I try to stroke her ego a bit. "This is your case. I'll just be there to help you out."

I want and need to be part of Graylin's defense team. The charges he's facing are much too serious for me to sit on the sidelines. If Jenny doesn't want to share her sandbox, I'll have Gus fire her ass.

Jenny crosses her arms and leans back in her chair. "How much juvenile court experience have you had?"

"Not much. Primarily representing child trafficking victims on solicitation charges. But I was an assistant U.S. Attorney before going out on my own. I know my way around a courtroom."

I don't like having to defend my experience and my pride is gently needling me to strike back. "Where'd you go to law school?" I ask.

Jenny smirks, which tells me her J.D. is no doubt from some third-rate law school that couldn't shine the shoes of my alma mater.

She takes a sip of water. "Harvard Law. Brown undergrad. I also picked up a master's in public policy from NYU in between. And you?"

I struggle to keep the shock off my face. "Stanford Law. San Francisco State undergrad."

Our respective law schools are often neck-and-neck in the national rankings, but Harvard Law is Harvard Law.

"Nice," Jenny says. "I love the Bay Area."

I take a bite of my cookie so I don't have to talk. Jenny's preference for solo work won't be our biggest problem. I don't particularly like this chick and that can wreak havoc on a defense team.

I decide to just put it out there. "Why are you so opposed to having me help out?"

"Attorneys who don't practice in juvenile court don't understand that representing a kid is very different from representing an adult client. Children are very emotional, their parents too. You're part attorney and part therapist. You also have to manage expectations, which you didn't do last night."

"Excuse me?"

"You told Gus that Graylin would get to go home when you had no idea whether that was the case."

"I was just trying to keep him upbeat."

Although Jenny Ungerman and I surely won't be developing any kind of girlfriend bond, I like the idea of Graylin having a Harvard-educated lawyer going to bat for him. But I want a place on his defense team too.

"How about this?" It feels like I'm groveling and I hate myself for it. "The minute something happens that makes you feel this isn't working out, say the word and I'll bow out."

Several tense seconds pass, then Jenny's thin lips flatten into a taut smile. "Okay, I guess. For now."

I figure that's the best I'm going to get, so I let it go. We start digging into Graylin's case.

"It doesn't seem like the detention hearing should be much of a problem for us," I say. "Graylin has a safe place to stay, he's not a troubled kid, he'll be properly supervised and there's no evidence that releasing him would put him or anyone else in danger."

I'm trying to impress Jenny with my knowledge of the legal standard for detaining a kid. I stayed up late researching it last night. If Jenny's impressed, she's not letting on.

"I've had cases where the prosecutor pushed hard to have my client locked up even though none of those factors were present. And if the girl's parents fight Graylin's release, the judge will take that into consideration as well. Is there anything about Graylin's family life that I need to know about?"

"Graylin's mother is out of the picture. She's had a drug problem for years. Gus is raising him with the help of his mother and sister. He has a felony drug conviction and did some time at Corcoran. But that's all behind him now."

I hesitate. She's going to eventually find out the rest, so I might as well spill it now. "That's where he met Dre. They both did time."

Jenny tries to play it off, but I see a flicker of judgment in her eyes. I change the subject.

"How did you end up on the juvenile side?" I ask.

With a Harvard Law degree, Jenny could've been doing something far more financially lucrative and prestigious than defending juveniles.

"I thought I was going to change the world." She laughs. "My older brother, who I idolized, got arrested for possession of forty bucks worth of marijuana when he was sixteen. He ended up with a prosecutor who threw the book at him and a public defender who was too overworked to give his case any real attention. The crazy part is, my parents could've hired an attorney to represent him. But they were tired of him getting into trouble and wanted to teach him a lesson.

"He spent a year at a juvenile camp and was never the same after that. He's been in and out of prison most of his life. I went to law school because I was on a mission to keep that from happening to other kids."

"Sounds like you're doing it."

"Not the way I'd hoped. The juvenile system is just as overburdened as the adult side. And all this energy the D.A.'s Office is putting into crucifying kids for sexting is nuts."

"Is sexting really a major problem?"

Instead of answering, Jenny pulls her iPad from her purse, taps the screen a few times, then hands it to me. "Take a look at that."

The screen shows the Los Angeles Unified School District's website. Several pages are dedicated to warning students and parents about sexting. They even have an official campaign, *Now Matters Later*, to educate students about using social media responsibly.

"If the district is putting this much emphasis on it," I say, "it must be a problem."

"Yep. Schools all across the country are doing the same thing. Our kids are bombarded with sexual images on TV, in movies and music videos. As a consequence, they're desensitized. They don't think sexting is a big deal."

Jenny retrieves her iPad, taps the screen a few more times and slides it back across the table. "If this doesn't tell you we have a crisis on our hands, nothing will."

This time she's pulled up an open letter written by the L.A. County Sheriff posted on the department's Facebook page entitled: *Nude #Selfies and the Need to Protect Our Children.*

I quickly read it, then gaze across the table, dumbfounded. "Is this for real?"

"Crazy, isn't it? When you have the sheriff of the largest county in the nation effectively begging parents to stop their kids from sexting, you know there's a problem."

I had no idea how prevalent this was. "But the child pornography statutes were passed to catch pedophiles. Why are they charging kids?"

"Because they can. Also the law hasn't caught up with technology. Some states recognize that. In New York, a kid caught with a picture of a naked minor on his phone would have to participate in a counseling program warning him about the legal consequences of sexting. California and most other states haven't gotten on board yet."

All I can do is shake my head.

"I blame prosecutors," Jenny continues. "They aren't exercising enough discretion. Some of them will treat the immature fifteen-year-old who sends a picture of his penis to his girlfriend as harshly as the malicious bully who forces a classmate to strip and posts her picture all over Instagram."

Jenny stops to take a sip of coffee. "And in the process, they're needlessly destroying a whole lot of young lives."

CHAPTER 23

The Shepherd

I'm relaxing in my cell, checking the most recent deposits into my Citibank account. Old School is standing in the doorway, poised to signal me to hide my phone if he sees the police in the vicinity. Another twenty-three grand hit my account yesterday. Birmingham is serving me well.

When I'm done, I spend a little time educating myself. I'm a history buff at heart. I particularly enjoy studying little-known historical figures. Yesterday, I read up on Louise Wooster, a Birmingham madam whose brothels earned her a fortune in the late 1800s. How ironic that centuries later, I now satisfy the sexual desires of the gentlemen of Birmingham. Unlike Madam Wooster, however, I won't be donating any of my profits to charity. I wonder if little Brianna is on her way down south yet.

"I'm done," I say, ending my web surfing.

Old School steps back into my cell. I hand him two books of postage stamps.

Inmates aren't allowed to have money in prison, so stamps have become our black market currency. They limit us to no more than 60 stamps at a time, but that rule is routinely violated since stamps are so easy to hide. While the face value of a book of stamps is about ten bucks, in the prison bartering system, it could be worth much more or far less, depending on what's up for trade and how many stamps are in circulation at a given time. For instance, a dude might charge one book of stamps for the extra pizza he pilfers from the chow hall. Or a haircut from an inmate with real skills could cost you two books. Four books of stamps might be enough for somebody to make your bed and do your laundry for two weeks. Old School usually trades his stamps for extra food.

Dudes with a good side hustle have been known to rack up thousands of dollars during their time at The Low. When they earn a few books, they mail them home, where a friend or family member sells the stamps for their full face value and either puts the money on their books or deposits it into a bank account. Some inmates have left The Low with thousands of dollars waiting for them.

Once Old School leaves, I place my phone back in its hiding place—velcroed inside my bath towel, hanging on my towel rack.

I'm about to lie back down when an announcement changes that.

"Four p.m. count call! Four p.m. count call!" a C.O. blares over the speaker system.

Inmates are counted four or five times a day in the federal prison system. The 4 p.m. count is the one sent to the Bureau of Prisons, so the big shots in D.C. have an accurate count of how many people they have locked up on a given day.

Every inmate needs to be in his room, standing by his bed by the time the two C.O.s conducting the count enter their cell. All across the yard right now inmates are hustling to get back to their cells in the allotted 15 minutes. Failure to make it on time means you get sent to the SHU—the Special Housing Unit—also known as the hole.

Years ago, you could be stretched out on your bed during a count. That changed after one inmate was counted for a couple of days before a C.O. realized he was dead.

Wallstreet hustles into the room, making it seconds before the C.O.s enter and check us off. We have to stay in our cells until the count of the entire facility is complete.

When it's over, Wallstreet's about to head back out to the yard. He's obsessed with the game of chess and would play 24/7 if he could. Considering all the time he spends on the game, he should be a lot better at it.

"Hang on," I say, stopping him in the doorway. "I need you to look out for the police while I make a quick call. It'll only be a second."

Wallstreet scratches the back of his neck. Even though he's the reason I have a phone, he doesn't like bucking the rules. Any day now, he'll be bumped down to a camp—the lowest level in the federal prison system—to serve out the remaining two years of his sentence. He doesn't want an infraction delaying his transfer.

"C'mon, Cali. I can't—"

Before he can balk, I'm on the phone talking to Willie. Wallstreet reluctantly stays put.

"Status," I say into the phone.

I sense a nervousness on the other end of the line.

"Uh, I need to tell you something," Willie says.

I close my eyes as tiny prickles of anxiety shoot down my spine. Has he screwed up already? Life at The Low is a privilege I don't want to lose. Exposure of my outside activities could earn me more time, or worse, get me kicked up to a medium or maximum security prison.

"I think I need to start working on another project," Willie sputters. "This one ain't working out like it should."

I don't respond for some time. Dead silence will send more of a chill to this minion than a raised voice. I'm not clear yet what he's trying to tell me. "Go on."

"The new guy had an accident while he was working on the project," Willie explains. "Scared him so bad, he screamed like an Apache."

I freeze. Apache was the nutcase who nearly beat Clint, my No. 2 man, to death. Clint turned on me at trial to shave some time off his own sentence. I almost wish Apache had killed him.

"Did your guy get hurt?"

"Nothing serious. But he got the message that it might not be a good idea for him to be handling this project."

I remain quiet, trying to put all the pieces together.

"So, since they're under twenty-four-hour surveillance right now, I have another idea for a project."

"I'm listening."

"The guy on the project has a girlfriend. She's an attorney. Maybe we should concentrate on her instead."

I remember seeing a chick in court with Dre Thomas during my trial. I assumed she was his woman because after he finished testifying against me, she hugged him. My attorney told me she used to be a federal prosecutor. It surprises me, but I like Willie's proposal.

"I like it," I say, grinning now. "I like it a lot."

This time, we won't be announcing our intentions. Now that our focus is on this lady lawyer, I need to carefully plot out exactly how we should proceed.

"Chill for a minute and let me reevaluate," I tell Willie. "I'll call you in a few days."

CHAPTER 24

Angela

When we arrive at juvenile hall, Graylin hugs us like we're his long-lost sisters.

"My dad was here," he says, beaming. "But they only let him stay for three hours. Tomorrow he can stay for four hours because it's Sunday."

Visiting hours for parents are limited to weekends and following court appearances, but there are no restrictions on lawyer visits.

"Have you talked to anybody about your case since we spoke to you last night?" Jenny asks.

Graylin looks down at the floor. "Um, well, not really."

"What do you mean *not really*?"

"Um, my friend Andrew asked me what I was in for. I had to say something because he was being friendly. So I just said I was accused of sexting and that was it. I swear."

"What about your dad? Did you talk to him about your case?"

"I told him you said I wasn't supposed to, but he made me. He only wanted to know whether I took the picture and I told him I didn't. Please don't tell him I told you. He'll be mad at me."

"Don't worry," I say. "I'll handle him."

Jenny pins a stern look on Graylin. "Going forward, it's important that you don't talk to *anybody* else about your case. Okay?"

Graylin nods. "Okay. I won't."

She pulls a pamphlet from her satchel and hands it to Graylin. "I want you to read this after I leave. It explains how the juvenile court process works."

She hands another copy to me. "You should read it too."

I glance at the title and stiffen. *Understanding the Juvenile Delinquency System*. Is she trying to belittle me in front of *our* client?

"Why does Ms. Angela need one?" Graylin asks. "Doesn't she know this stuff?"

"Of course I do," I reply with a phony smile. "I'm going to give my copy to your father."

Jenny takes out a yellow legal pad. "I want you to tell me everything you can remember about what happened on Friday. The police report says you had a naked picture of a girl from your school on your phone. Is that true?"

Graylin blows out a breath.

"It's okay to talk to us," I prod him. "Whatever you tell us is protected by the attorney-client privilege."

Graylin squints. "What does that mean?"

Jenny hurls a chiding look my way and I instantly realize my mistake. I'm talking to Graylin as if he were an adult, not a kid.

"That means whatever you tell me, even if it's something you did that's bad," Jenny explains, "I have to keep it a secret. I can't tell *anybody* about it unless you give me permission."

"And Ms. Angela too? She can't tell anybody either, right?"

I nod. "That's correct." Maybe if Jenny would use the word *we* instead of *I*, Graylin would understand that.

"Not even my dad or my granny or my Uncle Dre?"

"Not even them," Jenny confirms. "That's one of the rules attorneys have to follow."

He doesn't look at us. "Um, yeah. I had the naked picture of Kennedy on my phone."

"Did you take it?" Jenny asks.

"No, ma'am." Graylin raises his right hand. "I swear on the Bible."

"Then how did it get on your phone?"

"Somebody sent it to me on Snapchat."

"But Snapchat pictures disappear," I say.

"As soon as I saw it, I took a screenshot of it."

"Do you know who sent it to you?" Jenny asks.

Graylin shakes his head.

"You have to click on the sender's name to open the picture, don't you?"

"Yeah. But I didn't recognize the person."

Jenny scribbles something down on her legal pad. "Do you remember the name?"

"It wasn't a name. Just some letters and a number. I don't remember what they were."

"When did you first see it?"

"Right before first period ended."

"Describe the picture to us," I say. "Could you tell where it was taken?"

Jenny stretches her palm out toward me, her eyes still on Graylin. "Let's slow down. It's best if we ask him one question at a time. Describe the picture for us, Graylin?"

My jaw tightens from her rebuke. I keep my mouth shut and let the prima donna do her thing.

"It looked like she was in somebody's house and she didn't have any clothes on."

"What part of the house?" Jenny asks.

"A bedroom, I think."

"Was she posing for the picture? Like a selfie?"

"No. It looked like it was taken through a window because it was kinda far away."

"And you have no idea who sent it to you?"

"No, ma'am."

"Do you think Kennedy sent it to you? Maybe she likes you."

"Naw. There're some sluts at our school, but not Kennedy."

Jenny takes Graylin through every second of his day on Friday, starting with his arrival at school, his discovery of the Snapchat message and ending with his arrest.

"Ms. Jenny, how did the principal know I had the picture?"

"Someone left an anonymous note in the administration office saying you had a naked picture of Kennedy on your phone and that you were going to beat her up and post her picture all over Instagram."

Graylin rockets to his feet. "That's a lie! Somebody's lying on me!"

"We know Graylin." I rub his arm and guide him back to his seat. "And we're going to prove it."

"Did you have any other pictures of Kennedy on your phone?" Jenny asks.

"No, ma'am."

"Did you have naked pictures of anyone else on your phone?"

"No way."

Jenny scans the questions on her legal pad. "Did you send the picture to anyone?"

"No, ma'am. Nobody."

"Did you show it to anyone?"

"No, ma'am."

"Did you tell anyone about it?"

Graylin pauses for the first time and averts his eyes. "No, ma'am."

"We need you to be honest with us," Jenny says. "If you tell us something that isn't true, it might hurt your case because we won't be prepared."

He starts rubbing his palms up and down his thighs. "I was going to show it to my friend Crayvon, but I didn't get the chance."

"What's Crayvon's last name?"

"Little."

"So did you show it to him?"

"No, but I sort of told him about it."

"What do you mean *sort of*?"

"I saw him when we were leaving first period. I told him I had something I wanted to show him. But I didn't get the chance."

"Why not?"

"He had to go to the administration office to—"

Light fills his eyes and Graylin springs to his feet again. "Crayvon must've been the one who sent me the picture and left that note! He's supposed to be my friend. Why would he do that to me?" He starts to cry.

"Hold on Graylin," Jenny says. "You said you didn't get a chance to tell Crayvon about it. How would he know you even had it?"

"Because he must've sent it to me! He set me up!"

I stand up and hug him. "We don't know that for sure, but we'll look into it."

It takes us a few minutes to calm Graylin down.

It's clear that Jenny is much more skilled at retrieving information from child clients than I am. I want to know more about Crayvon Little. But since that subject upset him, she moves on to another topic and will likely return to it later.

"Let's go over how the police got your phone again."

Graylin hangs his head in an exaggerated show of exhaustion. "We already did. I'm getting tired, Ms. Jenny."

"I know. We'll take a break in a minute."

He exhales. "At first, when they asked me for it, I said it was in my locker. But then it started ringing."

"And then what happened?

"The Asian cop made me take it out of my pocket and give it to them, so I did."

Both of us jerk to attention at the same time. The first time Graylin recounted what happened, he made it sound like he willingly handed over his phone.

"What do you mean he *made* you give it to him?" Jenny asks.

"The Asian cop was really mean. He said, *Give me the damn phone* and pounded the table with his fist."

Jenny and I eye each other with lawyerly glee.

"Did they read you your rights before they started talking to you?"

"Nope. I kept telling them that my dad told me not to talk to the police without his permission, but they wouldn't stop asking me questions. So can you get me out because they didn't read me my rights?"

"We'll see," Jenny says.

"Let's take a break." She motions me toward the door. "We'll be right back."

Once we're outside in the hallway, Jenny bites her lip and starts pacing. "The biggest problem we have is that Graylin saved the picture to his phone. That makes the possession charge hard for us to kick."

Progress! She's finally using the pronouns *we* and *us* as if we're a team.

"Sounds like our best shot is filing a motion to suppress the picture and Graylin's statements because the police violated his Fourth and Fifth Amendment rights."

"That's not our best shot," Jenny says. "It's our only shot."

CHAPTER 25

Kennedy

I hate it *so* much when my parents argue.

I crack my bedroom door and take a few steps into the hallway so I can see into the living room. My parents are standing nose-to-nose.

"This is a decision *both* of us have to make," my dad says.

"I understand that," my mom spits at him. "What I don't understand is why you want to sweep everything under the rug."

"I just don't think it's a good idea to make our daughter the poster child for sexting. You had no right to call the mayor's office throwing around *my* name without *my* permission."

"We've raised a ton of money for that man. He owes us."

"Don't you understand that pushing this case means the media could pick up on it. That could cause even more embarrassment for her."

"There's nothing for Kennedy to be embarrassed about. Some pervert took a picture of her through her bedroom window. I want to teach my daughter to stand up for herself."

My dad throws up his hands and slumps to the couch.

I don't understand how my mom and dad started hating each other. Last Christmas, everyone was so happy. Then out of the blue, my dad sat me down and told me he was moving out.

"And why won't you go to counseling with us?" my mom asks. "Lord knows everybody in this house could use it."

He stands up, his hands at his waist. "I'm fine with Kennedy getting counseling, but I have no desire to air our dirty laundry before some stranger. So don't ask me again."

"I get it," my mom says, folding her arms. "Going to counseling would take too much time away from your little slut."

"Whatever."

"Oh, so you're not denying it this time."

"I'm not denying it because it doesn't do me any good. Think what you want to think."

I don't believe my dad is having an affair. He isn't like that. Sometimes my mom overreacts to stuff. Like when she cursed out my sixth-grade teacher for saying it would've been better if we'd made homemade cupcakes for the bake sale rather than buying the expensive ones from Sprinkles.

They're both quiet now, staring at each other like two frozen statues. I don't want to be like other kids at my school who have to go back and forth between their divorced parents like ping-pong balls.

"There's something I need to tell you," my dad says. "Please have a seat." He pats the space on the couch next to him.

"Oh, so you're finally going to admit that you're having an affair with that little Mexican slut."

"I'm not having an affair! For Christ's sake! Will you please sit down?"

My mom takes the armchair across from him.

My dad starts rubbing his palms together. He always does that when he's nervous.

"I want to come home."

I knew my dad was a good man and this proves it!

My mom softens like melted ice cream. "Why now? Is it because of what happened to Kennedy?"

My dad rubs his hands together again. "I do want to be here for Kennedy, but I want to be upfront with you. The governor is about to appoint me to the Superior Court bench. They're going to be examining every area of my life. It'd be better if I didn't have to explain the state of my marriage and it wouldn't look good for my daughter to be in the middle of a criminal case."

My mom's mouth gapes open, but no words come out.

"So can you do me this one favor? Just let the D.A.'s Office handle this without our active involvement."

When she's super mad, my mom doesn't raise her voice. Her next words are extra soft. "Sounds like you want to come home for *your* benefit, not for your daughter's and certainly not for mine." She leans back in the chair and crosses her legs.

My dad doesn't say anything and lets my mom keep talking.

"I couldn't care less about you being appointed to the bench. As soon as you're confirmed you're going to run off with your little slut. We might as well just end this charade now. I'm contacting a divorce attorney tomorrow. I'm done."

"C'mon, Simone, can't we—"

"And for the record, in addition to taking you to the cleaners, I'm going to make sure that boy gets put in jail for as long as they'll have him. Then I'm suing his family in civil court."

"That's a waste of time. They probably don't have a dime."

"I don't care if we never recover a penny. I want to make a point." She stands up. "I'd appreciate it if you'd leave."

My dad slowly gets to his feet. "I want to see Kennedy."

"She's asleep and I don't want to wake her. Please leave."

I go back into my room, tears streaming down my face. My mother is right. My dad only cares about himself.

As I sink onto my bed, my phone chirps. I pick it up and read the text from my best friend LaShay. When I hear screaming, I don't even realize that it's me.

My parents rush into the room, nearly tripping over each other in the doorway. My mom throws her arms around me. "What's the matter, baby?"

I can't speak, so I hand her my phone.

"Oh my God!" she shrieks after reading the text, then shoves the phone into my dad's face.

When my dad reads it, he looks like he wants to scream too.

"Now are you ready to fight for your daughter?" my mom yells at him. "Or is everything still all about you?"

CHAPTER 26

It's around dinnertime when Mossy and I walk into Craps. The place is nearly empty. An older couple is sitting at a cocktail table in the back while two young dudes are loud-talking each other at the bar. What we're about to do is pretty ballsy. I'm glad there won't be much of an audience.

We ease into a red leather booth near the entrance.

"You cool?" Mossy asks.

I smile. "As a cucumber."

I'm lying. My guts are doing somersaults and my underarms are damp with perspiration. The Shepherd wants me dead. Who's to say he wouldn't have someone take me out right here? But after Apache caught that dude casing my sister's house, he left me no choice but to go rogue.

I persuaded my sister to take Brianna and move in with a girlfriend in Lancaster, about an hour away. Donna initially balked, but after I told her about the guy in the black Escalade, she freaked and was packed up and on the road three hours later.

Donna's reaction only heightened my reluctance to come clean with Angela. She won't just freak, she'll run as far away from me as possible.

Mossy orders a cognac and Coke. I ask for a Pepsi straight, which causes the waitress to raise an eyebrow. It's been years since I've had a drink. During my dealing days, I made the decision to never partake of any substance that alters the senses. If you're a drug dealer, a good one, you need to be mentally alert at all times. I need the full use of my faculties right now.

"What's the latest with Graylin?" Mossy asks. His eyes conduct a 360-degree review of the club.

"A bunch of craziness." I explain the situation Graylin's facing and how the cops pulled a gun on Gus right there in the principal's office.

"Man, he's lucky that cop's trigger finger didn't slip. I can't believe they arrested Graylin just for having a naked picture on his phone."

"That ain't the kicker. They're charging him with possession of child pornography."

"You serious?"

"Yep. We gotta stick close to Gus, man. I think he's close to the breaking point. I remember how hard it was to keep it together when they snatched Brianna. He's going through the same thing. Except it ain't some pimp messing with his kid, it's the system."

"Have you told Angela about your situation yet?"

I shake my head.

"Man, your girl needs to know what's going on."

"I don't want her all stressed out about it. I've been staying at her place at night and she's in a busy office building during the day. So she's good."

"You better hope so."

When the door opens and Apache steps into the club, Mossy grimaces. "Man, you sure you want your crazy-ass cousin in on this one?"

"I wouldn't even know about The Shepherd's threat if it wasn't for him."

Before Mossy can protest further, Apache slides into the booth across from us.

"What up, cuz? Moss man? Y'all ready to get this show on the road?"

"This ain't no show," Mossy says. "We're here to deliver a message. That's it."

"Don't worry, I got this," Apache says.

"Who's running this place?" I ask.

"A dude named Buzz. I'ma go tell the bartender we wanna talk to him."

Apache trots over to the bar, says a few words to the female bartender, then returns to the table. "He'll be over in a minute."

"Let me do the talking," I remind him.

"This is your show, cuz. You'll be happy to know I already started putting my plan into action."

"And what plan is that?" Mossy asks.

Apache hurls a hurt look at me. "C'mon, cuz, you didn't tell him?"

"Didn't get the chance. Apache came up with a plan for us to take The Shepherd out from behind bars without any fingerprints leading back to us."

"Wow," Mossy says facetiously, "I bet his plan is brilliant."

"Actually," I say, "it is. So brilliant, in fact, I wished I'd come up with it myself."

Before I can explain, a rotund man in cheap slacks and a white shirt walks over to us. "One of y'all wanted to see me?"

"You Buzz?" Apache asks.

"Yeah."

"Why don't you take a seat?" I say.

"I'm working." Buzz's eyes dart to the left where a bouncer is now leaning against the bar. He must've warned the guy that something might go down.

"Don't worry," I say. "I'm not here to cause any problems. I need you to deliver a message to the man who owns this place. The Shepherd."

"This is my bar." Buzz's bloodshot eyes blink several times. "And I don't know nobody named Shepherd."

Before I can respond, Apache jumps in. "C'mon, man, we ain't tryin' to hear no bull. We both know—"

I give my cousin a silencing look and he flops back against the booth and sulks.

"If that's the company line you need to recite," I say, "so be it. But like I said, I have a message I'd like you to deliver to The Shepherd."

Buzz ain't no poker player. His eyes flash bravado, but I see nothing but fear seeping through. If the cops knew The Shepherd was associated with this place, they'd shut it down, confiscate everything in it and throw Buzz in jail too.

"My name is Dre Thomas. I hear Shep's got a target on my back."

I pause to wait for the man to plead lack of knowledge again. When he doesn't, I continue.

"Tell Shep that I've also got a target on *his* back. I know he's enjoying life in the safety of that federal penitentiary outside Dallas, but I know people on the inside. So if anything happens to me or my niece, my peeps will be coming for him. That's it."

Buzz struggles to keep his game face on. "Like I told you, I-I, uh, I don't know nobody named The Shepherd or Shep or nothing like that. This is my place. And I don't like people coming into my establishment threatening me. You need to leave."

"Ain't nobody threatening you," I say calmly. "I'm threatening Shep, a man you supposedly don't know." I hold up my Pepsi and flash him a smile. "We'll be leaving as soon as we finish our drinks."

"I want you to leave now," Buzz says.

Apache sets his 9mm on the table. "We'll leave when we're ready to leave."

"Aw shit!" Mossy says under his breath.

Buzz stares at the gun, then over at the bouncer. "We don't allow weapons in here. Get out!"

By the time the bouncer reaches our table, Apache is on his feet, his gun pressed to Buzz's head. The bouncer points his glock at me and Mossy.

"Apache!" I yell, holding out my hands. "Cool it, man!"

"I don't like the way this dude is talking to us." Apache's gun is pressed so deep into Buzz's temple the man's right ear can almost touch his shoulder. "You need to show your customers a little more hospitality."

Buzz's false teeth start chattering. "Look, y'all, I don't want no trouble!"

"Neither do we," Apache says. "That's why you need to let Shep know he needs to back off from messin' with my peeps."

"Leave!" the bouncer commands, his gun still on us.

Mossy and I stand up and start backing out of the club. Once we make it to the door, Apache shoves Buzz forward and calmly sticks his gun inside his waistband.

"My name's Apache," he says, before turning to leave. "Make sure Shep gets our message."

CHAPTER 27

Angela

Jenny and I spend most of Monday morning at her Echo Park office preparing for Graylin's arraignment and detention hearing.

We interview Graylin's minister and two of his teachers by phone and review every report card and accolade Gus could find. We scour Graylin's Snapchat, Instagram, Facebook, Twitter and Tumblr accounts, as well as his laptop and emails. Without his phone, however, we can't check his text messages. We find nothing that could come back to bite him at the hearing.

Jenny already has a Snapchat account. I create one too so I can familiarize myself with how the app works. We spend over an hour sending pictures back and forth. You can set the picture to disappear anywhere from one to ten seconds after a Snapchat message is opened.

"When do you think we're going to get a look at the picture and Graylin's phone?" I ask.

Jenny found out that the case is assigned to Deputy D.A. Miguel Martinez.

"Some prosecutors like to play hide-the-ball with the evidence," Jenny says. "The fact that Martinez hasn't returned my calls isn't a good sign. And I'm a little worried because he filed the possession charge as a felony. It's a wobbler, so he had the option to file it as a misdemeanor. I put a few feelers out and they came back mixed. He hates putting away kids for sexting, but he thinks juvenile court is beneath him."

My brain needs a break. I walk over to the window, which looks out onto busy Alvarado Boulevard. Echo Park used to be predominantly Latino. Now it seems as if every other brown face had been replaced by a hip, young white one. The bodegas and taco stands are now coffee shops, art galleries, health food stores and vintage clothing boutiques.

"You live near here?" I ask.

"Yep. I have a condo two blocks away. It's nice to be able to walk to work."

"The neighborhood sure has changed. How much are condos around here going for now?"

"I got mine for five. A guy who moved next door about a month ago paid seven."

"Seven as in *seven hundred thousand*?"

"Yep. Gentrification at its finest."

"The same thing is happening in South L.A. It's sad because the people being forced out of their apartments to make way for condos could never afford to buy one."

"I bought my place years ago." Jenny's tone is defensive. "Long before it became trendy to be here."

"I'm not judging you. I was only making an observation."

"Sure, you're judging me. Most of the long-time Echo Park residents seem to resent whites moving in."

I shrug. "They're just concerned about preserving the culture of their community."

Jenny chuckles. "No, they're being just as racist as the whites who try to keep them out of their neighborhoods."

"I don't think it's the same thing. They—"

"Why don't we change the subject?" Jenny snaps.

I stand up and start gathering my papers. She's right. Taking the conversation any further would be a mistake.

Forty minutes later we're back at juvenile hall sitting with Graylin. We have Gus on speakerphone.

"We want to explain what's going to happen at the arraignment and detention hearing tomorrow," Jenny begins, looking Graylin in the eyes. "It's going to be like a mini-trial. Even though there won't be a jury, you need to understand that the judge is the jury. So sit up straight, don't make any faces and respond clearly when the judge asks you a question."

Graylin begins to fidget, thumping his fingers on the desk. "What are they going to ask me?"

"The judge is going to read the charges against you and ask if you understand them." Jenny pulls out a piece of paper. "The first charge is possession of child pornography. Do you know what that means?"

"Um, yeah. Child pornography is having naked pictures, right?"

"Yes, of someone under the age of eighteen. The judge is going to ask whether you admit or deny the petition? You need to respond *deny*. I'll give you a signal when it's time to say that."

"Is deny the same thing as not guilty?"

"Exactly. And the second charge is making a criminal threat. You're going to say *deny* to both."

"Can I tell the judge that I didn't write that note and that Crayvon set me up?"

"No," Jenny says. "We're still looking into that."

"What's Crayvon got to do with this?" Gus' voice booms through the phone.

"Nothing that we're sure of yet," I say.

"Ms. Jenny, if they're charging me with having a naked picture on my phone, how do I get off since I *did* have a naked picture?"

Graylin is indeed a smart kid.

"You leave that to me. The only issue the court is going to deal with tomorrow is whether your home is a suitable place for you to be while your case is pending."

Jenny expresses surprise that the Probation Department hasn't contacted Gus yet and tells him to expect a call sometime today. "They're going to ask you a bunch of questions about Graylin's home life. You must show that he'll be under twenty-four-hour supervision."

"My mother will be home with him while I'm at work. My sister's going to help homeschool him."

"I can't go back to school?" Graylin says, crestfallen.

"No, not until your case is resolved."

He folds his arms and slides down in his chair.

Jenny points a finger at him. "You can't do that in court tomorrow. Please sit up. If something happens that you don't like, you have to ignore it. I know this is hard on you, but I need you to follow my instructions, okay?"

"Yeah, okay."

"C'mon, Little Man," Gus says. "Everything's gonna be fine. You gotta do what your attorneys say."

"Is Kennedy going to be there?" Graylin asks.

"I doubt it. I've never had a victim show up at a detention hearing, but you never know."

"Everything'll be fine," I say. "I wouldn't worry about it. You'll get to go home tomorrow."

The instant my words are out, Jenny purses her lips and rolls her eyes. I did it again. Telling Graylin something I don't know for sure. I'll apologize to Jenny later.

We spend the next hour taking Gus and Graylin through mock questioning. After Jenny lobs all the softball questions, I play the role of prosecutor and take them through the wringer.

One of the staff arrives to escort Graylin back to his unit and Jenny and I head for our cars, which are parked behind each other on Eastlake Avenue.

Jenny gets into her car, then abruptly jumps out and marches up to me.

"Please don't do that again." Her lips are twisted up like a pretzel.

"Do what again?"

"You told Graylin everything's going to be fine and that he's going home tomorrow. We don't know that for sure. You can't keep saying stuff just to make him feel good."

"I'm sorry. It kind of slipped out. But based on the facts, Graylin should—"

"That's the operative word, *should*. You can't make promises to a child client. They take you at your word and when you can't deliver, it destroys their trust. If you want to stay on this defense team, then stop undercutting me."

Before I can respond, Jenny struts back to her car and screeches off.

CHAPTER 28

The Shepherd

I'm sitting in the middle of my bunk in the lotus position, my eyes closed, taking in long deep breaths. I need a sense of calm to come to terms with the ultimate disrespect from Dre Thomas. To walk into my establishment and threaten me warrants immediate and serious action.

I meditate for upwards of thirty minutes before opening my eyes and coming back to my surroundings.

It's another hour before Old School shows up to serve as my lookout. Willie picks up on the second ring.

"I've had a chance to think things through," I say. "I like your idea about the new project."

"So we're going forward?" Willie asks.

I pause. Snatching a child is one thing, but kidnapping an adult—a lawyer no less—could present a whole host of problems. And I don't have total trust in Willie. He's the type of man who'd do anything for a buck. That means somebody else could lure him away for a buck more. But for the time being, Willie's all I've got.

"Not yet," I say. "I want to send a message first. A strong one."

"Okay, okay. I got it."

Our first salvo is all about intimidation. Mental anguish can sometimes be more menacing than a physical attack. I still remember the way Dre Thomas tore up the streets searching for his niece. I want him and his woman so spooked they can't function.

"I want to let them know who they're dealing with."

I hope Willie truly understands what I want him to do.

"I got you, boss."

I hate the man's slip-ups. "Don't call me that."

"Oh, yeah. Sorry."

"Take your time with this thing. Make your point loud and clear. No more mistakes."

As I hang up, another idea comes to mind. Simply terrorizing Angela Evans isn't good enough. After we play with her head a bit, I'll have Willie find somebody to rape her.

CHAPTER 29

Graylin

It's dinnertime, but I'm not hungry. I stare at my hamburger and wish I was home. I miss my granny's cooking, especially her fried chicken.

"You too good to eat, Smart Boy?"

Tyke is sitting down across from me. I don't look up and just keep ignoring him like I've been doing.

"I'm talkin' to you, Smart Boy."

I didn't know I had a nickname, but I kinda of like it. Tyke needs to leave me alone. I have a headache and my stomach hurts because I'm nervous about going to court tomorrow.

"Well, I ain't talking to you, Dumb Boy."

"Whoa!" all the other boys exclaim at once.

I've just embarrassed Tyke, but I don't care. I have too many other problems to worry about. Besides, Tyke can't do anything to me with Mr. Dennison so close by. That makes me feel even bolder.

"Dude, do you know who I am?" Tyke's face twists with rage.

"I'm not messing with you. So don't mess with me."

I take a bite of my hamburger just as Tyke hurls his milk carton across the table. The corner of the carton hits me below my right eye. The whole right side of my face goes numb. When I press my hand to my cheek and see a spot of blood on my finger, I explode.

Diving across the table, I start pounding Tyke in the face with a force I didn't know I had.

Mr. Dennison snatches me by my sweatshirt and pulls me away while another man grabs Tyke. I break free and jump on top of Tyke. I'm sitting on his chest now, pounding him in the face with both fists. He screams like a girl and tries to cover his face.

It takes both Mr. Dennison and Mr. Morris to pull me off of him. I'm still crying and swinging at the air as they drag me to the opposite side of the day room.

"I didn't even do anything to him and he threw his milk at me and tried to put my eye out!" I sob.

"I didn't do nothin' to him," Tyke yells from the floor. "He just jumped up and started wailin' on me. I swear!"

"Don't matter who threw the first punch," Mr. Dennison barks. "You know the rules. No fighting. Both of you are in big trouble!"

CHAPTER **30**

Angela

Jenny is already at the courthouse when I arrive the next morning. We haven't spoken since her little hissy fit yesterday. She greets me with such a gigantic smile I'm beginning to think she might be bipolar.

"You look awful happy," I say as I step into the attorney meeting room.

"That's because I just finished reading this." Jenny dangles a document in the air. "The detention report recommends that Graylin go home!"

"Thank God." Jenny hands it to me and I start reading it.

"Graylin should be here any minute," she says.

The negative residue from our tiff needs to be addressed. If we're going to handle this case successfully, we need to get along. I decide to eat crow for Graylin's sake.

"Hey, Jenny," I begin, "I wanted to say that I'm sorry about—"

She flashes me her palm. "Just don't let it happen again."

I don't like her dismissiveness and I'm about to tell her as much when the door opens and a sheriff's deputy shows Graylin into the room.

"Oh my God!" I run over and cup Graylin's face. "What happened to you?" His right eye is almost swollen shut and there's a long, red gash underneath it.

"This boy named Tyke threw a carton of milk at me. But I got him good. He won't be messing with me again."

The door opens and Gus enters the room. When his eyes land on Graylin, he cringes. "What in the hell happened to your face?"

Graylin hurls his arms around his dad. "This bully started messing with me for nothing."

"This is not good," Jenny says. "The detention report recommends sending you home. But it was obviously completed before the fight. This could change things."

"That's not fair!" Graylin whines. "Tyke was the one messing with me. I was only defending myself."

"The fact that somebody nearly put his eye out shows we need to get him the hell out of here for his own safety," Gus says.

"I need you to step outside," Jenny says to Gus. "We need to find out what happened so we're not hit with any surprises."

"He just needs to tell the truth," Gus says. "He—"

"I need you to step outside," Jenny says firmly.

"Please, Gus," I press, "we don't have a lot of time."

He sulks out like an angry kid.

As Graylin starts talking, Jenny takes furious notes. "That prosecutor is going to bring up the fight and say some bad things about you," she tells him. "I want you to try as hard as you can not to get upset at anything he says. And don't say a word unless I ask you to speak, okay?"

Graylin nods.

Jenny squeezes his shoulder. "I need you to be strong. Let's go in there and win, okay?"

"Okay." Graylin rubs his good eye with the heel of his hand just as a deputy knocks on the door to tell us his case is being called.

Juvenile court operates in a more casual atmosphere than adult court. In this one, the judge sits on an elevated bench, next to the witness box. There's no jury box and the court reporter sits below the bench facing the judge.

The three of us take seats at the defense table with Graylin in the middle. Gus and Dre are on the back row, along the wall. A well-dressed black couple is seated on the opposite side of the courtroom. Juvenile proceedings are closed to the public. They must be the girl's parents.

Jenny reads my mind. She leans over to whisper into my ear. "That's not a good sign."

I take a peek at the woman, who boldly scowls back at me. The man is busy with his cell phone.

When a GQ-looking Hispanic man carrying a thick stack of folders walks in, Jenny rises and approaches him.

"I'm Jenny Ungerman, Graylin Alexander's attorney. I left a couple of messages for you. Any idea when we can get a copy of the picture and the note? We'd also like to examine Graylin's phone."

"Oh, yeah, sorry. Crazy schedule," Miguel Martinez says. "I should have the picture and note to you by the end of the week. I'll need more time with the phone. We sent it to an outside firm to take a look at it."

He's about to sit down when he notices Graylin's face. His expression tells me it's as much of a surprise to him as it was to us.

"I'm concerned that they're doing outside analysis on the phone," Jenny says, when she sits back down. "The D.A.'s Office doesn't spend that kind of money on a case like this. Something's up."

The bailiff calls the courtroom to order and everyone stands as Judge Jaynie Miller enters from a side door and takes the bench. "Good morning, everyone!"

I've never seen a judge walk into court with such a cheerful disposition. The judge looks so happy I almost expect her to start waving like she's on a parade float. I guess she's thrilled to have escaped from corporate America. Her short brown hair is lightly sprinkled with blonde high-lights and her cheeks are a soft rosy color that's natural, not brushed on.

Judge Miller examines the paperwork in front of her. "Looks like we're here for an arraignment and detention hearing." She rattles off the charges. "Does the minor—" Graylin's swollen face stops her mid-sentence. "Does the minor admit or deny the petition?"

Jenny gently elbows Graylin.

"I deny," he says loudly.

"I've read the detention report. Mr. Martinez, do you wish to be heard?"

"Yes, Your Honor. We feel strongly that the minor should be detained. We believe that he is indeed a danger to others. The victim's parents—who are here in court today—fear that the minor presents a very real threat to their daughter. Simone Carlyle, the victim's mother, would like to be heard regarding the trauma her daughter has suffered due to the minor's conduct. In addition, Mrs. Carlyle recently advised me that the picture has gone viral. Our tech people were also able to confirm that."

I place a gentle hand on Graylin's shoulder. I can feel him shaking.

Jenny scribbles something on a Post-it note, folds it and passes it to me behind Graylin's back.

I cringe when I read it. *Viral=Problem!*

"Okay," Judge Miller says. "I'll briefly hear from the mother."

Martinez turns around. "Mrs. Carlyle, please stand."

Mrs. Carlyle rises and smooths her hands over her red St. John jacket. "I'm Mrs. Simone Carlyle. The victim is my daughter. I want the court to know that my baby is very distraught and embarrassed over this invasion of her privacy. Both physically and psychologically she's a wreck. She cries every day, all day." The woman stops to dab at the corner of her eye with a tissue. "And ever since my baby's friend texted her with the news that the picture has gone viral, she's been afraid to leave the house. It's probably in the hands of pedophiles now. My husband and I are here today to beg the court to keep the defendant locked up so my child is safe."

"But I didn't do nothing, Ms. Angela," Graylin mutters.

"Please be quiet," I whisper.

The judge directs a question to Martinez. "Any prior contact between the minor and the victim?"

"Nothing beyond attending the same school and having a couple of classes together."

The judge turns to Jenny. "Any questions for Mrs. Carlyle?"

"Just one," Jenny says.

"Mrs. Carlyle, has your daughter seen a counselor as a result of this incident?"

Simone tilts her head. "Excuse me, but this isn't an incident?"

"I'm sorry. Has your daughter seen a counselor?"

"No, not yet."

"No further questions, Your Honor."

I'm done with her, but Mrs. Carlyle isn't done with me.

"You're trying to make it seem like my daughter wasn't damaged by that little pervert!"

"Mrs. Carlyle," the judge says, "there isn't a question pending."

"Your Honor," Jenny exclaims, "I object to—"

"But I didn't do nothing," Graylin cries out. "I'm innocent. I swear!"

The judge gently taps her gavel. "Young man, you are not allowed to speak unless a question is directed to you. Do you understand?"

A tear falls from Graylin's swollen eye and in seconds, his hiccupping sobs fill the courtroom.

"Your Honor," Jenny says. "Can we take a short break to give my client a chance to collect himself."

Judge Miller twists her lips to the side. "Let's take fifteen."

CHAPTER 31

Apache

I just got off the phone with my cousin Dre. I can't believe what they doing to Gus' kid. Got him locked up like a criminal just for having a naked picture of some girl.

"You know anybody got a kid at Eastlake Juvenile Hall?" Dre asked me. "Somebody needs to have Graylin's back. I'm not sure they're going to let him come home."

Without a thought, I told him I was on it. I dig it when people, especially family, come to me for help. Makes me feel like a powerful mafia boss. I'm sure one of my partners has a little criminal-in-the-making on lockdown in juvie jail who can look out for Graylin. That's what family does, and Gus and Graylin are like family.

It only took me two calls to get things in motion. My homeboy Luke has a kid at Eastlake facing assault charges. Luke said he would get word to his son ASAP to have Graylin's back. When I hang up, I'm feeling quite pleased with myself. If you want the job done, and done right, I'm your fix-it man.

Now, I have to seriously focus on my plan to shut down The Shepherd. I jump in and out of the shower and thirty minutes later I'm rolling down Normandie in my Benz. I pull into the driveway of a house off 51st Street.

I bang on the door for a good minute before somebody answers.

Ronny Boy opens the door wearing only his boxers. "Man, do you know what time it is?"

"Negro, it's almost eleven o'clock. Get your ass up." I walk past him into the house. "I need some help."

He rubs his eyes. "You got some nerve bogarting me this time of the morning. I work nights. What you want?"

"I got some serious business that needs handling and you're going to help me do it."

"Dude, I'm on the up and up now. Got me a job at Home Depot, if you can believe that. Even got me a 401K."

"Good for you. But you owe me."

"C'mon, man, cut me some slack." Ronny Boy walks into the kitchen and I follow. "I'm not down with the streets no more. Got me a nice woman, a nurse. She makes good money. I ain't trying to mess that up."

"I hear you. But what I need you to do ain't nothing illegal. I just need you to make a contact for me."

Ronny Boy gives me a skeptical look, but doesn't say more. He slumps into a chair at the kitchen table.

I'm sure whatever you want me to do gonna lead right back to me if something goes down. Man, I ain't trying to go back to prison."

"You heard of The Shepherd?"

Ronny Boy nods. "The dude who got locked up for pimpin' little girls?"

"That would be the one. He's on lockdown in the federal pen in Texas right now, but that didn't stop him from putting the word out on the street that he wants my cousin Dre dead. But I got a plan to shut him down." I smile. "From the inside."

"Negro, you must be crazy. How you plan to get to him when he's in prison? Federal prison ain't like state."

"You don't need to know all the specifics. I just wanna know if you know that dude Blaze, who's doing life at Corcoran."

Ronny Boy's eyes flash like strobe lights. He hops up from his seat and starts waving his hands back and forth like a high-speed windshield wiper.

"Hell naw, dude! I ain't doing nothing got to do with Blaze. That dude is a stone-cold killer. He's still ruling these streets like a free man. And he got connections from here to China. Nobody messes with Blaze unless they wanna die."

"Calm down, calm down. I know what a lunatic the brother is. I need somebody to get a message to him."

"Well, I ain't delivering it."

"I don't want you to deliver it. But you gotta know some dudes who're still in Corcoran. You just got out six months ago."

"Yeah, so what?"

"I want you to get a message to one of them so they can get a message to Blaze."

"Man, I ain't tryin' to get mixed up in no madness. You know other dudes that done time at Corcoran. Call one of them."

"I plan to. But I need multiple sources. That way, when Blaze hears the same thing over and over again, he'll know it's the truth."

"Hears what?"

I tell him the message I want delivered to Blaze.

"Is it true?"

"Yep," I lie without hesitation. I know the criminal mind. When Blaze hears the same story from three or four sources, he won't take the time to check for factual validity.

"And that's all you want me to do? Just have one of my boys tell him that?"

"Yep. But it's gotta be when somebody visits him. Not on the phone."

"Man, ain't nobody going up there. Once you get out, you don't go back for nothing."

"Okay, what about this? I heard he's still down with LaRhonda Jenkins. She visits him on the regular even though he'll never see the light of day. You know anybody who can get word to her?"

He pauses to think. "LaRhonda got a beauty salon on Manchester. My sister goes there. I guess she could tell her."

I slap him on the back. "See, I knew you could help a brutha out."

"Man, Blaze is crazy. Once he hears that he's gonna…" Ronny Boy's words trail off as the realization of my ultimate intent crests like a gentle wave inside his feeble brain.

This time, Ronny Boy smiles. "Dang, man. You one smart-ass dude."

"Yeah, I am, ain't I? So how about calling your sister right now?"

CHAPTER 32

Dre

My buddy Gus is close to a meltdown.

"That girl's parents act like Graylin killed somebody!"

He's sitting next to me with his head in his hands. We're the only ones in the courtroom now besides the clerk and the bailiff. Angela and Jenny took Graylin outside to calm him down.

"Just keep it together, man. It's gonna be okay."

"Graylin's a good kid. I don't understand why they came at him like that." His right knee is bouncing up and down.

I nudge his arm. "Let's step outside and get some air."

Without responding, Gus follows me out of the courtroom. We maneuver down a wide hallway packed with kids and parents.

I'm exiting the courthouse before I realize that Gus isn't behind me. To get back to him, I have to go through the metal detectors again. Only four people are ahead of me in line, but it takes forever for the sheriff's deputy to wave me through.

As I scan the lobby, alarm sets in. Gus is walking toward a corner of the building where the girl's parents are standing. I make it over there just as Gus reaches them.

"I'm Graylin's father," Gus says, directing his attention to the man. "I wonder if I could speak to you for a minute. My son is a good kid. He—"

His wife gets in Gus' face. "Your son is a predator and a pervert who belongs behind bars."

Gus recoils like he's just been slapped. It takes a couple of seconds for him to respond.

"Ma'am, I know what they charged him with, but he's innocent. His life shouldn't be ruined because someone sent him that picture."

"You apparently don't know your child," the woman spits back at him. "If I have anything to say about it, he's going away for a long, long time. And when the criminal case is over I'm suing you for emotional distress."

I've never seen Gus speechless, but I *have* seen him on the verge of exploding, and he's almost there. I step in and turn to the father. "I'm Dre, a family friend. We're sorry about what happened to your daughter. But the police have this all wrong."

The man runs a hand down his face. I can tell he don't wear the pants in his house.

"To be honest," he says, "I agree with you. I don't think this situation warrants the death penalty either and I'm shocked at how it's being handled."

His wife looks as if she's about to swallow her tongue. "Percy! Have you lost your mind? You're going to stand right here in front of me and undercut not just me, but your own daughter?"

Her voice is so loud one of the sheriff's deputies begins stalking toward us. "Is everything okay over here?"

"No, it isn't. This man threatened us. He's trying to force us to drop the charges against his son."

Gus' eyes widen. "What? I didn't—"

"This will have to be reported to the judge." The deputy takes out a small notepad from his shirt pocket. "Ma'am, what's your name?"

"Simone Carlyle."

"I'll also need the name of your judge?"

"No, you won't." The words from the girl's father surprise everyone. "This man didn't threaten anybody. My wife's overreacting. He's just concerned about his son and wanted us to know that he's a good kid."

The woman's hands fly to her hips and she sneers at her husband with such disgust that the sheriff's deputy takes a step back.

"I understand that you're trying to protect your kid," the husband says to Gus, "but you need to make your case to the judge or the prosecutor, not us. This is out of our hands."

He takes his wife by the forearm, but she jerks away and struts off down the hallway. After a couple of seconds, he follows.

Angela and Jenny rush over. "What happened?" Angela asks.

"I just wanted to talk to them," Gus says, rubbing his chin. "To tell them Graylin was a good kid. That he didn't deserve any of this. But that bitch lied and told the sheriff I was threatening them."

Jenny presses three fingers to her temples. "You shouldn't have approached them. If they report this to the judge, the only person who's going to suffer is Graylin."

"But she's lying. Her husband even backed me up."

"Doesn't matter," Jenny says. "We don't need any distractions. So please don't say another word to them." She turns to Angela. "Call Graylin's minister and teacher and find out how fast they can get here. We're going to need their testimony."

Angela pulls out her phone, then freezes as she stares down the hallway. We all follow her gaze.

Simone Carlyle is standing at the end of the hallway, arms flailing, as she speaks to Deputy D.A. Martinez. Her husband is holding out his hands, palms down as if he's bouncing two invisible basketballs. We're too far away to hear what's being said, but there is no doubt that Mrs. Carlyle is speaking in anger.

"This isn't good," Jenny says glumly. "If they tell the judge you threatened them, there's a good chance Graylin won't be going home today."

CHAPTER 33

Angela

We're collectively holding our breath as we head back into the courtroom. We expect Martinez to report the hallway confrontation, but the judge beats him to the punch.

"I understand from one of the deputies that there was some kind of commotion between the parents during the break," Judge Miller says. "Is there anything we need to discuss?"

Martinez stands and to my surprise says, "No, Your Honor."

There's a gasp from Mrs. Carlyle, who springs up from her seat, shoots a dirty look at Martinez, then sashays her way out of the courtroom. Her husband shakes his head.

I'm relieved, but not for long. Martinez calls one of the Eastlake staff to testify. The detention services officer tells the judge that he managed to separate the fighting boys, but Graylin was so enraged that he charged at the other kid a second time, pounding him in the face while he lay on the ground. It took two adults, the man testified, to pull Graylin off of him. The other boy ended up with a broken jaw.

On cross, Jenny establishes that the kid has bullied other boys at Eastlake and that Graylin didn't start the fight.

Martinez has no other witnesses and hands the floor to Jenny, who expertly rolls through a short examination of Graylin's science teacher, then his minister. They credibly testify that Graylin is a smart, responsible young man who is always respectful. They tell the judge that he's never been in any trouble and that Gus is a great father who's always on hand for parent-teacher meetings and who attends church regularly with his son.

On cross, Martinez makes a half-hearted attempt to elicit negative information from the teacher but fails. He passes on even trying to cross the minister.

It's close to noon by the time Gus takes the stand. His hands are trembling and he continuously cracks his knuckles.

"What do you do for a living, Mr. Alexander?" Jenny begins.

"I rehab houses?"

"How long have you done that?"

"Two years?"

"And what did you do before that?"

Gus pauses.

We thoroughly prepped him for this question. It's always best to get negative information out on direct—so you can control how it's presented—rather than allowing your opponent to use it to score points on cross.

"I was in prison for three years. For possession of cocaine."

"Were you dealing cocaine?"

"No. Just a user. Had a bad habit, but I kicked it. Been clean for five years."

"Are you close to your son?"

"Yes. Very close. His mother," he pauses again. "His mother's a crack addict. We don't know where she is. I'm raising Graylin with my mother's and sister's help. He's a good kid. An A student. Never gives me any trouble. Very mannerable. Always says *yes, sir* and *no, sir*. His grandmother, my moms, makes sure of that."

Gus is relaxed and almost smiling.

"If Graylin is released who would supervise him?"

"I would be there in the mornings and after work. And during the day my mother or my sister Macie would be at the house with him. He'll be homeschooled for now."

"So there would be no time during the day when he would be left unsupervised?"

"That's correct."

"What about his schoolwork? How would he get that done?"

"Graylin's very self-motivated. I've never had to push him to do his homework. He likes school."

The second Jenny turns Gus over to Martinez, he stiffens like a slab of granite.

"Mr. Alexander, were you ever in any fights when you were in Corcoran State Prison?"

Jenny is on her feet before I can even process the question.

"Objection, Your Honor. That's irrelevant to this proceeding."

"Your Honor, the custodial parent's propensity for violence is quite relevant to whether his home is a fit place for the defendant."

"Mr. Alexander hasn't been in any trouble since his release three years ago," Jenny counters.

Judge Miller seems to wobble. "I'd like to hear it. Go ahead, Mr. Alexander."

Anger edges Gus' face. "I was in one fight."

"You broke another inmate's nose, correct?"

"I was defending myself from an attack. Prison isn't a great place. Neither is juvenile hall."

I inhale. Gus needs to answer the questions without the added commentary. If Martinez sees that he can get him angry, he'll keep pushing his buttons until he does. I've done that enough times with a witness myself.

"When you were out doing drugs, who was home with your then nine or ten-year-old son?"

"My mother or my sister."

"Were there times when Graylin was left home alone while you were off someplace smoking crack?"

"Objection," Jenny says. "What happened three years ago, isn't relevant to Graylin's current home life."

"I'll hear it," Judge Miller says.

Gus' lips press together as if he's trying to prevent something from escaping. "I was a different person back then. I don't understand why you're doing this. Why are you trying to make my son out to be a criminal? He's just a kid. A damn near perfect kid. He should be at home with me."

The judge peers over at Gus. "Just answer the question, Mr. Alexander. And please watch your language."

Gus' knuckles protrude as he grips the arms of the chair. "Yes, ma'am, sorry. Yeah, there were probably a couple of times when he was home alone, but nothing happened. That's all in the past. I've been a model citizen since I got out of prison."

"Is it true that your best friend," Martinez looks down at his notes, "Andre Thomas is a convicted drug dealer?"

"Yes," Gus says tightly. "And he's turned his life around too. He's the guy I work for."

"And Mr. Thomas—a convicted drug dealer—spends time with Graylin too, correct? He's even here in court today." Martinez gazes toward Dre at the back of the courtroom. So does the judge.

Martinez's questions are pissing me off. So I know Gus is having an even harder time.

He bites his lower lip. "Yeah. He's a good dude."

"Do you drink alcohol, Mr. Alexander?"

Gus squints. "I'm a social drinker. Nothing excessive."

"What about weed? Do you smoke weed, Mr. Alexander?"

"Um…" Gus looks at Jenny as if he needs some signal telling him whether he should answer honestly. "Not really."

"Not really? Your son told his intake officer that you do indeed smoke weed."

Graylin lowers his head and starts wringing his hands.

"Weed is legal now," Gus says. "Yeah, I smoke occasionally, but never in front of my son."

"Then how would your son know you smoked weed if you didn't do it in front of him."

"I don't know. Maybe he smelled it on me."

Martinez seems to be waiting for an explosion that doesn't come. I'm proud of Gus for keeping his cool.

"What's your monthly income, Mr. Alexander?"

"It depends on how many houses we flip. And sometimes I do tile work for a couple of real estate agents. But on average, not including flipping a house, I make about six hundred a week."

"Do you pay taxes on that money or are you paid under the table?"

"What does that have to do with anything?" Gus' jawline hardens.

"Can you answer my question, please?"

"Yeah, I pay my taxes."

"How are you able to send Graylin to an expensive private school like Marcus Preparatory Academy if you only make six hundred dollars a week?"

Gus looks up at Martinez with furious hooded eyes. "Because I make extra money when we flip a house. He also has a scholarship and my sister helps out when I'm running short."

"Are you certain that extra money came from flipping houses and not from selling drugs?"

"Objection!" Jenny yells, her cheeks are flaming red. "There's no foundation for that question!"

Before the judge can rule on the objection, Gus loses it.

"This is some bullshit!"

The judge taps her gavel. "Mr. Alexander, I've warned you once. You will not use that kind of disrespectful language in my courtroom. Your inability to control your temper is clearly a reflection of the kind of home Graylin would be released to. And I'll tell you right now, I'm having my reservations."

I see tears begin to puddle in Gus' eyes.

"This ain't right. Y'all trying to railroad my son. He didn't do nothing to deserve this. God knows this ain't right!"

The judge bangs her gavel so hard, I think it might crack. "One more outburst from you, Mr. Alexander, and you'll be back behind bars for contempt of court."

A tear falls from Gus' right eye. Graylin places his head on the table and cries.

Martinez moves back toward the prosecution table. Instead of gloating, he almost looks as if he feels sorry for Gus.

"I have no further questions, Your Honor."

Chapter 34

Angela

Judge Miller dismisses us for lunch following Gus' testimony. It's after one o'clock when we reconvene to hear her decision. It's anybody's guess how she's going to rule.

With Graylin sandwiched between us, everyone stands as the judge mounts the bench. She wastes no time getting to her decision.

"The purpose of a detention hearing is to determine whether it's in the best interest of the minor to remain in custody or return home. To keep a minor detained, there must be evidence that being in the parent's custody is contrary to the child's welfare."

I glance over at Graylin. He's squinting and leaning forward as if he can't quite hear. I'm trying to steel myself. The care with which the judge is explaining things makes me think she's not going our way.

"In most cases, I find it's best to have a child in a familiar, stable home environment pending adjudication. I'm impressed with this young man on many fronts. He's an excellent student, and based on the testimony of his teacher and minister, he's responsible, motivated and very mannerable. That's quite commendable, especially in these times. So Mr. Alexander, I applaud you for the job you've done raising your son as a single parent."

I begin to relax. I catch Jenny's eye and there's a contained smile on her face. The judge is going to do the right thing and send Graylin home.

"However, there are three issues that concern me. First, this isn't the typical sexting case. The picture of the victim—which has now gone viral—was taken through the bedroom window of her home, an incredible invasion of privacy. As you know, I must consider the allegations before me to be true. As such, the manner in which this victim was violated evidences predatory conduct. Because the minor is so young, I fear this could be a precursor to other, more serious and violent behavior."

Graylin turns to look at me, his face a kaleidoscope of confusion. "But I didn't take that picture, Ms. Angela," he whispers. "I swear I didn't."

I squeeze his forearm and continue focusing on the judge.

"Another issue of concern for me is the protection of the victim. I'm obligated to consider the victim's wishes in making my decision. This has been a very traumatic experience for her, as indicated by her mother's testimony. Mrs. Carlyle honestly fears the impact on her daughter if the minor is released. In addition, the victim's physical safety was also threatened, as set forth in the note.

"Finally, the fact that the minor was involved in a fight while in custody shows that he has violent tendencies. I also have concerns about the father's ability to supervise the child, due to his use of alcohol and marijuana, his close relationship with a convicted drug dealer, his own criminal past and his obvious inability to control his temper."

The judge's disparagement of Dre feels like an attack against me. How are they supposed to move on if nobody lets them forget their past?

"For these reasons, I don't believe it's in the best interest of the minor to return home. Therefore, I'm ordering that the minor be detained until final adjudication."

"Your Honor," Jenny says, standing up. "May I be heard?"

"You may, but it's not going to change my mind."

"My client has never been in trouble before and makes excellent grades. He was attacked by a known bully and didn't initiate the fight. Graylin will also be homeschooled and supervised twenty-four hours a day, so he wouldn't be in contact with the victim and, therefore, is no threat to her. And it's understandable why his father would be upset, considering what's happening to his son. Graylin has always thrived in his home environment and we think he will continue to do so if released. Would you consider house arrest, Your Honor?"

"I've made my decision, counselor." The judge turns to the bailiff. "Let's take a fifteen-minute break before we hear the next case." She rises and disappears through a door behind the bench.

I look over my shoulder, surprised to see that a gloating Simone Carlyle has returned. She was out for blood and today she got it.

On the back row, Gus sits forward with his head in his hands.

"I don't understand," Graylin says, weeping. "Why can't go I home? I didn't do anything. Why are they doing this to me?"

I embrace him in a tight hug. I have no words to soothe him. Jenny doesn't either.

Martinez approaches the defense table. He avoids making eye contact as he hands Jenny a document. "Since the picture of Kennedy has gone viral, we're amending the charges."

Jenny starts reading it as I glance over her shoulder.

"You're adding distribution of child pornography *and* invasion of privacy charges?" Jenny says. "Really? You have no evidence that Graylin took that picture or that he sent it to anyone."

"You don't know what evidence we have," Martinez says.

"Are you friggin' serious!" Gus exclaims.

I didn't realize he was standing behind us.

Gus rushes up to Martinez, who takes several steps back. "Why are you doing this? My son is a good kid!"

Dre pulls Gus away as I whisper into his ear. "If you go off in here, it's only going to make things worse for Graylin. Please don't say another word!"

When the bailiff walks up, Dre starts tugging Gus out of the courtroom.

"The facts of this case don't warrant these charges," Jenny says. "What kind of game are you playing?"

Martinez shuffles from one foot to the other. "No game at all. The D.A.'s Office is serious about sending a strong message to perpetrators of child pornography no matter how old they are."

Jenny glowers at him. "So what you're saying is, you're making an example out of Graylin."

Martinez shrugs. "No. I'm just doing my job."

CHAPTER 35

My head feels like it's going to blow up by the time I get back to my unit. I'm lying down in my cell—I don't care what they say, it's a cell, not a room—when Mr. Dennison announces that dinner's here.

I walk into the day room and stand in line to pick up a plate. All the kids are happy because we're having pepperoni pizza. I like pizza, but I'm mad at that judge for not letting me go home. I don't care what my attorneys say, this is all Crayvon's fault. He should be the one in here, not me.

"You Graylin, right?"

I turn around to see a tall kid with dreadlocks who looks at least fifteen or sixteen.

"How do you know my name?" I can't handle another bully messing with me so if I have to beat him up too, I will.

"You got a lot of props for going toe-to-toe with Tyke last night. Everybody around here is scared of him. Except me, of course."

I want to tell him that I'm scared of Tyke too. Instead, I turn around and wait for my pizza.

"They moved Tyke to the other side of the unit and put me over here so y'all can't fight no more. But you still gotta watch your back cuz he'll come at you again."

"I don't care." And I don't. I don't care about nothing anymore.

Kemal, a boy who was tight with Tyke is throwing me shade. Just to show I'm not scared, I get my pizza and sit down right across from him.

"Tyke want you to know it ain't over," Kemal whispers, after looking over his shoulder to make sure Mr. Dennison isn't watching. "He still gonna kick your ass."

I'm about to tell him to bring it on when someone cuts me off.

"Tyke ain't gonna do nothin' to nobody," says the boy who was talking to me in line. "If Tyke got a beef with Graylin, then he got a beef with me and I know he don't want that. And what about you? You got a beef with me?"

Kemal shakes his head about ten times. "Naw, man, I'm just the messenger." He slides down to the far end of the bench.

"You good now," the other boy says, sitting down next to me. "I got your back."

I'm so relieved I almost want to kiss him. "Thanks," I mumble.

"My pops told me to have your back. He and Apache go way back. They both OG's."

My dad calls Apache a career criminal. And I'm thankful that he is. "What's your name?"

"Dontay. But they call me Little Slice on the street."

"Why do they call you that?"

"Because if you cross me, I'll slice you up into tiny little pieces."

Little Slice laughs but I don't.

"Dude, I'ma keep it one hundred with you. If you wanna keep these bitches off your ass, you gotta act tough. You kicked Tyke's ass, but you walkin' around here lookin' like a little pussy. You gotta man up."

I want to ask Little Slice how I'm supposed to do that, but I don't want to look like a punk.

"What you locked up for?" he asks me.

"They said I had child pornography on my phone."

"Dude, that's messed up. Three of my boys got locked up for that. Your public defender probably don't even care about your case."

"I don't have a public defender. My dad hired me two lawyers."

"You could have ten lawyers and it still ain't gonna do you no good. So what you gonna do about your case?"

"What do you mean?"

"You can't leave it up to your attorneys."

"I have to. What can I do?"

Little Slice squints and starts smiling like he knows a secret. "You can do a lot. In fact, I know how to guarantee you don't get convicted cuz I got all kinda connections."

Yeah, right. If you were so smart, you wouldn't be in here with me. I can tell Little Slice likes to brag and act all hard, so I let him.

"So did you send that girl a picture of your penis or did she sext you?"

"I didn't sext nobody!"

Little Slice leans back. "Hold up, little bruh. I was just askin'. Turn down the volume."

"My attorneys are going to get me off."

"Believe that lie if you want to. I don't trust attorneys. They never tell you the real deal. They in it for the money."

I don't know for sure about Ms. Jenny, but I know Ms. Angela's not like that. I need to stop talking to Little Slice because he's making me depressed.

"You oughta let me help you," he says.

"How?"

"Just kick back and let me do my magic. What's the girl's name?"

I hesitate.

"Dude, you can trust me. My pops told me to look out for you."

"Kennedy Carlyle."

"Does she go to your school?"

"Yeah."

"What's the name of your school?"

I hesitate again.

"Do you want my help or not?" Little Slice says.

"Um, Marcus Preparatory Academy."

"Dang, bruh, you gotta be rich *and* smart to go there."

"I'm not rich. I got a scholarship."

"You think she sent that picture to you?" Little Slice asks. "Some of these ho's are scandalous."

"I think my best friend Crayvon sent it to me. But I don't know for sure."

"Aw, that's cold if one of your boys set you up like that."

"I'ma talk to my peeps and handle things for you."
"How are you gonna do that?"
"Just trust me, bruh. I told you. I got connections."

CHAPTER 36

Dre

I'm winding up for the day at a house we're rehabbing off University Street in Carson. Gus was here for a few hours laying some kitchen tile, but I told him to split. His head is so messed up right now, having him on the job is next to useless. The last five tiles he laid were all crooked.

I text Apache to see what's up with our plan. I'm not pleased with his response.

Chill. I got you.

Angela's working late tonight, so I pick up cheeseburgers and fries from In-N-Out Burger and head over there. Sometimes that girl will work all day without stopping to take a sip of water. I wish I could get the guys I hire to work half as hard.

As I pull into the parking garage, I can't help but frown. The place is way too dark for her to be walking to her car alone. I make a mental note to remind Angela for the umpteenth time to make sure a security guard escorts her to her car at night.

I watch as a well-dressed man climbs out of a Lincoln. My heart skips. I don't know why, it just does.

I tell myself to cool out. He's probably a lawyer returning to his office. The cat is surely dressed the part. The criminals I know don't wear suits or ties. Besides, the man Apache caught was a beefy dude driving an Escalade. This guy is trim and fit.

Turning off the engine, I grab our burgers and get out of the car. Giving in to my paranoia, I take a quick picture of the dude's license plate as I walk past his Lincoln. The Shepherd surely has enough money to have more than one thug doing his dirty work.

By the time I get to the lobby, the man is signing in at the reception desk. Having somebody sign a piece of paper ain't much of a security measure. I wait until he steps into the elevator before adding my own name. I notice that he signed in as John Wells and that he's headed to the fourth floor—Angela's floor.

Calm down. There are at least ten offices on the fourth floor. I stalk over to the elevators and jab the button. Ten seconds later, I jab it again.

After a wait that seems to last minutes but was probably only seconds, the elevator arrives and whizzes me to the fourth floor. I take giant steps toward Angela's office and charge inside.

Normally there's a receptionist manning the front desk, but she splits at six. I step into the hallway leading into the attorneys' individual offices and bang on Angela's closed door.

I hear muffled voices, then Angela sticks her head through the door.

"Hey," she says with a baffled smile. "What are you doing here?"

Relieved that she's okay, I hold up the In-N-Out bags. "I brought you some grub."

I peer past her and see the man who'd been driving the Lincoln. He turns around. When our eyes meet, I see instant panic in his. I don't recognize him, but he apparently recognizes me.

Angela steps outside, closing the door behind her.

"It'll be another hour or so before I can take a break. I wish you'd called first."

"Who's that?"

"A new client."

"So you never met him before?"

"Uh, no. Why?"

"Why're you meeting a new client this late at night?"

"What's up with the fifty questions?"

I repeat my question.

"Because I've been spending my days working on Graylin's case. This was the only time I could meet and it happened to be convenient for him too. What's going on?"

"What kind of case is it?"

"None of your business, Dre. Are you okay?"

"I'm fine." I reach behind her and throw open the door. "I'm sorry for the interruption," I say to the dude. "I'll be waiting out here until you guys are done."

Angela frowns. "What? You don't have to do that."

My eyes remain locked on the guy. "Yes, I do."

Angela picks up on the knowing glances between us. She looks from the man to me. "Do you two know each other?"

"Do we?" I ask.

The man stands up. "Uh, I don't think so. Is there a problem?"

"Nope," I step inside the office. "No problem at all. Like I said, I'll be waiting outside until you're done."

Embarrassment floods Angela's face. "Mr. Wells, I'm sorry for the interruption." She turns to me. "Dre, there's no need for you to wait. I'll call you when I'm done."

My eyes stay on the man. "Like I said, I'm not leaving. I'll be right outside."

"I'm not sure what's going on here," the man mumbles, "but maybe I should leave."

"Maybe you should," I say.

"Ms. Evans, I'll give you a call another time."

Angela stands there with her arms crossed. She doesn't say a word until we hear the main office door close.

"You tell me what's going on right now!" she says angrily. "You may've cost me a new client and I want to know why. And don't tell me it's nothing!"

I collapse into the chair the man just abandoned. "I'm sorry. Apache caught someone casing my sister's house and I'm worried that The Shepherd might try to have someone snatch Brianna again. I've been on edge ever since."

Alarm shatters Angela's face. "Okay, but why come down here and scare off my new client?"

"When I saw that guy, I started thinking Shep might've sent someone after you too."

"And why would he do that?"

"To get back at me for rescuing Brianna. For testifying against him. I don't know."

"Why're you being so paranoid, Dre?" Angela's eyes suddenly flare with fear. "Did someone tell you that The Shepherd was after Brianna again? Is that why you're so concerned?"

I want to tell her the truth and I almost do.

"No. I just—" I look down at my hands. "I couldn't handle anything happening to you or Brianna. I guess I *am* being paranoid."

Angela sits in my lap, loops her arms around my neck and kisses me.

"I'm fine. We have a security guard who walks the halls every hour. Whenever I'm here late, he always checks on me."

"Hey, Miss A?" someone calls out. "You still here?"

"Speak of the devil," Angela says smugly. She hops up and returns with a man who barely reaches my chin.

"Prentiss, this is my boyfriend, Dre. He's worried about me working late by myself. I was telling him how you always look out for me."

"Got that right," Prentiss says. "Everything's all good when I'm on the job. Nothing for you to worry about. I got her back." He pauses to give Angela a playful wink. "Miss A gets special treatment because she's the only tenant who brings me cookies."

Neither one of them understands the danger at hand. If that Wells guy was one of The Shepherd's henchmen, he could've knocked the unarmed Prentiss out with a simple backhand.

After Prentiss leaves, I convince Angela to take a break to eat. While she's in the back grabbing sodas from the fridge, I send Apache a text. He's been casing the Craps parking lot from time to time looking for the dude driving the black Escalade. That would confirm that he's tied to The Shepherd. I send him the picture of Wells' license plate and ask if he's seen the black Lincoln at Craps.

Just as Angela returns, I read Apache's response and the blood drains from my face.

CHAPTER 37

Martinez

It's twenty minutes after two and the Carlyles are late. I'm hoping they won't be a no-show. With the pressure I'm under to make this case stick, I don't need a recalcitrant victim.

I've asked Teresa, our investigator, to join us. She has amazing instincts. I've been pushing her to go to law school, but she's more interested in a low-stress life than a bigger paycheck.

We finally get a call that the Carlyles have arrived. We enter the conference room and find Kennedy wedged between her parents. She's going to make a very sympathetic witness. The girl's eyes are sad and she can't make eye contact for more than a second or two. She's wearing the pain of Graylin Alexander's violation like a fresh coat of paint.

"Thanks for coming down," I begin. "We—"

"It's not like we had much of a choice." Simone's voice is infused with sarcasm. "You ordered us down here like *we're* the criminals."

I don't take her bait. "This is Teresa Clump," I continue, as if she hadn't interrupted me. "She's one of our best investigators. Her help will be crucial in gathering the evidence we need to prove Graylin took that picture. We're still waiting for the forensics on his phone. Teresa will need to come out to your home sometime this week. We want to simulate taking a picture through Kennedy's bedroom window to give us an idea of where Graylin Alexander was standing when he invaded your daughter's privacy."

"Since you have to come out to the house anyway, why couldn't you interview her there?" Simone wants to know. "It's not like the case is going to trial tomorrow."

I don't care for Simone Carlyle. Fortunately, I'm very good at dismissing people I don't like.

"I'd like to begin by asking Kennedy a few questions." I take out the photograph, but don't slide it across the table yet. "This is an enlargement of the picture we found on Graylin's phone."

The girl's eyes dart over to the picture, then back down at the table.

"I want you to see it because I'm hoping you can provide some details about when it might've been taken. Can you handle it?"

It takes a moment, but Kennedy nods.

Simone shifts in her seat. "Is that really necessary?"

"Yes, it is."

Her husband might as well be a deaf-mute. He has yet to say one word.

When I hand Kennedy the picture she glances at it, winces, then looks away.

"Can you confirm that's you in the picture?" I ask.

"Yes," Kennedy says meekly.

"Do you recognize where it was taken?"

"It looks like my bedroom." Her eyes return to the picture, remaining there a little longer this time. "So he was peeking in my bedroom window?"

"Yes, he was," her mother says, answering a question that wasn't addressed to her.

I study Kennedy's reaction. She doesn't say more, at least not in words. A tear slides down the right side of her face. "That picture is all over the internet. It's so embarrassing."

I want to give Kennedy a chance to compose herself, so I turn to her parents. "Is Kennedy in counseling yet?"

For the first time, Simone drops her icy glare. Percy tugs at the cuffs of his monogrammed shirt.

"Not yet," Simone says. "We're still looking for the right therapist."

"I'm okay," Kennedy ekes out in a squeaky voice. "I don't want to talk to some stranger."

The Carlyles' delay in getting their daughter into counseling is inconsistent with the loving, protective parents they attempt to portray. Their daughter needs some professional help to deal with this violation.

"Do you have any idea when the picture might've been taken?" I ask.

Simone interrupts. "How would she know—"

I hold up my hand. "I need Kennedy to respond."

Her eyes still avoid the picture. "I don't know."

"It looks like you're about to get dressed."

"Maybe." She steals another quick peek. "I think maybe I'd just gotten out of the shower."

"Do you shower in the morning or at night?"

"Both."

"Which do you do most often?"

"Mornings, I guess."

"Do you normally stand in front of the window to get dressed?"

Her eyebrows fuse into one. "But I wasn't standing in front of the window."

"I'm sorry. What I should've said is do you normally get dressed in your bedroom or the bathroom?"

Simone throws a protective arm around her daughter. "What are you trying to imply?"

Teresa decides to jump in. "There's a pink sweater lying on the bed," she says. "Do you remember wearing that sweater recently?"

That's a great question and one that isn't on my list.

Kennedy's pensive expression tells me she's trying to remember. "It's one of my favorites. I wear it a lot."

"Can you remember the last time?" Teresa gently pushes.

Kennedy hunches her shoulder. "I'm not sure."

"We'd like you to think about it some more when you get home. And if you remember, please call Mr. Martinez."

She nods.

"Do you know if Graylin knows where you live?" I ask.

"Yeah. I've seen him on my block before. He's best friends with Crayvon, who lives up the street."

Eight pairs of eyes zoom in on Kennedy. This is crucial circumstantial information. "When was the last time you saw Graylin on your street?"

"I don't know. He's at Crayvon's house all the time."

Excitement starts to build in my chest. If this kid is a peeping Tom, that changes my perspective of the case. A lot of rapists start out peeking through bedroom windows. "Do you know if you saw him during the week he was arrested?"

Kennedy squints. "Maybe."

"Was it on a school day or a weekend day?"

"A school day."

"Do you remember if it was during the day or night?"

"It was probably after school."

"Did you talk to him when you saw him?"

"No."

"Did you talk to his friend Crayvon?"

"No."

"What were they doing?"

"Walking down the street."

"Have you ever seen Graylin or Crayvon in your backyard?"

"No."

"Do you know if Graylin has a crush on you?"

Kennedy frowns. "No. I barely know him. But a lot of girls like him."

"Can you tell me which girls?"

Kennedy rattles off five names which Teresa writes down since she'll be the one contacting them.

"Were any of them his girlfriends?"

"I don't know."

"Have any girls told you about"—I temper my words, fearing a hostile reaction from Mrs. Carlyle—"being with Graylin?"

"Being with him?" The girl looks confused.

What I want to know is whether young Graylin Alexander is sexually active. I'm about to ask her that question when I remember what the kids call it now. "Have you ever heard of him smashing any girls at your school?"

The two adult Carlyles look more confused than Kennedy was a second ago. I'm relieved when they don't ask for a translation.

"No," Kennedy blushes. "Graylin's not like that."

I suspect I'm not getting the truth. I need to know the real deal without Kennedy filtering the facts for her parents. Since Percy is a non-entity, I address my next question to his wife and prepare for the coming firestorm.

"Is it okay if we take a few minutes to talk to Kennedy alone?"

"Absolutely not." The response isn't a surprise, only the fact that the words come from the voiceless Mr. Carlyle, not his abrasive wife.

I rub my eyes with my thumb and index finger, then stare across the table at Mr. Carlyle. "As an attorney, I'm sure you understand the need for me to get honest responses. Kennedy is likely to speak more candidly with us without her parents present."

"Kennedy, is that true?" Simone asks. "Would you feel better talking to the prosecutor without us here?"

Kennedy shakes her head. "No. I'm okay if you're here."

"See," Simone says with a smirk. "We have a very open relationship. She tells us everything."

Lady, if you only knew. I hear that delusional statement from parents so often it no longer fazes me. In reality, kids don't tell their parents a thing. I certainly didn't and neither did they.

Percy checks the Breitling on his wrist. His watch had to cost upwards of five grand. "Please continue. You're not interrogating our daughter without us present."

I find his use of the word *interrogating* almost offensive. I'm not a cop. I'm here to right a wrong. This would be a whole lot easier if they would join my side of this fight.

"That's fine for now," I say, "but when she testifies in court, we'll need to—"

"My daughter won't be testifying," Percy says with deadly finality. "You don't need her testimony. That boy had the picture in his possession. That's a slam dunk case for possession of child pornography. The distribution charge is superfluous. No need to unnecessarily traumatize Kennedy by putting her on the witness stand."

"We also have the criminal threat and invasion of privacy charges. We'll definitely need—"

"My wife can testify to any resulting harm."

Simone looks adoringly at her husband. "I agree."

I know I won't gain any ground if I push the issue now, so I don't. I ask a few more questions about Graylin, then end the meeting.

The Carlyles have only been gone a couple of minutes when Percy returns to the conference room and closes the door behind him.

"Kennedy and Simone are in the ladies' room." He glances over his shoulder as if he's worried they'll walk back in and catch him talking to us. "I wanted to speak privately with you. The governor is about to appoint me to the superior court bench. If some reporter found out about this case, the publicity would be a further invasion of my daughter's privacy. We need you to resolve this as soon as possible."

"I'm doing everything I can to move it forward."

"Then cut the kid a deal and be done with it. Kennedy needs to move on with her life."

Mr. Carlyle seems far more concerned about his pending judgeship than his daughter's well-being.

"That poor kid," Teresa says once he's gone. "Mama and Papa Carlyle won't be picking up any awards for parents of the year."

I laugh. "Yeah, I guess they are a bit uptight."

"Ya think?" Teresa's wry smile quickly turns somber. "I'm not feeling Papa Carlyle. He's hiding something."

"He's obviously worried about his judicial appointment getting waylaid."

Teresa shakes her head. "It's more than that. He didn't open his mouth until you mentioned questioning Kennedy alone. And there's no excuse for them not having her in therapy yet. There's something going on in that house that he doesn't want anybody to find out."

"What are you saying?"

"C'mon, Miguel, we've both been doing this long enough to know that the picture-perfect family on the outside, is rarely as perfect on the inside."

The door reopens and all three of the Carlyles bolt back into the conference room.

"Kennedy just confided something to us," Simone says, her face flush. "Something you need to address A-S-A-P!"

"What happened?"

"Go ahead, baby," Simone says, "tell them."

Kennedy opens her mouth, but only a sob comes out. She collapses into her mother's arms.

"You were right," Simone says. "Kennedy *doesn't* tell us everything. That boy had somebody call my baby last night and threaten her to drop this case. If that doesn't prove he's guilty, nothing will."

Chapter **38**

Graylin

I get excited when I find out my attorneys are here to visit me. I didn't even know they were coming today. Nobody in my unit gets as many visitors and phone calls as I do.

When I step into the room, I know something bad has happened because Ms. Jenny and Ms. Angela have sad faces. I'm wondering if they're going to tell me that prosecutor has already convicted me. My dad is on speakerphone, which gets me even more worried.

"What's the matter, Ms. Jenny? Is something wrong?" I immediately start wondering if somebody died. "Are my mama and my granny okay?"

Ms. Jenny tells me to sit down. Her sad face is scaring me.

"They're both okay," she says. "We're here because somebody called Kennedy at home and threatened her. Was it you?"

I shake my head. I didn't do it, but I know who did.

Ms. Jenny is staring me down like she's trying to tell whether I'm lying. "Did you ask anyone to call Kennedy?"

"No. I swear I didn't."

"Do you know who might have called her?"

I rub my hands together. "Um, yeah. My friend Little Slice said he would take care of things for me. But I didn't know he was going to do that."

"Who the hell is Little Slice?" my dad yells. "I told you them thugs in there ain't your friends!"

I flinch. I almost forgot my dad was on the phone.

"He's in my unit. His real name is Dontay. His dad and Apache are friends. He's been looking out for me. That's the only reason nobody bothers me anymore."

"Apache? How'd that fool even know you were in there?"

Ms. Jenny asks me a whole bunch of questions about Little Slice. She asks me to repeat all of my conversations with him. She says what Little Slice did has made things worse for me.

I don't understand how things can be worse since I didn't do anything.

"Certain charges make it possible for the prosecutor to transfer your case out of juvenile court," Ms. Jenny says. "Intimidating a witness is one of those charges. The prosecutor has filed a motion to have you tried as an adult."

"Are you friggin' kidding me?" my dad yells.

I don't understand how I can be tried as an adult when I'm a kid. "Why do they want to do that?"

"So they can put you in an adult prison!" my dad shouts.

I don't say anything for a long time because I'm still trying to understand. "But I'm only fourteen."

"They wouldn't put a fourteen-year-old in an adult prison," Ms. Angela says, then turns to Ms. Jenny. "He'd go to the Youth Authority, right?"

She nods. "Yeah. And it's not called the Youth Authority anymore. Now that they're under the Department of Corrections, it's the Division of Juvenile Justice."

My dad is so mad it sounds like he might have a heart attack. "I don't care what they call it. It's still prison!"

"But I didn't threaten anybody."

"The prosecutor will claim that you asked Little Slice to do it," Ms. Jenny says.

"But I didn't. Why can't I just tell the judge that?"

"That's not going to fix it, Graylin," Ms. Jenny says, her voice extra soft. "Now we have to have what's called a fitness hearing. The judge will decide if your case should be transferred to adult court."

"This ain't right! You also told us he'd be going home!" my dad shouts at her through the phone, even though it was Ms. Angela, not

Ms. Jenny who said that. "And now you're telling me they're gonna try my son as an adult. What in the hell am I paying you twenty grand for?"

Ms. Jenny starts saying a lot of stuff to calm down my dad, but it's not working. I'm not listening anymore because I can't stop staring at Ms. Angela. She's not saying anything and that's freaking me out. Ms. Angela is always telling me everything's going to be okay. Now, she won't even look at me.

When I get back to my unit, I go straight to my room. I'm really, really mad. At everybody. Especially Little Slice. I don't understand how that prosecutor can do this to me when all I did was save a stupid picture to my phone.

During recreation time, I find a bench where I can sit by myself. Yesterday, when my granny called, she said she was praying for me three times a day and told me to pray too. I close my eyes and look up at the sky. I try to pray, but I can't. I'm mad at God too.

I open my eyes and see Little Slice coming toward me. All I want to do is wail on him like I did Tyke.

He props his foot up on the bench. "What up, bruh?"

Ms. Jenny told me not to have any more conversations with Little Slice, but I can't help myself.

"You got me in trouble! You didn't tell me you were going to call Kennedy. You made my case worse!"

"Dude, what you talkin' 'bout?"

I tell him everything Ms. Jenny told me and how they're adding a new charge against me for intimidating a witness.

"Hold up, bruh. I didn't call that ho, but I did put one of my boys on it. What happened? Did she drop the case?"

"No! And now that prosecutor thinks I threatened her even though I didn't do anything!"

"Dude, that ho is lying. My peeps know what to say and what not to say."

"Well, I'm the one in trouble now. That prosecutor is trying to get me tried as an adult."

"Whoa. That prosecutor's going deep in your ass."

I want to sock him in the jaw.

"But if I was you, I'd be glad. At least now you have a chance of gettin' off."

I look at him like he's crazy. "You're buggin'."

"No, I'm serious. If you get transferred to adult court," Little Slice says, "your peeps can post bail and get you outta here. But the best thing is you get to have a jury. I'd rather go with a jury than a juvie judge any day. Ninety-nine percent of the time a kid loses in juvie court cuz the judge decides everything. But if you have a jury, all you need is one juror to believe you and you get off with a hung jury. So I don't know why you lookin' so sad."

I replay everything Little Slice just said. I *would* be better off with a jury. If I testify, I can tell them that I didn't do it. All I have to do is get a few mothers or even some teachers on the jury. When they find out I'm a good student, they'll believe me.

"I can see the wheels spinning in your big water head," Little Slice says, laughing. "But I'm tellin' you right now, your attorneys are gonna fight you on this. They ain't gonna want you to be tried as an adult."

I feel my sadness floating away. "My attorneys told me I get to make all the decisions about my case."

"Yeah, but your dad and your attorneys ain't gonna be down with this," Little Slice continues. "But you gotta stand up for yourself."

What Little Slice is saying makes sense. I *would* be better off in adult court. And that's exactly where I'm going.

CHAPTER **39**

Apache

From everything I can tell, my plan is coming together like clock-work. Dre is constantly on my ass, wanting me to snap my fingers and make everything happen as of yesterday. That's not how it works. This mission requires plotting and patience.

He freaked out like a mug when I told him I saw that dude's Lincoln in the Craps parking lot. Not only that, I actually saw the well-dressed dude talking to the guy I caught casing Brianna's house. Now we got some peeps watching Angela too.

I park my Benz in front of Special Touch Beauty Salon on Manchester Boulevard and hop out. This is the last piece of my plan and the most important.

I have an appointment with LaRhonda, Blaze's woman. If anybody'll know if Blaze got the word, she will. I see her at a booth near the back of the salon. I ain't never had my hair done in a beauty shop before. But I gotta do what I gotta do for my cuz.

My hair is usually in a long braid, but today it's hanging loose down my back. Every sista in the joint is checking me out. I'm a good-looking dude, but I know they're looking at my hair, not me.

LaRhonda's wearing a crooked grin as I approach her booth. "Are you my two o'clock appointment?"

"Yep. I'm here for a conditioner and a hot oil treatment."

She starts running her fingers through my hair before I'm even settled good in her chair. "Boy, where you get all this gorgeous hair from?"

"My great-grandmother was a full-blooded Apache."

"I gotta hurry up and get you outta here. Some of these heffas might try to scalp you for a new weave."

She leads me to the shampoo bowl and we start an easy conversation.

"So, you said on the phone that you know Blaze."

"Yeah. Everybody know Blaze. How's he doing?"

"Making it the best he can. I visited him last weekend."

"I heard you was still down with him. I wish I could find a woman as true-blue as you."

LaRhonda smiles.

"Is what they saying on the street about the dude who took his daughter true?"

She stops massaging my head and looks down at me. "You heard it too?"

"Yep."

LaRhonda shakes her head. "That girl was Blaze's heart. Had a good head on her shoulders too. When she first went missing, we had everybody looking for her. We figured she might've been trafficked, but we didn't know for sure. About three months later, they found her in a crack house off Figueroa with a heroin needle stuck in her arm. I was the one who had to tell Blaze. When I did, it was like he died too."

"They say it was one of The Shepherd's dudes who snatched her and turned her out. Is that true?"

LaRhonda nods. "That's the word on the street."

"Does Blaze know?"

"When I saw him last week, I told him about what I'd heard, but some guys on the inside had already told him."

"That's crazy. So what's he gonna do about it?"

A hint of a smile tinges her lips. "What can he do? He's in prison. So is The Shepherd."

I don't say nothing and neither does she. LaRhonda's been Blaze's woman all this time because she knows how to keep her mouth shut.

"But if I was The Shepherd," she continues, "I'd be worried. Bars or no bars."

That's all I need to hear. Everything is in motion.

I settle back, close my eyes, and enjoy my head massage.

CHAPTER 40

Graylin

As one of the staff leads me to the attorney meeting room, I can hardly walk. My legs feel as flimsy as a bowl of Ramen noodles. I know Ms. Angela and Ms. Jenny won't agree with what I have to say, but this is *my* case and *my* life. So I'm going to do this *my* way.

When I enter the room and see my dad, I freeze.

"Hey, Little Man." My dad pulls me into a bear hug. "Angela got special permission for me to visit you today."

I'm not sure I can do this with my dad present. At least he's in a good mood. For now.

"Have a seat, Graylin." Ms. Jenny pulls out a chair for me. "We wanted to meet with you and your father to prepare you for the fitness hearing."

I suddenly have a headache. Probably because of what I have to do.

"During a fitness hearing," Ms. Jenny says, "the prosecutor has to prove that you can't be rehabilitated by the juvenile system. And if you can't, your case will be transferred to adult court."

I peer over at my dad. He looks as puzzled as I am.

"So how do they figure that out?" my dad asks.

"The judge will look at things like the type of crime, the child's criminal history, the potential for the child to improve and the seriousness of the crime. It's all about whether the judge thinks the kid is such a hopeless case, that he should be treated like an adult."

"Why do I need to be rehabilitated when I didn't do anything in the first place?" I ask, but nobody answers my question.

"That sounds like a piece of cake for us then." My dad is acting so happy. "My son's not some thug."

"Nothing is a piece of cake where the legal system is concerned," Ms. Jenny says, then glances at Ms. Angela as if it's her turn to speak. There's a short pause before she does.

"There's something else we need to advise you of," Ms. Angela says, mainly to my dad. "If Graylin is convicted on the pornography charges, be it juvenile or adult court, he'll have to register as a sex offender."

Sex offender? "What does that mean?" I ask.

My dad's not happy anymore. His face is all scrunched up. "It means they're saying you're a pedophile, which is bullshit!"

I don't know what a pedophile is either.

Ms. Angela turns to me. "Registering as a sex offender means you'll have to comply with certain requirements. For instance, every year, you have to advise local law enforcement of your address, where you go to school and where you work, so they can keep track of you at all times. You also have to provide your DNA."

"And don't it mean he can't even be alone around kids?" my dad says angrily.

All of this is confusing. How can I not be around other kids when I'm a kid myself? "Why would they want to keep track of me like that?"

My dad doesn't let Ms. Angela answer my question.

"So they can publish your name on a list of perverts!" I can see the veins in his forehead popping out. "Anybody can go on a computer and look at the list. So no college is going to accept you and nobody's going to rent you an apartment and no company is ever going to hire you because people don't want to work with a pervert. So what it really means is that you're screwed for life." My dad lowers his head and wipes his hand down his face.

I wait for Ms. Angela and Ms. Jenny to say my dad is overreacting, but they don't.

I can't believe this. "Just because I saved Kennedy's picture on my phone?"

Ms. Angela nods.

"How long will I have to be a sex offender?"

Ms. Angela looks away.

"Forever," Ms. Jenny says.

My dad starts bouncing his knee up and down like I do when I get nervous or upset. "That's nuts! He's only fourteen. Every day it feels like we're walking deeper and deeper into a nightmare."

"This is only if there's a conviction," Jenny says, trying to make it sound like it's not a big deal. "Even if he's convicted, we might be able to get his record expunged if he doesn't get into trouble again. But you can only apply for that seven years after a conviction."

"Thanks," my dad says. "Now we have something to look forward to."

I still don't understand why anyone would do this to a kid just for having a naked picture. How can they convict me for something I didn't even know was against the law?

"We're going to fight this fitness hearing with everything we've got," Ms. Jenny says.

I take a deep breath and blurt out, "I don't want to fight it."

A puzzled look glazes my dad's face. "What? What're you talking about? Of course you do."

I try to remember everything Little Slice told me. "In juvie court, kids get convicted ninety-nine percent of the time because a judge decides everything. It's better for me to be in adult court because I get to have a jury. I'll only need one juror to believe me and I can get a hung jury and get off."

My dad is staring at me so hard I can almost feel his gaze touch my cheek. "What? That's crazy. We ain't taking that kind of chance."

"Little Slice said—"

"Don't you mention that fool's name to me again!" my dad yells. "That thug's got you in enough trouble. Don't you understand that?"

Ms. Angela holds up her hands. "Gus, please calm down. Shouting at him isn't helping the situation."

I'm glad Ms. Angela's on my side, so I focus only on her. My words gush out like a flood. "I want to take my chances in adult court. I want a jury. And in adult court I can also get out on bail."

My dad ignores Ms. Angela. "Boy, you don't know what you're talking about!"

"Little Slice told me you would try to talk me out of it. But this is my life and this is what I want to do."

My dad's eyes are about to pop out of his head. "Boy, I'll—"

Ms. Jenny stands up. "Gus, let's take a breather and hear Graylin out."

"Hear him out, my ass! This boy is talking nonsense and you need to tell him that. If I have to knock some sense into him, I will."

I don't look at my dad. I'm trying to find the courage to do something else Little Slice told me to do, but the words are stuck in my throat.

"Let's discuss the pros and cons with Graylin," Ms. Jenny says, "and then—"

"Lady," my dad barks, "are you out of your friggin' mind! There ain't no pros to this!"

My stomach feels like it's full of bricks. What I'm about to say next is really going to make my dad have a meltdown. But I don't have any other choice.

I swallow hard, then blurt out, "I want to talk to my attorneys alone."

My dad jumps to his feet and leans over me. His face is so twisted up he looks like a monster. "I ain't going nowhere! You don't know what the hell you're talking about! I'm here to protect your stupid ass!"

I turn to Ms. Jenny. "You told me in the beginning that I'm the client and that I get to make the decisions about my case. So that's what I'm doing." I stop and take a deep breath. "I want a private meeting with my attorneys."

"Boy, I'll—"

Ms. Angela grabs my dad's arm and pulls him across the room. "Gus, just give us a few minutes to talk to him alone. We'll work this out."

My dad acts like he didn't hear her. "What's wrong with you? Have you lost your mind? I want you to stay away from this Slice fool. He's filling your head with nonsense." He sneers at Ms. Jenny. "This is not my child. He's never been disrespectful like this. You need to get him out of this place!"

I stare down at the floor, too scared to look up at my dad.

"Gus, please." Ms. Angela is begging him now. "Step outside for a minute and let us talk to Graylin."

My dad jerks the doorknob so hard the window rattles. As soon as he's gone, I can breathe again.

Ms. Jenny starts to say something, but I cut her off. I don't want to hear what my attorneys have to say either.

"Don't invite my dad to our meetings anymore," I tell them. "I want to be tried as an adult so I can have a jury. And no matter what you say, I'm not going to change my mind."

CHAPTER **41**

Angela

It takes some doing, but we finally convince Gus to go home and let us talk to Graylin alone. Jenny and I spend another hour with him, but he won't budge.

"But Graylin, if you're convicted," I say, "you could end up doing more time. You can't take that risk."

"It's not a risk because I'm not going to get convicted. All you have to do is get one juror to believe me and I'll get a hung jury."

I close my eyes and try to clear my head. This entire conversation is unnecessary. There's no way the judge would send a kid with Graylin's spotless record to adult court.

"We want you to sleep on this, Graylin," Jenny says. "We'll talk to you again tomorrow."

"I'm not going to change my mind."

Jenny pats him on the back. "That's fine. We'll still talk tomorrow."

After a staff member escorts Graylin back to his unit, I stand up and press my forehead against the wall.

"Having an adult client who won't accept my legal advice is one thing," I say. "But having to wrestle with this naïve child who doesn't understand that he could be throwing his life away scares me to death."

"I think he's a very gutsy little guy," Jenny says.

I spin around. "What? How can you say that?"

"He's right about the juvenile system. A lot of judges are so jaded they think a kid is guilty as charged even before he walks into the courtroom. And with Martinez piling on the charges and Kennedy's parents pushing the way they are, he doesn't have much of a chance."

I can't possibly be hearing her correctly. "So what are you saying?"

"I'm saying he does have a better chance in the adult system. Even on the possession charge."

"Are you nuts?"

"There'll certainly be a few parents on his jury. They're going to look at Graylin's record and see that he's a good kid. They're going to see their kids in him and it's going to scare the heck out of them because under the same circumstance, their kid would've done the same thing he did."

"No way. It's too much of a risk. If his case is transferred to adult court, we might as well walk him over to juvie prison right now."

"I hear you're an amazing attorney. Adult court is your domain. I think you can get him off."

"He can't win on the possession charge. He had the picture on his phone. How can I get him off?"

She smiles and waits a beat. "Jury nullification. No matter what the law says, no jury will want to lock up a great kid like Graylin just for saving a picture on his phone."

"Have you lost your mind? That's a complete crapshoot."

"Parents have no idea prosecutors are going after kids like this. The jury will be outraged. All he needs is one juror to go his way and he walks."

"It's fine for you to propose all these what-ifs, but if Graylin was your kid, I doubt you'd be supporting this."

"Whether he's in juvenile court or adult court, the stakes are the same," Jenny says. "If he's convicted, he's going to have to register as a sex offender for the rest of his life. He has a better shot in adult court because I don't think the prosecutor can find twelve people willing to convict him."

I cup my forehead. "If they think he took that picture, they'll convict him."

"But he didn't take the picture and the prosecution won't be able to prove that he did."

"You can't say that. We don't know what evidence they have."

Jenny rears back. "Are you saying you think he took it?"

"No. But I've been practicing law long enough to know that just because somebody's innocent doesn't mean they won't be convicted."

"I know this is a very scary roll of the dice," Jenny insists, "but at least there's a chance."

"No way. What Graylin wants to do is crazy, and his father agrees. So we're going to fight like hell at that fitness hearing."

"Gus isn't the deciding factor here. Graylin's our client, not Gus."

"Graylin's a naïve kid who thinks life is fair. I'm not letting him destroy his life."

Jenny reaches for her satchel, pulls out a book and starts flipping pages. "The juvenile court rules are crystal clear on this." She has the audacity to start reading to me like I'm a first-year law student.

Role of counsel: An attorney's ethical allegiance is to the child and not to the parent or guardian paying you for representation. Parents are not allowed to waive rights for their children since they may have conflicting interests. Parents need not be present when lawyers interview clients and cannot be present if the child objects. The lawyer is ethically required to present the child's position to the court.

She slams the book on the desk in front of me.

"Screw the rules!" I say. "Graylin's a fourteen-year-old kid who's getting bad advice from some fool in juvenile hall. It's our job to do what's best for him, regardless of what he wants."

"Did you just hear what I read? It's our job to follow our client's wishes."

"You're talking theory. I'm talking real world. A jury might be hesitant to lock up a fourteen-year-old white kid, but it's a different ball game for a black kid. And I'm not taking that kind of chance. The stakes are way too high."

A curtain of red inches up Jenny's neck. "So you're making this a race thing?"

"No, I'm making this a reality thing."

Both of us are so worked up we have to pause to catch our breaths.

"Just so I'm clear," I say, "are you telling me you're not going to fight to keep Graylin in juvenile court?"

Jenny's hands are gripping her narrow hips and she's sneering at me. "I'm going to do what my client asks me to do."

"If you're not going to do what's best for Graylin, he may not be your client anymore."

Jenny snatches her book and stuffs it back into her satchel. "I'm pretty sure Graylin wants an attorney who's complying with his wishes," she says with a cunning smile. "So if anybody's getting removed from this case, it's you, not me."

CHAPTER 42

The Shepherd

Chess is a game that requires keen intellect, intense concentration, and extended patience. Skills I not only possess but excel at. I watch Wallstreet examine the board, determined to snare me in a trap. That, however, is not going to happen.

Roxbury—a young cat from the Boston area—sits down opposite me on Wallstreet's side of the table.

"We got a new king on campus," Roxbury says, with an annoying laugh. "Just got here from the Bay Area. They call him Oaktown."

Roxbury is a low-level drug dealer and the biggest gossip at The Low. He's worse than a teenage girl. We both ignore him, but Roxbury is the kind of guy who can have a conversation with himself.

"Yeah," he goes on, "and I hear he don't like pimps."

"C'mon, man," Wallstreet complains. "Can't you see we're busy right now."

I pretend not to care about what Roxbury is saying, but if this Oaktown cat means trouble for me, I need to take note. In a place like The Low, violence is rare for two reasons. First, the dudes sent here weren't convicted of violent crimes, so that's not part of their nature. Second, they recognize that it's a privilege to be able to kick back in this lax environment. Getting into a fight means points on your record. And too many points can keep you from getting transferred to a camp, which has even more privileges, like working off-site. And on the flip side, too many points mean you could get kicked upstairs to a medium or maximum-security prison. Now, I'm not saying violence doesn't happen at The Low. Just not the way it goes down on the regular at a state prison or a max facility.

Roxbury keeps stoking the fire. "He's in unit six. I hear he got lots of connections on the street. Even more than you."

I assume he's referring to me, not Wallstreet. I'm busy watching my cellie. I concentrate on his eyes as they dart from one side of the board to the other. The most enjoyable part of this game is predicting what my opponent's going to do next.

Wallstreet transitions one of his knights, which isn't what I expected him to do. There's a much smarter move he could've made, but he's focused only on trying to keep me from capturing his queen. You can't win if you're constantly playing defense. Sometimes you have to have the guts to go after your opponent.

I taunt him. "You can run, but you can't hide."

Roxbury gets tired of being ignored and leaves. His comments, however, have registered with me. I've settled comfortably into prison life. I don't need anyone disturbing my peace.

It takes only three more moves to whip Wallstreet yet again. As I head back to my cell, I scan the grounds, looking for C.O. Sims. I spot him just before I reach the doorway of my building. Without slowing, I signal him with a slight jutting forward of my chin.

By the time I reach my cell, he appears behind me.

"What's up?" he asks.

"Who's this new guy from Oakland in unit six?"

"Just another drug dealer is all I hear." Sims chuckles. "You worried about having to share your popularity?"

I want to tell him to screw himself, but I don't have it like that. C.O. Sims holds all the cards and he can pull his hand and walk away at any time.

"Just wondering what was up. I don't want any problems."

"Bodyguard work ain't in my job description." Sims shrugs and walks away.

Two hours later at the chow hall, I get my first look at Oaktown. He has an imposing, bad-ass look about him and neither smiles nor frowns. He's the size of a mountain with deep-set eyes that pull you in like a magnet. So many tattoos cover his dark arms you can barely see any skin. He doesn't look as if he belongs at The Low. The stench of violence emanates from his body like puddles of sweat.

Other inmates are staying clear of him. I can almost smell their fear. I feel a twang of jealousy. People used to fear me too.

As I'm leaving the chow hall, Oaktown walks up behind me.

"I don't like pimps," he says. I can feel his hot breath on the back of my neck. "A pimp beat my mama to death. You gotta be weak to make your money off a woman."

I don't turn around and just keep walking.

"My homeboy Blaze asked me to look you up." He's matching me step for step. "Says you snatched his daughter and pimped her out."

I have no idea what he's talking about, but I do know the name Blaze and that strikes even more fear in me. Blaze is behind bars for drug trafficking. But I know for a fact he did his share of killing when he was on the street. He just never got caught.

Why would Blaze think I snatched his daughter?

I want to speed up, but I don't want it to look like I'm running scared.

"How would you like it if somebody raped *you?*"

I have to walk outside and across the yard to get back to my unit. My legs feel as if they're going to give out any second.

"You a chomo," Oaktown says. "And I don't like chomos. Stay out of my way. I don't wanna even look at you." He brushes past me, shoving me with his shoulder.

I've never in my life been disrespected like this before. And I'd be lying if I said I wasn't scared. But I'm also fortunate. Nobody else was around to witness what this fool said to me. Respect is a big thing in prison. If you let a dude punk you, everybody will think you're a bitch. And in prison, the only thing worse than a bitch is a snitch. I pick up my pace, anxious to get back to my cell so I can think.

I'm not the kind of man to sit back and let somebody humiliate me. I have to find a way to let Oaktown know that.

CHAPTER 43

Graylin

I finish my breakfast and wait in the day room. My fitness hearing starts in one hour. I'm nervous, but I'm ready to do what I have to do.

My Uncle Dre spent two hours with me yesterday, telling me all the reasons why I don't want my case transferred to adult court. I finally said okay, just so he would leave.

Little Slice comes up to me in the day room and slaps me on the back. "You good to go?"

I nod, but I'm really not.

"Do what I told you to do and everything'll go down just like I said it would. And when you win your case, you gonna owe me."

One of the staff walks me and two other boys across the covered walkway that connects juvenile hall to the courthouse. Ms. Angela and Ms. Jenny are waiting for me. Both of them have sour looks on their faces like they're mad at somebody. Probably me.

Ms. Angela stands up and gives me a hug. "Dre told me you guys talked for a long time yesterday."

"Yep."

"So are you ready to fight this fitness hearing?"

"Yep."

Ms. Angela looks over at Ms. Jenny and smirks. "Good. I'm glad we're on the same page."

I'm sorry that I'm going to have to hurt Ms. Angela's feelings. But this is my life, not hers.

Ms. Jenny comes over and hugs me too.

"Just like at the detention hearing, you need to remember that the judge is watching you," Ms. Angela says. "So sit up straight and be respectful. It's more important than ever that the judge gets to see the kind of person you are. We know you're a great kid. We want the judge to know it too."

"Yeah, okay."

"And say *yes*, not *yeah*," Ms. Angela corrects me.

I want to roll my eyes, but instead I say, "Yes, Ms. Angela."

When we enter the courtroom, I see my dad and Uncle Dre sitting on the back row.

W-T-F!

My granny and my aunt Macie are here too! Why'd he have to bring them today of all days? I hurry to the front of the courtroom without even looking at them.

The asshole prosecutor is already at his table. If my eyes could shoot bullets, I'd put a dozen holes in his head right here in the middle of this courtroom. He's trying to put me in prison for nothing and I wish he would die.

The bailiff asks everyone to stand as Judge Miller takes the bench. Everyone stands up, except me.

Ms. Angela glares down at me and whispers, "What's wrong with you? Get up!"

I ignore her.

Ms. Jenny is peering down at me too. They must think I'm wigging out, but they haven't seen anything yet.

Ms. Angela squeezes my shoulder, but I still don't move. "Graylin, what are you doing? Stand up."

The judge props an elbow on her desk. "Ms. Ungerman, is there a reason your client's disregarding the bailiff's instruction to stand?"

"Yeah," I shout out, "cuz I don't want to."

Dead silence follows my words. It's as if somebody waved a magic wand and everybody is frozen in place.

Judge Miller narrows her eyes and wags her finger at me. "Young man, do you understand the seriousness of this hearing?"

"Yeah, I do. And it's bullshit, so I ain't participating." I fold my arms and slide down so low in my chair that my chin almost touches the table.

When I see Ms. Angela turn around and stick out her arm toward the back of the room, I know that's a signal for my dad. He wants to run up here and strangle me. But I'm not worried because I know the bailiff won't let him.

"Young man, that kind of language and the disrespect you're showing are not acceptable in my courtroom. Would you please stand?"

"Ain't no reason for me to stand cuz we don't need to have no fitness hearing," I shout at the judge. "I want to be tried as an adult. So go ahead and send me to adult court cuz I ain't staying here to get railroaded for something I didn't do."

Jenny's face is so red it looks like she got stung by a zillion bumblebees.

Nobody's saying anything, so I keep talking. "I want justice my way. I wanna be in adult court with a jury of my peers."

"Your Honor," Ms. Jenny sputters. "May we approach?"

"Counselor, that sounds like an excellent idea. Why don't you?"

Both of my attorneys and the prosecutor almost stumble over each other getting up to the bench. They're trying to talk low, but I can hear everything they're saying.

Ms. Jenny opens her mouth to say something, but Ms. Angela cuts in.

"Your Honor, since our client's been detained at juvenile hall, he's been unduly influenced by another juvenile there. That juvenile has convinced him that he'd be better off in adult court because he'd be entitled to a jury. And he's convinced that a jury won't convict him. We've tried to talk to him, but he won't listen. Please excuse his behavior today. This is all an act."

Ms. Jenny isn't saying anything. Her arms are crossed and her head is tilted to the side.

The stupid prosecutor throws up his hands. "Well, if the boy's own attorneys can't control him, the juvenile court system certainly can't rehabilitate him."

Judge Miller frowns. "Have you explained to your client the consequences of what could happen to him if this case is transferred to adult court?"

Ms. Angela and Ms. Jenny nod at the same time. "Repeatedly," Ms. Angela says.

The judge drums her fingers on a stack of papers on her desk. "From what I know of this young man's background, this is not a situation where I feel the minor should be sent to adult court." She eyes the prosecutor. "So unless Mr. Martinez puts on an unusually strong case, that's unlikely to happen. But the conduct he's displaying in my courtroom right now is very troubling and might cause me to change my mind."

"Your Honor, can we have a short break to speak with our client?" Ms. Angela says.

"Sounds like a great idea." The judge checks her watch. "I'll give you twenty minutes. But if your client comes back in here acting like this, I might be inclined to grant his wish."

CHAPTER 44

Angela

As soon as we're behind closed doors, Gus explodes. "What the hell is wrong with you? You have no idea what you're doing!"

Graylin slouches down further in his chair, his hands clasped, staring at the wall.

"Sit up and look at me!" Gus yells.

Graylin takes his time sitting up. His eyes remain focused on the wall, not his dad.

"Please lower your voice," Jenny warns him. "We don't want one of the deputies coming in here. And it's not helping things when you yell at him. We need to talk this out."

Gus whirls around to face Jenny. "Lady, there ain't nothing for us to talk about. My son is black. He don't get the same chances a white kid might get. I'm handling this my way, not yours. And he's gonna do what I tell him to do. Even if I have to beat his ass to make him do it."

"But I can get a jury in adult court," Graylin pleads, "Little Slice said—"

"I don't care what that fool said. Do you understand that you're facing felony charges? You're gonna go back into that courtroom and act like you got some home training. I didn't raise you this way."

Graylin flies out of his chair and stands chest-to-chest with his father. Both of their faces are distorted with rage.

"This ain't your life! It's *my* life!" Graylin's eyes are glassy with tears. "That judge is going to lock me up for something I didn't do. I want a jury trial. At least that way I'll have a chance to show them I'm innocent. I don't have a chance in here. You're always telling me to man up. Well, that's what I'm doing. I'm being a man. And a man makes his own decisions."

Gus is momentarily stunned into silence by his son's defiance. Before he can respond, I step between them.

"Let's all calm down." I grab Graylin by the arm and pull him away. "I'm going to ask for a continuance."

Graylin jerks his arm away from me. "I don't want a continuance. I'm not going to change my mind and nobody in this room can make me."

Gus reaches around me and tries to grab his son, but Graylin jumps back out of his reach. "Boy, are you—"

"Both of you cut it out!" Jenny yells. "Let's give Graylin a few minutes alone to think about what he's about to do."

I pull Gus toward the door and Jenny follows. We walk a few feet down the hallway, away from the clusters of parents and kids waiting for their cases to be heard. "When we go back into court," I say, "we need to press the judge hard for her help. Maybe she'll do the right thing despite Graylin's behavior."

Jenny exhales. "But that's not what Graylin wants."

"Screw what Graylin wants!" Gus says. "What are you going to say to me when my fourteen-year-old son gets locked up?"

Everyone in the hallway is staring at us now. I'm surprised that one of the sheriff's deputies hasn't come over.

"If you're going to prevent me from following Graylin's wishes," Jenny says, "then I'll have to resign from the case."

Gus spreads his hands, palms up. "See ya."

Jenny starts to walk away. "Wait!" Now I'm the one yelling. "This is not the time for you to bail. Graylin needs you in there. Both of you need to chill!"

When I see the bailiff walking toward us, I know he's about to tell us to quiet down. Instead he says, "Judge Miller wants everybody back in the courtroom."

***

When we return, Martinez is sitting on the edge of the prosecution table. The judge is standing nearby. She's not wearing her robe.

"Did you two work things out with your client?" the judge asks.

Her question is directed to Jenny, but I'm the one who responds. "Your Honor, we can't seem to get him to change his mind."

The judge marches over to where Graylin is standing and pins him with a gaze intense enough to spark a fire.

"Young man, do you understand what you're doing?"

Graylin has resumed his gangbanger persona. His arms are locked across his chest and his head is arrogantly cocked to the side. "Yep. I want me some justice."

His right leg is trembling, but he's otherwise staying in character.

"If you're convicted in adult court," Judge Miller tells him, "the consequences are much more serious. You could end up with multiple felonies on your record that might never go away. It's best for you to have your case heard in juvenile court."

"Sounds like you already decided to convict me," Graylin says, just as surly as before. "This is why we need Black Lives Matter cuz the black man keeps getting fucked by the system. I said I don't wanna be here. So send me to adult court, damn it!"

The judge's pert lips flatten into a straight line.

I immediately start pleading Graylin's case. "Your Honor, my client is not himself. You've read the detention report. He's a great kid. This is an act. We'd like you to take into account that he's been influenced by—"

"Counselor, I don't care who influenced him," Judge Miller bristles. "If one of my sons talked to me like this, I'd—" She catches herself. "Well, that's beside the point."

"But, Your Honor," I continue, "he's pretending to—"

"I don't care if he's pretending. Your client's disrespectful behavior and his failure to listen to your advice tell me better than that detention report ever could that he's unfit for the juvenile justice system. So trying to rehabilitate him would indeed be a waste of this court's time. Since he wants to be in adult court, that's precisely where I'm sending him. Let me get my robe so we can put this on the record."

CHAPTER 45

Angela

Graylin is smiling like it's Christmas morning and Santa brought him everything on his wish list.

"Now I can get out on bail, right, Ms. Angela? Can I go home now?" He grins over at me with hopeful, glistening eyes.

I'm not a proponent of child abuse, but right now I want to slap him upside his big naïve head. He has no idea what he's just done. Gus storms out of the courtroom. I can hear his aunt and grandmother weeping as they trail behind him.

"No, Graylin, you can't go home now. Your case has to be transferred to adult court first. A Superior Court judge has to set bail."

"When is that going to happen?"

"It could take several days."

Shock rocks his face. "So I have to stay at juvenile hall until then?"

"Yes, you do. And there's no guarantee that the court's going to even let you out on bail."

He turns to Jenny as if she might contradict me. She meets his stunned eyes with silence.

Graylin's voice starts to quiver like he's about to cry. "But Little Slice said I would get out on bail."

"I guess this proves Little Slice doesn't know everything, huh?"

"But I thought I could get out right away."

"I never told you that."

"But Little Slice said—"

"If you mention Little Slice to me one more time, I swear I'm going to slice you up into little pieces."

Graylin smiles. "That's funny, Ms. Angela."

"There's nothing funny about what you did. The first thing you need to do is apologize to your father for your behavior. He may not even want to post your bail."

For the first time, Graylin seems to realize that Gus is holding the keys to his freedom.

Martinez walks over. "It's been nice working with you, counselors. On the adult side, the case will be assigned to Lorelei Sullivan. Child pornography cases are her forte."

I want to slap Martinez upside the head too. "Thanks for everything."

Jenny picks up her satchel and is about to leave.

"Hold up," I say. "Why don't we have lunch? We need to clear the air."

***

Thirty minutes later, we're seated at a sandwich shop, not far from the courthouse. We place our orders and take seats until our food is ready.

"I'm sorry about getting so upset," I begin. "But I couldn't agree with you about letting Graylin make the decision on this."

Jenny hunches her shoulders. "Well, he did anyway. Now that you'll be in adult court, you'll be in familiar territory. Good luck."

What I'm about to say will no doubt come as a surprise to her. It's a surprise to me too. "I'd like you to stay on the case."

Jenny blinks.

"You know these sexting cases backward and forward," I continue. "I know the adult system. We'll make a great team."

"No, we won't. Even though he's in adult court, the same rules still apply. Graylin is the client and he gets to make the ultimate decisions. I'm not going to disregard my obligations to my client just because you want to act like his mother."

I remind myself that this is not about me. I need to do what's best for Graylin, and Graylin needs Jenny fighting for him. I need her too.

"I wasn't trying to act like his mother. I was trying to keep him from ruining his life. The fact that he thinks he did something good shows that he's not mature enough to make a decision like this."

Jenny rolls her eyes and looks away. Instead of convincing her that we can continue to work as a team, I've just reconfirmed that we'll still be tugging at opposite ends of the same rope.

As I'm about to apologize for the second time, someone calls out my ticket number and I get up to retrieve my turkey sandwich. Jenny's number is called next. We both ignore the cloud of distrust hanging over us and start eating.

"If we can find out who took that picture and who sent it to him," I say after several bites, "I think we have a chance of getting him off. Even on the possession charge." I hope Jenny notices that I'm still using the plural *we*. "I didn't want to admit it before, but I do think we have a shot at jury nullification. Frankly, it's our best shot."

Jenny reaches for her phone. "I have an excellent investigator. Her name's Mei Lau. If anybody can find out who took that picture, she can. She's great at navigating in juvenile circles. Even though she's in her thirties, she could easily pass for fourteen or fifteen. I just texted you her contact information."

"I'm sure I can use her, but I also need you. Graylin does too. Will you please stay on the case?"

Rather than answer me, Jenny takes a bite of her sandwich. I put mine down and stare across the table at her. If I have to grovel for Graylin's sake, I will.

"Look, Jenny, let's make this about Graylin. Not about—"

"I don't know," she says. "Let me think about it and get back to you."

CHAPTER 46

Angela

As usual, arraignment court is a zoo. Being back here fills me with a strange, yet familiar calm. This is *my t*erritory. I look toward the cage and spot Graylin in his gray sweat suit. He looks like a small ferret next to the five grown men in the cage with him. He waves at me. I don't wave back because that isn't allowed. There's a sign to that effect on the wall inside the cage.

When the judge calls Graylin's case, a deputy escorts him to the table where I'm standing.

"How are you doing?" I ask.

"I'm good," Graylin says, hugging me. "Can you get me out today, Ms. Angela?"

"Maybe."

I don't say any more than that because the truth would crush him. His aunt Macie agreed to put up her house. Assuming the judge grants bail, it could still be two or three days, maybe longer, before all the paperwork is processed.

"Your dad's supposed to be here," I say, looking over my shoulder.

"He's still mad at me. But when I win my trial, he'll understand."

I'm still mad at Graylin too. A fourteen-year-old can't drink, drive, smoke, vote or even sign a contract, but the law says he can make his own legal decisions? Whoever came up with that jewel was smoking something.

"When the judge asks how do you plead, say *not guilty* and not a word more," I tell him. "And you better not pull any of that disrespectful crap you did in juvenile court."

Graylin grins. "Okay, Ms. Angela. I won't."

The judge opens a folder, then stares out at me. "You're kidding me. Another sexting case? How old is the defendant?"

"Fourteen," I say.

The exasperation on the judge's face matches mine. "How do you plead?"

I give Graylin a nudge.

"Not guilty," he calls out in a loud, clear voice.

"My client has never been in trouble before. We'd like to ask that the defendant be released on O-R to his father. He'll be under twenty-four-hour supervision at home."

The judge turns to the prosecutor. "You okay with that?"

The deputy D.A. handling arraignments today is a fifty-plus, hard ass who plays it by the book. When I tried to talk to him earlier this morning, he said he didn't have time. I'm glad he won't be the prosecutor trying the case.

"We object, Your Honor," the prosecutor says. "The defendant's in adult court because he tried to intimidate a witness. We're asking that he remain in custody without bail."

Without bail? My heart starts to palpitate.

"Your Honor, that's unfairly excessive for a case of this nature. This young man is an excellent student with no prior criminal record. And the charge of witness intimidation is a farce."

The judge looks down at the papers on his desk. "Counselor, since a juvenile court judge sent his case here, he's obviously not the angel you want me to think he is."

The prosecutor interrupts. "I'd like to direct your attention to the judge's certification and the transcript of how disrespectfully the defendant behaved toward the court."

The judge pauses to read. "I see that here."

"In addition," the prosecutor continues, "the victim's mother is in court today. She'd like to see the defendant remain in custody because she fears for her daughter's safety."

All eyes turn to Simone Carlyle, who's dressed in black like she's here for a funeral. She stands up even though she wasn't asked to. Gus and Dre are sitting four rows behind her.

"Your Honor, I strongly disagree. I'm requesting house arrest, ankle monitoring and no computer access except for completion of his school-work, which will be supervised."

"I'll split the baby," the judge says. "Bail is granted at fifty thousand dollars. The defendant will also be under house arrest and required to wear an ankle monitor. Next case."

"Fifty thousand dollars!" Graylin looks as if he's about to crumple into tears. "My dad doesn't have that much money!"

"He only has to have a portion of it. Don't worry. We've already worked it out. I'll come back to talk to you after I speak with your father."

A deputy appears to escort Graylin away.

I motion Gus into the hallway and explain everything I need him to do to get the bail taken care of. I'm about to head back inside when I see Jenny standing a few feet away.

"Nice job in there," she says.

She has no idea how happy I am to see her.

"So is this just a coincidence or can I interpret your being here as a good sign?"

Jenny smiles. "I'm in."

I give her a hug.

"What made you change your mind?"

"Good old-fashioned outrage. I'm sick and tired of the D.A.'s Office filing these cases and labeling good kids as sex offenders for the rest of their lives. I'm ready to help you kick some butt."

CHAPTER 47

Angela

Jenny and I are in my office waiting for her investigator to arrive. The three of us are going to discuss case strategy and outline the evidence we need to get Graylin acquitted.

There's a gentle knock on the door and a cute Asian girl with a nose ring and a purple streak in her bangs steps into the room. Jenny's right. Mei doesn't look anywhere close to thirty.

After introductions and some quick background on the case for Mei, we start tossing around ideas.

"We need someone else to point the finger at," Jenny says. "And that someone is the person who took the picture and sent it to Graylin."

"Are you certain it's the same person?" Mei asks.

Jenny stops to think. "I just assumed it was, but you make a good point."

"So you're confident your client didn't take it?"

"Yes," I say before Jenny can answer.

"I'll need to interview him." Mei scribbles in her notebook. "He can help me determine which of his classmates I should talk to."

I feel a twinge of discomfort. Despite my response just now, what if I'm wrong about Graylin not taking that picture? I've certainly had clients look me in the eyes and flat out lie to me. Is my closeness to Graylin clouding my legal judgment?

"Since the note was left at school," Mei says, as she examines it, "one of his classmates is probably involved. And it sounds like it was written by a kid."

I glance down at my copy and reread it.

Dear Mrs. Keller,

Graylin Alexander should be ashamed of himself. He took a naked picture of Kennedy Carlyle with his iPhone. He also said he was going to beat her up and embarrass her by posting the picture on Instagram so it could go viral. Please stop him from doing this!

Signed, Anonymous

"What makes you think it was written by a kid?" I ask.

"Because of the *Dear Mrs. Keller* part and because it says he took the picture with his *iPhone*, not *phone* or *cell phone*. Kids are more conscious about brands. I don't think an adult would've been that specific."

"The exclamation mark at the end also seems like something a kid would use," Jenny adds.

I tug at a swatch of my hair. "I just wish we knew which kid."

"Don't worry," Jenny says. "Mei will find out. She's amazing."

Mei puts the note away and starts examining the photograph found on Graylin's phone. In the picture, Kennedy Carlyle appears to have been captured mid-stride in what looks like a bedroom. Her breasts and pubic area are clearly visible.

"Can't you argue that the picture doesn't meet the definition of obscenity under the statute?" Mei asks. "In another case I worked on, the attorney got an acquittal by arguing that."

I reach for my iPad and reread California Penal Code Section 311.

"Obscene matter" means matter, taken as a whole, that to the average person, applying contemporary statewide standards, appeals to the prurient interest, that, taken as a whole, depicts or describes sexual

conduct in a patently offensive way, and that, taken as a whole,
lacks serious literary, artistic, political or scientific value.

"If this is the legal standard," I say, growing excited, "the charge can't
possibly stick. That picture doesn't show any sexual conduct."

Jenny shakes her head. "I wish it was going to be that easy. You
have to read section 311 in conjunction with the section that defines
sexual conduct."

I scroll down to that section, which provides multiple definitions of
sexual conduct, including sexual intercourse, masturbation, and sado-
masochistic abuse. Kennedy's picture still doesn't fit. My excitement
starts to build again but crashes when I get to the fifth definition.

As used in this section, "sexual conduct" means . . .(5) Exhibition of
the genitals or the pubic or rectal area of any person for the purpose
of sexual stimulation of the viewer.

I glance back up at Jenny. "Can't we argue that it wasn't for the
purpose of sexual stimulation?"

"I've tried that argument before," Jenny says. "And it didn't go well.
This picture definitely falls within the statute."

I turn to Mei. "How did the attorney in your other case get the kid off?"

"Sorry," she says. "It wasn't a kid. The guy was an artist. I guess they
must've used the artistic exception. I'll take a look at Kennedy's social media
pages as soon as I leave. That should give us some helpful information."

"Her pages are all shut down now," Jenny says. "But I took a look
at her Snapchat, Pinterest, Instagram, Tumblr and Facebook pages the
same day I got the case." She hands several pages to Mei. "Here are my
notes and some screenshots. I wrote down the names of the kids who
seemed to communicate with her the most."

Mei quickly scans them. "It amazes me that kids can find the time
to manage all of these sites. Find anything interesting?"

Jenny shakes her head. "She loves hot pink, puppies, owls, all things
Paris and has a big-time crush on Drake and Katy Perry. My first thought

after spending two hours on her social media pages was that she's a nice little girl."

"So who does Graylin think sent him the picture?" Mei asks.

"His best friend Crayvon Little," Jenny says. "I didn't find anything helpful on his social media pages. And I don't know about motive, but he certainly had means and opportunity. Not only does he live across the street from Kennedy, he just happens to have made a trip to the administration office right before a school clerk found the note lying on a counter. Unfortunately, no one saw him or anyone else put it there."

Mei asks for the spelling of Crayvon's name and writes it down.

"Is there any way to subpoena Snapchat's records?" I ask. "Then we could find out whose account the picture came from."

Mei shakes her head. "Snapchat only gives that information to law enforcement. We can check to find out if the prosecution subpoenaed them, but I doubt it. They aren't going to spend that kind of time and money on a minor case like this."

I understand what she means, but Mei's calling this a minor case rubs me the wrong way. There's nothing minor about the possibility of Graylin being labeled a sexual predator for life.

"If we're going to win this," Jenny says, "we have to pull at the heartstrings of the jury. Every juror in that courtroom has to see their son, grandson, or nephew in Graylin and understand that the same thing could happen to them."

"How do you guys get around the possession charge since the picture was on Graylin's phone?"

"It's a specific intent crime," Jenny explains. "We're going to argue that he lacked intent. He saved it to his phone, but he didn't know it was pornography."

Mei frowns. "Ignorance of the law is no defense. Have you won with that argument before?"

"Nope. But there's always a first time."

"And you're sure Graylin's telling you the truth when he says he didn't take the picture?" Mei asks again.

"Yes," Jenny and I say in unison.

"I know Graylin pretty well," I add. "I don't think he's lying to us."

Jenny quickly concurs. "I've been doing juvenile criminal defense for close to ten years. There's a sense of righteous indignation in a child who's been falsely accused. I see that in Graylin. An adult understands that life isn't always fair, especially when you're talking about the justice system. But a kid thinks that if they're telling the truth, everything will turn out fine. And that's precisely what Graylin believes."

CHAPTER 48

The Shepherd

Wallstreet and I are kicked back on our bunks shooting the breeze. When the door opens and Oaktown steps inside our cell, I immediately spring up.

He closes the door behind him and walks over to Wallstreet, who's on the bottom bunk.

"Why you always hangin' out with this chomo?"

My cellie says nothing. I don't have to see his face to know that he's so petrified his lips won't work.

"I'm talkin' to you," Oaktown repeats.

"I-I…this is my cell. I'm just in my cell."

"Why you always playin' chess with him?"

Wallstreet is too terrified to answer, so Oaktown raises his gaze to me.

"Anybody who sells little girls is a pervert and I don't like perverts. Especially a pervert who turned out my homeboy's little girl."

"Man, you got your facts wrong," I say. "I'm out of the trafficking business. And I don't know nothing about Blaze's daughter."

"Don't lie to me. The way I hear it, you still goin' long and strong in the pimpin' game. I heard you pimpin' little girls down south now."

"Uh, I-I gotta go." Wallstreet eases his way around Oaktown and disappears through the door.

I need to talk to this thug on his level, which means I can't show any sign of fear.

"You've received some incorrect information. And I don't appreciate you disrespecting me by coming into my cell like this."

Oaktown crosses his massive arms. "You made the mistake of snatchin' the wrong little girl. Blaze's kid didn't start hittin' the needle until after you put her on the street. Blaze is holdin' you responsible for her death. He asked me to kill you. The only reason you're still breathin' is cuz I haven't decided yet how I'm gonna do it."

This is a place for non-violent offenders. How did this psychopath get in here?

"I hear you got lots of dough. I'ma need a few stamps and I also want you to get some of your peeps to put some money on my books."

If I have to pay this guy to leave me alone, so be it.

"I might be able to do that," I say, forcing fearlessness into my voice, "but I can't have you threatening me all the time. You show me some respect and I'll do the same to you."

Oaktown responds with a deep guttural laugh.

"Oh, so you wanna be the tough man, huh? I bet you wasn't tough when you was snatchin' little girls off the street and selling 'em like crack. You a pervert."

"You have your business and I have mine. Anyway, I don't do that anymore."

"I told you not to lie to me!" His saliva peppers my face.

Oaktown leans in so close I can see the red veins in his yellow eyes. Even though I'm sitting on the top bunk, we're almost eye-to-eye. I want to climb down, but I don't know that my legs will hold me up.

"Put three hundred dollars on my books. I hear you got a phone, so I'll give you a couple of hours to get it done." He stretches out his hand. "Ten books of stamps should hold me for now."

I don't have a choice. I jump down from my bunk and retrieve the stamps from my hiding place. When I hand them to him, he stands there and recounts them, even though he just saw me do that.

He turns away as if he's leaving, then swings back around and punches me in the side with the whole force of his body. I'm sure I hear my ribs crack.

I cry out and reach for the bed to keep from falling to the floor.

"Catch you later, pervert." He slips back out of the door.

Wallstreet must've been waiting for Oaktown to leave because he returns only seconds later.

"You okay?" He helps me sit on his bed.

"Thanks for having my back." I'm still doubled over in pain.

"I-I told you, I don't do violence. That maniac is going around telling everybody you're a chomo. If I defend you, he'll turn on me."

Oaktown is a problem that's only going to get worse. Paying him off will likely increase his threats. *Would he really kill me?* No, that wouldn't make sense. I'm much more valuable to him alive. But I can't sit around being his punching bag and personal ATM. I have to find a way to make this problem go away.

"I need you to help me find somebody who can get Oaktown off my ass. I can pay them."

Wallstreet starts waving his hands in the air like a referee calling a foul. "I told you, I can't get involved. And everybody's scared of him. The guy's nuts. You should report him and ask the guards to put you in protective custody."

"Then I'll be labeled a snitch and locked up with the gays and cho-mos. I'd rather go to the hole."

Almost any infraction can get you put in the hole, which means twenty-three hours a day of solitary confinement. No human contact other than a guard, no books or magazines, and only three showers a week. Your food is slid through a slot in the door. No one asks to go there.

But an idea comes to me. The hole may well serve two purposes—getting me some relief from Oaktown's harassment and restoring my rep.

CHAPTER 49

My friends are always telling me I should be glad that I look half my age. Maybe I'll be grateful when I'm fifty, but right now, it's mostly annoying. Except when I'm trying to pass myself off as a middle-school student.

I knock on Crayvon Little's front door and wait for the response I've heard a million times.

Mrs. Little opens the door, looks me up and down and says, "You're the investigator? You don't even look old enough to drive."

I flash a smile that hides my irritation. "I assure you I am." I shake her hand and step into her living room.

Sharon Little is a thin, fair-skinned woman who wears her hair short and her attitude strong. She has the sturdy stance of a woman you don't mess with, despite her lithe frame.

"Crayvon's back there on that dang computer. My son lives on that thing. I couldn't pay him to go outside and play in the yard. It's such a shame."

Since deciding to focus my investigative talents on juvenile cases, I've become a bit of a technology whiz. Social media plays some role in nearly all of my cases. Kids often convict themselves with their own posts. If parents took half a second to monitor what their kids are doing online, my business would be cut in half.

Mrs. Little yells down the hall and a tall, waif-like kid bounces into the room dressed in jeans and an oversized Stephen Curry jersey.

"This is Ms. Lau, Graylin's investigator. She wants to see if you know anything that can help Graylin's case."

She takes a seat on the living room couch. Crayvon sits next to her, while I settle into a cushy arm chair.

"It's a shame what they're doing to that boy. Ruining his life for nothing. I don't believe for a minute that Graylin took a picture of that girl through her bedroom window. That boy is an angel. I heard that girl's mama is trying to throw the book at him. She better be careful because what goes around always comes right back to you. Go get Ms. Lau a bottle of water," she tells her son.

"Do you know Mrs. Carlyle?" I ask.

"Just in passing. The Carlyles have lived on this street for at least five years, but she barely waves and never participates in any of our block parties."

"Which house is it?" I ask, although I already know.

She steps over to the picture window. It's the beige house with the white trim four houses down on the opposite side of the street. I'm pretty sure the Carlyles are recently separated."

"Really?"

"Yep. I never see him come home in the evenings anymore. His black BMW used to be parked in the driveway every night, but I haven't seen it in weeks."

I nod, happy to let Mrs. Little keep blabbing away.

"Simone—that's the wife—thinks she's all that because she's a vice president at some company. Raised her daughter to think that too. That's why her husband ran off. She's always traveling. Never home. Got some African nanny raising that child. That's the problem."

"Have you had much contact with Kennedy?"

"Not really. She keeps that child protected, too protected. Anyway, you're not here to talk to me."

Mrs. Little suggests that we move into the dining room. I don't object even though I prefer the more relaxed setting of the living room. A comfortable witness is a more talkative witness. I follow her and take a seat at the dining room table.

Crayvon hands me a bottle of water and places a coaster on the table. I start by asking him general questions about his classes. He isn't a shy kid, but he's not overly forthcoming either.

"Is everybody at school talking about the picture?"

"Yep."

"Have you seen it?"

He pauses as his eyes steal a glance at his mother.

"Go on, boy," Mrs. Little says. "I know you looked at it just like everybody else."

"Yeah, I've seen it."

"Who showed it to you?"

He pauses again. "Kenya."

"What's Kenya's last name?"

"Morris."

"Do you know how she got the picture?"

"From Instagram. But it's not up there anymore. Kenya saved it on her phone like Graylin did. A lot of people did. But when everybody started talking about Graylin getting arrested, they got scared and deleted it off their phones. Everybody saw it though. It went viral."

"Do you know who took the picture?"

"Nope."

"Do you know who posted it on Instagram?"

"Nope. But I know Graylin didn't. He wouldn't do that."

"Do you know of anybody who didn't like Kennedy and might've wanted to embarrass her?"

"Nope."

"Do you know of anybody who didn't like Graylin?"

"Nope. He's popular and really smart too. He always helps me with my algebra."

"Does Graylin ever come over to your house?"

"Yep."

"What do you guys usually do?"

He shrugs. "Mostly play Nintendo. Or just hang out."

The phone rings and Mrs. Little gets up to answer it.

"I understand that Kennedy lives across the street. Do you ever go over to her house?"

Crayvon freezes, then steals a glance down the hallway, where his mother is on the phone. "Um, no."

His stricken face sends off a warning signal. *He's lying.* If I'm going to get any admissions out of Crayvon, I need to do it before Mrs. Little returns.

"Have you and Graylin ever gone over to Kennedy's house when he came over to hang out with you?"

I include Graylin in my question so Crayvon thinks I'm focusing on Graylin's conduct, not his.

"Um," he tugs at a loose thread on the hem of his T-shirt, "not that I can recall?"

Not that I can recall? He sounds like a well-coached witness.

Before coming here, I looked up Kennedy's house on Google Earth to see if I could figure out where the picture was taken from. Whoever shot it had to be standing outside her bedroom window. I lucked up and found pictures of the interior of the Carlyles' home on a real estate website. Those pictures and the Google Earth view show that the bedrooms are in the back on the ground floor, which means the shooter had to enter the backyard.

"Have you and Graylin ever gone into Kennedy's backyard?"

Once again, Crayvon's face flashes panic. "Nope. Never."

"So you guys have never looked into Kennedy's bedroom window before?"

"Of course not. I wouldn't do that. Neither would Graylin."

Mrs. Little returns just as I'm asking my next question.

"Do you like Kennedy? I mean, as a friend?"

"Nope. Nobody likes her. She's too fake. Thinks she's all that because her parents buy her anything she wants. She has some Nikes that cost over four hundred dollars. Most girls don't care about expensive tennis shoes, but she tries to outdo the boys."

"She gets that snootiness from her mama," Mrs. Little chimes in.

"Does Kennedy have many friends?"

"Not really. She only hangs out with LaShay Thornton."

"Is LaShay in the eighth grade too?"

Crayvon nods.

"Where does she live?"

"In the Jungle with her grandmother. Her mama and daddy are both in the military."

"That's a surprise," Mrs. Little says. "I'm shocked that Simone lets her daughter hang out with somebody who's in a lower economic class."

"What's the Jungle?" I ask.

"It's a neighborhood with a bunch of apartment buildings," Crayvon explains. "And they have lots of trees like in a jungle. It's kinda rough over there."

"Where is it?"

"Not far from here." Mrs. Little points over her shoulder. "If you're going north, back down LaBrea, you make a right on Coliseum. If you get to Rodeo, you've gone too far."

I turn back to Crayvon. "And you're sure you don't know who might've taken that picture of Kennedy?"

His eyes dart everywhere except in my direction. "Nope. I have no idea."

CHAPTER 50

Willie

I don't realize it until I look over at Bones, but I've chosen a complete imbecile to partner with me on this gig. It's 70 degrees outside and he's sweating like he just walked out of a sauna. That means he's scared.

"Man, you okay?" I ask.

"Yeah. Let's do this."

Bones is the worst kind of criminal, a dude who wears his bravado like a badge, but is the first one to crap on himself when something goes wrong. I'm going to dump him as soon as this job is done.

Our rented truck is headed west on Florence Avenue toward Angela Evans' office. We're both dressed as handymen in dark-green coveralls with *Roscoe's Electrical Repair* stitched on the pockets. We park on the street instead of the building's parking garage and hop out. I grab a large tool box from the cab of the truck.

It's after eight at night, so there shouldn't be much foot traffic in the building. I look around again for security cameras. If there are any here, somebody did a good job camouflaging them. We're wearing fake mustaches and baseball caps pulled low over our foreheads just in case. We walk up to the reception desk where a young security guard is busy tapping the screen of his phone. He barely looks up at us.

I sign in, prepared to give a spiel about the building management calling us to check out the hallway lights on the fourth floor. I'd even practiced it with Bones. But this cat doesn't care who enters the building. He's all into his phone.

"We have to fix the—"

I kick Bones in the ankle, cutting him off mid-sentence.

The guy is still glued to his phone. "Yeah, okay." He never looks up at us.

Bones hobbles behind me over to the bank of elevators.

"What you do that for?" He stoops to massage his ankle.

"Because you opened your big mouth."

"I just figured we should tell the guy what we're doin' to make it look good."

"Did that dude look like he was concerned about us? Keep your fat trap shut. I told you, I'll do the talking."

When the elevator opens, we take it to the fourth floor. After getting off, I look up and down the hallway. No one in sight.

"Stay here and signal me if anybody comes."

I walk the few steps to the door of Angela Evan's office suite and knock. When no one answers, I stick a long tool into the lock and it easily pops open.

"Is anyone here?" I call out. "It's the electricians."

I've been following Angela nearly every day. Since my first visit to her office, she hasn't worked past five, probably on directions from Dre. I still can't believe he almost busted me. Tonight's mission is as much for him as it is for his woman.

I check to make sure nobody's in the other interior offices, then wave Bones in. "Hurry up."

"Which office is it?" Bones asks.

I ignore his question, walk up to the first door on the right and quickly pop the lock. We step inside and close the door.

"Let's get to work," I say. "Miss Angela Evans is gonna get quite a surprise when she comes to work tomorrow morning."

CHAPTER 51

"Aw, Dad, this is whack."

My son, Little Dre, is standing in front of me with his lips poked out as I scroll through the text messages on his cell phone. After what Graylin's going through, it's time I have a serious talk with my own kid.

"You can't be doing anything crazy with this phone. If you do, I'm taking it." I tell him for the third time what happened to Graylin.

"A lot of my friends sext, Dad. It's not a big deal."

I can't believe my ten-year-old just said that. I must be stuck in a time warp.

"Yes, it is a big deal! And it's illegal. Did you hear what I said about Graylin? And I don't care what your friends do. You better not do it. Your ass could end up in jail!"

"Leave that boy alone," Sheila calls out from the kitchen. "You're scaring him."

"Nobody's talking to you. I still say he's too young to have a cell phone in the first place."

A cell phone led to Brianna being kidnapped. If I have anything to say about it, she'll be thirty before she gets another one.

"I need to be able to reach him," Sheila yells back. "And it's only a TracFone. He can't even go on the internet."

My son's mother is and always will be the biggest one-night mistake of my life. My son was the only good thing that came out of hooking up with her.

I grab Little Dre by the arm. "Have you sexted anybody before?"

"Ow, Dad, you're hurting me. I haven't sexted nobody. I promise."

I realize how tight I'm squeezing his arm and loosen my grip. If I overreact, he's not going to tell me the truth. "Has anybody ever sexted you?"

Little Dre takes way too long to answer. "Yeah," he admits. "But I always delete 'em."

WTF? I try not to show my shock. "Who sexted you?"

"Aw, Dad. I don't wanna get nobody in trouble."

"I'm not going to tell anybody. I swear. Just tell me."

He hangs his head. "Some of the girls in my class." He smiles deviously. "Moneequa sends naked selfies all the time."

"A girl sent you a naked picture?"

"Not all the way naked, Dad. Just her breasts."

My son might as well have punched me in the face. *Does a fourth grader even have breasts?*

"And my friend Colton sent a picture of his you know what back to Moneequa. He showed it to me."

I'm so floored my brain can't even form another question.

"Dre, that's just what kids do with them phones these days," Sheila interrupts us again. "It ain't that serious. They're just being kids."

Sheila's dumb-ass remark is why Little Dre is coming to live with me as soon as me and Angela get straight.

My phone rings and Apache's name appears on the screen. My pulse takes a leap. Maybe he has some good news for me.

"Hate to have to tell you this, cuz, but the guy I asked to keep an eye on Angela's office, just called me. Somebody trashed the place last night."

***

The reception area of Angela's office suite is spotless, but when I step inside her office, I feel tingles of anger. Nothing is *untouched*. The place looks like a tornado ripped through it. The desk is on its side and the two guest chairs are broken into pieces. The printer looks as if it's been smashed with a hammer. Paper is everywhere. Cotton stuffing sticks out of the gutted couch like clusters of clouds. The blood-red words spray-painted on the wall make me shiver: *YOU R NEXT!*

There's no way I can avoid coming clean with Angela now. The problem won't be telling her that this is the handiwork of The Shepherd, but admitting that once again I lied to her.

"Sir, you shouldn't be in here."

I look over my shoulder to find Prentiss, the clown of a security guard. "This is a crime scene. You shouldn't be in here."

"Yeah, okay."

When I step back into the hallway, I hear the chime of the elevator. Angela steps off, her face full of anguish. Jenny is right behind her.

"I was a block away when the police called me," she says. "How'd you find out?"

Luckily, she doesn't wait for my response. She brushes past me and tries to enter the office, but Prentiss stops her. "I'm sorry, Miss A, but you can't go inside until the police have processed the crime scene."

He spreads his arms, blocking the doorway like a comical rent-a-cop straight out of central casting.

"But it's *my* office. I need to see how bad it is. C'mon, Prentiss. I'll only be a second and I won't touch anything."

His lips twist in frustration and his arms fall to his side. "Okay, but hurry up. If the cops ask me, I'm telling them you went in there against my orders."

She darts inside, followed by me and Jenny.

Angela gasps and covers her mouth with both hands. Her eyes linger on the words scrawled in red. "Why would somebody do this?"

As I pull her back into the hallway, Jenny walks up to Prentiss. "Were any other offices in the building vandalized?"

"No, just Miss A's."

Jenny squeezes Angela's shoulder. "Is there a problem with one of your clients?"

"No way. Besides Graylin's case, I only have one active criminal matter plus a couple of sexual harassment lawsuits. I don't think this has anything to do with anybody I'm representing."

Angela stares at me. I want to look away, but I don't. Her probing eyes tell me she knows that I know exactly why her office was trashed.

"Did Graylin make bail?" I try to change the subject. To pretend this didn't happen.

"Yeah, but the paperwork is still being processed. He'll likely be home tomorrow."

"That's good to hear."

Angela turns to Jenny. "I need a minute to talk to Dre. Can you excuse us?"

CHAPTER 52

Sullivan

The new case I received today throws me for a loop. Graylin Alexander. Fourteen years old. No prior record. It's my job to put him away for possession of child pornography. Cases like this make me want to rethink my career choice.

Ten years ago, there were only a handful of women in the D.A.'s Sex Crime Unit. Now, more than half are women. My colleagues are smart, tough and ambitious. The cream of the crop. We enjoy taking pedophiles off the streets and putting them behind bars where they belong. But in the last few years, the defendants facing charges for possession and distribution of child pornography have been getting increasingly younger. Somebody decided to start reading the laws literally and that means going after teens who have no concept of the danger they face when they take a seductive selfie and post it online or send it to a friend. They're simply kids being kids with a technological spin no one could have predicted.

I flip through the detention report and frown. This boy reads like an angel. Stellar grades, a stable home life, and no record of truancy. The affidavits from his minister and teacher would qualify him for sainthood.

Picking up the phone, I dial Martinez's office.

"I just got the Graylin Alexander file. This kid doesn't belong in adult court. Even the detention report says so. What's the deal? How did he end up on my desk?"

"The kid got it into his head that he'd be better off in adult court because he'd have a jury and his attorneys couldn't talk him out of it," Martinez explains. "You should've seen how he acted out at the fitness hearing. Refused to stand up, ignored the judge's instructions, even swore at her. So, she granted his wish. I thought his father was going to have an aneurysm."

Martinez didn't answer my question. A kid can't just act out and end up in adult court. Martinez had to file a motion for a fitness hearing. "Why'd you even push to have this kid tried as an adult? He's sounds like a choir boy. I wish my eighth grader had his grades."

"There's some heat on the case."

"What does that mean?"

"The parents of the girl are politically connected. I got an order to go for the jugular. And if you haven't felt the heat, don't worry, it's coming."

As I think about it, maybe I already had, but didn't realize it. It's rare for my boss to inquire about a minor case like this. In the hallway this morning, he asked me what I thought of it. I told him it was too soon to know. My boss is far savvier than Martinez's. If he tried to force me to pursue a case for political reasons, he knows I'd balk.

"So what's going on?"

"That's why I filed the pornography charges as felonies rather than misdemeanors."

"Can we prove he took the picture?"

"We don't have any evidence of that yet, but he admitted to the police that he saved it from Snapchat. So, the possession charge is your clear winner. The witness intimidation charge isn't as solid, but it's still doable. A kid at Eastlake named Dontay Davis was bragging that Graylin Alexander asked him to threaten the girl to drop the case. Unless you can find some evidence to show he took the picture, the distribution and invasion of privacy charges are losers. I planned to drop them down the line anyway."

"What about the criminal threat charge? Is that based solely on the anonymous note?"

"Yeah. If no evidence turns up, you might have to drop that one too."

This is not how I operate. I don't file charges and then hope that the evidence to support them somehow magically appears.

"What about the victim? Is she in bad shape? Suicidal or anything like that?"

"No."

"Any negatives on our side that I need to know about?"

"Something's up with the victim's dad. He doesn't want her to testify."

"Why?"

"Claims it would be too traumatic for her. He's about to be appointed to the bench and wants the case to disappear. He tried to pressure me to offer the kid a plea. But I think the guy's hiding something."

"You're talking in code. What are you saying? You think he's molesting the girl?"

"My investigator sat in on our interview. She thinks that's a possibility. I don't know what's going on. But something's not right with him."

"Thanks a lot for such a wonderful case."

Martinez chuckles. "Unless the jury goes rogue, the possession charge is your clear winner, even without the girl's testimony. The mother can testify about the effect on her, but it'll be a stronger sell if the jury can see the devastated victim herself."

"What do you know about the kid's attorney?"

"He has two. Angela Evans and Jenny Ungerman. Both of them are excellent lawyers and fairly reasonable to deal with. Jenny knows the juvenile court system inside and out. Very committed to her clients. Angela used to be a federal prosecutor. They're going to give you a run for your money."

I hang up and try to psyche myself up for this case. I miss the good old days when there were no cell phones, texts, tweets or kids posting provocative selfies online every five seconds. You can't watch ten minutes of TV without seeing two strangers jump into bed and start humping each other's brains out. So why would our kids think there's anything wrong with sharing pictures of their privates?

Cases like this make me ultra-paranoid about keeping my own house in order. I open my laptop and dial into Net Nanny. I'm determined not to become one of those naïve, helicopter parents who control every aspect of their kids' lives. Successful professionals who spend more time making money than raising their kids. Their heads are so deep in the sand, they have no idea what their kids are doing online. And the kids are so shielded from real life, they have no idea how to think for themselves.

Protecting my two kids and protecting my career go hand in hand. Considering what I do for a living, it would be more than embarrassing if one of my kids were accused of sexting.

I punch in the password and go through my son's texts, emails and social media accounts. I can see in real time everything he's doing online. At thirteen, Jonathan is still into video games and has recently become fascinated with rattle snakes. As long as he doesn't bring one home, his new hobby is fine with me.

With a greater sense of trepidation, I switch over to my daughter's account. My fifteen-year-old is growing more and more obsessed with the number of likes she receives on Instagram. She came home in tears last week because her friends teased her about only getting twelve likes for the picture of a new blouse she'd posted.

I've been giving serious thought to taking away Nina's cell phone and limiting her computer use to schoolwork. But I know from firsthand experience that the helicopter-parenting model is doomed to fail. I've sat across the table from far too many devastated parents who'd banned their kids from social media, only to find out they used a Snapchat or Instagram account their parents knew nothing about to post the tweets and pictures that landed them in court. At least this way, I can monitor everything she's doing.

I quickly scan all of Nina's social media accounts, ending with Instagram. Finding nothing objectionable, I'm about to log off when I decide to click on the page of Nina's best friend, Brooke. The first picture that catches my attention is a shot of Nina, Brooke, and Zoey. All three girls are bent at the waist, looking back over their shoulders with puck-ered pink lips. They're wearing identical butt-exposing shorts—shorts I didn't buy for Nina—their tight little rear ends pointed directly at the camera. It's the perfect shot for a pedophile to zero in on. They might as well have written the caption *Mr. Pedophile, please come and get me!* underneath the picture.

I snatch the receiver from my desk phone, then slam it back into the cradle. I grab my keys and cell phone instead and head for the elevator. I need to have a talk with my darling little daughter in the safety of my car. It wouldn't look good for the deputy D.A. prosecuting Graylin Alexander to be overheard screaming at her daughter for her pornographic post.

CHAPTER 53

Dre

Angela and I ride the elevator in silence. When we reach the lobby, I finally speak. "Why don't we go to your apartment? This could take a minute."

"No," she says. "My car will do."

We head for the parking garage.

Angela hits her key fob, opening the door of her Saab and climbs into the driver's seat. I take my time getting into the passenger seat.

"So what's going on?" she demands before I can even shut the door.

"It's The Shepherd."

Fear crinkles the corners of her eyes. "The Shepherd's in prison."

"Yeah, but I got word that he's put a price on my head."

"Word from who?"

"He put the word out on the street. Apache brought it to me."

She suddenly softens. "He's trying to kill you?"

"Yes. And apparently threatening me too." I pause. "By going after you. That dude I confronted in your office was one of The Shepherd's guys."

Her face clouds with fear. "How do you know that?"

"Apache connected him to the guy who was casing Donna's house. Because of that, I had Donna take Brianna to stay with her girlfriend in Lancaster for a few weeks."

"Oh, so you thought it was fine to tell Donna what was up, but not me? I asked you more than once what was going on and you said nothing. Is that the reason you've been staying at my place all the time? Because you knew The Shepherd might try to come after me?"

I nod.

"So you lied to me. Again."

I don't respond.

"You didn't think I deserved to know what was going on? At least for my own safety?"

"You were under a lot of pressure from Graylin's case. Besides, I was watching out for you and I had somebody else looking out too."

"But why didn't you tell *me* what was going on?"

"Because I knew you'd freak out." I inhale. "Like I said, you've been crazy busy with Graylin's case. I wanted to solve the problem without you ever finding out there was a problem."

"Nice job on that plan."

I turn and look out of the passenger window.

"Look, Dre, I made the decision to stay with you despite your past because you told me all of that was behind you."

"And it is. I haven't—"

"I understand that what The Shepherd decides to do is not within your control. I don't blame you for my office being trashed. I blame you for not being honest with me about what was going on. This is the same problem we've had over and over and over again. You trying to be Superman and not being truthful with me."

"I thought I could handle it. Shut it down. And I will."

"How?"

I look away.

"You're not trying to go after him in prison, are you?"

"I can't spend the rest of my life looking over my shoulder."

"So what are you going to do?"

"You don't wanna know."

She stares at me. "You're right. I don't." She throws open the car door and starts a brisk walk back toward the building.

I go after her, grab her by the arm and spin her around. "I'm going to handle this."

"How? By having somebody kill him in prison so you can end up there too?"

"That's not going to happen."

"Which part? Having somebody kill him or you ending up in prison? What are you planning to do, Dre?"

"I'm going to handle my business. That's all you need to know."

"I'm done. I can't have this craziness in my life. We never should've gotten back together!"

We stand there, eye-to-eye, saying nothing.

"I'm going to protect you," I tell her. "So you don't need to worry about anything."

"Really?" she snickers. "I feel so safe right now. Since the price is on your head, I guess breaking up with you will solve all of my problems. Maybe you should put the word out on the street that we're no longer together."

Angela turns and walks away, and I let her.

CHAPTER 54

The day after my interview with Crayvon, I decide to return to his street to nose around Kennedy's house. I need to figure out how someone took that picture through her bedroom window.

I'm leaning toward siding with Graylin that Crayvon was the one who set him up. I haven't shared this with Angela or Jenny yet. I'd like to have something a little more concrete than a gut feeling before I finger Crayvon as our guy.

I park my Prius a few houses east of Kennedy's house and climb out carrying a clipboard and my Nikon. If anyone asks, I'm a photographer hired by a local builder to take pictures of homes in the area. The builder wants to make sure his new construction stays consistent with the neighborhood.

I approach Kennedy's house and knock lightly on the front door. When I get no answer, I ring the doorbell. To my relief, no one answers. I know from the pictures on that real estate site that the bedrooms are facing the back of the house. I walk around to the side and see a gate leading into the backyard. I check to see if it's locked, but the latch opens easily.

After gazing over my shoulder to make sure no one is watching, I squeeze through the gate, waiting a second or two to make sure the Carlyles don't have a vicious guard dog before going all the way inside. I snap a wide shot of the backyard, take a couple pictures of the two bedroom windows and scurry back out.

I'm almost at the end of the driveway when I notice a young girl sitting on the steps of a house across the street. I wave. The girl waves back.

"What's your name?" I ask, after crossing the street.

"Taisha."

"Why aren't you in school today?"

"I had a bad asthma attack this morning. But I'm better now. What were you doing in Kennedy's backyard?"

I wish the girl hadn't seen that. Something tells me she won't buy my spiel about new construction, so I act like a politician and pretend I didn't hear the question. "Do you know Kennedy Carlyle?"

"Yep."

"Since Kennedy lives right across the street, she must be a good friend of yours?"

The girl puckers her lips with attitude. "We used to be best friends, but not no more. Now LaShay is her only friend. But I don't care. Kennedy's being homeschooled now. I bet she's too embarrassed to go back to school since everybody's talking about that naked picture of her."

"So you go to Marcus Prep?"

"No. You have to be rich to go there."

"Then how do you know about the picture?"

"Because everybody was talking about it in my Sunday school class."

"Where do you go to Sunday school?"

"Greater Mount Calvary."

"Did you see the picture?"

"Nope. I didn't wanna see it. You sure ask a lot of questions. You must be a private investigator working for Graylin. He goes to my church too."

I nod. This little girl is sharp.

"Do you know anybody who saw the picture?"

"Yeah, lots of people. It was all over Instagram. But it's gone now."

I don't buy her claim that she didn't want to see it. Since she knows that it's no longer on Instagram, that means she must've at least searched for it.

"Does anybody at your Sunday school know who took it?"

"Nope." She pauses. "But I do."

My heart skips three beats. "So who took it?"

"Crayvon." She points up the street. "He lives in that yellow house with the red car in the driveway."

"How do you know Crayvon took it?"

"Because I saw them sneaking into Kennedy's backyard like you did a minute ago."

"Them who?"

"Graylin and Crayvon."

"If both of them went back there, how do you know Crayvon was the one who took it?"

"I just do."

"Do you remember which day it was?"

"I think it was Wednesday. Graylin got arrested on Friday."

"Did you tell anybody?"

"Nope. I didn't want to get them in trouble. Nobody likes Kennedy. She acts like that's her real hair, but it's not. It's just a three-hundred-dollar weave that looks like real hair."

Kennedy's weave is not something I want to know about. "What time of day was it?"

"Hmmm," Taisha puts a finger to her chin. "Around five o'clock maybe. It wasn't dark yet."

"Do you know how long they were back there?"

"About five minutes. They both ran out laughing."

I can't believe I stumbled upon this witness. I'm so stunned my mind goes blank.

"I hope you have some more questions for me. Otherwise, you're not that good of an investigator."

I laugh. "Well, help me out. What other questions should I be asking you?"

Taisha smiles deviously. "You should ask me if I saw anybody else go back into Kennedy's backyard that same day after Crayvon and Graylin came out."

"Did you?"

"Yep?"

"Who?"

"Crayvon. And this time, Graylin wasn't with him. I bet you anything Crayvon took that picture and is trying to pin it on Graylin. Graylin's nice. He always says hi to me. Crayvon's the one who would do something like that. Not Graylin."

"Tai, who are you talking to out there?" A woman opens the screen door and steps onto the porch.

"Hi, my name is Mei." I'm worried that this woman won't like the idea of a stranger talking to her daughter. "I'm an investigator hired by Graylin Alexander's attorneys. He's the boy—"

"I know who he is. His family goes to my church. It's a shame what they're doing to that child."

"I didn't get your name," I say.

"Betty. Betty Taylor. And I guess you've met my daughter Taisha. She's quite a little talker."

"Yes, she is. She gave me some information that could be very important to Graylin's defense."

"Oh, did she?" Betty says with raised eyebrows.

"Tai, why don't you go inside and wash your hands? We'll be eating in a minute."

Betty waits until Taisha is inside and motions me back down the walkway. I assume to make sure Taisha doesn't overhear us.

"I don't know what Taisha told you, but whatever she said, I'd take it with a grain of salt. She's my foster daughter. A very troubled kid. Half of what comes out of her mouth is pure fantasy. I've had dozens of foster children over the years, but I've never had one who lies as much as this one."

I'm not sure what to say. "She told me she saw Crayvon sneaking into Kennedy's backyard a couple of days before Graylin was arrested." I decide not to mention the part about Graylin going in with him earlier. "Did she tell you that?"

"No, and I wouldn't put any stock in it. She lies the way you and I breathe. She can't help it. I think it's a cry for attention."

"Taisha said she and Kennedy use to be best friends. Is that true?"

"Yes. You know how teenagers are. Friends one day, enemies the next. Taisha took it pretty hard when Kennedy stopped inviting her over. Once she became friends with that other girl—I can't think of her name."

"LaShay?"

"Yes, LaShay. She all but stopped speaking to Taisha."

If Taisha told the truth about that, why can't she also be telling the truth about Crayvon? I've interviewed tons of people. Liars often display red flags, like not making eye contact, excessive blinking or shifting their eyes to the left or right. I picked up no such flags from Taisha.

"I think I'd sense it if Taisha wasn't telling me the truth," I say, unwilling to disregard the goldmine of information she'd given me.

"Oh, no you wouldn't." Betty rests a hand on her hip and smiles. "When it comes to telling lies, Taisha is very, very good at it."

CHAPTER 55

The Shepherd

I haven't had a decent night's sleep since Oaktown's arrival at The Low. I have nightmares about someone breaking into my cell and shanking me. I woke up this morning dripping with sweat, patting my body for stab wounds.

Now Oaktown is going around telling everybody I'm a chomo and that I trafficked Blaze's daughter. I used to be someone respected around here. Now other inmates despise me.

All of my efforts to find someone willing to take on Oaktown came up empty. I've finally admitted to myself that I only have one option. If I want to stay alive, I have to go to the hole. But I refuse to go there as a snitch.

I leave Willie a message letting him know that he won't be able to contact me for a while. I hide my phone in a ceiling vent in the Education Department and prepare myself for what I have to do.

Fortunately, I understand the culture of criminals. Most are small-minded bullies underneath the bravado. They're like an undefeated boxer who's never taken a real punch. Once somebody lands one, he falls like raindrops. I convince myself that's how it will be with Oaktown.

All week I've been hibernating in my room, avoiding Oaktown. But today, I head to the chow hall with my head held high. I'm sitting down with my food when he walks over.

"Ain't no money on my books this week?" he says. "Where's my money at?"

I take a long time to respond. "Can't you see I'm eating?"

He chuckles. So do the handful of inmates sitting around me.

Oaktown grins and looks around. "Did you hear what this chomo just said to me?"

"Who you calling a chomo?"

Before he can react, from my seated position I head-butt him in the groin. He doubles over and falls to the floor. That's when I hop up and start stomping on his head.

In seconds, three C.O.s converge on us. One of them pulls me away and cuffs me.

"You're going to the hole!" he yells at me.

I continue to resist as the C.O. drags me away while Oaktown lies curled up on the ground, wincing in pain.

The inmates are all staring at me. I see respect in their eyes and that pleases me. I could have done something less dramatic to get put in the hole, like failing to show up for a count or going off on a C.O., but I had to restore my rep.

And now I've done just that.

CHAPTER 56

Angela

Jenny and I are taking a pizza break in her office. We've been bouncing around ideas about Graylin's defense for the past three hours. Earlier in the day, Jenny got a call from a friend who passed on some information he thought she should know. Kennedy's parents are using their political connections to get the book thrown at Graylin.

I'm not naïve, but the news stuns me. That's not how the justice system is supposed to work. Graylin is a good kid. He's not a sexual predator and I'm going to do everything in my power to make sure he's not branded as one. There's no way I can tell Gus what the Carlyles have done because he'd likely try to confront them again.

The only good news we've had lately is that our new prosecutor, Lorelei Sullivan, is a straight shooter.

"I haven't been up against her before," I tell Jenny, "but I checked around and she has a good rep. No oversized ego and she's not into dirty tricks or hiding evidence. If something happens mid-case that says the defendant didn't do it, she'll readily dismiss the case."

"That's good to hear."

Jenny looks over at me as if there's something she wants to say.

I wait her out.

"So when are we going to deal with the elephant in the room?" Jenny asks.

"And what elephant would that be?"

"The break-in at your office. By the way you pulled Dre out of there, I assume it had some connection to him."

I remain silent.

"Look," she pushes, "we'll be spending a lot of time together trying this case. If somebody has a beef with you or Dre, I could end up in the line of fire. I need to know what's going on."

She's right, of course. "How much do you know about why I left the U.S. Attorney's Office?"

"A little."

"Yeah, right. The situation with my ex was all over the news. I'm sure you Googled me just like I did you."

"Okay, okay," Jenny admits. "I know a lot. You were engaged to some judge who was abusive. Then you hooked up with Dre. When it came out that he was a drug dealer, you resigned from your job."

"So you *do* know a lot. Except my boyfriend is an *ex*-drug dealer."

"So is Dre's past connected to the break-in?"

"Kind of. What wasn't reported in the media, at least not linking me or Dre to the case, was the conviction of a pimp named Rodney Merriweather. Everybody called him The Shepherd. He kidnapped Dre's niece Brianna. Dre testified against him in court and he got locked up for trafficking children. Now it appears that from behind prison walls, he's put a contract out on Dre. The trashing of my office was really a message for Dre."

"Oh, wow." Jenny leans back in her chair. "This sounds like something right out of *Power.*

I laugh. "You watch that?"

"Yep. I love it."

"Me too."

Neither one of us says anything for a couple of minutes.

"So what's Dre going to do?"

"I don't know. And I don't want to know. We're not on speaking terms right now, even though we're kinda living together."

"How are you *kinda* living together?"

"Dre's been sleeping at my place. He's concerned that The Shepherd's goons may come after me."

"But why aren't you speaking to him? It doesn't sound like he caused any of this."

"He wasn't honest with me. And this isn't the first time that's happened."

"Men always think they can handle things themselves. For you to date him knowing his past, he must be a special guy."

I shrug. "So now that you know I could be taken out at any moment, are you still okay trying this case with me?"

"It'll take more than a potential hit from a prison inmate to keep me from clearing Graylin's name. But from now on, if we're working any late nights, let's do it at my office."

We both laugh as Jenny's cell phone chimes, signaling a text. Her face lights up as she reads the screen.

"You win the lottery?"

"Perhaps." She starts typing on her phone. "Mei wants to know if it's okay to drop by."

"This late? Please tell me it's good news. I can't handle any more bad news."

"The best news ever," Jenny beams. "Mei thinks she knows who took that picture of Kennedy."

CHAPTER 57

The Shepherd

After a week in the hole, I'm beginning to feel like my old self again. My meditation and yoga practice have made my situation bearable. Being beyond the clutches of Oaktown has brought me nothing but peace.

I was even able to find a replacement for C.O. Sims. Barker Phillips is a disgruntled correctional officer with twenty-plus years on the job who feels he should've been promoted over his white colleagues years ago. Slipping me some decent food and getting me access to a cell phone is his way of sticking it to the system while making some extra cash on the side.

I finally have a chance to call Willie.

"I've been waiting for your call," he says anxiously. "That project went very well."

That brings a smile to my face.

"And, um, well…that Apache dude dropped by again. He left another message for you." I hear him take a deep breath. "But I didn't understand what he was talking about. He said, *Enjoy the blaze.* What does that mean?"

An intense urge to slam my fist against the wall rattles through me. But I cannot let Willie detect that I have lost control of my emotions. I feign a laugh. This all makes sense now. My guys would never knowingly snatch Blaze's daughter. Dre Thomas planted that lie.

I'm about to give Willie an order when I hear footsteps.

It's C.O. Phillips. His shift's about to end and he needs to retrieve the phone before his replacement comes on duty. I hand it over and sit there, contemplating how to address the news from Willie.

Later that night, just as I've fallen asleep. I hear my cell door open. Two inmates are standing in the doorway, just behind a correctional officer I don't recognize.

"We're here to deliver a message from Oaktown," says one of the men, who's half the size of the other one. "He needs his money."

I'm still groggy and the words don't compute.

The C.O. lets the men inside and closes the door.

The big man grabs me from the bed and hurls me headfirst against the wall. "You better not scream!" he yells as I crumple to the floor.

I'm in so much pain I can barely breathe, much less find the strength to scream. He lifts me back up by the throat and slams me into the wall again. My entire face puffs up like a volleyball. I can no longer see out of my right eye.

"I have money! Please don't hurt me. I can pay you." My voice sounds garbled and blood spurts from my mouth.

The big man lets me fall to the ground again, but the other one pulls me right back up to my feet.

"We don't like chomos," says the smaller man, who seems to possess super-human strength. He has me pinned to the wall with a single hand.

I try to break free, but the more I struggle, the harder he smashes my face against the cold cement wall.

"No! Please don't hurt me!" I scream out of the side of my mouth. "Why are you doing this?"

"We deliverin' a message from Oaktown," one of them says. I don't know which one because I can't see out of either eye now. "He wants you to know that you can run, but you can't hide, even in the hole."

I feel a fist to my stomach and a pain more intense than anything I've ever felt shoots a raging fire through my body. They start tossing me around like a rag doll, alternately, punching me and slamming me into the wall.

All I can do is pray that I pass out.

CHAPTER 58

Angela

Graylin's preliminary hearing starts in fifty-two minutes. Jenny, Graylin and I march into the Criminal Courts Building in downtown Los Angeles like soldiers heading off to war. In a way, we are.

If things don't go our way at the hearing and the case proceeds to trial, all isn't lost thanks to Mei. The information she got from Taisha about Crayvon going into Kennedy's backyard alone lifted our spirits. All we need to raise reasonable doubt is the possibility that someone *other* than Graylin took that picture of Kennedy. Of course, the information about Graylin also being in Kennedy's backyard does concern us. We haven't discussed it with him yet for fear of distracting him. We need Graylin one hundred percent focused on the prelim.

"You ready to testify," Jenny asks as we all clear the metal detectors.

"Yep," Graylin says, smiling. He's dressed in one of his church suits with a light-blue tie. His hair has been freshly cut and he's even wearing a lemony-smelling cologne. So much of it, in fact, that it stings my nose.

Jenny squeezes his shoulder. "Don't forget that Angela's going to lead you every step of the way. Just like we practiced."

"I know," Graylin says, showing not a lick of nervousness. "I told you, I got this."

I press the elevator button. "And I want short answers," I remind him. "Not long ones. And remember that the prosecutor is going to be very nice when she asks you questions. But she's not on your side. So listen very carefully to her questions before you answer."

"Don't worry, Ms. Angela. I watched three episodes of *Law & Order* last night. I know how prosecutors try to trick people. She's not going to trip me up. I'm too smart for that."

It's a quick ride to the fifth floor. As we step off the elevator, Graylin suddenly clutches my arm with the desperation of a drowning swimmer.

"What's the matter?" I say.

His face is ashen and his lips are quivering. I follow his gaze and see two uniformed police officers sitting on a bench down the hallway.

Graylin's grasp on my arm tightens even more. "Those are the cops who arrested me!"

He darts behind my back, almost tripping me. I try to pull my arm free, but Graylin won't let go.

"Calm down," Jenny says. "They can't do anything to you."

"Are they going to be in the courtroom looking at me when I testify?" he whimpers.

"No," Jenny assures him. "They'll have to wait outside."

The tension doesn't leave Graylin's face. He's been upbeat since getting out of juvenile hall. The obnoxious teenager who disrupted the fitness hearing quickly morphed back into the sweet kid I know and love. Today, he's like a frightened rabbit.

"Everything's going to be fine." I free my aching arm and throw it around Graylin's shoulder. "Don't even look their way."

Jenny and I surround him, blocking his view of the cops as we walk past them.

Dre and Gus are seated on the back row of the gallery. I'm glad to see that the Carlyles aren't here.

Graylin stops to give his worried father a hug. Dre hugs him too. Graylin's relationship with Gus has definitely been fractured. I can see the weight of Gus' fear for his son written all over his face. I swear he's aged a few years since Graylin's arrest.

We all take a seat at the defense table with Graylin sitting between us.

"When is the jury coming in?" Graylin asks.

Jenny and I exchange a cryptic glance. We've told Graylin there's no jury for this hearing.

"This is just a hearing where the prosecutor has to convince the judge there's enough evidence to take your case to trial, remember?" Jenny says. "So there's no jury. The judge will decide everything."

"Oh, yeah." Graylin slaps his forehead. "I forgot. Sorry."

The prosecutor walks in, sets her files down on the table, then comes over to introduce herself. Lorelei Sullivan is short with fiery-red hair and a friendly smile. She conveys the kind of self-assurance that would make you automatically gravitate toward her at a cocktail party.

A rear door opens and Judge Calvin Fuller takes the bench. "I understand we're here for a preliminary hearing," the judge says after we've stated our appearances for the record.

He's a good draw for us. A fiftyish, South Central native and Hastings Law School grad, he's smart, socially conscious and knows from experience that all cops aren't good cops. He's tall with salt-and-pepper hair and a distinctive goatee.

"Call your first witness, Ms. Sullivan," Judge Fuller says.

I interrupt. "The defendant also has a suppression motion, Your Honor."

Judge Fuller stares down at the papers on his desk.

"Okay, I see that here."

"We'd like an instruction from the court limiting the prosecution's questioning of the defendant to the Fourth and Fifth Amendment issues raised in our motion to suppress."

The judge nods and looks over at the prosecutor. "Got that? Limit your cross of the defendant to the factual issues identified in the motion."

"Understood," Sullivan says.

It's risky to put a defendant on the stand in a criminal case, even at a prelim. But without Graylin's testimony, there's no way we can show his rights were violated.

I expect Sullivan to call one of the cops who arrested Graylin, but instead, Gino Rivera, a young Hispanic boy, is her first witness.

"Who's that?" I whisper to Graylin.

"I don't know him, Ms. Angela. I never saw him before."

As it turns out, the kid is a current resident at juvenile hall. He testifies that according to Little Slice, Graylin was in on the plan to threaten Kennedy to drop the case. This kid would never be allowed to testify at trial because his testimony is all hearsay. But hearsay is admissible at a prelim.

Graylin insists the kid is lying and is about to jump out of his skin. Rivera's testimony doesn't freak me out nearly as much as it should. The fact that Sullivan didn't call Little Slice to testify tells me he won't back up this story. Without Little Slice or someone else tying Graylin directly to the threats against Kennedy, the prosecution won't be able to prove the witness intimidation charge. I spend a few minutes eliciting testimony that the boy has no direct evidence of anything he testified to and that Little Slice—who's been in and out of juvie since he was ten—is a liar and braggart.

Sullivan's next witness is L.A.P.D. Officer Alan Chin. The bailiff steps outside and escorts Chin into the courtroom. Sullivan asks only a handful of questions about his background, then moves to the salient points.

"When you showed up at Marcus Preparatory Academy on May tenth, what was your understanding of the reason the police were called?"

"The principal received a report that the defendant had a naked picture of another student, Kennedy Carlyle, on his phone. Child pornography is a very serious issue these days. The report also said that the defendant threatened to post the picture all over the internet to embarrass the girl."

"What happened when you arrived at the school?"

"The defendant was waiting for us in the principal's office. We asked him if he wanted to speak to us and he agreed, so we took him into the principal's conference room."

Graylin is squirming like a worm, whispering to us that the cop is lying on him. Jenny is trying to calm him down so I can concentrate on taking notes for my cross.

"Did you identify yourself as a police officer?" Sullivan asks.

"Yes."

"Was anyone else with you?"

"Yes, my partner, Officer Fenton."

"What happened once you went into the conference room?"

"We told—I mean—we asked Graylin to take a seat. I asked him if he had a naked picture of Kennedy Carlyle on his phone and he lied and said no. He also lied to the principal when she asked him about it."

"Did you ask him if you could look at his phone?"

"Yes. He lied again and said it was in his locker, but then the phone started ringing."

"Then what happened?"

"I asked him if I could see his phone and he said okay. So he put in his password and handed it to my partner. Fenton didn't see anything on it, but when I checked his deleted pictures, I found the picture. He probably deleted it right before we got there."

"Objection," I say. "Lack of foundation, calls for speculation."

"Sustained."

"Could you describe the picture?"

"It appeared to be a young girl in a bedroom. She was standing and was completely naked."

"Did you later confirm the identity of the girl in the picture?"

"Yes, the principal confirmed that it was Kennedy Carlyle, a classmate of the defendant."

"When the defendant voluntarily entered the conference room to speak with you, was he under arrest?"

"No."

"So he was free to leave at any time?"

"Of course."

"At any time during your meeting with the defendant, did you tell him that he couldn't leave the room?"

"No. And he never once asked to leave."

"And did you force him to hand over his phone?"

"No. He willingly gave it to us."

"And how long did the interview last?"

"Fifteen, twenty minutes, tops."

"No further questions," Sullivan says.

I'm standing even before the judge gives me the go-ahead.

"Officer Chin, since you knew that you were being called to Marcus Prep because a student allegedly had a naked picture on his phone, did you obtain a search warrant for my client's phone before showing up at the school?"

"No."

"Did you read my client his Miranda rights before commencing your interrogation?"

"It wasn't an interrogation. We were just talking to him."

"Did you read him his Miranda rights?"

"No. I didn't need to because he wasn't under arrest."

"Did you examine the so-called report that my client had a naked picture on his phone?"

He shrugs. "Yeah. The principal showed the note to me."

"Was that note signed by anyone?"

"No."

"And you felt you had probable cause to interrogate my client based on a simple anonymous note?"

"It wasn't an interrogation. Anyway, we didn't need probable cause since your client agreed to talk to us."

"Isn't it correct that you ordered my client into the conference room?"

"No. We asked him if he wanted to talk to us and he agreed."

"What were your exact words?"

Officer Chin repositions himself in the chair. "It was something like, *Would you like to talk with us?* And he said, *Okay.*"

I hear the muffled voice of Graylin behind me and I'm praying Jenny can quiet him down.

"Did you identify yourself as a police officer?"

"Yeah. I said, *I'm Officer Chin.* And I was also in uniform, so there's no doubt he knew."

"Did you tell Graylin he didn't have to go into the conference room to talk to you?"

"No, but he was free to decline."

"You testified that Graylin wasn't under arrest. So was he free to leave the conference room?"

"Yes."

"Did you tell him that?"

"I'm not sure. I may have."

"Didn't Graylin tell you that his father told him not to talk to the police without his permission?"

"I think he may have mentioned that."

"How many times?"

"At least once."

"Wasn't it more like four or five times?"

"No, I don't think it was that many."

"So why did you continue to question him after he told you that his father told him not to speak to the police without his permission?"

"We're only required to suspend questioning if someone asks for an attorney and he didn't do that. And, like I said, it wasn't like he was under arrest or anything. If he didn't want to talk to us, he could've left."

"So you think a fourteen-year-old boy locked in a conference room with two police officers would think he could just get up and walk out?"

"Well, he could."

"Was he also free to leave school grounds anytime he felt like it?"

"Objection, calls for speculation," Sullivan says.

Judge Fuller takes two beats before responding. "Overruled. The witness can answer."

Chin is bright enough to follow Sullivan's lead and avoid speculating. "I don't know the school's rules. I only know that the defendant was free to leave the conference room."

"Did you pound the table with your fist and say, *Give me the damn phone?*"

"I asked for the phone. I don't recall pounding the table, but I do recall him telling me his phone was in his locker, which was a lie and—"

That's not what I asked you, asshole.

"Officer Chin, my question was whether you pounded the table with your fist and said, *Give me the damn phone.*"

"I don't recall."

Graylin's voice disrupts my focus. "But he's lying on me, Ms. Jenny!"

I turn around and give him the meanest look I can muster. I'm grateful the judge didn't hear him.

"Isn't it correct that you demanded that my client give you his password?"

"No, we didn't demand anything."

"Did Graylin type in his password?"

"I don't remember."

"And for the record, you have no proof that Graylin deleted the picture from his phone that day or any other day, correct?"

He shrugs.

"I didn't hear your answer, Officer Chin."

"It's his phone. He must've done it."

"But you have no proof of that, correct?"

"Yeah."

"I have no further questions."

As soon as I return to the defense table, Graylin grabs my arm. "He's lying, Ms. Angela," he says, near tears. "He made me give him the phone! I didn't know I could leave!"

"I know. I need you to calm down. Getting upset won't help your case. The judge knows he's lying." *At least I hope he does.*

Sullivan doesn't do a redirect, so Officer Chin is dismissed. The bailiff calls Officer Fenton from the hallway. Sullivan only asks him enough questions to back up Officer Chin's statements, then hands him over to me.

"Officer Fenton, didn't my client repeatedly say that his father had instructed him not to talk to the police without his permission?"

"Yes, he did mention that."

"How many times?"

"I'm not quite sure."

"At least three?"

"Probably."

"At least four times?"

"Maybe."

"So if your partner testified that it was only one time, you would disagree with that, correct?"

His shoulders hunch and his eyes dart toward the prosecutor. "It's hard to remember the exact number."

"But it was at least four times, correct?"

"Yeah."

"And why didn't you stop your interrogation when he told you he couldn't talk to you without his father's permission?"

"It wasn't an interrogation and he wasn't under arrest. It wasn't like he was invoking his Miranda rights. He never asked for an attorney."

"Do you think a fourteen-year-old-boy dragged into a conference room by two police officers would know to invoke his Miranda rights?"

Before Sullivan can object, Fenton does it for her.

"We didn't *drag* him anywhere."

"How close were you sitting to my client while you were interrogating him?"

"I was sitting next to him."

"And your chair was turned sideways so you were facing the side of his body, correct?"

"Yes."

"And your knee was touching his leg, correct?

Officer Fenton stutters. "I-I don't remember."

"You don't remember touching his leg?"

"Well, I may have."

"Did Officer Chin pound the table with his fist during the interrogation of Graylin?"

"He might have."

"He might have or he did?"

"Yeah, I guess he did."

"Do you think Graylin was intimidated by that?"

Sullivan jumps in before he can answer. "Objection, calls for speculation."

"Sustained," the judge says.

"Did Graylin look scared when Officer Chin pounded the table?"

"Yeah, a little. I guess."

"Didn't he start crying?"

Fenton shrugs again. "Yeah, after we found out he was lying about having his phone with him."

"And didn't he even wet his pants?"

"Yeah, but we weren't aware of that until we put him in the squad car."

"When Officer Chin pounded the table with his fist, did he say to Graylin, *Give me the damn phone?*"

"Yeah, something like that."

"And you typed in Graylin's password, not him, correct?"

"Yeah, but he gave it to us."

"I have no further questions, Your Honor."

I take my seat. Jenny nods approvingly. Graylin's knee is bouncing, probably because he knows what's coming next.

Sullivan doesn't do a redirect and tells the judge she has no further witnesses.

Judge Fuller turns to me. "Call your first witness."

I say a quick prayer and return to my feet. "The defense calls Graylin Alexander."

Chapter 59

Angela

As Graylin trudges toward the witness stand, I pray he sticks to our script. It's always risky to have a defendant testify at the prelim because his statements can be used against him at trial. Having a child witness, who can be easily manipulated by a skilled prosecutor, is doubly risky. I plan to zero in on the police interrogation and get him off the stand as quickly as possible.

Graylin looks like a miniature country preacher sitting in the witness box. His tightly clasped hands highlight his nervousness.

"Did your teacher take you to the principal's office on May tenth?" I begin.

"Yes, ma'am."

"Did you believe you could say no when your teacher told you she was taking you to the principal's office?"

"No, ma'am. I have to do what my teachers tell me to do or I'll get in trouble."

"Did two police officers come into the principal's office while you were there?"

"Yes."

"What did they say to you?"

"The Asian one, Officer Chin, told me to go into the principal's conference room."

"Did you think you could disobey his order?"

Sullivan is on her feet. "Objection to the use of the word _order_."

The judge grunts. "Sustained."

I rephrase my question. "When Officer Chin told you to go into the principal's conference room, did you think you could refuse to go?"

"No, ma'am. I had to do what the police officer told me to do. Just like I have to obey my teachers."

"Did the police officers tell you that you didn't have to go into the principal's office if you didn't want to?"

"No."

"Did they close the door when you went into the principal's office?"

"Yes."

"Did you think you could leave?"

"No. I had to stay there until they said I could go. I thought I was under arrest."

"When they started asking you questions, did you tell them you didn't want to talk to them?"

"Yes. I kept telling them that my dad told me not to speak to the police without his permission. But they ignored what I was saying and kept asking me questions."

"How many times did you tell them that your dad told you not to speak to the police without his permission?"

"A lot."

That wasn't the answer we had rehearsed.

"Do you remember how many times?"

There's a flash of recognition in his eyes as he suddenly recalls our prep session. "At least four or five times."

"So when Officer Chin testified that it was only once, that wasn't the truth?"

"No, it wasn't. He said a lot of things that weren't true like—"

I hold up my hand. We instructed Graylin to follow my lead and not jump ahead of me. We also told him that if I raise my hand, that means he isn't following my instructions.

"Hold on a minute. We'll get there."

Graylin lowers his head and tucks in his chin. I smile at him, so he's not devastated by my rebuke.

"When the police officers asked you for your phone, did you think you could refuse to give it to them?"

"No, ma'am. That's why I didn't tell the truth and told them it was in my locker because I didn't want to give it to them. But when it started ringing, Officer Chin pounded the table with his fist and said, *Give me the damn phone.*"

"How did you feel when Officer Chin pounded the table with his fist and said, *Give me the damn phone*?" I plan to repeat the cop's command as many times as I can.

"I was scared. I knew I had to do what he said."

"Where were the two officers sitting?"

"Officer Chin was sitting on the other side of the table, but Officer Fenton was sitting on my left, really close to me. He was facing me and his knee was bumping my thigh. Like on *The First 48* when they're in a tiny room interrogating somebody trying to get them to confess."

I give Graylin a look. We don't need his embellishment.

"How did that make you feel?"

"Scared."

"I have no further questions."

Sullivan walks over to the witness box and stands even closer to Graylin than I was.

"Good afternoon, Graylin, my name is Lorelei Sullivan and I'm the prosecutor. I only have a few questions for you. Do you watch legal shows on TV?"

"Yes."

"Have you ever seen *Law & Order*?"

"Yes."

"What about *Boston Legal*?"

"Yes. But *Law & Order* is a lot better."

Jesus. He's letting his guard down already.

"And you already mentioned *The First 48*. So you're familiar with Miranda rights, correct?"

"Yes. That's when you have the right to remain silent."

My stomach flips. We instructed Graylin to answer yes or no to Sullivan's questions whenever possible. Nothing more.

"That's right. Did you ever tell the officers that you didn't want to talk to them?"

"Um, yes. But not in those exact words. I told them that my dad told me not to speak to the police without his permission. So that's the same thing."

Sullivan wasn't expecting that response. She moves on.

"When Officer Chin asked for your phone, what did you think would happen if you didn't give it to him?"

Jenny glances over at me. We're both holding our breath.

"That he would arrest me."

"Okay, so then you didn't think you were already under arrest when you were in the principal's conference room, correct?"

Graylin squints and does exactly what we told him to do if a question confused him. He pauses and thinks about his response before speaking.

"No, ma'am, that's not correct. He didn't tell me I was under arrest yet, but I knew I couldn't leave the room, so that's the same thing as being under arrest."

"But you said you thought the officers would arrest you if you didn't give them the phone. So it doesn't sound like you thought you were under arrest yet."

Graylin sits taller in the chair. "What I meant to say is that I thought they would take me to jail. I knew I was already under arrest since they had me locked up in the conference room with them."

You go, boy! Jenny and I trade a glance that's the equivalent of a high-five.

Sullivan rolls her eyes and plows ahead.

"When you first sat down to talk to the two officers, you wanted to explain your side of the story so you wouldn't get in trouble, right?"

Graylin pauses. "Um, yes."

I wince.

"But not until after I spoke to my dad," Graylin quickly adds.

He's following our directions better than some of my adult clients.

"Now, didn't you lie to the police about having a naked picture—"

Like twin Jack in the boxes, Jenny and I shoot to our feet, shouting in unison, "Objection!"

"That question is outside the scope of our motion," I say. "The prosecutor is violating the court's instruction."

Judge Fuller gives Sullivan a chiding look. "Sustained. Don't test me, counselor." Then he turns to the defense table. "I only need objections from one of you at a time."

Sullivan steps even closer to Graylin and rests her forearm on the corner of the witness box. "You're a good student, aren't you, Graylin?"

"Yes, I get mostly A's."

"Would you say that you're mature for your age?"

Graylin squints. "Um, everybody says I'm big for my age. Is that what you mean?"

I don't like the path Sullivan is heading down.

"Not exactly. Do you consider yourself to be very responsible?"

"Yes."

"Give me some examples of how you're responsible."

I tap my fingers on the desk. We didn't prep Graylin for this line of questioning. I get to my feet.

"Your Honor, I object to the question as beyond the scope of our motion."

Sullivan doesn't wait for the judge's response. "I disagree. The defendant's maturity level is directly relevant to whether his actions were voluntary."

"Overruled," the judge says.

Sullivan turns back to Graylin. "Can you give me some examples of how you're mature?"

"Um," Graylin looks out at me, but I can't help him. "Um, I do my chores and my homework without being told. I babysit my little cousin, Keesha." He stops and looks up at the ceiling. "I go with my granny to the grocery store and help her with the shopping. I also put a schedule on her calendar so she knows when to take her blood pressure and thyroid pills. Stuff like that."

"Wow, that's wonderful," Sullivan says, exaggerating her praise. "When you went into the conference room with Officers Chin and Fenton, did they lock the door?"

Graylin pauses. "I don't know if they locked it, but they closed it."

"Did the officers ever tell you that you couldn't leave the room?"

"No. But the way police are always shooting innocent black men, I knew I had to do everything they told me to do, which means I couldn't leave the room. And I had to give them my phone when they asked for it."

I can't help but smile. He's not supposed to go off script, but that little zinger was fine with me.

Sullivan frowns and walks back over to the prosecution table to look at her notes. After a few seconds, she says, "No further questions."

Graylin rushes off the stand and returns to his seat. "Did I do good, Ms. Angela?" he whispers.

"You did great. The best witness I've ever had. And I mean it."

"Ms. Evans, call your next witness," the judge says.

"That's it, Your Honor. I have no further witnesses."

"Let's take a ten-minute break," Judge Fuller says. "When we return, I'll hear brief oral arguments."

CHAPTER 60

The Shepherd

When I wake up, I have no idea what time it is or how long I've been lying on the hard cement floor. Every inch of my body is on fire. My head throbs and even blinking causes me intense pain. I can't swallow because my mouth is full of dried blood.

I try to stand, but I'm only able to crawl over to my bed. My knees feel like someone pounded them with a hammer. There's no way I can protect myself.

How did Dre Thomas orchestrate this?

An hour or so later, C.O. Phillips comes with my food. He takes one look at me through the bars and cringes. "What happened to you?"

"That C.O. on duty last night let two inmates in here to attack me! Oaktown sent them!"

He opens the door and steps inside. "You want to file a complaint?"

"You know I can't snitch! You have to protect me."

"I can't watch you every minute."

"I'll give you whatever you want! Please! I need your help!"

"Like I said, you wanna file a complaint?"

"That'll only make it worse. I'm supposed to be safe in here!"

"I don't know what to tell you."

"I don't understand why you won't help me. I can pay you. Don't let them kill me!"

Phillips sets my tray on the floor and turns to leave.

I sit up, wincing in pain. I have no choice. I have to use my final trump card.

"If I tell the warden about the cell phones, the drugs and everything else you sneak in here for inmates, you'll have a real problem on your hands. And that goes for your buddy Sims too. I suggest the two of you put your heads together and figure out how you're going to protect me."

The man's jaw tightens. "You shouldn't make threats you can't back up."

I can't back down now.

Oh, I can back them up," I tell him. "And if I have to, I will."

CHAPTER 61

Angela

As we wait to begin oral arguments, I now regret eating breakfast this morning, something I never do before an important court appearance. There's a strong possibility my scrambled eggs could end up splattered on the courtroom floor.

"You did great," Jenny tells me. "You got Fenton to contradict his partner more than once. That has to weigh heavily with the judge."

"We'll see."

When oral argument commences, I'm first up to bat.

"Your Honor, the defendant's motion to suppress should be granted for a number of reasons. First, the police officers conducted a custodial interrogation of the defendant and failed to read him his Miranda rights. Graylin Alexander is a fourteen-year-old kid. No child locked behind closed doors in his principal's private conference room, with two police officers sitting close to him, bumping his leg, cursing at him and pounding the table, would feel free to leave in such an intimidating situation."

Sullivan interrupts me. "Your Honor, there's no evidence that the door was locked."

I ignore her and keep going.

"In addition, contrary to Ms. Sullivan's claim, my client did not voluntarily agree to speak to the officers, nor did he just hand over his phone. He was clearly in police custody and should have been read his Miranda rights."

Judge Fuller interrupts. "So, Ms. Sullivan, what's your response? Was this a custodial interrogation?"

"No, Your Honor, the defendant was not in custody. The officers asked him to come into the room. They didn't order him in there and at no time was he told he couldn't leave or that he was under arrest."

"Your Honor," I continue, "my client was marched off to the principal's office by his teacher and then ordered into a conference room by the two officers. He wasn't given a choice. This was indeed a custodial interrogation."

When the judge doesn't say anything more on this point, I'm emboldened. "And even if he wasn't in custody, his actions weren't voluntary. My client stated—some four or five times—that he didn't want to talk to the officers without his father's permission. Still, they ignored his pleas and continued brow-beating him until he answered their questions."

Sullivan butts in. "Counsel is misstating the facts. The police officers didn't—"

I intentionally talk over her. "Nor did my client voluntarily give them his phone. The fact that he told them it was in his locker when it was actually in his pocket, shows that he didn't want to give it to them. Their actions in taking it, demanding his password, and looking through it constitute an unlawful search and seizure in violation of the Fourth Amendment. Any evidence they found is inadmissible as fruit of the poisonous tree."

Sullivan jumps back in.

"The officers did nothing improper here, Your Honor. What occurred in that conference room does not meet the level of a custodial interrogation because they didn't engage in any coercive behavior. The officers didn't physically harm the defendant. They questioned him for only fifteen minutes. They didn't deprive him of sleep or food. They didn't threaten that he was going to spend years in prison. And the defendant is a bright, mature fourteen-year-old. He takes care of his young cousin. He even helps his grandmother with her medicine. He knows how to speak up for himself. He could've very easily asked to leave the room or, better yet, he could've asked for an attorney. The defendant not only voluntarily gave the officers his cell phone, he even turned over his password. If he didn't want them to look at it, he could've refused."

"That's ridiculous," I say. "He's a child." I turn away from the judge and glare at Sullivan. "He didn't think he *had* a choice. Even an adult in his situation wouldn't have felt free to leave the room. My client wasn't even free to leave school grounds. He repeatedly told the police that he didn't want to speak to them without his father's permission. There would've been no need for him to say that over and over again if he wanted to speak to the police as you claim."

"Your Honor," Sullivan counters, "the courts have consistently held that a child's request for a parent is not the same as asking for an attorney. In any event, the defendant didn't ask for his father. He stated only that his father told him not to speak to the police without his permission. Yet he chose to disregard his father's wishes. There's no Fourth or Fifth Amendment violation here."

I'm looking at Judge Fuller, but he's not giving me any clues about where he stands. I take a breath and continue.

"I'd like to direct the court's attention to *J.D.B. v. North Carolina*, which is cited in our moving papers. That case involved a thirteen-year-old boy interrogated at school. The Supreme Court held that interrogations occurring on school grounds are inherently coercive in nature. The court also held that the police must take into account the age of a suspect when determining whether Miranda rights are warranted. No middle school student in the intimidating situation my client was in would feel free to leave."

"Your Honor," Sullivan fires back, "In *J.D.B.* the Supreme Court did not find interrogations of minors on school grounds *per se* coercive, as opposing counsel is trying to make out. I assert that—"

The judge taps his gavel. "Okay, counsel, I've heard enough. I'm ready to rule. You may be seated."

My legs are wobbling as I return to my chair. Jenny gives me a covert thumbs-up.

"In *J.D.B. v. North Carolina*," Judge Fuller begins, "the U.S. Supreme Court did indeed point out that children will often feel bound to submit to police questioning whereas an adult in the same circumstances would feel free to leave. The courts are clear, however, that even when a minor asks for a parent, that does not mean the minor has invoked his or her constitutional right to remain silent."

My stomach drops. Graylin looks over at me, his forehead etched with deep lines of confusion.

"While the defendant did say that his father told him not to talk to the police without his permission, he continued talking to them anyway, and even turned over his phone to them. On the issue of whether he acted voluntarily, I must side with the prosecution. I also don't find that the circumstances of the interrogation were sufficiently coercive to rise to the level of a custodial interrogation. The police did nothing to prevent the defendant from leaving the room. It was a relatively short interrogation and he wasn't deprived of sleep or food.

"As such, defense counsel's motion to suppress the defendant's statements, his phone and any evidence retrieved from the phone is denied. I also find that the prosecution has met its burden of demonstrating probable cause as to each of the charges filed against the defendant."

The judge rises and disappears into his chambers.

Graylin's lips are quivering as a tear rolls down his cheek. "The police lied on me, Ms. Angela. I didn't want to talk to them. They made me do it!"

"I know."

We walk toward the back of the courtroom and he rushes into his father's arms.

"You were really good up there," Dre says. "I couldn't follow all of that legal mumbo jumbo, but it sounded to me like the judge made the wrong call."

I want to fall into Dre's arms the same way Graylin collapsed into Gus'.

"Thanks," I say and brush past him out of the courtroom.

CHAPTER 62

Dre

With The Shepherd still on my ass and Angela giving me the cold shoulder, I decide to do something that feels good. I hit the road and head for Lancaster to hang out with my sister and Brianna. The ninety-minute drive is taking a lot longer. Normally, that would cause me stress, but I'm listening to some old school R&B that's helping me mellow out.

It irks me that Angela is ignoring me even though we're living under the same roof. You'd think she'd be grateful for my willingness to protect her. All I have to show for my gallantry is a stiff neck and a sore back from sleeping on her trendy-looking, hard-as-rocks couch. No matter how she treats me, until this thing with The Shepherd is a wrap, I ain't budging.

Once I get to Lancaster, I shoot the breeze with my sister and her friend for a while. Donna doesn't ask me anything about The Shepherd. That's her way. She'd rather pretend the problem doesn't exist. Then again, she knows me. There's no need to ask. If the threat had been eradicated, I would've told her it was safe to return home. I go into the backyard to look for my niece.

"Hey, Bree."

She runs over and jumps into my arms. Her excitement is precisely the lift I need.

"I'm working on a science project," she brags. Colorful sheets of construction paper are spread out all over an iron table. "I'm making the solar system."

"Looks good. So you're going to be a scientist?" Brianna scrunches up her face. "No. I hate science. I'm going to be a commentator on CNN so I can tell people what I think."

I chuckle. "Okay, that sounds like a winner."

"Is Graylin doing okay?" She picks up a pair of scissors.

I specifically asked my sister not to tell Brianna about Graylin's situation. Considering how overprotective she is, I'm surprised that she did.

"Your mother told you about Graylin?"

She glances toward the back door to the house and gives me a sheepish grin. "Nope. I heard her talking on the phone. She tries to keep me away from anything bad. She won't even watch the news in front of me. But I'm okay. I can handle it."

"If Donna didn't tell you, how'd you find out?"

"All the kids at Sunday school are talking about it. Graylin didn't do what they're accusing him of, Uncle Dre. He's not like that."

"I know. Angela's his attorney and she's working real hard on his case."

"Oh, good. If anybody can get him off, Angela can. I've been praying for him."

I grab a lawn chair and watch Brianna cut a circle out of a yellow piece of paper. "So what are the kids saying about Graylin?"

"That he wouldn't peek through somebody's bedroom window and take a picture of them naked. That sounds like something his friend Crayvon would do."

My ears open up like the large end of a funnel. I remember seeing Crayvon at Graylin's apartment a few times.

"Why do you think it sounds like something Crayvon would do?"

"Because he's a pervert."

"And why is he a pervert?"

"One time at church, he put his hand under Nedra Johnson's dress. And when she told the Sunday school teacher, he said he didn't do it. But he's a liar because I saw him. The Sunday school teacher told his mother, but she didn't believe it either. Everybody thinks he's so innocent, but he's not. Graylin thinks that's his best friend, but if you ask me, he's jealous of Graylin."

"Why is he jealous?"

"Because Graylin's smart and gets good grades without even studying hard and because all the teachers like him. He's also jealous because Graylin and his daddy are super close. Crayvon never sees his father."

"Does Crayvon go to Graylin's school?"

"Yep. My friend Analla told me Crayvon lives right across the street from that girl."

"What girl?"

"The girl whose naked picture Graylin had on his phone."

I hop up and pull out my phone.

"Who're you calling, Uncle Dre?"

"Angela. What you just told me could help Graylin's case."

Chapter 63

Angela

During the course of a case, there are both up days and often even bigger down days. For me, the down days get my blood pumping the hardest. Losing that suppression motion gave me an emotional shot of adrenalin. I'm determined to do everything in my power to make sure Graylin gets justice.

We're at Jenny's office getting a recap of some additional interviews Mei conducted with Graylin's classmates. Of the seven or eight kids she's talked to, Crayvon Little and Taisha Mitchell will be the most crucial. Mei's convinced that Crayvon took the picture of Kennedy and sent it to Graylin. Based on all the evidence she's gathered, Jenny and I agree.

Even if it turns out that he didn't, the information we have about Crayvon is still a positive for Graylin. In a case like this, it's important to have another potential suspect. That's the foundation of reasonable doubt. Is it reasonable for the jury to believe someone other than Graylin took that picture? We think it is. Before proceeding down Crayvon's path, however, I want to talk to him myself.

I check the time on my cell phone. We need to start wrapping up. We have an interview with Crayvon in about an hour.

When we arrive, Crayvon's mother greets us warmly and shows us into the dining room. "Crayvon'll be here in a minute. He went to Home Depot with my sister. I'll be right back with some coffee."

"I don't think she's going to be so nice to us once she realizes we're here to throw her son under the bus," Jenny whispers.

If Crayvon took that picture and set up Graylin, he deserves to be under a bus.

Mrs. Little sets a plate with several slices of pound cake in the middle of the table, then returns with cream, sugar and three mugs of coffee.

"I've been praying every night for Graylin and his family," Mrs. Little says. "It's not right what they're doing to him. They're just kids. I tell Crayvon all the time, he better not be doing that sexting stuff."

A tall, skinny kid charges through the front door and into the dining room, almost out of breath. He immediately reaches for a piece of cake, but his mother slaps his hand.

"Boy, where are your manners? Say hello, then go wash your hands."

After quick introductions, Crayvon dashes out and returns in seconds. He sits on one side of the table with his mother. Jenny and I are on the other.

Jenny is chomping on Mrs. Little's pound cake as if it's a foreign delicacy. "Mrs. Little, this is the best pound cake I've ever tasted. You must give me the recipe."

"It's the coconut and pineapple that make the difference," she says proudly. "Sorry, though. It's a family secret."

We know we have to ease into our questioning, so we take it slow, asking a series of softball questions about Crayvon's school activities and his friendship with Graylin. Every few seconds, Mrs. Little interrupts.

"Those boys are closer than two peas in a pod. I almost feel like he's my son. You know, his mother isn't around, right?"

We nod and continue with our questions.

"Do you know Taisha Mitchell?" Jenny asks.

Crayvon takes a bite of pound cake. "Yeah. She lives up the street. She's a foster kid. She's weird."

"Boy, don't talk with your mouth full," his mother scolds him. "And don't be calling that child weird. You're blessed that you have a family."

"Tell us what you know about her," Jenny says.

"Nothing really. She doesn't go to our school."

"Is she friends with Kennedy?"

"She used to be, but not anymore. Now LaShay is Kennedy's best friend."

"What do you know about LaShay?"

"She's in my algebra and English classes. She's kinda quiet."

Jenny reaches for her second piece of pound cake.

"What about Kennedy? Are you friends with her?" I ask.

"Nope."

"Do you have any idea who might've taken that picture of her?"

"Nope."

"Right before your second-period class, you told Graylin you had to go to the administration office. Why?"

"My first-period teacher, Mrs. Bosley, asked me to drop off some papers for her."

I make a note for Mei to confirm that with the teacher.

I inhale, knowing that my next line of questioning is likely to spark a change in demeanor from both Crayvon and Mrs. Little. Jenny senses where I'm about to go and gives me an out.

"Mrs. Little, could I bother you for some more coffee?"

"Of course." She stands up and retrieves Jenny's mug. "It'll take a couple of minutes. Since I'm the only one who drinks coffee, I bought one of those single-cup coffeemakers."

I wink at Jenny. She intentionally guzzled down her coffee like it was water so Mrs. Little would have to go get her a refill.

When Mrs. Little leaves the room, I lower my voice a bit, praying she can't hear us from the kitchen. "Taisha says she saw you and Graylin going into Kennedy's backyard a couple of days before Graylin was arrested. Is that true?"

Crayvon stops chewing and his eyes dart toward the kitchen. He seems as concerned about his mother overhearing us as we are.

"Um, well, we went back there, but we didn't do anything."

Mrs. Little must have dog ears. She flies back into the room, no mug in hand. "Wait a minute. When were you in the Carlyles' backyard?"

"Um, I don't remember. But Graylin went with me."

"What were you guys doing back there?" I ask.

"Nothing. We were just messing around. We snuck back there and ran right back out."

Mrs. Little pulls out her chair and sits back down next to her son. Her lips are on the edge of a frown.

"Taisha told us you two were back there about five minutes," I say.

"Yeah. We were looking around. Kennedy's backyard is huge. They have a real waterfall."

Mrs. Little's arms are folded now and she's giving her son a look to kill.

I know we're going to get that same look in about two seconds.

"Taisha said that after Graylin left, you came back a little later by yourself and went back there again."

Crayvon jumps to his feet. "No, I—"

Before he can finish, Mrs. Little blows a fuse. "Oh, hell no!" She pushes her chair back, plants her hands flat on the table and leans over. "You're not going to pin this on my baby!"

I hold up my palms. "We're just following up on what Taisha told our investigator. We—"

"I know what you're trying to do." Her smooth face is now wrinkled with rage. "I'm sorry about what happened to Graylin, but you are *not* going to make my child his scapegoat. Get out of my house!"

Jenny reaches for another piece of pound cake, but Mrs. Little snatches the plate away.

"Get out. Now!"

CHAPTER 64

The Shepherd

It's hard for me to believe, but I'm enjoying life at The Low again. My threat against the two C.O.s worked. They have a lot more to lose than I do. Oaktown hasn't even crossed my path since I got out of the hole two days ago.

After returning to my cell, I found out that Wallstreet asked to move to another unit. As it stands now, I don't have a cellie and that works for me. Other inmates avoid me since they know Oaktown despises me, and that's fine and dandy too. At least I'm not a snitch.

I still haven't spotted the two goons who attacked me in the hole. Maybe they're in the hole now.

I call Willie for an update.

"We took care of that project," Willie says. "And everything's running smooth down south."

"I want to go back to the original project."

"The big project or the little project?" Willie asks.

"Both." I want Dre Thomas dead as of yesterday and his niece in Birmingham as soon as possible.

"Who should we go after first?"

What we need is a plan to do it simultaneously. But can Willie pull that off?

I hear someone approaching. "Hold off on everything until I can get back to you." I hang up and slide the phone underneath my leg.

C.O. Phillips steps into my cell. "How's it going?" he asks.

"It's going."

I don't like the look on his face. He's angry, but he's trying to keep his temper in check.

"I wanted to give you a heads-up that Oaktown is being moved to this unit."

"What? Why?"

"It's out of my control."

"I never would've snitched on you and Phillips," I say. "I only said that out of desperation. You have to make sure that fool stays away from me."

"We will," Phillips says. "But it's going to cost you. We want another ten grand. Each."

Now they're getting greedy.

"I don't have that kind of money."

Phillips chuckles. "Yes, you do."

"And if I don't?"

"Then we won't be able to keep Oaktown off your ass."

It suddenly hits me that they may be moving Oaktown back over here to kill me. That would solve things for them. It was a mistake to threaten the C.O.s. They could turn out to be an even bigger problem for me than that psychopath.

"I'll see what I can do to get you the money."

"No, you'll get it."

"If you let Oaktown kill me, it's going to come back on you."

"No, it won't."

That wasn't the response I'd hoped to hear. I wanted him to say he'd never let Oaktown kill me.

"I'll get you the money."

"I know you will." He steps closer to my bunk. "I'll wait right here while you transfer the money to our accounts. And when you're done, I'm taking your phone."

Chapter 65

Angela

I park in front of Graylin's apartment building on Hillcrest and turn off the engine. I'm waiting for Jenny to arrive before going inside. After getting thrown out of Crayvon's house, we decide it's finally time to talk to Graylin about being in Kennedy's backyard.

My cell phone rings as Jenny pulls up behind me. I glance at the screen, see that it's Dre and let the call go to voicemail. I can't deal with our relationship drama and this case too. So Dre's been pushed to the back burner.

I grab my purse and iPad and climb out.

"Hey," Jenny says, holding up a bag. "I picked up some donuts."

"I'm surprised you didn't go back to Crayvon's house and ask for some more of that pound cake."

Jenny laughs. "I would've if I thought Mrs. Little would've given me another piece."

My phone chimes, signaling a text as we head toward the entrance of Graylin's apartment building.

I don't even bother to look at the phone. "It's Dre," I say. "He's been blowing me up. You know how men are when you ignore them."

"You still aren't speaking to him?"

"Nope."

"You have some nerve. He's serving as your personal bodyguard and you're treating him like crap. So you're not even going to read his text?"

"Nope. Let's go inside."

Graylin greets both of us with hugs and wastes no time digging into the donuts.

"Is someone here with you?" Jenny asks. Graylin is supposed to be under twenty-four-hour supervision.

"Yep. My granny's in her bedroom watching *The Haves and the Have Nots*. When that show comes on nobody can bother her."

Being in the same house with Graylin isn't proper supervision. He's wearing an ankle monitor, but even so, he could've sneaked out and returned without his grandmother ever knowing. I plan to talk to Gus about this.

"Okay," Jenny begins, as we settle into the living room, "we want to talk to you about some new information we discovered."

Hope floods Graylin's face. "You found out who sent me the picture?"

"No, not yet," Jenny says. "We have some questions to ask you and you need to be honest with us."

Graylin bites into a jelly donut and a blob of strawberry jelly dribbles onto his white T-shirt. "Okay."

We've agreed that Jenny will take the lead on questioning Graylin so that I can pay closer attention to his demeanor. We have to be certain he's telling us the truth. We're not happy Graylin neglected to mention being in Kennedy's backyard. That's the kind of circumstantial evidence Sullivan could use to convict him. I'm thankful that we know about it now. It would've been devastating to be hit with that bombshell during the middle of trial.

"Do you know Taisha Mitchell?" Jenny asks.

He stops to think. "Yeah. She lives on Crayvon's street with a foster family. She goes to my church."

"Our investigator interviewed her and she said she saw you and Crayvon going into Kennedy's backyard a few days before you got arrested. Is that true?"

Graylin almost chokes on his donut. "Um, yeah."

"Why didn't you tell us that?"

He lowers his head. "You didn't ask me, Ms. Jenny. And if I'd told you I'd gone back there, you would've thought I'd taken that picture of her."

"Did you take the picture?" she asks.

His head shoots back up. "No ma'am! I swear! You have to believe me, Ms. Jenny. We were only playing around. They have a huge waterfall. We weren't even back there that long. Crayvon's the one who likes her, not me."

"Crayvon likes Kennedy?"

"Yeah."

"You didn't tell us that either."

"You didn't ask me."

That's the problem with a child client. They often don't understand the relevance of certain information.

"Do you remember when you went back there?"

"Yes, it was on Tuesday, that same week that I got arrested."

"How do you remember that?"

"Because we have Math Club meetings after school on Tuesdays and sometimes I go to Crayvon's house afterward to help him with his algebra."

"After you two came out of Kennedy's backyard," Jenny continues, "what did you do?"

"I went home."

"What time did you go home?"

"I don't remember. But I'm sure it wasn't dark yet because I'm not allowed to ride the bus at night."

"Did you take any pictures while you were back there?"

"No, Ms. Jenny. You have to believe me. And Crayvon didn't take any pictures either."

"Taisha said she saw Crayvon go back into Kennedy's backyard by himself a few minutes after you left."

Graylin shrugs. "I wouldn't know. I went home."

It takes a couple of seconds for his brain to process the implication of Jenny's statement. And when he does, outrage crawls across his face like an ugly rash.

"I told you! I knew it was Crayvon! He took that picture! He set me up!"

"We don't know that for sure," Jenny says. "We spoke to him too. He says he didn't take it."

Graylin didn't seem to hear Jenny's words. "I was wondering why he hasn't called or come by to see me since I've been out. That's why! Because he set me up!"

"Calm down, Graylin," I say. "We don't know that for sure."

"I do! Crayvon's the only one who could've taken that picture. He lives right across the street from Kennedy. I thought he was my best friend." He starts to cry. "How could he do this to me? You have to tell the police it was Crayvon and not me!"

My phone chimes again. I pull it from my purse. It's Dre again. This time I read his text.

IMPORTANT RE GRAYLIN. CALL ME!!!

While Jenny tries to calm Graylin down, I step into the hallway to call Dre back. If this is a ploy to get me to talk to him, I'm going to be pissed.

"I got your text," I say, as detached as ever. "What's up?"

I listen as Dre speaks at twice his normal pace, clearly revved up about what he has to share. When he's done telling me about his conversation with Brianna, I'm more excited than he is. It won't be a stretch for the jury to believe that a kid who puts his hands underneath a girl's dress at church could also be a peeping Tom.

Graylin is absolutely right. Crayvon took that picture and set him up to take the fall.

CHAPTER 66

Angela

Graylin's trial is two short weeks away. Now that we have another plausible suspect, our energy level is off the charts.

Jenny and I are parked outside the apartment of LaShay Baker, Kennedy's best friend. When we called to set up the interview, the girl's grandmother was more than receptive.

Naomi Baker opens the front door before we can even knock.

"Get on in here and give me a hug!" she says, throwing her arms wide open.

Mrs. Baker is a tall, bulky woman with a gracious smile who speaks in a booming female baritone.

She squeezes me so hard I gasp for air. When she gives Jenny the same treatment, I almost burst out laughing.

"I'm so proud of you girls. Graylin's a good boy and I'm glad he has you two fighting for him. C'mon in here and have a seat."

She shows us into a living room that's a throwback to the 1970s. There's beige shag carpeting and her antique couch has plastic slip covers.

"Thank you," Jenny says, massaging her ribcage. "So you know Graylin?"

"No, but LaShay told me all about him. And the Holy Spirit tells me things. He's a good boy. I can feel it."

Jenny throws me a bewildered glance. She's wondering if Mrs. Baker is playing with a full deck.

"Mrs. Baker," I begin, "we wanted to talk with LaShay about—"

"Everybody calls me Mama Baker," the woman says. "So you girls should call me that too. I made some coffee." She points to a white decanter sitting on the coffee table. "Let me go get the rest of the food I prepared."

Mama Baker returns carrying a silver platter with finger sandwiches and chocolate cake cut into neat squares. Jenny eyes the food like she just ended a ten-day fast. She reaches for the cake first and immediately starts gushing.

"This cake is absolutely amazing!"

"Is LaShay here?" I ask as Jenny chows down. Cake must be her thing. I'm jealous that she can eat like a pig and remain as thin as a straw.

"Oh, I'm sorry. I guess y'all didn't come here to chit-chat with me." She yells down the hallway. "LaShay! Come in here, baby!"

A petite girl wearing cornrows appears in the entryway.

Mama Baker pats the couch next to her. "Graylin's attorneys wanna talk to you, baby."

LaShay perches herself on the edge of the couch, across from Jenny and I. She rests her hands in her lap, which is also where she keeps her gaze.

I take the lead since Jenny is too busy munching. "We understand that you're friends with Kennedy Carlyle."

The girl nods. "Yes. She's my best friend."

"Then you know about the picture that was taken of her?"

LaShay nods.

"Can you think of anybody who might've wanted to hurt Kennedy by taking that picture of her."

"Nope."

"Did Kennedy ever tell you she thought she knew who took it?"

"Yeah. She said Graylin took it."

"Do you know why she thinks that?"

"Because he had it on his phone and because that's what everybody is saying at school."

"Do you know Crayvon Little?"

"Yes."

"Did Crayvon like Kennedy?"

"Yep, he told me he wanted her to be his girlfriend. But she can't stand him because he's always making jokes about her."

Jenny takes a break from her orgasm over the cake to ask a question. "When did he do that?"

"All the time. He's always trying to embarrass her."

"Can you give us an example of something he did to embarrass her?" I ask.

"One time, in the cafeteria in front of everybody, he called her stuck-up and said her breasts were flatter than pancakes. Everybody laughed. It really hurt Kennedy's feelings."

Mama Baker shakes her head. "These kids today are a mess with all this bullying stuff."

For the next thirty minutes or so we listen to LaShay's depiction of eighth-grade behavior.

"Did Kennedy ever report Crayvon to a teacher or anyone else at school?"

"Nope. She was too afraid."

"Afraid of what?"

"If she reported him and he got in trouble, he might start teasing her more."

"Did Kennedy ever tell you she saw Crayvon or Graylin in her backyard before?"

"No."

Jenny asks a few more questions, then gives me a look that says she's all out. I'm about to announce that we're done when another question comes to mind.

"I have one more question. Do you know if Kennedy has started counseling yet?"

"Nope," LaShay says.

"Why not?"

"Because her daddy doesn't believe in it. He says he doesn't like telling strangers their business."

"You don't take your problems to man," Mama Baker says. "You take them to Jesus."

With that, we begin packing up to leave. Mama Baker asks if we'd like to take some cake to go. Jenny doesn't even let the woman get the words out before saying yes.

Mama Baker leaves the room and returns carrying two Ziploc bags with the cake wrapped in foil inside.

"Would you girls mind if I lay hands on you?" Mama Baker asks, moving in without waiting for our consent.

Jenny's eyes blaze with uncertainty. She has no idea what that means.

"That's fine," I say. Jenny remains mum, clutching her cake.

Mama Baker stands facing us. She grips the front of our heads, curling the heel of her large hands underneath our foreheads, and starts to pray.

"Father, I ask you today to bless these two women with the power to bring justice where justice is long overdue. Give them all your power, Father, to help young Graylin out of this mess. Father, give these girls the insight of Perry Mason and the oratory gifts of Johnny Cochran. Help them convince that jury that if the glove don't fit, they must acquit."

I glance over at Jenny, who has one eye open. She looks petrified. Mama Baker goes on for what seems like another five minutes.

"That I ask of you in Jesus' name. Amen! Hallelujah!" She squeezes both our heads then gently pushes us, sending us stumbling backward a step or two.

"Thank you so much," I say.

"You're welcome, baby. Give Mama Baker a hug."

She pulls me into her arms, then turns to Jenny, who crosses her eyes at me over Mama Baker's shoulder.

"What was that head-grabbing thing?" Jenny says as we're walking to our cars. "I should've told her I'm Jewish."

"I'm glad you didn't. She might've tried to pray you into a Christian."

We both have a good laugh.

"I still can't believe the Carlyles haven't gotten Kennedy into counseling yet," I say.

"Maybe they're afraid of something coming out during the sessions," Jenny replies.

"Like what?"

"I don't know, but I hope we're not missing something obvious. I don't have a good feeling about the father."

"So you think Mr. Carlyle had something to do with this?"

"Maybe."

I shake my head. "That would be way too weird. I don't buy it and neither would a jury. It's Crayvon. A kid who puts his hand underneath a girl's dress—in church no less—is a predator in the making. We just have to convince the jury of that."

CHAPTER 67

The Shepherd

I transferred ten grand to Sims' and Phillips' accounts and so far, it's been worth every penny. I see Oaktown from time to time in the chow hall, but he hasn't even looked my way. My only gripe is not having a cell phone. The two C.O.s are trying to teach me a lesson for threatening them.

Staying in my room is making me stir crazy, so I decide to catch a movie. There's rarely anything playing that I want to see, but tonight they're showing *Sully* with Tom Hanks. I've always been interested in how that dude landed that big bird on the Hudson River. I don't know if I could've been as cool under that kind of pressure.

I enter the TV room and take a seat near the back, always careful to watch my surroundings. The racial divide in prison is deep. There are separate TVs for the blacks, Mexicans, and whites.

A few minutes into the movie, I feel a tap on my shoulder. It's C.O. Phillips. He signals me to come outside.

I grunt, angry that I'm going to miss part of the movie. We walk over to the exercise room and enter a small backroom.

"Sims and I are still a little concerned about you threatening us," Phillips says.

I exhale. I paid them ten grand and now they're trying to extort me for more?

"I thought that was all behind us. I didn't mean any harm. I was desperate." *Just like you're desperate right now.*

I realize that I hold all the power and it feels good. If the warden found out about their misdeeds, they wouldn't just lose their jobs, they'd end up in prison like me.

"You and Sims got the ten grand I sent, right?"

A C.O. at their level makes about fifty thousand a year. That's a twenty percent bonus.

"Yeah, we got it. But you need to understand that money can't buy everything."

I wish this buffoon would hurry up and finish messing with me so I can get back to the movie.

The door opens and C.O. Sims steps into the room. That's when I sense that something's about to go down. Before I can gather my thoughts, Sims charges forward, punching me in the face.

I retreat to the nearest corner.

"You messed up by threatening us," Sims says. He pulls a rag from his back pocket while Phillips rushes me, pinning my back against the wall. Sims stuffs the rag into my mouth so deep I start gagging.

When I turn my head, I see one of the monsters, the bigger one, who attacked me in the hole. There's another man—a known chomo—standing behind him. His eyes are glistening like he's about to enjoy a tasty meal. And then I see Oaktown.

"No, no!" I yell, but my words are muffled by the rag. "You can't do this! Help!"

"Scream all you want," Oaktown says. "Nobody can hear you. Everybody's enjoyin' the movie. Except you."

I manage to spit out the rag just as Phillips releases me. I fall to the floor and scrunch up in the fetal position.

"Please, please don't hurt me. I can pay you. I have lots of money. I can help your family!"

Sims turns to Oaktown. "He's all yours. Have fun." The two C.O.s walk out and shut the door.

Oaktown signals the monster with a simple nod. He immediately drops his pants and urinates in my face. I hold up my hands to block the stream, fearful and incensed at the same time.

"I can pay you!" I plead, crab-walking away. "I can pay you anything you want!"

The monster snatches me up from the ground, rips my pants off and slams me chest first into the wall. "He's all yours," he says to the chomo, still holding me against the wall.

The chomo strips off his clothes and rushes toward me. I try to wrestle free, but in seconds I feel a searing pain pierce my buttocks. "Owww!"

"Is this what you did to Blaze's daughter and a whole bunch of other dudes' kids?" Oaktown asks. "I thought you outta know what it felt like."

The chomo moans with pleasure as his hairy chest presses into my back. He's sweaty and smells like rotting garbage. I vomit into the wall. The pain of this violation is so intense I'm close to blacking out.

"Please, please," I whimper, "help me!" My eyes meet Oaktown's and I see nothing but disgust.

"Hurry up and finish rapin' that fool," Oaktown says, holding up a long, rusty-looking shank. "So I can kill his ass and get back to the movie."

CHAPTER 68

Angela

It's close to midnight the day before trial and we've just finished putting the finishing touches on our exhibits, examination outlines, and my opening statement.

"I'm so tired, I can't see straight," Jenny says, scratching her forehead.

I'm stretched out on the couch across from her desk. "At least you can see crooked. I can't see at all."

"So how do you feel about our case?" she asks, yawning.

"Pretty good. They have nothing to support the invasion of privacy and distribution charges and the criminal threat count is just as weak. And unless Little Slice testifies, the witness intimidation charge is a loser too."

The prosecution turned over the forensic analysis of Graylin's phone. It definitively showed that the picture was not taken on the phone, nor did Graylin forward it to anyone. The Snapchat account that sent him the picture was linked to a website that allows users to create untraceable email addresses. So there's no way for us to identify the sender.

I'm pissed that Sullivan hasn't dropped everything except the possession charge. She's trying to muddy the waters. Even if the jury acquits him on the other charges and finds him guilty on the possession charge, he could still be locked up for a year.

"I'm just glad Taisha and Crayvon aren't on Sullivan's witness list," Jenny says.

Her cell phone rings. A call this late at night can't be good. As she listens, her expression turns gloomy. "What?" She springs forward in her chair.

I'm sitting up now, praying that whatever she's hearing has nothing to do with Graylin.

Jenny hangs up and props her elbows on the desk.

"What's the matter? Is Graylin okay?"

"That call wasn't about Graylin."

"Then what? What happened?"

"You need to call your boyfriend."

"Dre?" I stand up so fast my head starts swimming. "You got a call about Dre?"

"Yeah. You need to call him. Now."

"Why?"

"To ask him if he had anything to do with The Shepherd being murdered in prison two nights ago."

It takes a minute before I speak.

"I don't have to ask him. He didn't have anything to do with it." I have no idea why I just said that.

Jenny sighs. "You don't know that."

"Yes, I do because I know him."

"You're barely speaking to the guy, and now you're defending him?"

"Of course I'm defending him."

"You said he told you he was going to solve the problem. Apparently, he did."

"Hold on. Who was that on the phone?"

"My brother-in-law's an L.A.P.D. detective. After the break-in at your office, I asked him to ask around about The Shepherd. He knows an administrator with the Federal Bureau of Prisons. The Shepherd was raped, beaten and stabbed to death."

"You had no right to do that."

"*No right?* The Shepherd threatened you. I'm working closely with you. That means my life was also in danger."

"So what are you saying? You think Dre broke into a federal prison and killed him?"

"No. But maybe he paid somebody to do it."

"Just because the man is dead, doesn't mean Dre had anything to do with it."

"It seems awfully coincidental to me."

I look around for my purse. I need to discuss this with Dre, not Jenny.

"Can you make sure all the exhibits and outlines are packed up?" I say, heading for the door. "I'll meet you back here in the morning at seven."

CHAPTER 69

Dre

I'm whistling as I park in front of Angela's apartment building. Apache called me yesterday with the news that The Shepherd is dead and now my woman needs me. Life is beginning to taste sweet again.

When Angela opens the door, she's not wearing a face that welcomes me. Her eyes are cold and her expression is hard. I can tell she's been crying. Except for the faint light coming from a floor lamp in the living room, the apartment is dark.

"What's the matter? Are you okay? Did something happen with Graylin's case?"

Angela doesn't respond.

I step inside and close the door behind me. "Angela, say something. What's the matter?"

"Did you have anything to do with The Shepherd's murder?"

I suck in a breath and don't let it out. "How'd you find out?"

"Doesn't matter how I found out. Answer my question."

"I need to know who told you."

"Jenny."

"Jenny? How did she know?"

"Her family's full of law enforcement. After the break-in, I told her The Shepherd was behind it. She asked her brother-in-law to look into it."

I wish she hadn't done that. His nosing around could cause us some problems. "I think we need to sit down," I say.

"Just answer my question, Dre. Did you have anything to do with his murder? And don't lie to me."

"No." I pause. "Not directly."

"Not directly!" Angela yells. "Did you put a hit on the man? Please, God, tell me you didn't."

"I'm not going to talk to you until you calm down. Let's go into the living room."

Angela stays put for several seconds, then turns and flops down on the living room couch.

I ease into an armchair facing her.

"I'm going to tell you everything. The whole truth and nothing but. But before you start bombarding me with questions, let me get it all out."

Angela's arms are locked across her bosom. "Fine."

I run my palm down my face, move to the edge of the chair, then sit back again.

"No, I didn't put a hit out on The Shepherd. But I guess you can say I did have an indirect role in his murder."

I expect Angela to fire off some more questions at me, but she doesn't.

"After we got word that The Shepherd's guys were after me, and possibly Brianna, Apache came up with a plan to shut him down. For good."

I'm shocked that Angela's abiding by my request not to interrupt. I almost wish she would.

"Apache knows a drug dealer named Blaze who's doing life at Corcoran for cocaine trafficking. He was way up there in the drug game. Did millions of dollars in business. After he got locked up, his daughter got trafficked. Snatched off the street just like Brianna. She was sixteen. A couple of months after she went missing, they found her in a crack house, dead from an overdose. She was a good kid and Blaze loved her to death."

I pause to evaluate how Angela is taking this. Her entire face is one big frown.

"Apache put the word out that The Shepherd's guys snatched Blaze's daughter. That's it. That's all he did. But Apache figured that once Blaze heard that, he'd take revenge against The Shepherd. Blaze has all kinds of connections inside and outside of prison. And that's exactly what he did."

Angela pinches the bridge of her nose. "Did The Shepherd actually traffic Blaze's daughter?"

"I have no idea and neither does Apache. But we didn't care. We wanted him dead. And the plan worked. As a matter of fact, it worked like a charm."

Neither one of us says anything for the next few minutes.

"You can't tell Jenny any of this. If she talks to anyone, that could cause us problems."

She inhales slowly. "I know that."

I wait for another question, but Angela is staring off into space.

"I know I promised you my criminal past was behind me," I say. "But I'm not the kind of dude who can sit back and let somebody threaten me or anybody I care about. It's not in me. I'm always gonna protect mine. And that includes you. And for the record, I'm not sorry he's dead. He was pure evil. After all the young girls he destroyed, he didn't deserve to live."

I take my time standing up, hoping she'll tell me to sit back down. When she doesn't, I start making my way toward the door. My hand is on the doorknob when Angela calls out to me.

"Wait a minute."

I turn around as she walks over. "Yeah?"

"Nobody has the right to play God. I've never believed in an eye for an eye."

My body braces for more condemnation from the woman I love. I wait patiently for her words, the final detonation that will blow up our relationship for good.

"I don't condone what you did," Angela says, "but I'm glad The Shepherd's dead."

Relieved, I reach for her, but she backs away, out of my reach.

"But that doesn't mean I forgive you for lying to me."

CHAPTER 70

Angela

When I arrive at Jenny's office the next morning, I quickly put The Shepherd issue to bed.

"Dre told me he didn't have anything to do with The Shepherd's murder and I believe him."

Jenny smacks her lips. "If you say so."

"I do."

I know she doesn't believe me, but we don't have time for distractions. Graylin's trial is about to start in a couple of hours. Any strife between us could impact the defense of our client. I need to concentrate on my opening statement. I practice it for the umpteenth time and we head to court.

Judge Erik "The Electric" Lipscomb runs his courtroom like a drill sergeant. He's a tall, handsome guy with an athletic build. He was a cop before going to law school. His claim to fame is an article he wrote calling for a return to the electric chair, along with televised executions, as a deterrent to crime. Hence his nickname. The judge takes the bench promptly at nine and gets things rolling.

Sullivan's opening statement is brief and to the point. In my opinion, she spends way too much time on reasonable doubt and little time on what she's going to prove. She doesn't tell the juror that she has evidence that will show Graylin took the picture of Kennedy or that he tried to intimidate her into dropping the case. That means she doesn't have any such evidence. Sullivan's final appeal, tells me she senses that we're banking on jury nullification because she practically begs the jury to follow the law, not their personal feelings.

"In deciding this case, I ask that you put your personal feelings aside and focus on the law," she urges the jury. "You may not like the fact that minors are being prosecuted for possession of child pornography, but I'm asking you to look at the larger implications if this crime is not punished. In our society, we protect our children. Child pornography is a danger we cannot allow to spread.

"The evidence will show, beyond a reasonable doubt, that the defendant was in possession of child pornography. We need to send a strong message to him and to other kids who might also think it's okay to use their cell phones to invade the privacy of others. What the defendant did is wrong and it shouldn't be tolerated, regardless of whether he's an adult sex offender or a fourteen-year-old child predator. This is not a victimless crime. There's a young girl whose naked picture has been circulated all over the internet. She deserves justice. And the only way to give her justice is to listen to all the evidence, apply the law and find the defendant guilty as charged on all counts."

My take is totally different. As a very young attorney, I learned that a trial is basically a story. Whoever has the best story and the most believable witnesses wins. I take a quick sip of water before standing up. I round the defense table and face the jury.

I do the perfunctory introduction of myself and thank the jury for their service.

"Contrary to what you just heard from the prosecutor," I begin, "this case is not about a child predator or about protecting children. This is a case about a kid being a kid. My client, Graylin Alexander," I turn to face him, "received a picture via a popular social media app called Snapchat, something you'll hear a lot more about over the next few days. Maybe you've used it before. If you have teenage kids, there's a good chance they have a Snapchat account. Graylin opened a Snapchat message and, to his surprise, someone had sent him a naked picture. A naked picture of one of his classmates.

"What did he do? What any fourteen-year-old might do. He saved the picture to his cell phone. He didn't show the picture to anyone. He didn't send the picture to anyone. He didn't post it on social media. He simply took a screenshot of it. That's it. That's why he's here. Graylin Alexander—an A student who's active in his church, who's loved and respected by his teachers and classmates, who's never had any contact with the criminal justice system—took a screenshot of a picture someone sent him. That's why the prosecutor charged him with a number of sex-related crimes that will change his life forever."

I stop and dramatically shake my head to show my dismay.

"You're going to hear several witnesses over the next few days. I want you to listen very carefully to each one of them. And not only my witnesses, but the prosecution's as well. Graylin Alexander doesn't have to prove he's innocent. The prosecution must prove he's guilty. The prosecution must prove beyond a reasonable doubt that this cherub-faced young boy"—I face Graylin again—"is a sex offender.

"Many people think that if someone is charged with a crime, they must be guilty of something. But you must give my client the presumption of innocence. If I asked every one of you right now, if you thought Graylin was innocent and you hesitated, even for a split second, then you wouldn't be giving him the presumption of innocence he is entitled to by law. As you listen to this case, my client has to be as innocent as your next-door neighbor, who you know didn't take that picture.

"Like the prosecutor, I want you to listen carefully to every witness and follow the law. But I also want you to use your common sense. If what you hear doesn't seem right, then maybe it isn't."

I pause. This is as close as I can get to asking for jury nullification. I'll hit it harder in my closing. I'm not looking in her direction, but I can feel Sullivan ready to pounce with an objection. I let the silence hang in the air until it's almost uncomfortable.

"Graylin Alexander is a kid," I finally say. "He did something any kid—even your kid—might do in the same situation. He expressed his adolescent curiosity. He's not a criminal. Don't punish this kid for simply being a kid."

I take a few seconds to look into the eyes of as many jurors as I can, then walk back to my seat.

"You did good, Ms. Angela!" Graylin reaches over and gives me a hug as soon as I sit down. He's already forgotten my admonition about not showing emotion in front of the jury. But his hug gives me a boost of confidence.

I assumed Sullivan's first witness would be one of the cops. Instead, she calls Simone Carlyle to the stand. This time, Kennedy is in the courtroom to witness her mother's testimony. This is the first time I've had a chance to see the girl. She looks small and frail sitting next to her father. All this time, my focus has been on Graylin, not Kennedy, the victim. And today, my heart goes out to her.

Mrs. Carlyle testifies along the same lines as she did during the detention hearing, her testimony intended to elicit sympathy for her daughter.

"What impact has this tragic invasion of privacy had on your daughter?" Sullivan asks.

"My baby hasn't been the same since," Simone Carlyle says with a sniffle. She wipes at a non-existent tear with a tissue. "This has been so devastating for her. Teenagers are so sensitive. What that boy did to my baby was the worst kind of crime."

"Objection," I say. "The witness has no evidence that my client committed any crime."

"Sustained," declares the judge.

Every time she utters the words *my baby*, Mrs. Carlyle glances out at Kennedy and so does the jury. If Sullivan wants the jurors to feel sorry for the girl, Mrs. Carlyle's performance is getting the job done.

On cross, I know I have to be delicate with Mrs. Carlyle or the jury could turn on me. I have only one area to pursue.

"Mrs. Carlyle, is Kennedy seeing a therapist?"

Sullivan cuts in. "Objection, rule 352, Your Honor. The probative value of this question is outweighed by its prejudicial effect. Also, this line of questioning is irrelevant and an invasion of the victim's privacy."

"I don't plan to inquire about the specifics of her therapy," I protest. "This line of questioning goes to whether the victim has suffered the degree of emotional distress that her mother claims."

"This isn't a civil case," Sullivan counters. "The state doesn't have to prove the victim suffered emotional distress."

"Your Honor, my question goes to the truthfulness of Mrs. Carlyle's statements on direct."

The judge mulls over our objections. "I'll allow it. Overruled."

When I turn back to her, Mrs. Carlyle gawks at me as if she hasn't heard my question. "Could you repeat the question?" she sniffs.

"My question is simple, Mrs. Carlyle. Has your daughter been seeing a therapist?"

"No, she hasn't."

I love her snippiness and I pray she gives me a lot more of it.

"If she was so devastated by what happened, why hasn't she been in therapy?"

"Are you trying to say this didn't affect my baby?"

"I'm sorry, Mrs. Carlyle, I'm the one asking the questions. I'm trying to understand why you haven't placed your daughter in therapy since she's suffering so much emotionally."

"We haven't found the right therapist."

"How many therapists have you interviewed?"

She glares over at Sullivan as if she's being derelict for not objecting. "Isn't that confidential information?"

"Again, Mrs. Carlyle, I'm the one asking the questions. I don't want to know any specifics about her therapy—which *would* be confidential—only how many therapists you've spoken to in an effort to get help for your daughter."

Mrs. Carlyle puckers her lips and shifts in her seat. She steals another look at Sullivan, who's looking quite alarmed herself. Her opening witness was supposed to pull at the jury's heartstrings.

"If you must know, my husband doesn't believe in therapy. He's a very private person. We're dealing with this through our faith."

I peek over my shoulder at Mr. Carlyle, knowing the jurors will follow my gaze. Percy Carlyle looks even more uncomfortable than his wife. He tugs at his tie for the third time.

"Okay, what church do you attend?"

"Objection, Your Honor," Sullivan says. "This is really going far afield."

"No, Your Honor, it isn't. Mrs. Carlyle just testified that they're dealing with the situation through their faith. I'm just trying to confirm that."

"I'll allow it," Lipscomb says, "but not for too much longer."

"Holman United Methodist Church," she says proudly.

I don't see the Carlyles as a church-going family. Holman is one of the most prominent black churches in L.A. Something tells me Simone just snatched that name out of the air.

"And where is that church located?"

"In Los Angeles."

"On what street?"

"I don't understand why that's relevant," Simone snarls.

It's relevant because you don't even know where the church is, which proves you're a big fat liar.

"Do you know what street the church is on, Mrs. Carlyle?"

She shoots daggers at me. "It's very stressful sitting up here in this witness box. I'm sorry, but I can't remember right now."

"Does Adams Boulevard ring a bell?"

She smiles. "Oh, yes, it's on Adams."

"And who's the head minister there?"

If looks could kill, I'd be dead. She doesn't know that either.

"Isn't Reverend Sauls the minister there?" I say, helping her out again.

"Yes, that's it. Reverend Sauls."

"And when is the last time your family went to church?"

"Just because we don't go to church every Sunday doesn't mean we don't have faith."

C'mon, girlfriend, keep it coming!

"That wasn't my question, Mrs. Carlyle. I asked when your family last visited Holman United Methodist Church."

"I don't remember."

"Have you been since May tenth, the day you learned about the picture of your daughter?"

"No, we haven't and I don't appreciate what you're trying to imply. My daughter is suffering and we're doing everything we can to help her."

I stand there long enough to check out the frowns in the jury box. A couple of women even shake their heads. I've done my job.

"I have no further questions for this witness."

As soon as I'm seated, Jenny leans across Graylin. "Great cross," she says. "How'd you know they didn't go to church?"

"Because that woman is too evil to step foot into a church."

Sullivan asks for a short break before calling her next witness. Jenny takes me aside, out of Graylin's earshot.

"Did you notice how rigid Kennedy looks sitting next to her father?"

I glance back at them. Actually, I *had* noticed.

"It's strange," Jenny continues. "He didn't even have his arms around her."

Now that Mrs. Carlyle has returned to her seat, she has Kennedy wrapped in a close embrace.

"I hate to beat a dead horse," Jenny says, "but Simone's testimony just reignited my suspicion that the Carlyles have some dirt to hide."

This is a distraction I don't need. "We're in the middle of trial. Even if you're right, it's a little late to do something about it now."

"I'm going to give Mei a call to see what she can dig up on Daddy Carlyle. We should've done it days ago."

"Go for it," I say with a shrug. "But I think it's a complete waste of time."

CHAPTER 71

Jenny's call throws me. The possibility that Percy Carlyle may have something to do with that naked picture of his daughter is unsettling.

As I head up the walkway to the Carlyles' home, I'm still not sure what my approach is going to be. Whatever it is, I don't have a lot of time. The family will be returning home from court soon.

I ring the doorbell and an attractive, narrow-faced woman in her twenties answers the door.

"Hi, you must be Kennedy's nanny."

"I'm the family's *au pair*." She corrects me in a soft Ethiopian accent. "How can I help you?"

I didn't know there was a difference and I hope I didn't offend her.

"My name is Mei. Are the Carlyles home?"

"No, they're in court today?"

"Oh, my goodness. Has the trial started already? I need to speak with them about the case. How's Kennedy doing?"

"She's getting better. But it hasn't been easy. She's a very emotional child."

"I didn't get your name," I say.

"I'm Zala."

"Zala, I guess I'll have to come back later. I hope the Carlyles will be getting back together. That would be so good for their daughter."

Zala's eyes dart from left to right. "To tell the truth," she says, lowering her voice although no one else is in earshot, "I think Kennedy would be better off if they went ahead and got a divorce. Those two argue all day long. Mrs. Carlyle isn't a very nice woman. She's so demanding and treats Mr. Carlyle very badly."

"Is Kennedy close to her father?"

"Not really. He's a strange man."

"Strange how?"

"Very distant. When he was living here, he kept to himself. Stayed in his office most of the time. They didn't even have family dinner together."

"Wow, that's not good for Kennedy."

"No, it isn't." Zala shakes her head. "I have to finish dinner. They'll be home soon."

"Okay," I say, taking a step back. "Did you ever notice anything inappropriate between Kennedy and her father?"

"Inappropriate? What do you mean?"

I try to choose my words carefully. "Did Mr. Carlyle ever behave in a sexually inappropriate way toward his daughter?"

When the question registers with Zala, her eyes expand and she goes from chatty to close-mouthed.

"Of course not! Mr. Carlyle is not *that* kind of man. I'm insulted that you would ask such a question. Mrs. Carlyle would never permit that kind of behavior toward her daughter. You must go now." She slams the door in my face.

I walk back to my car a bit perplexed.

If anyone is in a position to detect inappropriate behavior by Percy Carlyle toward his daughter, it would be their live-in help. Still, I'm not throwing in the towel. I need to hit the internet to see what interesting tidbits I can dig up on him.

I've worked with Jenny long enough to know that when that woman has a hunch about something, nine times out of ten, she's right.

CHAPTER 72

Angela

After the break, Sullivan calls Officer Fenton to the witness stand. His testimony on direct and cross is much the same as it was during the preliminary hearing. Sullivan doesn't call Officer Chin, at all. Probably because she doesn't want the jury to see him for the liar that he is.

To support the witness intimidation charge, Sullivan produces Little Slice's cousin, who claims he made the call to Kennedy on Graylin's behalf. On cross, I establish that he never spoke to Graylin and that the prosecution dropped the charges against him in exchange for his testimony.

I'm surprised when Kennedy and her father don't return to the courtroom after the break, but minutes later, I understand why. Sullivan calls a computer specialist from the D.A.'s Office to verify that the naked picture of Kennedy was retrieved from Graylin's phone. When the picture appears on the huge courtroom screen, her breasts and groin area are blacked out.

I hate the reaction of the jurors. More than a few shake their heads. Graylin stares down at his hands, never looking at the picture. Mrs. Carlyle, of course, is there to put on a weeping show.

Sullivan's next witness is LaShay Baker, who's accompanied by her grandmother. Mama Baker strolls into court wearing her Sunday best. She's decked out in a red, hip-clinging knit skirt suit with a hat so enormous it resembles a sombrero.

When the bailiff calls LaShay to the stand, the whole courtroom can hear Mama Baker's raspy voice even though she's trying to whisper. "Don't be afraid, baby. Just tell the truth. The truth shall set you free."

LaShay states her name for the record and explains that she's Kennedy's best friend. Sullivan starts with an area that catches us totally by surprise.

"Did you ever see the defendant bullying Kennedy?"

"Um, yes."

"How did he bully Kennedy?"

"He and Crayvon, that's another boy in our class, they would make jokes about her."

Graylin *and* Crayvon. This is news to us.

Graylin is incensed. "She's lying on me, Ms. Angela!" he whispers.

I place my hand on Graylin's forearm. He responds to my signal and calms down, but I know it won't be for long.

"What kind of jokes?"

"They would say she's skinny and that her weave looks like horse hair and that she's stuck-up."

"And how did Kennedy react when they did that?"

"She would cry because her feelings would be hurt."

Right on cue, I can hear Simone Carlyle sniffling.

"Do you know if Graylin ever showed the picture of Kennedy to anyone?"

"Yes."

Jenny and I lean forward at the same time.

"Who did he show it to?"

"I was walking behind Graylin as we were leaving first-period class. I heard him tell Crayvon he had a picture he wanted to show him."

"And then what happened?"

"Crayvon said he couldn't look right then because he had to go to the administration office."

Graylin told us he tried to stop Crayvon right before class but said he didn't specifically mention the picture, just that he had something to show him. Why didn't LaShay tell us this?

"And was there another time when Graylin tried to get Crayvon to look at the picture?"

"Yes. During first period when we were taking our algebra test. Graylin made a spitball and threw it at Crayvon. When he turned around, Graylin held up his phone and pointed at it. But Crayvon was trying to finish his test and ignored him."

I look over at Graylin. Whenever someone says something that isn't true, Graylin reacts with pure outrage. Right now, he's quiet, which tells me that LaShay is speaking the truth.

"Thank you, LaShay," Sullivan says. "I have no further questions."

I'm not quite sure how I want to play this. It's almost four o'clock and the jury looks as exhausted as I am. I need to make it quick.

"LaShay, how long have you known Graylin?"

"Since elementary school."

"Do you think Graylin's a nice boy?"

"Yes, ma'am, he's pretty nice. And he's smart too."

"When you said Graylin and Crayvon made jokes about Kennedy, wasn't it only Crayvon making those jokes?"

"Yes, ma'am. Graylin was just there with him."

"Then why did you say Graylin and Crayvon made jokes about Kennedy?"

She looks over at Sullivan. "Um, Miss Prosecutor asked me if Graylin was there when Crayvon made the jokes and I said yes. So she said that means they were doing it together."

Sullivan cringes like she wants to crawl under the table. The judge is glaring at her, and so is the entire jury.

"So, you never heard Graylin make any jokes about Kennedy, correct?"

"Yes, that's correct."

"You testified that Graylin told Crayvon he had a picture to show him. But isn't it true that Graylin only said he had something to show Crayvon, never mentioning a picture?"

She stops to think. "Yeah, maybe."

It's too dangerous to question her about Graylin holding up his phone in class. So I move on.

"Do you think Crayvon has a crush on Kennedy?"

"Yes, he—"

"Objection, calls for speculation."

"Sustained."

I quickly rephrase the question. "Did Crayvon ever do anything that made you think he liked Kennedy."

"Yes, ma'am. He was always liking her pictures on Instagram. He tried to get her to instant message him, but she wouldn't. She doesn't like him."

I know I'm going to get an objection to my next question, but I ask it anyway. "Do you think Crayvon tried to embarrass Kennedy because she rejected him?"

"Objection, Your Honor." This time Sullivan is more than pissed. "Calls for speculation."

"Sustained."

"Did you ever see Graylin do anything to hurt Kennedy's feelings?"

"Um, no ma'am. Graylin's nice. Everybody likes him."

That's the best I'm going to get. I slowly walk back to the defense table.

"I have no further questions of this witness, Your Honor."

Chapter 73

Mei

Despite my conversation with Zala, I'm not convinced that Percy Carlyle is on the up and up. But two hours of internet sleuthing also reveals nothing. That doesn't deter me. Good investigators keep looking even when the chips are down.

After taking a screenshot of Percy Carlyle's picture from his law firm's website, I plant myself in the underground garage of his law office in downtown Los Angeles. Jenny texted me that Percy didn't attend the afternoon session, so I'm hoping he returned to his office. Thanks to Crayvon's mother, I know that he drives a black BMW. I scan all five floors of the underground garage and count only three black BMWs. I take a guess that the one on the first level belongs to Percy Carlyle. Not because it's the newest model, but because parking on the first floor is a perk given to law firm partners, not lowly associates.

I pull into a nearby parking spot and wait. I'm hoping he doesn't plan to work too late tonight. I take out my laptop and continue my online search.

Around seven I spot a man who looks like Percy Carlyle enter the garage. I watch and pray he's going to the black BMW. And luckily he does. He starts his car and I do the same, determined to leave the garage ahead of him. I'll have to pay the attendant to get out, which is going to take some time. I'm sure Percy has a card key and can drive right out.

I get to the booth and when the woman tells me I owe forty-five dollars, I'm speechless. I hand her my credit card as I check my rearview mirror. I see Percy headed for the lane to my right.

"Do you need a receipt?" the attendant asks.

"No, thanks." I need to hurry. Jenny won't sweat me for a receipt.

Percy is easing out of the garage onto Olive Street. It seems to take forever for the guard gate to lift.

By the time I spot Percy's BMW again, he's four cars away. He makes a right onto Fifth Street and gets on the Harbor Freeway headed south. Since I have no idea where he's going, I try to stay close. When he bypasses the Santa Monica Freeway exchange which would take him home, I have to cut off a couple of cars to keep up with him. Several miles ahead, he transitions to the San Diego Freeway south, then south on the Long Beach Freeway. It's another twenty minutes before Percy pulls up in front of a bar called the Crest on Cherry Avenue. Maybe he's meeting some woman. And I bet she's not a client.

I park across the street and watch him enter the bar. I give him a few minutes to get situated before following him inside. Ten minutes later, I walk in, take a seat at the bar, and order a Diet Coke. I scan the place, looking for Percy, trying not to appear too obvious. The club is full, but not packed. I get up and start roaming around.

That's when I spot him. Percy Carlyle, his tie unknotted, is smiling and sipping wine in a corner booth. He's also snuggled up with someone who definitely isn't his wife.

CHAPTER 74

Angela

I've been expecting a surprise or two from Sullivan, but not this one. As soon as we enter the courtroom for day two of the trial, Sullivan hands me a revised witness list.

"We just discovered two new witnesses," she says with a surprisingly straight face. "The late notice shouldn't be a problem since you or your investigator have interviewed both of them."

"Who are they?" Jenny says, reading the document over my shoulder as Sullivan walks away.

"Taisha and Crayvon."

"Why would Sullivan want to call either of them?" Jenny asks. "Especially Taisha. It's going to hurt her case when she testifies that Crayvon went into Kennedy's backyard by himself."

I have a bad feeling. Sullivan's a very skilled attorney. She wouldn't knowingly offer testimony that could raise reasonable doubt. We could object, but there's no way Judge Lipscomb isn't going to let them testify, particularly since we've already interviewed them.

Ten minutes later, Taisha saunters down the center aisle of the courtroom like a mutant ninja midget. She's dressed in green from head to toe. Green pants, green blouse, green earrings, even green eye shadow. From the smile on her face, it's clear that she loves being the center of attention.

Taisha Davis is sworn in and Sullivan approaches her like they're old friends.

"Good morning. May I call you Taisha?"

"Yes, you may." Taisha daintily clasps her hands in her lap.

"Do you know the defendant Graylin Alexander?"

"Yes, he's best friends with a boy who lives on my street named Crayvon and he goes to my church, Greater Mount Calvary."

"Do you know Kennedy Carlyle?"

"Yes, she lives on my street too."

"Have you ever been in her house?"

"Yep, lots of times."

Sullivan puts a picture up on the courtroom screen.

"Is this Kennedy's house?"

"Yes."

"Where is Kennedy's bedroom?"

"In the back on the first floor, just like at my house."

Sullivan draws Taisha's attention to another picture. "And is this a picture of Kennedy's backyard?"

"Yes."

"Can you point to Kennedy's bedroom?"

"It's the window on the right."

"During the week of May tenth, did you see Graylin sneaking into Kennedy's backyard?"

"I sure did."

A couple of jurors gasp. Taisha smiles and pauses like she's taking cues from a Hollywood director.

I place a hand on Graylin's forearm. "Remember, the jury is watching you. Don't show your emotions. Stay calm."

"Can you tell us what you saw?"

"I was looking out of our living room window and I saw Graylin and his friend Crayvon sneaking into Kennedy's backyard. Her house is right across the street from mine."

"How long were they in the backyard?"

"About five minutes, I guess."

"After they came out, did one of them go back there alone?"

"Yep, Crayvon went home. Then Graylin went back there a few minutes later by himself."

"Ms. Angela!" Graylin whispers way too loudly. "She's lying on me!"

Jenny admonishes him before I can. "We know, Graylin. You have to be quiet so we can hear what she's saying."

"And did you learn that Graylin was arrested for having a naked picture of Kennedy Carlyle a couple of days later?" Sullivan asks.

"Yes."

"I have no further questions."

I'm stunned by Sullivan's lightning-fast examination. She has to know she's only getting half of the story.

Graylin is near tears. "I never went back there by myself, Ms. Angela. I swear! Why is Taisha lying on me?"

"I don't know," I say, getting to my feet. "But I'm about to find out."

I walk close to the jury box and face Taisha. Jenny blasts out of her seat like a missile.

"Your Honor, please forgive me for the interruption. I need to speak to my co-counsel. Right now."

What the—

Judge Lipscomb grimaces. "Make it quick."

Jenny's interruption has wrecked my rhythm. Whatever she has to say better be important. As I turn around, I pray the jury doesn't see the angst on my face.

I take the few short steps back to the defense table.

Before I can ask her what's up, Jenny grips my forearm so hard I think it might snap in two. "We missed it!" she whispers into my ear.

"Missed what? And why couldn't you wait until I—"

"Crayvon didn't do it!" Jenny declares. "It's Taisha. Taisha took that picture and sent it to Graylin!"

CHAPTER 75

Angela

It takes me a few seconds to process this. Taisha lives across the street from Kennedy. Taisha was the one Kennedy kicked to the curb. Taisha lies like a rug. Taisha had means, motive, and opportunity.

I turn back around to face the witness box, my heart racing. "May I also call you Taisha?"

"Yes, you may."

"Did you speak with my investigator, a woman named, Mei?"

"Yep. A cute Asian girl, right?"

"Yes."

"Yep, I spoke to her. I saw her sneaking into Kennedy's backyard too. The same day she interviewed me."

This little girl is dangerous. I have to keep this moving.

"Didn't you tell the investigator that it was Crayvon who returned and went back there by himself, not Graylin?"

"Nope."

"And didn't—" I'm on to another question before I realize that Taisha didn't give me the answer I was expecting.

"What did you say?"

"You have your facts wrong. I never saw Crayvon go into Kennedy's backyard by himself. Just Graylin."

"You do understand that you're under oath, correct?"

"Yes."

Since I'm facing a lying witness, I have to tread lightly.

"You have no idea whether Kennedy was home on the day you *claim* you saw Graylin and Crayvon going into her backyard, correct?"

"Nope. I'm pretty sure she was home."

You little tart.

"Didn't you tell my investigator that you didn't know whether she was home or not?"

"Nope. I told her Kennedy was at home."

"Taisha, you're in foster care, correct?"

"Yes."

"Who is your foster mother?"

"Mrs. Betty Taylor."

Mrs. Taylor isn't in the courtroom. Maybe Taisha wouldn't be lying if she were here.

"Was your foster mother home the day you spoke with our investigator?"

"Yes."

"And didn't your foster mother tell her that you have a habit of lying?"

"I don't know what she told her. I wasn't listening to their conversation. They told me to go back inside."

"Well, do you have a habit of lying?"

For the first time, Taisha pauses to think about her answer. "I wouldn't call it lying. Sometimes I remember things or forget things."

"Are you forgetting something about the day you claim you saw Graylin and Crayvon going into Kennedy's backyard?"

"Nope. I saw Graylin go back there by himself with his cell phone in his hand. That's what I saw with my own two eyes."

"You don't know what Graylin and Crayvon were doing in Kennedy's backyard, correct?"

"Not really. But when Graylin went back there by himself, I did see a phone in his hand."

I cross my arms and pause. I can't let the jury see how irritated I am with this little girl.

"You have no evidence that Graylin took any pictures in Kennedy's backyard, correct?"

"He must've. Kennedy's picture ended up on his phone."

"Objection," I say. "Move to strike the witness' statement as speculation."

"Sustained."

"You didn't actually see Graylin take a picture. You're just guessing, correct?"

She shrugs.

"I didn't hear you."

"No, I didn't see him do it. But the police must've arrested him for a reason."

"Again, Your Honor, move to strike."

"Sustained," Judge Lipscomb says. "Young lady, we don't want you to guess."

Taisha smiles up at him. "Okay, judge."

It's time for me to turn on her. "You took that picture of Kennedy, didn't you?"

Taisha doesn't even blink. "Nope."

"You were upset with Kennedy for not being your friend, weren't you?"

"I don't care about her. I have lots of friends."

"Name them?"

"What?"

"Name your friends."

Taisha flubs.

Sullivan jumps to her defense. "Your Honor, I object to this line of questioning. Counsel's badgering the witness."

"Sustained."

"You wanted to hurt Kennedy, didn't you?"

"You're not going to pin this on me," Taisha says calmly. "I didn't do it. Graylin did."

I stare at her a few seconds, then turn away, shaking my head in an exaggerated show of disgust.

"I have no further questions."

Sullivan almost crashes into the witness box in her rush to rehabilitate her star witness.

"Just a few questions, Taisha. Do you have a computer at home?"

"No."

"Do you have a cell phone?"

"No."

"Do you have a Snapchat account?"

"Nope."

"No more questions, Your Honor."

As Taisha saunters past our table, she looks as if she's about to stick out her tongue at me. Instead, she flashes me a cheeky smile.

Judge Lipscomb bangs his gavel. "Let's take a ten-minute break. And I mean ten minutes, not a second longer."

"She's lying!" Graylin bursts into a full-blown crying fit as soon as the jury is ushered out of the courtroom. "I never went back there by myself. Why did she lie on me like that, Ms. Angela?"

"I don't know," I say, pointing him toward the back of the courtroom. "Why don't you go talk to your dad and your granny?"

After Graylin walks away, I tell Jenny we need to call Taisha's foster mother to testify about her proclivity for lying. "How do you think the jury reacted to us going after her?"

"I'm sure they don't think she's credible. I can't believe we didn't focus on her earlier."

I'm not entirely onboard with Jenny's theory about Taisha. My bet is still on Crayvon and I hope we haven't hurt ourselves by zeroing in on her. I don't want the jury to think we're carelessly slinging mud in the hope that something sticks.

"Something's not right," I say.

Jenny furrows her perfectly arched eyebrows. "What are you talking about?"

"I have a bad feeling that Sullivan has an even bigger surprise for us when Crayvon takes the witness stand."

CHAPTER 76

Angela

When we reconvene, Judge Lipscomb announces that another matter requires his attention, so he's ending court early today. Jenny and I are grateful for the reprieve. Gus rushes a distraught Graylin out of the courtroom, while Jenny and I remain behind to collect our files and exhibits.

Other than the court clerk, we're the only ones left in the courtroom.

"This has certainly been a crazy day," I say. "I'm not sure we did the right thing by going after Taisha."

Jenny is quick to disagree. "As far as I'm concerned, the more potential suspects, the better."

I let out a long sigh. "I hope you're right."

"We haven't even had a chance to talk about what Mei told us about Percy Carlyle," Jenny says with a devious twinkle in her eyes.

"What's there to talk about? It's clear now why he wasn't big on family counseling. And it's not because he's a child molester."

"Yeah, but—"

Simone Carlyle barges back into the courtroom, enters the well and doesn't stop until she's standing in front of our table.

"You'll do anything to get your client off," she says, leaning in close enough to kiss me. "Even try to frame another child. You're not going to get away with this."

"Excuse me?" I push my chair back to get some breathing room.

"First you have your investigator trespass on my property and—"

"I don't think Taisha Davis is a credible witness," I say. "So I wouldn't put any stock in anything she said on the witness stand today."

Mei had indeed gone into the Carlyles' backyard and taken pictures, but I'll never admit that to this witch.

I turn away and continue packing up our documents. My abrupt dismissal of Mrs. Carlyle seems to further enrage her.

"And not only did you have that woman trespass on my property just once, you had her come back and start asking our *au pair* all kind of inappropriate personal questions about my husband."

Jenny decides to step in and rescue me. "Mrs. Carlyle, this isn't the time or the place for this. You should—"

Simone's lips angle into an ugly sneer. "Nobody's talking to you!"

"If you're talking to my colleague," Jenny fires back, "then you're talking to me. Anything that goes on in this case, we're *both* responsible for."

I want to hug Jenny for coming to my defense. It's been such a stressful day I don't have the extra brain cells for this.

"Fine then. I'll sue both of you."

"Go for it," Jenny says. "But you need to be spending your time keeping better track of your husband."

"How dare you! What is *that* supposed to mean?"

A smile dances across Jenny's lips. I know where she wants to go, but that's on her. I duck my head and continue packing up our stuff.

"It means whatever you think it means," Jenny says.

"I don't know who you think you are. But I'll tell you this—"

Jenny points a pink fingernail in the woman's face. "Since you want to berate somebody, go home and scold your husband. And while you're at it, ask him who he was hugged up with at a bar yesterday."

"How dare you say something so outrageous!" she sputters. "My husband—"

"He was at The Crest. It's a bar on Cherry Avenue in Long Beach. And just so you know, he wasn't hugged up with a woman. It's a gay bar."

Simone is finally rendered speechless. She opens her mouth, but no words follow.

"Enjoy your afternoon," Jenny says.

We each grab a box and walk out of the courtroom. Neither one of us makes a sound until we step into the elevator. When the doors close, we burst out laughing.

"Oh, my God, that was priceless!" I say. "Did you see her face?"

Jenny presses a palm to her cheek. "I don't believe I did that. It's not right to out people, but I couldn't help myself. That woman deserved it."

"Please remind me not to get you upset."

We're still laughing as we walk out of the building.

"I was right about Mr. Carlyle having something to hide," Jenny says. "But way wrong about what it was.

"And I'm glad you were. If he'd had something to do with that picture, that would've been way too weird."

"It's going to be another long night," Jenny sighs. "I'll pick up some Starbucks on the way."

"Add three extra shots to mine."

"You're going to OD on caffeine," Jenny cautions me.

"You better do the same because it's going to be a long night prepping for Crayvon's cross. I plan to be over-prepared since what he says on the witness stand tomorrow could make or break our case."

CHAPTER 77

Angela

The trial is taking its toll on Graylin. All morning, he's been asking us the same question over and over again.

"Ms. Angela, if Crayvon lies on me too, you have to let me testify so I can tell the jury I didn't do it. You're going to let me testify, right?"

"We'll see," I say yet again.

We've explained to Graylin that it's not a good idea for him to testify. Sullivan would tear him apart. But since Taisha's testimony, getting the truth out is all he's been able to focus on. Too bad this process has very little to do with the truth.

Once the jurors are seated, Judge Lipscomb instructs Sullivan to call her next witness.

The bailiff retrieves Crayvon Little from the hallway. Unlike Taisha, he walks unsteadily down the aisle toward the witness stand. He's wearing a brown suit and shoes that look as if they've been polished with Vaseline. He stops right outside the box, raises his right hand and swears to tell the truth. While LaShay and Taisha were almost swallowed up by the witness box, Crayvon sits tall.

After establishing his age, where he lives and attends school, Sullivan moves on to questions that will score her some points.

"Crayvon, how long have you known Graylin Alexander?"

Crayvon clears his throat. "A long time. Since third grade."

"Is he one of your closest friends?"

"Yes."

"Not anymore," Graylin mutters under his breath.

"To your knowledge, did Graylin have a crush on Kennedy Carlyle?"

Crayvon sits up straighter. "Yes."

Graylin flinches. "He's lying, Ms. Angela! He likes her, not me!"

I squeeze Graylin's arm. He says something indecipherable and quiets down.

"How did you know Graylin had a crush on Kennedy?"

"Because he's always talking about her and he told me he liked her."

"Did you like Kennedy?"

"No. I have a girlfriend. Her name is Danielle. She goes to my church."

"Did Graylin ever visit your home?"

"Yep, all the time."

"Do you live on the same street as Kennedy Carlyle?"

"Yes, up the street, about four houses down, but on the other side of the street."

"During the week of May tenth, did you and the defendant, Graylin Alexander, sneak into Kennedy's backyard?"

"Yes."

"Why did you do that?"

"We were just looking around. We ran back out after a few minutes."

"Was Kennedy at home?"

"I don't know."

"Did you look into her bedroom window?"

"No."

"How long were you and Graylin in her backyard?"

"Not long. Only a few minutes."

"Did you have your cell phone with you?"

"No."

"Did Graylin have his cell phone with him?"

"Yes."

"After you left the backyard, what did you do?"

"We went back to my house and watched TV, but then Graylin had to leave so he could get home before it got dark."

"Did Graylin have to pass by Kennedy's house on his way home?"

"Yes."

"Did Graylin ever tell you he had a naked picture of Kennedy on his phone?"

"Yeah, on the same day he got arrested."

"Did he show it to you?"

"He wanted to, but I had to take something to the administration office for my teacher, so I couldn't see it."

"When was this?"

"The same day he got arrested. Right before our second-period class started. In first period, when we were taking our algebra test, he threw a spitball at me to get my attention. When I looked back at him, he was holding up his phone and pointing at it. He was trying to tell me something, but I didn't understand at the time. But now I know he was—"

Jenny is on her feet. "Objection, calls for speculation. The witness just testified that he didn't understand what Graylin was trying to tell him."

We decided last night that Jenny would handle the cross of Crayvon since she has more experience with child witnesses.

"Sustained," Judge Lipscomb says.

Sullivan doesn't mind the objection. The jury will infer that Graylin was trying to show him the picture of Kennedy.

"What did you do when Graylin tried to get your attention?"

"I didn't want to talk because I was trying to concentrate on my test. So I ignored him."

"Did you take the picture of Kennedy and send it to Graylin?"

"No. I didn't have nothing to do with any of this."

"I have no further questions of this witness."

Jenny stands, smiles and approaches Crayvon.

"Crayvon, do you believe Graylin took a naked picture of Kennedy?"

He shrugs. "I don't know."

"How many days was it between the time the two of you went into Kennedy's backyard and Graylin's arrest."

"I don't know. I think three days."

"So if someone else testified that it was two days, would they be wrong?"

"Yep. I know it was three days because I watched *NCIS* later that night and it comes on on Tuesday nights."

"Do you talk to Graylin on the phone?"

"No, we usually text."

"Did Graylin text you after he left your house that day?"

"Probably."

"Did he mention taking a picture of Kennedy?"

"Nope."

"When was the next time you saw Graylin?"

"The next day in first period."

"Did he mention taking a picture of Kennedy?"

"No."

"And when you saw him in the cafeteria at lunchtime, did he tell you that he had a picture of Kennedy?"

"No."

"Did he tell you anytime that day that he had a picture of Kennedy?"

"No."

"Did he tell you anytime on Thursday that he had a picture of Kennedy?"

"No."

"What about before your algebra test on Friday? Did Graylin tell you then that he had a picture of Kennedy?"

"No."

"So if Graylin had taken a picture of Kennedy after school on Tuesday, do you think he would've waited all the way until Friday to show it to you?"

This time Sullivan interrupts. "Objection, calls for speculation."

"Sustained."

"Probably not," Crayvon says, not understanding the objection.

"Young man," the judge says, "if I say an objection is sustained, that means you shouldn't answer the question."

"Okay, sorry."

"Did you ever tease Kennedy about being skinny?"

He scratches his jaw. "Sometimes, but I was only playing around."

"Did you ever tease her about wearing a weave?"

"Yeah, but I didn't mean any harm."

"Did you ever call her stuck-up?"

"I guess so."

"Did you ever tell LaShay that you wanted Kennedy to be your girlfriend?"

"No. I already have a girlfriend."

"It made you mad that Kennedy rejected you, didn't it?"

Crayvon's nose twitches and his lips protrude. "No! I didn't like her. Nobody likes her. She thinks she's better than everybody else because her parents have lots of money."

Jenny walks over to the defense table and lifts a few pages of her legal pad. She's not looking up anything in particular. She wants Crayvon's heated words to hang in the air.

"Did a girl at your church named Nedra Johnson accuse you of putting your hand under her dress?"

This question catches both Crayvon and Sullivan off guard.

Crayvon's head whips back. "That was—I was—she lied on me."

"So did you put your hand under her dress?"

He briefly averts his eyes, making him look like the liar that he is. "No, I didn't!"

Sullivan finally snaps out of her fog. "Objection, Your Honor. Asking this witness about an unfounded allegation is far more prejudicial than probative. I move to strike the witness' answer and request an instruction to the jury."

"Sustained." Judge Lipscomb glances over at the jurors. "The jury should disregard the young man's response."

I smile. Sullivan's late objection was a gift to us. The stammering denial from Crayvon makes him look like the pervert that he is.

"Did you ever go into Kennedy's backyard and take a picture through her bedroom window?"

"No, I did not." This time, he looks more convincing.

"Do you have a Snapchat account?"

"I used to. But my mama made me get off Snapchat after what happened to Graylin."

"Did you ever send a naked picture of Kennedy to Graylin on Snapchat?"

"No!"

"You didn't want to see the picture Graylin was trying to show you because you were the one who sent it to him, isn't that correct?"

"No, it's not!"

"You were the one who left that anonymous note in the administration office, weren't you?"

His eyes expand and he's on the verge of tears. "No! I told you I had nothing to do with it!"

Jenny backs off and asks him about his grades. At first I'm stunned, then I get it. If Crayvon starts crying, the jury's likely to feel sorry for him. I'm glad that Jenny's doing the cross. She asks a few more benign questions, then moves on to motive.

"When is the last time you saw your father?"

He shrugs. "I don't know."

"Are you close to your father?"

"Not really."

"Is Graylin close to his father?"

"Yeah."

"Did Graylin's father"—Jenny turns to smile at Gus, who we positioned one row behind the defense table today—"often take you along when he took Graylin out?"

Crayvon shrugs. "Yeah, I guess so."

"Where did Gus take you two?"

"The movies."

"And where else?"

"The park and fishing and stuff like that."

"Didn't Graylin's father buy him a leather jacket and get you one too?"

"Yeah."

"You're jealous of Graylin because he's close to his father, aren't you?"

Crayvon's anger resurfaces like a high tide. "I'm not jealous of him! At least my father's not an ex-con!"

Jenny stifles a smile. Crayvon couldn't sound more envious if we'd written him a script. She walks back to her notes, waits a long beat, then turns to the judge.

"Your Honor, I have no more questions for this witness."

CHAPTER 78

Angela

Jenny and I are standing at the defense table during a break when Sullivan walks over.

"We're dropping the criminal threat and distribution charges," she says, in the same tone she might use to tell us what she had for lunch.

This is good news, but not quite good enough. "The witness intimidation and invasion of privacy charges should go too?" I say. "There's no evidence to support them either."

Sullivan shrugs. "Those stay."

I feel like an angry bull taunted by a flash of red. She's produced no evidence showing Graylin took the picture of Kennedy. Nor has any witness credibly tied Graylin to the threatening call Kennedy received. The only reason she's not dropping the witness intimidation charge is because without it, Judge Lipscomb would no longer have jurisdiction over this case and we'd be kicked back to juvenile court.

"You must get some kind of perverse pleasure playing with people's lives," I say. "Both you and Martinez knew you couldn't prove the witness intimidation charge from day one. Graylin has no business in adult court."

"He's here because the judge found him unfit as a result of his own conduct. Don't blame that on me."

Yes, Graylin's outrageous behavior landed him here, but we never would've gotten to that point if they hadn't added the bogus witness intimidation charge in the first place.

I take a step into Sullivan's personal space. "How do you sleep at night? You can't just—"

Jenny slips between us. "Thanks for the heads-up," she tells Sullivan as she drags me out of the courtroom and into the hallway.

My eyes well with tears. It's not like me to behave that way toward an opposing counsel. The stress is getting to me.

"Please chill," Jenny says, throwing an arm around my shoulder. "You've been kicking butt. No matter how many games the prosecution plays, we're still winning."

I only wish I had Jenny's confidence.

When court resumes, Sullivan rests her case and I make my perfunctory request for a directed verdict. I ask the judge to dismiss the remaining charges—possession of child pornography, witness intimidation and invasion of privacy—arguing that the prosecution hasn't met its burden of proof. As expected, the judge denies the motion and we break for lunch.

We all gather at a sandwich shop, where I tell Gus and Graylin about two of the charges being dropped. Graylin's thrilled and more convinced than ever that he's going to win. Gus, however, understands the significance of Sullivan's refusal to drop the witness intimidation charge and he's livid. But like Jenny, he also thinks we're ahead.

When it's time to return to court, Jenny tries to cheer me up. "Let it go. Sullivan hasn't met her burden and she knows it. We scored some major points with Crayvon today."

"What major points?"

"What fourteen-year-old boy who takes a naked picture of his classmate is going to wait three days, or even two days, if you believe Taisha's timeline, to show it to his best friend. If that doesn't raise reasonable doubt, I don't know what will."

I can't help being Debbie Downer. "That helps us with the invasion of privacy charge, and the witness intimidation allegation is weak, but there's still the possession charge."

"If that jury thinks Crayvon took the picture and sent it to Graylin, they're not going to find him guilty of possession either."

"I hope you're right."

By the time the jury is called back in, it's well after one o'clock. The judge directs me to call my first witness. We only have three. Taisha's foster mother, Graylin's minister, and one of his teachers.

Betty Taylor does an excellent job of explaining that her foster daughter's excessive lying is a cry for attention. Next, Graylin's science teacher calls him one of the best students she's had in her twenty-plus years of teaching. For almost fifteen minutes, Reverend Ball praises Graylin as a real leader and a blessing to his church. I'm about to move on to the allegation that Crayvon stuck his hand underneath Nedra Johnson's dress when the courtroom doors burst open with a loud bang.

Mama Baker storms down the center aisle, dragging her granddaughter LaShay by the forearm.

"The devil is a lie! The devil is a lie!" she yells. "Mama Baker don't raise no heathens!"

Judge Lipscomb bangs his gavel. "What the hell? Order in the court! Order in the court!"

"Judge," Mama Baker says, waving her free hand, "we need to talk because Mama Baker don't raise no heathens. My granddaughter needs to get back up on that witness stand. And the sooner the better!"

Mama Baker is about to step into the well of the courtroom when the slow-moving bailiff jogs over and blocks her path.

"I need to talk to the judge," she says. "Because the devil is a lie!"

Judge Lipscomb looks as flustered as the bailiff. "Ma'am, you can't interrupt a court proceeding like this. Please leave my courtroom."

"I prayed on this all night, judge, and this is what the Lord told me to do."

"Get the jury out of here!" Judge Lipscomb says to the bailiff. "Ma'am, please don't say another word."

The bailiff is still standing guard over Mama Baker. He seems uncertain about leaving her unsupervised. He yells across the courtroom. "I need the jurors back in the jury room."

The jurors snicker as they file through the door behind the jury box. Once they're gone, the judge erupts.

"Ma'am, this is highly inappropriate! You can't disrupt my courtroom like this. I just may find you in contempt of court."

"That's good and well, but you should know that Jesus is the only judge I fear. My granddaughter didn't tell the truth up there on that witness stand. And I can't let that be. She needs to redo her testimony because Mama Baker don't raise no heathens."

LaShay cowers behind her grandmother, her face wet with tears.

The judge is at a loss for words. He's obviously never had to face anyone like Mama Baker before.

"I'd like to see counsel and Mrs. Baker in my chambers. Now!"

CHAPTER 79

Angela

When we finish listening to what Mama Baker has to say, everybody in Judge Lipscomb's chambers is flabbergasted.

The judge orders Mama Baker back to the courtroom. He looks at Sullivan, then at Jenny and me. "How would you like to proceed?"

"I'd like to request a mistrial," Sullivan says in a voice stripped of emotion.

"We don't want a mistrial," I say. "We want a dismissal."

Sullivan hesitates. "What we just heard doesn't impact all of the charges."

"Then let's proceed," I say, more fired up than ever. "I'd like to recall LaShay to the witness stand right now. I can finish up the reverend later."

The judge shakes his head. "In my twenty-three years on the bench this is the craziest thing I've ever seen."

He gives us ten minutes to talk to Gus and Graylin, who also don't want a mistrial.

"What did LaShay's granny say, Ms. Angela? Did she tell the judge Crayvon and Taisha lied on me?"

"Hold on. You'll find out everything in a second."

I start scribbling down notes for my cross-examination of LaShay. I don't have time to write down complete questions, so I jot down key words as reminders of the areas I want to cover. I pass my legal pad to Jenny. She peruses it then scribbles down another topic for me to address.

Judge Lipscomb calls the jury back in and LaShay walks to the jury box. The judge reminds her that she's still under oath. The little girl's eyes are puffy and red and it appears that she's been crying for some time.

"LaShay, when you testified in this courtroom yesterday, did you tell the truth?" I ask.

Her head is bowed so low that her chin grazes her chest. "No, ma'am," she sniffs.

"Are you ready to tell the truth now?"

"Yes, ma'am."

"Do you know who took the naked picture of your friend Kennedy Carlyle?"

LaShay nods.

"I'm sorry, LaShay. Nodding your head won't work. You'll need to speak up so the jury and the court reporter can hear you."

"Um, yes, I know."

"Please tell the jury who took it."

"I did."

The collective gasp is so loud it sounds like the courtroom is equipped with surround sound. I wait for the commotion to die down before continuing.

"And why did you take a naked picture of Kennedy?"

"Because she asked me to."

Mrs. Carlyle jumps to her feet. "That's a lie! You framed that boy, and now you're trying to frame my baby!"

The bailiff trots over to Simone just as Mama Baker revs up.

"The devil is a lie!" she yells from the front row. "The truth shall set you free. Go ahead, baby. Bare your soul. Jesus loves you."

The judge bangs his gavel and points it first at Mrs. Carlyle, then at Mama Baker. "If I hear a peep from either one of you, you're out of here!"

While Mama Baker sits taller in her chair, Simone slumps back to the bench. The bailiff remains standing in the middle of the aisle, an arm's reach away from both of them.

I move closer to the witness box, hoping to make LaShay feel more at ease.

"So why did Kennedy ask you to take a naked picture of her?"

"She wanted to get back at Graylin for not liking her. She knew he would get in trouble if he had a naked picture of her. She also thought her parents might get back together if something bad happened to her."

"Do you know who left the note for the principal?"

She nods, then catches herself. "Um, yes. Kennedy typed it up, but I left it on the counter when nobody was looking."

"When did you do that?"

"Right before second period started."

"Do you know who sent Graylin the picture on Snapchat?"

"Yeah. Kennedy did that part. She made up a fake Snapchat account. There's a website you can go to and get a fake email address that nobody can trace."

"Did she send the picture to anybody else besides Graylin?"

"Yeah, lots of people, but Graylin got it first. She told me she wanted it to go viral so she would get famous like Kim Kardashian. But people started making fun of her online, calling her skinny and stuff and that hurt her feelings. I don't think she thought it would really go viral because when it did, she got scared. We also didn't know Graylin would get in trouble with the police. We thought he might get detention or something like that."

I think I have everything I need. I glance back at Jenny for confirmation. She nods.

"I have no further questions, Your Honor."

For the first time, Sullivan looks deflated. She places both hands flat on the table and pushes herself to her feet.

"LaShay, are you certain you're telling the truth?"

"Yes, ma'am."

"Is this the truth or is this what your grandmother told you to say?"

Mama Baker is on her feet. "The devil is a lie! The truth—"

The judge bangs his gavel. "That's it. Bailiff, show Mrs. Baker out of my courtroom."

Mama Baker keeps talking as she waddles down the aisle. "That's okay, baby. You just tell 'em the truth. The truth shall set you free."

Sullivan swallows and resumes. "You claim Kennedy wanted to get Graylin in trouble, correct?"

"Yes."

"If she wanted to get him in trouble, why didn't she just send him the picture in a text or an email?"

"Because he would've known she sent it."

"How did she know he would take a screenshot of it?"

LaShay looks at Sullivan as if the question doesn't make sense. "Because everybody does."

Sullivan struggles to recover. She opens her mouth to speak, then apparently thinks better of it. "I have no further questions of this witness, Your Honor."

"I think that's enough for today," the judge says. "I'm dismissing the jury and I'd like to see counsel and the defendant in chambers."

"Did we win, Ms. Angela?" Graylin says, excited. "Is that why we have to go talk to the judge?"

I'm praying that's the case, but I don't want to get his hopes up. "I don't know, Graylin. We'll have to see."

I feel a hand on my shoulder and turn around to an embrace from Gus. "Dre told me you would do it!"

I eye Dre over my shoulder at the back of the courtroom. He's smiling with such pride that it warms me up inside. Gus reaches out and hugs Jenny too.

"Let's not count our chickens before they're hatched," I say. "I wish I could take credit, but this was nothing short of divine intervention."

When we enter the judge's chambers, he's stripping off his robe. He tells Graylin to take a seat in one of the chairs in front of his desk. The attorneys remain standing.

"Ms. Sullivan," Judge Lipscomb says, as he rolls up the cuffs of his white shirt, "you have some decisions to make regarding the charges against this defendant." He sits down behind his desk.

Sullivan looks down at the floor.

"Do you want to proceed with this prosecution," the judge asks, "or dismiss the charges?"

"Let me talk to my boss," Sullivan says, as if all the life has been sucked out of her. "I'll have a decision in the morning."

I can tell Graylin is about to burst with excitement. I place a hand on his shoulder as we walk back into the courtroom which is empty except for Gus, Dre and the bailiff.

"I told you guys! Little Slice was right! If I had stayed in juvenile court, that judge would've locked me up and made me a sex offender! Now I'm going free!"

"What happened in there?" Gus asks anxiously.

"I have a strong feeling the charges are going to be dismissed," I say. "The prosecutor has to check with her boss. We'll know for sure in the morning."

Jenny smiles. "I don't know about y'all, but I think we should do some early celebrating."

CHAPTER 80

Angela

We give Graylin the honor of picking the restaurant and he chooses El Torito in Marina Del Rey. Jenny calls Mei with the good news and invites her to join us. An hour later, we're all seated at a long table, munching on chips and salsa, drinking margaritas and gazing at the sailboats docked along the Marina.

I can't explain how great it feels to see Graylin so happy.

"The devil is a lie! The devil is a lie!" he exclaims every few minutes. *"Mama Baker don't raise no heathens!* LaShay's mama was so funny."

"You need to be thanking God that she's an honest woman," I tell him. "Not everybody would've done what she did."

"I can't believe this nightmare is finally over," Gus says. "If I ever catch a case again, God forbid, I'm looking up the two of you."

A waitress sets a bowl of guacamole and two platters of chicken quesadillas in the middle of the table.

Graylin lifts his strawberry lemonade high in the air. "A toast to the two best attorneys in the whole wide world!"

We all raise our glasses in cheer.

"The person sitting next to you also deserves some applause," Jenny says, pointing across the table at Mei. "She tracked down all of our witnesses."

"Thank you, Ms. Mei," Graylin says, giving her a hug.

Mei blushes. "Thanks, but I had no clue that LaShay took that picture or that Kennedy asked her to."

"So what's going to happen to them?" Dre asks. "They're the ones who should face child pornography charges."

"I don't know," I say. "I suspect the D.A.'s Office just wants this case to go away."

"That D.A. better file charges against both of 'em," Gus bellows.

I don't say it out loud, but I feel sorry for Kennedy. Simone Carlyle's partly to blame for what her daughter did. The girl probably saw her mother bully people. So it was easy for her to manipulate LaShay and have no qualms about setting up Graylin.

"It's possible Kennedy and LaShay will be charged," Jenny says. "Especially if you push for it."

"I plan to," Gus says. "And I also plan to sue both of those girls and their parents in civil court, just like that witch Simone said she was going to do me. Me and my son want some emotional distress money for everything they put us through."

"You have a good case," I say. "But maybe you should move on. Turn the other cheek, so to speak."

"No way. They shouldn't be allowed to get away with this. Just because they're girls, people are probably going to be more sympathetic toward them. But what they did could've ruined my son's life."

Jenny nods. "I only wish prosecutors would exercise a little more discretion when they're filing these cases."

My phone rings and *Blocked* shows up on the caller ID display. My pulse speeds up. Calls from the prosecutor's office usually show up as blocked.

"Hey, everybody, this might be the prosecutor." I wave my hand in the air so they all quiet down. "Let's pray the charges are being dismissed."

I place the phone to my ear, but I'm having a hard time hearing over the restaurant noise.

"Hold on a minute," I say into the phone. "Let me put my earphones in so I can hear you better."

I listen intently for only about a minute, then hang up the phone. Everyone is smiling in anticipation of what I have to say. But Dre knows me and immediately senses that something is wrong.

He squeezes my shoulder. "Babe, what did she say?"

"They're dropping the charges." I pause, not wanting to relay the rest of the conversation. "All of them except for the possession of child pornography charge."

"What the fuck!" Gus slams his fist so hard on the table that water splashes out of his glass. Everybody in our corner of the restaurant is staring at us.

"Sullivan said Graylin's saving the picture to his phone was a criminal act. She's offering him a deferred entry of judgment deal."

"What's that?" Dre asks.

"Graylin has to plead guilty to the possession charge," I explain. "If he stays out of trouble for a year, the charge will be dismissed. But if he gets in any kind of trouble during that time, the deal is revoked and he'll be placed on probation." I pause. "Until he's twenty-one."

"Twenty-one!" Gus screeches. "So if he gets a friggin' traffic ticket, he'll be locked up for violating his probation? That's nuts!"

"Hold on," Jenny says. "The court has the option to retain jurisdiction until he's twenty-one, but it's rare for probation to last that long if a kid doesn't get into trouble again. This is just the worst-case scenario."

Dre's face shows nothing but incredulity. "And what does he have to do to avoid violating probation?"

"He'll have to go to school, maintain a C average, and avoid any additional charges," Jenny says. "None of that would be a problem for Graylin."

"And if he does violate probation," Dre presses, "then what happens?"

Jenny inhales long and hard. "He'll have to provide a sample of his DNA to police so that if he commits a crime in the future, it's in the system. The police will have the right to search his person and his home at any time without a warrant and without probable cause. He'll also have a felony on his record, have to serve time—probably in a juvenile camp—and have to register as a sex offender."

As I listened to Sullivan minutes ago, I sensed that she disagreed with the decision not to drop all of the charges. I suspect that her marching orders came from the top. Instead of walking away in defeat, the D.A.'s Office is trying to save face.

"We have to consider the offer," I say. "If Graylin's convicted, he could—"

"No!" Graylin yells. Tears dampen his cheeks. "I'm not pleading guilty to nothing because I'm not a child pornographer!"

I turn to Jenny and know instantly that we are on the same page. There's no disputing that Graylin was in possession of child pornography. The law doesn't care how he got it. The only way we can win on the remaining charge is via jury nullification, which always was and still is a gamble.

"Graylin," Jenny says gently, "this is a good thing."

"No it isn't!" he shouts, his tears streaming now. "That jury isn't going to convict me. Not after you showed them how everybody lied on me. You said I'm the client, so it's my decision. I want to take my chances with the jury."

CHAPTER 81

Angela

When Judge Lipscomb calls the attorneys into his chambers the next morning, it feels like we're marching in a funeral procession.

"So where do we stand?" he asks. He's sitting forward in his chair, his elbows propped on his desk.

Sullivan shuffles from one foot to the other. "We're dropping the invasion of privacy and witness intimidation charges," she says, then swallows. "But we're proceeding with the possession charge."

The judge squints up at her. "You're kidding me, right?"

Sullivan blows out a breath. "Your Honor, there's no disputing that the defendant saved the picture to his phone."

The judge isn't happy. "And there's also no disputing that Penal Code Section 311 was intended to go after pedophiles and this kid is no pedophile. If you're dropping the witness intimidation charge, that means I no longer have jurisdiction. I can send this thing back to juvenile court where it belongs."

"We did offer the defendant a deferred entry of judgment deal," Sullivan says. "One year, but he turned it down."

Now the judge is giving me the same chiding look he'd just given Sullivan.

"Ms. Evans, please tell me you didn't advise your client not to take the deal."

"Your Honor, we've tried everything, but Graylin won't agree to it. His father couldn't convince him either."

The judge grunts. "Get him in here. His father too."

I walk back into the courtroom and tell Graylin and Gus that the judge wants to speak to them in chambers.

"Why, Ms. Angela? Why does the judge want to speak to me?"

"Because he's not happy that you turned down the prosecutor's offer."

"I sure hope the judge can talk some sense into this stubborn fool," Gus mutters.

Graylin takes a seat in front of the judge's desk. Gus is standing behind him, gripping the back of his chair.

"Good morning, young man." Judge Lipscomb rounds his desk and sits on the edge, facing Graylin. "I understand you turned down Ms. Sullivan's offer of a deferred entry of judgment. Do you understand what she's offering you?"

Graylin squeezes the arms of his chair. "Yes, sir."

"I want to be sure you understand what you're doing. Explain to me what Ms. Sullivan offered you? I'd like to hear it in your own words."

"If I plead guilty and stay out of trouble for a year, then the possessing child pornography charge will be dismissed. But if I get in any trouble, I'll be on probation for a long time and have to give the police my DNA. And If I do something wrong while I'm on probation, then I'll be locked up and be a sex offender."

"I'm sure a good kid like you can stay out of trouble for a year. Don't you think the prosecutor is offering you a good deal?"

Graylin exhales. "No, sir."

"Why not?"

"Because I'm not a child pornographer and I shouldn't have to plead guilty to something I didn't do. And how do I know somebody won't set me up again? Then I'll get convicted on the child pornography charge because of that."

Judge Lipscomb's chest rises and falls. "Young man, you admit saving a naked picture of another minor on your phone, correct?"

"Yes, sir."

"Then under the law, you're guilty. Do you understand what it means to have to register as a sex offender?"

"Yes, sir."

"That's what could happen if you get convicted. You don't want to risk that. Everybody says you're a smart kid. You're not thinking too smart right now."

Graylin says nothing.

"I want you to give some serious thought to what you're doing. Would you like some time to think about it?"

"It's not right to put me in jail just for having that picture," Graylin says. "And I'm going to prove it to the jury."

"How are you going to do that?"

"I'm going to convince them that I'm innocent when I testify."

The judge glares up at me, then back down at Graylin. "Your attorneys are putting you on the witness stand?"

"I have the right to testify in my own defense," Graylin says. "It's the law."

"Jesus Christ!" the judge exclaims. He points a lean finger inches from Graylin's nose. "This is what you're going to do, young man. You're going to take the next thirty minutes to think about what you're doing. You're going to listen to your father and your attorneys and—"

Graylin politely interrupts the judge. "I'm sorry, Your Honor, but I don't need any time. I'm not going to change my mind."

He reaches into the inside pocket of his jacket and pulls out some papers. I can see that it's a wrinkled copy of the pamphlet Jenny gave him the day after his arrest. It looks so worn he must've read it a dozen times.

"This is the pamphlet that my attorney, Ms. Jenny, gave me about my rights," Graylin says. His hands are shaking so badly we can hear the paper rattle. "And it says right here on page six that I get to make the decisions about my case."

In a shaky voice, he starts reading from the pamphlet.

You are not required to accept a settlement offer. Your attorney must present the offer and tell you what he or she thinks of the offer. Your attorney should explain the pros and cons of the offer. It is important to remember that the decision to accept or reject the offer is only your decision. The defense attorney cannot make the decision

*for you, your parent or guardian cannot make the decision for you,
and the court cannot force you to take a settlement.*

Graylin refolds the pamphlet and looks back up at the judge. His
hands are no longer shaking.

The judge huffs loud enough to blow the curtains down. "Young
man, I have the power to dismiss this case and send you back to juvenile
court since I no longer have jurisdiction. Are you saying you don't want
me to do that?"

"That's right, sir. I want my day in court."

Gus curses under his breath.

Graylin meets the judge's stern glare with more defiance than ever.
"My granny always tells me to have faith," he says, putting the pamphlet
back inside his jacket pocket. "So that's what I'm going to do. I'm not
pleading guilty because I'm not a child pornographer. And when I testify,
I know the jury's going to believe me."

CHAPTER 82

Once Graylin's little speech is said and done, one thing is clear, Judge Lipscomb is pissed. Pissed at the prosecution for not dropping the case, pissed at the defense attorneys for not being able to talk some sense into our client and pissed at Graylin for being too young and too naïve to understand the incredible risk he's taking with his life. But to our surprise, he doesn't send the case back to juvenile court.

The judge denies my request for a three-day continuance but gives us the rest of the day off. He sends the jury home with instructions to return the following morning.

Jenny and I agree that we have to roll the dice and let Graylin testify. The jurors now know Kennedy set him up. If they're going to let him walk on the possession charge, they need to see for themselves, not through the testimony of others, what a great kid he is.

I take Graylin to Jenny's office where we spend the rest of the day going through mock questioning. Although only one charge remains, the stakes are still high. Except for a murder trial, I've never had a case with more serious consequences. Nor have I ever had a case where I wanted to win for my client more than this one.

After Gus drops by to pick up Graylin, Jenny and I sit in silence for a while.

"This is positively my last juvenile case," I say. "It's way too heart-wrenching."

Jenny smiles. "It is tough sometimes, but when I fight for these kids and win, there's no better feeling in the world." She stands up and pulls a large album from the top of a file cabinet. "This," she says, "makes it all worthwhile."

I open the album and find dozens of cards and letters, some hand-written, some typed. There are also a few pictures.

I look up at her. "Are these letters and cards from your former clients?"

"Yep."

I read a couple of them.

Dear Ms. J.,
Thank you for beleeving in me. Nobody ever beleeved in me like you did.

Dear Miss Jenny,
Thanks for fighting for me. I promise I'm going to get my GED and stay out of trouble.

There's a picture of Jenny posing with a gangly black kid in a cap and gown. "Who's he?"

"My star client," Jenny beams. "He graduated from El Camino Junior College last year. He'll be a junior at Long Beach State in the fall."

Reading the letters makes me feel hopeful and scared at the same time. I pray we'll see Graylin graduate from college one day.

"It'll be a good thing for the jury to hear from Graylin," Jenny says. "He's smart, kind and articulate. They'll see their own kids in him. They won't want to ruin his life."

I don't know how long I've been staring out of the window.

"Hey, are you even listening to me?" Jenny says.

I spin around. "I have an idea. Where's our witness list?" I frantically search for our trial binder.

"Why?"

"*Please* tell me we kept Dr. Mandell on the list."

Dr. Mandell is a child psychologist. We'd gone back and forth on whether we wanted to call an expert to testify.

"She's on there," Jenny says. "Why?"

I start scrolling through my phone for her number. "Because Dr. Mandell is going to help us get jury nullification."

"What do you need me to do?" Jenny asks.

"Pray that she's available on short notice."

CHAPTER 83

Angela

The next day, we complete the testimony of Graylin's minister, then call Dr. Faye Mandell to the stand.

The woman exudes professionalism. She's around sixty, slim and stylishly dressed in a hot pink Chenille pantsuit. After explaining that she specializes in child psychology, Dr. Mandell tells the jury that she has a master's degree in clinical social work and a Ph.D. in child psychology, both from USC. She's also written numerous books and articles on parenting and has appeared on CNN and MSNBC to discuss sexting among teens.

"Dr. Mandell, you've written several articles about the impact of technology on adolescent sexuality. Can you tell us how the two intersect?"

"Technology allows kids to explore their sexuality without doing it face-to-face. In my day, we talked in person or on the telephone. Today's kids send text messages. Technology is another part of their environment. The cell phone is the most widely used mode of communication among teens. They don't talk. They text and sext."

"Can you explain to the jury what sexting is?"

"It's sending or posting sexually suggestive text messages and images, including nude or semi-nude photos—usually of yourself—via cell phone, email or social media. The term sexting has been around for about twelve years."

"Is sexting a popular trend among teens?"

"Sadly, yes. A study published in the *Archives of Pediatric & Adolescent Medicine* found that thirty-nine percent of teens admit to having sent a sext. Another forty-eight percent say they've received one. A whopping eighty-six percent of teen sexters never get caught. And more girls sext than boys."

"And when you say teens, what ages are you referring to?"

"For the figures I just quoted you, thirteen to seventeen."

I hit a few buttons on my laptop, introducing an exhibit. An image of the brain appears on the courtroom screen.

"I'd like to ask you a few questions about childhood brain development. Is the brain of a teen, say a fourteen-year-old, the same as the brain of an adult?"

"No, it's not. The front part of the brain is called the prefrontal cortex. This area right here." She aims at the screen with a laser pointer. "It's responsible for problem solving, impulse control and weighing options. In children, this area isn't fully developed until the early to mid-twenties."

"What do you mean when you say a child's brain isn't fully developed?"

"As children enter adolescence around the age of twelve, a number of changes begin taking place in their brains. They start to develop sexually, which we call puberty. They start developing their own identity and move away from their parents and closer to their peers. During this phase, kids are more apt to experiment. Today's technology makes it easier for them to take risks based on hyper-rational thinking, which is—"

"Objection, Your Honor," Sullivan interrupts. "We're not here for a biology lesson. I don't think this is at all relevant. And it's far more prejudicial than it is probative."

"Counsel, please approach."

"Ms. Evans, I tend to agree with the prosecutor. How is this relevant to the possession charge?"

"Your Honor, this is a specific intent crime. The prosecution has to prove that my client had the intent to possess child pornography. His maturity level and the development of his brain in that regard are directly relevant."

"I agree with you, Ms. Evans. Overruled," he says loudly.

I'm stunned. I expected Judge Lipscomb to give me more of a fight. I smile inwardly. He's still pissed that the prosecution didn't drop all of the charges and he's cutting us some slack.

I turn back to Dr. Mandell. "You were about to explain what hyper-rational thinking is. Please continue."

"Children generally don't have the logical skillset we have as adults. They lack the ability to correlate potential cause and effect. This makes them more vulnerable to things like peer pressure, drugs, and sexting. Because of the undeveloped nature of the prefrontal cortex, teens are also more likely to take risks that an adult would never take. Like sending a naked selfie or saving one they may have received from a text or Snapchat."

Sullivan audibly groans.

"So are you saying, their maturity level impacts their behavior?"

"Absolutely. While we think they should know better, they don't. They aren't physiologically developed enough to understand the risks. Even when they're warned about it. They're children. There's a reason we don't let fourteen-year-olds drink, drive, vote or smoke. Kids are more impetuous and they're not cognizant of risks. Because of the developmental differences in their brains, they don't stop to consider the long-term consequences of their decisions."

"Do you believe children should be charged with possession of child pornography for—"

"Objection!" Sullivan yells.

"Sustained," Judge Lipscomb replies, giving me a chiding look that says I'm pushing the envelope. "Let's move this along, counselor."

"Dr. Mandell, why do you think sexting is so prevalent among teens these days?"

"In great part because our children are saturated with sexual images. TV, movies, music, advertising, everywhere they turn. If you have the exhibit I prepared, I can show you better than I can tell you."

"Your Honor, I'd like to refer the witness to defendant's exhibit six." I hit a key on my laptop and a collage of photographs fills the courtroom screen.

"This is a sampling of the kind of sexual images our children are bombarded with almost from the cradle." She points the laser at the screen. "This is an ad for mascara that I saw in Macy's. It touts the mascara as *Better Than Sex*. And we've all seen the Carl's Jr. hamburger commercials where the ketchup runs down the woman's breasts. These are shots from *The Bachelor* and *The Bachelorette* TV shows, which are extremely popular among teenage girls. They show people making out within minutes of meeting each other."

She aims the laser at a picture of the *Housewives of Atlanta*.

"This is another popular reality show. As you can see, the women routinely dress in an extremely provocative manner, exposing their breasts. These shows set the standards for our kids. Then there's *Dating Naked*. I still can't believe that's even on TV. And, of course, there's the ever-popular Kim Kardashian, whose claim to fame is a porn video. She's a wealthy pop culture icon—in part, because of that video—and millions of girls want to be like her. Even in cartoons like *Shrek*, there's sexual innuendo."

Dr. Mandell places the laser pointer along the edge of the witness box.

"I could go on and on, but I think you get my point. My generation grew up with *Father Knows Best* and *I Love Lucy*. Lucy and Ricky Ricardo slept in separate beds. And even when we progressed to *The Brady Bunch*, we saw Mr. and Mrs. Brady in bed but never having sex. We can't saturate our children with sexual images and then expect them to act like saints. What you see up there on that screen is the norm for today's kids. So, of course, they don't think it's any big deal to trade pictures of their genitals."

I see several members of the jury—both male and female—frowning, but at the same time, nodding in agreement.

After a few more questions, I hand my witness over to Sullivan.

"Ms. Mandell, do you believe that teens should be absolved of their crimes simply because their brains aren't fully developed?"

Dr. Mandell smiles. "I'm sorry, Ms. Sullivan, but it's *Dr.* Mandell. And no, I don't think that. But I do think that in the sexting area—"

"That's okay. You've answered my question."

I stand up. "Your Honor, Dr. Mandell should be allowed to finish her response."

The judge peers down at the witness box. "Were you finished, Dr. Mandell?"

"No, I wasn't."

"You can continue."

"What I wanted to say was, unfortunately for our kids, the law hasn't caught up with technology. We're using laws meant to protect children as a sword against them, rather than a shield to protect them. These kids shouldn't be prosecuted under laws intended to punish pedophiles. They're sexually curious children, not pedophiles. We're criminalizing normative adolescent behavior."

Sullivan pounces. "So you believe a kid who keeps sexual images on his phone is engaging in normal adolescent behavior?"

"I sure do. Over seventy percent of teens own a cell phone. You'd be surprised how many kids are sexting." She turns away from Sullivan and faces the jury. "Maybe even your own kids. As far as I'm concerned, any parent who hasn't had a frank, but stern talk with their teenagers about sexting is guilty of parental malpractice."

At least three of the female jurors have distressed looks on their faces. They're probably going to run straight home and check their kids' phones.

Sullivan groans. She seems uncertain about where to go next, but plows on.

"It sounds as if you think the only way we can keep kids from sexting is to confiscate their cell phones?"

"That's one way," Dr. Mandell says. "But until kids truly understand the consequences of doing this, it's ridiculous to lock them up and make them register as sex offenders for the rest of their lives."

A couple of jurors grimace. They didn't know finding Graylin guilty means he'll be branded an eternal sex offender. I could kiss Dr. Mandell for sneaking in that little jewel.

Sullivan asks a couple more questions that go just as badly, then gives up.

The judge dismisses Dr. Mandell then turns to me. "Who's your next witness, counsel?"

For some reason, I'm holding my breath as I slowly rise. "I'd like to call my client, Graylin Alexander."

CHAPTER 84

Angela

The judge gives us a fifteen-minute break. He must've seen the trepidation in my eyes and figured I needed it.

Jenny follows me to the ladies' room where I press cold paper towels to my face.

"I wish Mama Baker was here to lay hands on us," Jenny says.

I laugh. "Maybe we should give her a call to see if she can do it over the phone."

We're making jokes, but we both know this is no joking matter.

"I'm glad we teamed up on this case," Jenny says.

"Me too." I give her a long hug.

"I owe you an apology?" Jenny says.

"For what?"

"You were right. Dre didn't have anything to do with The Shepherd's death. According to my brother-in-law, he was paying off a couple of correctional officers who snuck in cell phones, food, and other stuff. After he threatened to expose them, the guards looked the other way when three inmates raped, beat and stabbed him. Hidden cameras showed the guards letting the inmates into the room where The Shepherd was found dead. All five of them are facing murder charges."

I wonder whether the inmates who killed him were Blaze's henchmen. I don't even care. I'm just glad The Shepherd's not around to ruin the lives of any more children.

"Thanks for telling me that," I say, and we hug again.

Jenny opens the bathroom door and steps aside to let me walk out first. "Let's go finish kicking Sullivan's butt."

Graylin, Gus, and Dre are standing outside the courtroom. I was so nervous about Graylin testifying today that I didn't notice his new suit.

"Wow, don't you look nice?"

For most of the trial he's been wearing the same blue suit with a different shirt and tie. Today he's in a spiffy double-breasted gray suit.

He smiles. "My aunt Macie bought it for me."

"You ready to testify?"

"Yep."

"Now remember—"

"You don't have to tell me again, Ms. Angela. I remember. Only answer the questions asked. Say *yes, ma'am*, not *yeah*. Sit up straight. Be respectful. Don't show my feelings. Look the jurors in the eye. Did I miss anything?"

I chuckle. "No, I think you got it all."

Five minutes later, when it's time for him to take the stand, Graylin's confidence has shriveled up like a grape on a hot griddle. He's even unsteady on his feet as he walks to the witness box.

"Can you state your name for the record?" I ask, once he's settled in.

"Graylin Michael Alexander."

"I'd like you to take a look at defendant's exhibit seven and tell us what it is."

"This is my last report card."

"And what is your grade point average?"

"Three-point-eight. I got mostly A's."

"Are you in the TAG Program?"

"Yes."

"Tell us what TAG stands for."

"The Talented and Gifted Program."

"And how long have you been in TAG?

"Always."

"Always?"

"Yes, since elementary school."

"Do you like school?"

"Yes. I'm going to be a lawyer when I grow up."

He must have come up with that overnight. When we prepped him, he told us he wanted to be a video gamer.

"Did you receive a picture via Snapchat on May tenth?"

"Yes."

"What did you do with it?"

"I took a screenshot of it."

"Why?"

"Because I was shocked to see it."

"Were you aware that having it on your phone meant you were guilty of being in possession of child pornography?"

"No, ma'am, I didn't know that."

"What did you intend to do with the picture?"

Graylin lowers his chin. "I was going to show it to my friend Crayvon, but that's it. But I didn't though."

"Were you going to put it on the internet?"

"No, ma'am."

"Did you put it on the internet?"

"No, ma'am. I wouldn't do that."

I ask him several more questions, not because I need to, but because I don't want to leave him in Sullivan's clutches. But ultimately, I have to.

Once I sit down, Graylin closes his eyes and his lips start moving. It looks like he's praying.

"Good morning, Graylin," Sullivan says.

"Good morning."

"I only have a few questions for you."

"Okay." Graylin rubs his palms together.

"Have you ever received any other inappropriate pictures on your cell phone besides the picture of Kennedy Carlyle?"

Jenny and I freeze, then nearly knock each other over jumping to our feet.

"Objection, irrelevant, vague and ambiguous as to *inappropriate*," Jenny says. "And the probative value is outweighed by its prejudicial effect."

I stand there mute, even though Graylin is *my* witness.

"Sustained," Lipscomb says, "but only because the question is a little vague. Ms. Sullivan, could you be a little more precise with your question?" He turns to us. "I don't need objections from both defense counsel."

Sullivan happily rephrases her question. "Have you ever received a naked picture of anyone else besides Kennedy Carlyle on your cell phone before?"

We asked Graylin that question and he said no. The fact that Sullivan is asking it means she knows something we don't. From the terrorized look on Graylin's face, he's either going to answer in the affirmative or lie.

"Um, yes, ma'am."

How did Sullivan know this? Is this information she got from Crayvon?

"How many times?"

"Two times?"

Graylin looks sheepishly at me. I'm trying not to look angry, so I don't make him any more nervous than he already is. But I want to strangle him for not telling us this.

"Who was in the pictures?"

"It was just two grown white ladies. I didn't know the ladies."

"When did you receive them?"

"I'm not sure. Last year some time."

"Who sent you the pictures?"

"I don't know. Somebody on Snapchat."

"Did you save those two pictures to your phone?"

Graylin sits up straighter, like he's proud to answer this question. "No, ma'am."

Sullivan hesitates as if she isn't sure she wants to ask the next question. "Why not?"

Graylin hunches his shoulders. "I don't know. I didn't know the ladies. And I also didn't know Snapchat that good back then."

"So if you'd known how to use Snapchat better, would you have saved those pictures too?"

"I don't know. Maybe."

"And why did you save Kennedy's picture?"

Graylin's chest starts to heave like he's entering the early stage of an asthma attack. He takes a long time to answer and Sullivan waits, not pressing him.

"Ma'am, I don't know, but I didn't mean any harm. I didn't know Kennedy's picture was child pornography. I wasn't—"

Sullivan dives in to cut him off. "I have no further questions of this witness."

"I wasn't trying to hurt anyone." Graylin turns to face the jury as tears trail down his cheeks. "I'm not a bad person—"

"Objection!" Sullivan screams, but her protest goes unheeded by both Graylin and the judge.

I can't believe it, but Judge Erik "The Electric" Lipscomb is staring down at Graylin with watery, empathetic eyes. He's actually biting his bottom lip as if to contain his emotions. He doesn't say one word and lets Graylin continue his emotional plea to the jury.

"I'm a good student," Graylin sobs. "And I go to church every Sunday. Please don't make me a child pornographer!"

By the time Graylin gathers himself and walks back to the defense table, I'm thrilled to see more than a few moist eyes in the jury box.

CHAPTER 85

Angela

I was hoping the judge would call a recess and let us do closing arguments in the morning, but Lipscomb wants this case over and done with as much as we do. So after lunch, Sullivan and I are set to make our final appeal to the jury.

The only reason I'm still on my feet is because I'm amped up on caffeine and adrenalin. In a matter of hours I plan to go home, pull the covers over my head and sleep for a week.

Sullivan's wearing a maroon suit that looks like she slept in it. Her eyes are bloodshot and she didn't wash her hair this morning or put on any makeup. When she stands to address the jury, I can relate to her weariness.

"Good afternoon, ladies and gentlemen," Sullivan begins. "I want to thank you for your service to this court. There is only one count before you, possession of child pornography. The state has met its burden as to this charge. The defendant testified that he saved a naked picture of Kennedy Carlyle to his phone. That is a fact. The defendant, therefore, is guilty.

"Please don't let the defendant's tearful plea prevent you from fulfilling your duty as a juror. Graylin Alexander is guilty of possession of child pornography. You should not allow your personal feelings to prevent you from carrying out your obligation to render a decision based on the facts and the law. There is no question that the defendant is guilty of this charge. I respectfully request that you return a guilty verdict."

I'm not surprised that Sullivan didn't try harder. I don't have that option. I have to step up to the plate and swing for a homerun.

I stand up, woozy from skipping breakfast and lunch. I paste a smile on my face and approach the jury box.

"When I first spoke to you about this case," I begin, "I told you it was about a kid simply being a kid. I think if you consider all the evidence you've heard—from both the prosecution and the defense—you'll agree with that characterization. Graylin Alexander is a kid who acted like a kid. He saved a salacious picture to his cell phone. He didn't take the picture. He didn't send it to anyone else. He simply saved it to his phone.

"You heard LaShay Baker testify that when she and Kennedy Carlyle set up this scheme to entrap Graylin, they knew he would save the picture to his phone because—in her words—everybody does. Graylin Alexander was just doing what kids do. You heard child psychologist Faye Mandell describe Graylin's conduct as normal adolescent behavior, something any kid might do. In fact, she testified that thirty-nine percent of teens admit to having sent a sext and a whopping forty-eight percent say they've received one. We might not like that. But it's indeed a sign of our times.

"My client is not a pedophile or sex offender despite the prosecution's attempt to saddle him with those labels for the rest of his life."

I walk over and stand behind Graylin's chair. His hands are folded and resting on the table and he's sitting as straight as a toy soldier.

"This cherub-faced, fourteen-year-old is a rather extraordinary young man. He's managed to make almost straight A's despite being raised by a single father and having a drug-addicted mother whose whereabouts he doesn't even know. Although the state is prosecuting my client under a statute designed to punish pedophiles, Graylin Alexander is not a pedophile. It's up to you to rectify this travesty. We can't raise our children in a super-sexualized society with erotic images everywhere they turn, and not expect them to be impacted. The adults of this world are to blame for this sexting phenomena. Not our children.

"We ask that you return a verdict of not guilty. Please don't punish this kid for simply being a kid."

As I sit down, a tidal wave of exhaustion consumes me.

"You did really, really good, Ms. Angela!" Graylin says, full of enthusiasm. "We won. I know it! We won!"

I'm not so sure, but I don't have the heart to dash his hopes. I keep quiet and return his hug. He leaves with Gus and Dre to pick up a snack, while Jenny and I remain at the defense table, too spent to move.

"I know you must be starving," Jenny says after a while. "Let's go across the street and grab a sandwich. I'm predicting a quick verdict in Graylin's favor."

I never make those kinds of predictions. The last time we all hugged and ran off to celebrate, we were in tears a few hours later. I don't want food. I want sleep. I'd love to go to my car and take a nap.

Sullivan walks over to us. "Nice job, counselors. You really fought hard for your client."

I don't want her olive branch. "We wouldn't have to fight so hard if the D.A.'s Office would exercise some discretion and stop filing pornography charges against kids who don't deserve it."

She shrugs and walks away.

Jenny and I are stepping into the hallway, when the judge's clerk calls my name.

"The judge wants both sides back in court," she says.

I glance at my phone. The jury hasn't even been out thirty minutes. "They can't be done deliberating already," I say to Jenny.

"Yes, they can." She's beaming like a *not guilty* verdict has already been rendered. "And a quick verdict in a case like this usually means good news for the defense. I'll go find Graylin."

CHAPTER 86

Angela

Judge Lipscomb walks out of his chambers, but doesn't take the bench. His expression is so stern it scares me. "The bailiff has informed me that the jury has a question."

I'm stunned. Questions mean confusion and confusion isn't good.

"What's the matter, Ms. Angela?" Graylin asks. "Why do they have a question?"

Before I can answer, the bailiff comes out of the jury room and hands Judge Lipscomb a piece of paper. He begins reading, then briefly closes his eyes.

"The jury wants to know if Graylin would serve time in an adult prison or a juvenile facility if he's convicted."

The judge's words feel like a punch in the stomach.

"I'm going to call them back in and tell them their question is inappropriate since their focus should be on the verdict, not the sentence, which is my job. Everybody should stay close. I suspect we could have a verdict very shortly."

I feel something vibrating and realize it's Graylin's bouncing knee. He starts to quietly sob. I'm doing everything in my power not to join him. I place my arm around his shoulders and gently rock him.

Jenny reaches across Graylin and grabs my free hand. "I've had a couple of cases where the jury asked the craziest questions, but still found my client not guilty," she says. "And even if they do find him guilty, there's always the possibility that Judge Lipscomb could throw out the verdict."

I wish Jenny would just shut up. I don't want her getting Graylin's hopes up for nothing. I failed him and now I have to deal with that. After a few more minutes, I hand a sobbing Graylin off to Jenny and walk to the back of the courtroom and fall into Dre's arms.

***

Another hour passes before we learn that the jury has reached a verdict. This time I'm sitting between Jenny and Graylin, instead of having him in the middle. Jenny probably thinks I want to be the one to console Graylin. I want the center spot so the two of them can console me. If Graylin is convicted, I'm going to be the biggest basket case in this courtroom.

The jury files back in. Nobody's looking at us.

The judge goes through all the perfunctory language, then asks the jury foreman to stand.

As it turns out, Juror No. 5 is the foreman. He has several family members in law enforcement. The foreman typically wields the most influence over other jurors. This is not a good sign.

I'm holding Graylin's hand to my right and Jenny's to my left.

"Have you reached a verdict?" Judge Lipscomb asks.

"Yes, we have," the jury foreman says sternly.

We watch as the verdict form is passed to the judge for an advance look, then back to the foreman, who begins to read. "We find the defendant Graylin Alexander not guilty of—"

I hear Gus cheer from the back of the room. A jubilant Graylin jumps to his feet and turns around to face his father. "I told you, Dad! I told you!"

Judge Lipscomb bangs his gavel. "Let's quiet down. Back in your seat, young man!"

I don't hear anything else because my own sobs drown out the foreman's voice. Graylin and Jenny are hugging me, but all I can do is press my forehead to the table and cry.

EPILOGUE

Angela

"Who's the man?" Graylin grins as he extends his arm for a fist bump with his dad.

"You're the man," Gus says, pulling his son into his arms.

The backyard of Graylin's aunt Macie is packed with friends and family. Dre and Apache are manning the barbecue grill while Mossy plays bartender.

In the ten days since the trial ended, Graylin returned to school and is back to his old self. As it turns out, there was only one juror who was on the fence, but he finally came around. It was his question about where Graylin would serve his time that had us thinking they were coming back with a guilty verdict.

Kennedy and LaShay were offered deferred entry of judgment deals, which they accepted. Both girls were expelled from Marcus Prep. I also filed a defamation and emotional distress lawsuit against LaShay and Kennedy on behalf of Graylin. Suing a kid means you're suing their parents. The Carlyles' attorney has already requested a meeting to discuss settlement. Graylin's going to have a hefty college fund when it's all said and done.

I walk over to Jenny, who's standing over the dessert table with a piece of cake in one hand and an apple martini in the other.

"You're the greediest white girl I've ever met," I tell her.

She takes a sip of her drink. "I thought Mama Baker's cake was amazing, but this red velvet is to die for." She takes a bite. "Do all black people make amazing cakes?"

"Excuse me, but I think that's a racist question."

She hugs me. "Naw, we're homegirls now."

"I'm going to tell Mossy no more drinks for you and I'm also driving you home."

"Hey, my brother," Jenny says when Dre walks up.

"*My brother?* Since when did you two become so cozy?"

Jenny abandons me and hurls an arm around Dre. "We're buddies now. You got yourself a pretty cool fella here, so you need to keep him around. Never know when I might need a favor from a guy with his kind of street cred."

"I can't believe Ms. Straight and Narrow said that."

Dre laughs.

Graylin steps into our semi-circle.

"Like I was telling you," he says to Jenny, "I'm going to be an attorney one day, so I want to get started early. I've been reading a lot about what paralegals do. I'm good at researching stuff online. Until I finish law school and pass the bar, can you hire me as your paralegal, Ms. Jenny?"

"Hey, wait a minute," I say. "What am I, chopped liver? How come you don't want to work for me?"

"You're good too, Ms. Angela. But I want to help kids and Ms. Jenny only represents kids. I'm going to be a juvenile defense attorney."

I give him a hug. "I'm so proud of you."

He turns back to Jenny. "So are you going to hire me?"

"How are you going to get to work?" Jenny says. "You're not even old enough to drive yet. And what about your schoolwork?"

"I can work from home and we can have meetings on FaceTime or Skype. And besides research, I can also take a look at your cases from a kid's perspective and give you my opinion. I can be your paralegal-slash-consultant."

"You know what? I think you've talked yourself into a job."

"Excellent. So when do I start?"

"Hold your horses. Let me take a look at my caseload and see if I have anything I need your help with."

"Okay," Graylin says. "I want twelve dollars an hour."

"Excuse me, but that's higher than the minimum wage."

"You can't get a paralegal *and* a consultant for minimum wage. And don't worry, you'll get your money's worth."

"Young man," Jenny says, amused, "you're going to make a great attorney one day."

We all laugh as Graylin runs off to tell Gus about his new job.

Jenny takes a sip of her martini. "I'm happy to see you two love birds have made up."

Dre throws an arm around me and plants a kiss on my neck.

"I keep trying," I say with a coy smile, "but I can't seem to shake this guy."

We haven't completely resolved things yet, but we're working on it. I know there's going to be another time when Dre's past enters our present. But I also know that I want him in my life.

"I have something for you." Dre pulls a red velvet, ring-sized box from his back pocket.

Jenny starts jumping up and down before I can even react. "Oh my God!"

I'm too shocked to move. We haven't resolved half of our problems and we've never talked seriously about marriage. I can't believe he'd do this in front of all these people.

"Dre...um, there's a lot of work we need to do before—"

Jenny gives me an incredulous look. "You are *not* going to embarrass him in front of all of us. Open that box and tell him *yes!*"

"Yeah, Ms. Angela," Graylin chimes in. "You can't dis my Uncle Dre like that."

"You sure can't," Brianna says.

Everyone at the entire party has crowded around us.

"At least open it," Dre says. There's a glint in his eye. This man knows me almost better than I know myself. How can he smile right now when he sees the apprehension on my face?

He's only putting me on blast like this because he knows I'd be hard-pressed to reject his proposal in front of family and friends.

"Uncle Dre," Brianna calls out, "you're supposed to get down on one knee."

"Yeah, man," Apache teases. "Do it right, cuz."

"I can't believe you going down for the count," Mossy says.

Dre stares at me, still all smiles. He forces the box into my hand. I take my time opening it.

"We wanna see!" Jenny gushes, peering over my shoulder. "How many carats is it?"

I push nosy Jenny out of the way and peek inside the box. I glare back up at Dre. "What's this?"

"Exactly what it looks like."

Dre takes the box from me and pulls out a key. "This," he says, dangling it in the air, "is the key to our new house. The one I rented for us. I've already signed the contract, so you can't back out. The owner also gave us a one-year lease with an option to buy."

I silently count to five to calm myself down. There are way too many people watching for me to go off on him.

"You rented a house for us without my seeing it?" He knows what a control freak I am.

"I'm sure you'll love it."

"I don't believe you did this." I smile and try not to sound upset since everybody seems to be so thrilled for us.

"Let me show you a picture of it."

He pulls his phone from his pocket, taps the screen and holds it up for me to see. When my eyes take in the place, all I can do is cry.

"Oh my God! That's the house in Leimert Park! The real estate agent said somebody else rented it!"

"That somebody was me," Dre says, wearing his smugness like a badge.

I throw my arms around him and plant a kiss on his lips.

He gives me a crooked smile. "So, I guess this means we're finally moving in together, right?"

Author's Note

"There can be no keener revelation of a society's soul than the way in which it treats its children."
— Nelson Mandela, Former President of South Africa

When a criminal defense attorney I know expressed his frustration about the number of kids he was defending who'd been charged with possession of child pornography arising from sexting, I was stunned. At that time, I had no idea that a child who sends or receives a sext could be charged with a sex-related crime. Far more disturbing was finding out that these children, some as young as twelve or thirteen, would be required to register as sex offenders *for the rest of their lives* if convicted. I instantly knew this was a topic I wanted to explore in a novel.

Parents and schools all across the country are grappling with this teen sexting crisis (yes, I'm calling it a crisis). A few states have moved to change their laws to treat sexting children less severely than adult perpetrators of child pornography. It's my hope that eventually all states will do the same. In my opinion, it's hypocritical for us to raise our children in a such a sexually permissive society and then turn around and label them sex offenders when they mimic what see in music, movies and on TV.

Please don't wait until a child you know ends up in Graylin's predicament. Educate yourself first, then talk to the kids in your life about sexting and online safety. And be proactive. Monitor what your children and grandchildren are doing with their cell phones and computers. Our kids need to understand both the social and legal consequences of sharing intimate photographs—photographs which never disappear from the web and often end up in the hands of human traffickers and other sexual predators.

The web is full of helpful information about sexting, online safety and the impact of labeling children as sex offenders. I've included a few resources below.

In the meantime, no matter how old you are, stay safe online!

Resources

Nude #Selfies and the Need to Protect Our Children
An open letter written by L.A. County Sheriff Jim McDonnell
(Google "Jim McDonnell" and "selfies")

National Center for Missing and Exploited Children
A great resource for information about the threats posed by sexual predators as well as tips on how to keep your kids safe online.
(http://www.missingkids.com/safety)

Raised on the Registry: The Irreparable Harm of Placing Children on Sex Offender Registries in the U.S
Human Rights Watch Report, 2013
An eye-opening report about the consequences of labeling children as sex offenders.
(www.hrw.org)

DISCUSSION QUESTIONS FOR *ABUSE OF DISCRETION*

1. Why is sexting so prevalent among teens today?

2. What is the earliest age a child should be allowed to have a cell phone?

3. Should sex education be taught in schools? If so, at what age?

4. What can be done to help children understand the life-changing repercussions of sexting and posting inappropriate content online?

5. Do you think children who sext should be charged with possession/distribution of child pornography?

6. Should all states change their child pornography laws so that children who sext are treated less severely than adult purveyors of child pornography?

7. Some parents believe that it is an inappropriate invasion of a child's privacy rights to monitor their online activities. Do you agree or disagree?

8. Have you spoken to the children in your life about sexting and online safety? Why or why not?

9. How do you feel about the fact that, in many states, the police can question a child without parental permission?

10. What were some of the things you liked/disliked most about *Abuse of Discretion*?

ACKNOWLEDGEMENTS

I'd like to start by thanking my diehard friends—some old, some new—who critiqued the early drafts of *Abuse of Discretion:* Analla Reid (my teen consultant), Dyanne Norris, Margarita Alejandro, Lauren Cook, Rev. Deborah Manns, Jerome Norris, Jabari Akil, Olivia Smith (I truly appreciate your eagle eye!), Julie Ungerman (my real-life Jenny!), Star Rice (my biggest fan in the ATL), Cynthia Hebron (my ride-or-die homegirl) and Alicia Evans (Girlfriend, I refused to send this book to press until I got your blessing!).

I'm also grateful for the experts who not only critiqued *Abuse of Discretion,* but took the time to answer my many, many questions about their area of expertise: Faye Mandell, psychotherapist and licensed clinical social worker, Jeffery Probasco, Director of Eastlake Juvenile Hall (thanks for the tour), Lori Lee Gray, L.A. County Deputy District Attorney (who's nothing like my imaginary prosecutors), Sherri L. Cunningham, dependency lawyer and Supervising Attorney with the Law Offices of Rachel Ewing, and the Honorable Catherine Pratt, Commissioner, Compton Juvenile Court.

To my friend and extraordinary publicist Ella Curry of EDC Creations Media Group, LLC, thanks for sending me back to the drawing board on this one. You always give it to me straight. Your honest critique was much appreciated and helped me create a much stronger story.

Many thanks to my assistant Lynel Washington and the members of my writing group, the Prize Writers, who were the first to lay eyes on this book, Arlene L. Walker, Darlene Hayes, Mark Jones and Dwayne Alexander Smith. Thanks for pushing me to become a better writer.

As always, thanks to my fans! I truly appreciate your support!

We hope you enjoyed *Abuse of Discretion*. All of Pamela's novels are available in print, e-book and audio book formats, everywhere books are sold.

To read an excerpt of all of Pamela's books, visit www.pamelasamuelsyoung.com.

Vernetta Henderson Mysteries
Every Reasonable Doubt (1st in series)
In Firm Pursuit (2nd in series)
Murder on the Down Low (3rd in series)
Attorney-Client Privilege (4th in series)
Lawful Deception (5th in series)

Angela Evans Mysteries
Buying Time (1st in series)
Anybody's Daughter (2nd in series)
Abuse of Discretion (3rd in series)

Short Stories
The Setup
Easy Money
Unlawful Greed

Non-Fiction
Kinky Coily: A Natural Hair Resource Guide

About the Author

Pamela Samuels Young is an attorney and award-winning author of multiple legal thrillers. A passionate advocate for sexually exploited children, Pamela speaks frequently on the topics of child sex trafficking, sexting, online safety, fiction writing and pursing your passion. Pamela is also a natural hair enthusiast and the author of *Kinky Coily: A Natural Hair Resource Guide.* The former journalist and Compton native is a graduate of USC, Northwestern University and UC Berkeley's School of Law. She resides in the Los Angeles area.

Pamela loves to hear from readers! There are a multitude of ways to connect with her.

Email: authorpamelasamuelsyoung@gmail.com
Website: www.pamelasamuelsyoung.com
Facebook: www.facebook.com/pamelasamuelsyoung and
          www.facebook.com/kinkycoilypamela
Twitter: www.twitter.com/pamsamuelsyoung
LinkedIn: www.linkedin.com/pamelasamuelsyoung
Pinterest: www.pinterest.com/kinkycoily
YouTube: www.youtube.com/kinkycoilypamela
BLAST (Book Lovers Against Sex Trafficking): www.blastunited.com

To schedule Pamela for a speaking engagement or book club meeting via speakerphone, Skype, FaceTime or in person, visit her website at www.pamelasamuelsyoung.com.

www.ingramcontent.com/pod-product-compliance
Lightning Source LLC
Chambersburg PA
CBHW020552120726
47903CB00001B/229